TAKING FLIGHT

Siera Maley

To my mother, who is my biggest fan and who has unabashedly and enthusiastically supported and encouraged me to do what I love, and to my beautiful girlfriend, who I hope I have inspired to write just as she has inspired me to do the same.

Chapter One

"And a sadder story this morning, now: tragedy struck late last night when actress Nicole Erickson was killed in a car accident after she swerved into another lane and was hit by oncoming traffic. Two others were injured in the wreck, but have reportedly been stabilized at a hospital nearby. Nicole got her start as a child with her role as the titular character on the 80s sitcom *Just Amanda*, but today she has become a household name, and it's truly very sad that she's passed away."

"You know, Amy, I actually met Nicole about a year ago and she really was a very nice woman. Very sweet."

"I've heard nothing but good things. Now, authorities have not released very many details on what may have caused the crash, but foul play is not suspected, and we expect to have more details later in the day. In other news—"

I raised my arm. It felt heavy, and I pointed the remote in my hand at the television and pressed "rewind." The newscasters on the screen froze, and then began to recite their lines in reverse and at double speed until I pressed "play" again.

"Two others were injured in the wreck—"

I paused it, and then rewound again.

"—anything quite like those fireworks. We hope you all enjoyed your Fourth of July weekend. And a sadder story this morning, now: Tragedy struck late last night when actress Nicole Erickson was killed in a car accident after she swerved-"

There was a knock on my bedroom door, and then it flew open before I could pause the television again. Caitlyn took me in as I lay on my bed with the remote in my hand and a sheet of paper beside me. She glanced to the television and her eyebrows shot up.

"What the hell, Lauren? Are you psychotic?" She moved quickly, turning the television off before I could protest, and then rounded on me. "Give me that." She snatched the remote away from me and tossed it aside, folding her arms across her chest after it landed on the floor nearby. "Watching it over and over's not going to help."

"It does help," I protested quietly. But Caitlyn had five years of friendship with me under her belt, and she easily saw through the lie. Sometimes it was nice having someone around who actually paid attention to the things that I said and did. This wasn't one of those times.

She sat down on my bed, and her lips turned down into a frown. "Delete the recording, Lauren. I know it's only been three months, but she wouldn't want you sitting at home alone every day rewatching two strangers discuss how your mom died. You're crazy for recording it in the first place."

"She wouldn't care what I do every day," I said. "She didn't care back when she was alive." Caitlyn looked like she wanted to argue, so I changed the subject. "Are there paps still outside?"

"They're still there," Caitlyn confirmed. "And they've got plenty of worthless shots of *me*, now, but you know it's you and your dad they really want."

"Where is he?"

"Passed out in the living room. How was court?"

I didn't answer her question at first. I'd had a court date this morning for skipping class, of all things. It was my fourth warning this year, but even back when I'd had two parents, my mother had always been busy working and my father had always been busy drinking, so there hadn't exactly been much parenting going on between the two of them. I'd had the freedom to do whatever I wanted for as long as I could remember.

That meant my school attendance hadn't exactly been stellar, but I'd understandably been even worse about going this year, and that led to four truancy violations in rapid succession. The first one was just a written warning. After the second, I was told to attend a weekend study program. I didn't bother with that, and honestly, I hadn't thought far ahead enough to care about what the consequences were. So they gave me a third warning and told me to attend some kind of attendance review board thing. I didn't.

I know it may have seemed like I deserved what I got, with a court date and an official sentencing and everything, but what no one seemed to understand was that I knew what I wanted to do with my high school career. I wanted to drop out, get my GED, and then get out of Los Angeles; daily public schooling had never been right for me, and I hated living where I did.

People across the country may not have known that I was my mother's daughter, but the people here in Los Angeles that went to school with me did, and that meant that from the moment I started high school, everyone was constantly watching the girl with the A-list mother to see what she'd do next. My every move and every slip-up was overanalyzed and I got a reputation before I was ready for one. I was the "bad girl" by the end of freshman year just because I hated school and wasn't afraid to argue with teachers if I thought I was right.

Or I was spoiled. I thought I was above the rules and could do what I wanted just because I had a famous mother. And I've found that when people tell you you're something for long enough, you start to believe it. Caitlyn was always my best friend, but I made other ones I shouldn't have, and they were bad influences on both myself and on Caitlyn before we finally toned it down a little and stopped hanging out with them, which only really happened right around the time of my mother's death three months ago.

So anyway, three years of high school, a little bit of drug use, and a lot of alcohol consumption later, here I am, with one toe too many out of line. My fourth warning sent me to juvenile court, which could've ended in a lot of different ways, but my judge chose what he called a "court-approved truancy prevention program." He told me my problem was behavioral, given my previous offenses, and that he knew just what to do to fix it.

Caitlyn was watching me expectantly now, so I simply reached over, picked up the sheet of paper on the bed beside me, and handed it to her.

Her eyes scanned the page, and then she looked up at me. "What the hell is this?"

"My punishment."

"Well, obviously." She shook her head. "Your dad won't let this happen."

"Are you kidding? It's *my* dad we're talking about here." Caitlyn was silent. "I mean, he's legally obligated either way, but I guess it's also a lot easier to blow your dead wife's money on alcohol without a kid around to take care of. And anyway, even if he didn't want me to go, the court's appointing someone to help personally escort me to the airport. I'm gone."

"To Georgia," Caitlyn deadpanned. "No way. It's not gonna happen."

"I'm leaving in three days." I took the paper from her and stared down at it distastefully. "The judge is college buddies with this guy. David Marshall. Meet my new dad."

"Bullshit. So you didn't go to school for three months. They can't ship you across the country for that."

"Well, the way the judge put it, my dad wasn't doing enough to make sure I was going. And our principal was there, and he decided to talk about the time I got caught with alcohol in my locker last year, so I was basically screwed after that. I'm supposed to stay with this guy until I graduate from my new high school."

"For seven months? Lauren, they live on a *farm*. Look at this!" She snatched the paper back from me and prodded it with horror, picking out a few choice phrases as she scanned it again. "Horses, cows, and chickens... *devout Baptists*... Lauren, they'll crucify you. You're gay!"

"Thanks for reminding me; I'd forgotten," I said flatly. "Obviously I'll just have to keep my mouth shut about it."

"Even if you could pull that off, you're gonna have to go to church with a bunch of hicks. This isn't even Atlanta, Georgia; they live in the mountains."

"Which is why I'm gonna try to find a way back here the instant I turn eighteen," I said. "They can't make me go to school or punish me for not going if I'm not legally required to go anymore. And I turn eighteen five months from now, in March."

"That still isn't much better than seven. And how would you get back across the country? You won't have any money."

I considered it. I highly doubted I could get a job while in Georgia, considering I'd be up to my ears in crap from David Marshall: counselor extraordinaire, so that ruled out booking a flight. And I'd still need a car to get to the airport. I had to assume there'd be no one in Georgia willing to help me.

I looked at Caitlyn as the solution came to me. It was simple. "Come get me."

She laughed at me. "Are you serious?"

"I'll give you anything you want. You can even have half my

trust fund," I insisted, a plan already formulating in my mind. "They won't let me take a cell phone, so I might not be able to contact you, but I can leave you my car keys. And then on my eighteenth birthday, you show up, and we Thelma and Louise it all the way back to Los Angeles and collect my stuff and my trust fund. Then I can legally drop out of high school and get my GED, and from there, we'll do whatever the hell we want. *Go* wherever we want."

"You do realize that's absolutely insane, right?" Caitlyn asked, but she grinned nonetheless. "So of course I'll do it."

"Yes!" I tackled her in a hug and we collapsed on my bed, pressed together until I sat up, straddling her hips. She smiled up at me and reached for my sides, her fingers pushing up under my shirt and pressing against my hipbones.

"I'll miss you, though," she told me.

"I know. Who'll give you the time of day after I'm gone?"

She laughed sarcastically and pinched me, making me jump. I got off of her and let her sit up. "So you and a grown man, living together," she sighed out. "That's not creepy at all."

"I'm sure he has a wife," I replied. I'd thought about this already. "And if he's taking in kids, he probably has some of his own too."

"Hmm. Maybe a hot daughter?" she suggested. Her way of trying to make me feel better.

I shrugged. "Doubt it. But she'd probably be homophobic, anyway."

"True." Caitlyn frowned at me. "I can't believe you're really going."

"Trust me; neither can I. But there's not exactly much I can do to stop it. I'll just have to be an asshole once I get there."

"It's not fair. Your mom just died. Can't they have a little sympathy?"

"Well, I wasn't exactly a model student beforehand either. And I don't know if the judge knew who my mom was. Our principal didn't mention it and you know she kept her maiden name. Lauren Lennox and Nicole Erickson... no relation unless you keep up with celebrity gossip. They did recognize my dad's name from his short stint on my mom's old show in the 80s, though, and that didn't really seem to affect their decision."

"It's still not fair."

"I don't know. Maybe everything balances out in the end. I have millions of dollars waiting for me when I turn eighteen, so this kind of pales in comparison, doesn't it? Not that I want to go, but I'm just gonna be a pain in the ass anyway. I feel sorrier for the Marshalls. If they think a little hard work, church, and therapy is gonna make me into a well-mannered robot, they've got another thing coming."

Caitlyn smirked at me. "That's true. I can't exactly visualize you working on a farm." She paused. "Actually, I take that back. I can, and it's hilarious. Do you even own shoes that aren't heels?"

I held up a finger. "One pair."

"Shit," she laughed. "I wish you could bring a phone! I want updates."

"From what was said in court, it sounds like I'll get monitored calls. Like jail."

"You're going to redneck jail," Caitlyn declared with disbelief.

"And redneck school," I added.

"Redneck church, redneck farm…"

"Is there any other kind?"

"Shhh. Ooh, redneck parties."

"Redneck kegger. I could be down with that."

"Okay, we need to stop," Caitlyn decided with another laugh. "So you have three days. We can't waste them."

"And what do you propose?"

She counted off on her fingers. "Clubbing for sure. Um… more clubbing. And getting you laid, since you'll be celibate for the next seven months."

"Five months, and says who?"

"You seriously think you'll find someone to hook up with? Everyone there'll be closet cases."

"I have gaydar, and I'm hot. I'll work it out."

"Well, let's make sure you get laid anyway. Just in case." She paused thoughtfully. "And I bet Zeke's replenished his vodka stash by now… At the very least, I'm gonna give you a proper send-off."

* * *

We did go clubbing, but it wasn't easy getting there. My family was a private one before my mom's death. She married my dad young; they met on the set of *Just Amanda* when my mom had the lead role and my dad played a recurring character that popped in and out every few episodes. Her career eventually took off afterward and his died, but they stayed friends as teens and she remained his claim to fame, particularly when they started dating and then married in their early twenties.

My mom took a career hiatus to have me shortly afterward, and then went right back to work a year after I was born. She didn't become *famous* famous until about a decade ago, though, when she played a supporting role in a movie that won a crazy amount of Oscars: like six or seven, I think.

The result was that I got lucky. My mom was watched by the media like a hawk in the years leading up to her death, but I was old news by then: a kid she'd had for over ten years. *Nicole Erickson's Kid Turns Thirteen* isn't a headline like *Nicole Erickson Due to Have Baby* is. I wouldn't ever complain about having the fortune half of "fame and fortune," but I was glad I didn't have to deal with the "fame" part of it. David Marshall, provided he wasn't obsessed with my mother's personal life, probably wouldn't make the connection between her and me.

My dad and I, however, was a coin toss, especially since David would probably be given my dad's name. If you were a huge fan of *Just Amanda* or a huge fan of my mom, you may have heard of him. Or if you were just constantly glued to TMZ and were one of those people who constantly knew which celebrities were dating or married to whom. I doubted David was like that. But his wife — assuming he had one — could be.

Being that I was completely fameless and my dad was a Z-lister by now, we normally didn't have to deal with paparazzi. That was my mom's problem, not ours. But it had certainly become ours now. Even three months later, there were still a few men that waited outside of our house, trying to get pictures of me and my dad looking distraught or wrecked or something. As if any high-profile magazines would want to publish pictures of a drunken-looking Z-lister and his no-name daughter three months after the death of their third family member. But they kept trying, and I was determined not to give them what they wanted. So on days like my court date and days like today, when I had to leave the house, I had one trick: to smile. They wanted me sad, so I was happy.

I was still thinking about the way they'd blinded Caitlyn and I with flashes back at my house as I danced with her at our favorite 16-and-up club. I would never understand how Mom had dealt with it on a daily basis. She wasn't around much when I was growing up, but she was ten times the person my dad was. He spent his time away from me drinking away the pain of being a failed child star. He was a complete and total cliché. It was pathetic. Mom wasn't around because she was busy raking in millions of dollars and putting in appearances at various events and ceremonies. I wondered now if she would've regretted the time she spent away from home if she'd known she'd be dead at 42.

It was probably a good thing that Caitlyn distracted me at that point. She nudged me and leaned forward, shouting into my ear over the music. "What are you doing?! Do you see anyone you like?!"

I glanced around half-heartedly, uninterested in trying to find a girl to hook up with. It felt stupid. If my mom had taught me anything, it was that life was fleeting in the grand scheme of things and that I should enjoy it while I had the chance, but I'd done this dozens of times, and it was meaningless in each and every instance.

The routine was always exactly the same. I'd hook up with a girl, and then I'd avoid her every time I came here, and if I were lucky, I'd never have to speak to her again. Rinse and repeat. If I really wanted to have sex, there were easier ways to get it. The fun for me was the chase. Getting a girl interested and making her feel brave enough to go for it. *That* was what I was good at. But that took effort, and I didn't feel like trying tonight. In fact, I really didn't feel like doing anything. Even dancing with Caitlyn felt like a chore. I wanted to go back to bed.

I didn't tell Caitlyn what I was thinking. I just shrugged instead. She read me correctly, though, and rolled her eyes as she pulled me closer. "C'mon! You love this! Go flirt with someone!"

I looked around again. There were a few gross couples nearby grinding on each other, and a few groups of girls dancing together while guys watched them from the shadows, no doubt trying to gather the courage to go ask them to dance.

Caitlyn was watching me, and so she saw me shake my head. Her hand slid into mine instantaneously, and she tugged, pulling me into a corner of the club, where it was a little easier to talk. "What are you doing? This is your last chance to have fun, remember?"

"I guess so." I struggled to put what I was feeling into words. "I just think maybe I've done this enough for now."

"What, slept with girls?" Caitlyn asked. "Okay, Lauren, there are a lot of things people say about you that aren't true, but the sleeping around part? That part's true, and we both know you own it. You are *never* not in the mood to hook up."

"It's not that." I rolled my eyes and forced a smile. "I just don't feel like making an effort tonight. I'm leaving in, like, two days and—"

"Which is what makes this perfect!" Caitlyn insisted, cutting me off. "You're guaranteed not to see any of these people for half a year."

"Why are you so invested in getting me laid?" I asked her, quirking an eyebrow.

She didn't reply at first, and let out a deep sigh instead. "I want my best friend back, Lauren. I know your mom died. I know that it's been hard. But we spent the majority of high school drunk or high and *still* managed to act like normal human beings: going to school, interacting with people, *leaving our houses*. We've been shitty students for years and now you're finally getting punished for it because you literally just wouldn't get out of bed and go to school. I tried to help and you ignored my texts—"

"That's not—" I tried to interrupt, feeling embarrassed, but she cut me off again and continued.

"Then, after you ignored me, I showed up in person to try and get you to do something fun, and you hardly ever took me up on that. And now you have two days left in Los Angeles and you'd still be at home in your bed right now if you could be, wouldn't you?"

She was right, but I shook my head at her in disbelief. "Caitlyn,

I lost a parent."

"And I lost my best friend," she countered. We stared at each other, the moment tense, and, at last, she stepped back. "I'm gonna go get us drinks," she mumbled, and then turned and walked away.

I stood alone, my back resting against the wall, and thought about what Caitlyn had said. It was true that I hadn't been myself for the past three months. But she couldn't expect me to stay the same after a death in the family. And it wasn't fair to try and put a rush job on my recovering from it, either.

But I knew how she felt. There was a part of me that missed my old self too. On the outside, at least, I'd been the confident girl that'd turned heads and turned straight girls bi for a night. I'd let insults roll off of my back and I was good at hiding when I was hurt. People hated me and loved to hate me, and I didn't care. I was untouchable; I wore a suit of emotional armor. Now I was just a shell of the girl I'd used to be.

I felt sorry for Caitlyn by the time she returned with two drinks in her hands. I knew she was only trying to help, and I knew she'd probably have a rough time without me in the months to come. In her own way, she was just trying to say goodbye in the best way she knew how.

She offered me one of the drinks and then took a flask out of her purse. We'd stopped by her house on the way here and gotten vodka from her brother. She opened the flask and dumped only a small amount into her drink; she was driving tonight. Then she handed it to me.

"Don't take all of it; I'm having more when we get back to

your place," she warned, seemingly convinced now that I wouldn't be spending any time with another girl tonight.

I considered the flask in my hand, then tilted it over my drink and poured a majority of the contents in before Caitlyn could protest. "We can steal some more from my dad tonight."

* * *

When I woke up the next morning, I couldn't remember most of my night, and Caitlyn and I were both nude in my bed.

I sat up, rubbing at my head as I glanced over at her and then at my room around us. The lamp on my nightstand had been knocked over, and I spotted Caitlyn's bra and my pants on the floor by my bedroom door. I looked at Caitlyn again, frowning. Her dirty-blonde hair was fanned out all over her pillow, and she looked pretty wrecked, honestly. But this wasn't the first time we'd woken up like this, and I doubted it'd be the last.

Caitlyn and I had been friends for a long time, and she'd never called herself anything but straight, but with enough alcohol in our systems, this happened sometimes. It wasn't a big deal, but it wasn't something I'd wanted to deal with right before I left for Georgia.

Our relationship was strange. There were times where we could go a week without talking and then be desperate to hang out, and then there were also times where things got a little too intense and I'd give anything for that one-week break.

There are moments I think everyone will experience during

their lives at some point where they're aware that something more than friendly is happening beneath the surface with someone, even if nothing ever actually comes of it. Caitlyn and I'd had a lot of those moments; we'd be pressed together, both knowing we'd slept together in the past and that I was gay, and for just a moment, I'd think it could happen for us while we were sober.

But it never did. The moment would pass, and then we'd end up naked and hung over in the same bed however many days later, trying to remember what exactly had happened the night before. It'd been happening since sophomore year, sometimes even while she'd had a boyfriend, and I supposed it'd keep happening until she finally got into a serious relationship. And it *would* be her that'd get into a serious relationship out of the two of us.

She stirred beside me and her eyes opened. I stared back at her, clearly topless as I sat up in bed beside her. She abruptly shut her eyes and let out a short, hoarse laugh. "Shit."

"Sorry about the boobs," I told her, sliding out of bed and moving to find some clothes to put on. "Oh, and the vagina."

That made her laugh again. "What happened last night?"

"I have no idea," I admitted even as I pulled on underwear and a top. I tossed Caitlyn a pair of shorts and a T-shirt, and she stayed under the covers as she wriggled the bottoms on. "How many times does this make, though?"

Caitlyn stuck her middle finger in the air, my shirt shielding her face from view as she pulled it on. "Shut up; I felt sorry for you... I'm sure."

"Probably," I admitted, even though she'd been kidding. I had a brief memory of a drunken Caitlyn declaring emphatically that even though I was being a loser, I still needed to have sex before I left for Georgia. "I think you volunteered yourself to be the one to bite the bullet and sleep with me. You poor, poor thing. Such a victim." I got another middle finger for that, and grinned at her.

"At least you're smiling," she said with a sigh. "That's an improvement. And now I need a shower. Can you please come out with me tonight and find a girl we don't know this time? We need to cleanse you."

"You need higher self-esteem."

She rolled her eyes at me, pointing a finger back and forth between us. "Drunk Me may have thought this was a good idea, but Sober Me is super uncomfortable with the idea of spending five months being your most recent lay."

"I can find someone to sleep with in Georgia!" I exclaimed through laughter. "Seriously!"

"Maybe, but after the way you acted last night, I'm not so sure you'll make an effort."

She had a point there. I scratched at my head as Caitlyn left for the bathroom, and frowned once she'd gone. A part of me was glad I couldn't remember anything with Caitlyn, but another part of me wished I could remember it all. That was a new feeling.

I tried to shake it off and headed downstairs. I was surprised to see my dad making pancakes in the kitchen. I was used to seeing him unconscious more often than conscious, and equally as surprising was that he also seemed to be sober.

"Are you hungry?" he asked me. I nodded truthfully and sat down at our breakfast bar, silently watching my dad as he cooked.

He'd let his hair grow out in the past few months; it was shaggy and long now, but remained the same dark brown color it'd always been. The color I'd inherited from him. I looked a lot more like my dad than my mom. I had his brown eyes too.

He served me a stack of three pancakes and asked, "Need me to make more?"

I knew what he was asking, albeit indirectly, and nodded anyway. "Yeah."

"Okay. So do I know this one?"

I picked at my pancakes awkwardly. "It's just Caitlyn."

He was silent for a moment, pouring batter into the pan on the stove. "Again?" he finally asked.

"It was stupid," I mumbled, growing uncomfortable. My dad wasn't completely oblivious; he knew that I was having sex. But it was rare that we talked so openly about it.

He finished with the pancakes and sat down next to me with a stack of his own, leaving a third stack on the counter for Caitlyn. I tried to ignore the way he'd chosen a beer for his drink. "Let me tell you something, kiddo," he said. "I met your mom when I was sixteen years old. A long time ago. But I still remember the way we looked at each other. We both just *knew*. It was this look, like… like we were the only two people that mattered. If you get that look, you don't let that go, understand?"

I took his words with a grain of salt. Most of the things he said lately didn't make sense, and this was him only slightly more coherent than usual. If his drinking habits were bad before my mom's death, they were horrible now.

"Okay, Dad," was all I said. On the bright side, if his words held even an ounce of truth, I would know that look when I saw it. I was used to being looked at like I was dirt, so it'd be a nice change, I suppose.

"Caitlyn's a very nice girl. I like Caitlyn," he told me. "Do you like Caitlyn?"

"Yep."

"So you like her, and then if you get the look from her... that's when you know." He pointed his beer at me knowingly, as though he'd just said something profound, and then tipped it back and downed the rest of its contents. I looked away from him to avoid watching him do it, but my stomach churned uncomfortably anyway, and I suddenly wasn't very hungry.

"Okay." I couldn't muster up the effort to explain to him that Caitlyn was just a friend, especially given that on mornings like this one, it didn't really feel like the truth.

* * *

I didn't go out with Caitlyn the night before I left for Georgia, even though she begged me to. Instead, we stayed in and she helped me pack, and afterward, we laid awake together talking about how stupid the whole Georgia thing was and how much it sucked that I had to go. We did more research too, and got a better idea of what exactly I'd be up against.

David Marshall had a Master's degree in Psychology, and his day job was as a school counselor. And not just a guidance counselor, like the ones that helped students work out their schedules, but the kind students also used as a substitute therapist.

He lived on a farm with his wife Wendy and two unnamed kids, according to his website. That was part of his shtick; he claimed that hard work on the farm would teach responsibility, weekly attendance at the local Baptist church would teach morals, and continuous therapy sessions with him would give kids a chance to talk through their issues. On top of that, the Marshalls would provide a comfortable and stable family environment to nurture the growth and change of their new member. And, in my case: they could make sure I actually attended school during my reformation.

It all just sounded like a load of bullshit to me, and I stayed up for most of that night, dreading my flight in the morning.

Chapter Two

Caitlyn came with me to the airport the next day. It was crowded, just as I'd been told Hartsfield-Jackson in Atlanta would be. I was also told that David would be waiting for me. I knew what he looked like, so I didn't expect it to be hard to find him, although a part of me wanted to ditch him and find a place to hide out for five months. But I didn't have the money for that. Only enough for one meal during a layover in Phoenix.

An older man appointed by the court to escort me drove us to the airport and came inside with us. My dad was there too, and for the brief time that we spent in the airport together, I finally sensed that he was somewhat sad to see me go. Or maybe it was guilt I was sensing. Either way, I made Caitlyn promise to check in on him now that he'd be alone for so long, and then I made her promise again that she'd come get me on my birthday.

"I'll be there," she assured me, and shook her purse for emphasis. The ring of keys I'd given her jingled inside, my car key amongst them. "And I'll bring my brother with me so I don't have to come alone. Zeke said he'd come."

"Good idea," I agreed, and pulled her in for a hug. We lingered, pressed together, and it struck me how intimate this gesture felt. It was an unfortunate after-effect of sexual contact with someone I actually cared about.

She laughed nervously after a few seconds and mumbled, "Okay," pulling away sooner than I wanted her to.

My dad hugged me goodbye next. It was brief and a little awkward, and I only stood with him for a moment before the court official made it clear that I needed to get ready to go through security. So I did. And just like that, I was on my own.

I made my way through the crowd without too much difficulty, and a short while later, I was on my flight.

The whole trip was very uneventful. I got lunch while I was waiting to switch flights in Phoenix, I listened to music on the plane in an effort to drown out crying babies, and by six o'clock in the evening eastern time, I was in Atlanta.

I brought one big suitcase that I had to retrieve from baggage claim, and between that, my carry-on, and my purse, my arms were full as I weaved in and out of the crowds at Hartsfield-Jackson airport. As I walked, I thought about what the next few months would bring. I planned to be difficult and uncooperative as often as I possibly could. Perhaps there was a chance I'd be too much for the Marshalls, and they'd send me back to California. Of course, that'd mean I'd have to take some other form of punishment instead, but it had to be better than being shipped across the continent to live with a bunch of country bumpkins. I was a rich girl from the city, for God's sake. The mountains were no place for a girl like me.

Yes, my best bet was absolutely to resist them as much as humanly possible. I'd refuse to do farm work, refuse to attend church, and refuse to reveal anything about myself to David Marshall. Maybe I'd even refuse school, if I really wanted to push their buttons. The opportunities were endless.

As much as the thought of defying David Marshall lifted my mood, reaching him at the airport dampened it far more. I caught sight of him just past security and took him in before he saw me.

The man hadn't looked intimidating on the paper I'd had, but I'd attributed that to the fact that it was an ad for his services. Now I had to admit that he genuinely looked like a nice guy. And also like a pushover. Maybe he'd cooperate with some of my demands after all. Like to not have to touch any farm animals. Or maybe he'd send me home early on good behavior if I promised to love Jesus instead of weed.

I finally gathered my courage and headed towards him, taking in the visible signs of age in his face as I approached. He had a lot of crease lines and wrinkles, which I figured had to be stress-related. It couldn't be easy repeatedly taking in troubled teens and shaping them up. I wondered briefly what his success rate was. Were there any who'd come out unchanged and unscathed?

He didn't see me until I was just a few feet away from him, but when he did, he offered me a smile and stepped toward me, folding up the paper in his hand with my name written on it in bold, black letters and tucking it into his pocket. "Lauren. It's good to meet you."

"Hey," I grunted, not meeting his eyes. He seemed unsurprised by my attitude, which was frustrating.

"Here, let me take your suitcase," he offered, and took the bigger one from me, leaving me with my carry-on and my purse. "I trust your flight went well?"

I didn't reply. Instead, I took note of his lack of a Southern accent. So he wasn't from the South: at least not originally. That made sense. He went to college with the judge that sentenced me to this whole bullshit reform trip, so at some point he must've chosen to live where he did now. I couldn't fathom why anyone would choose a location in the middle of nowhere though.

David kept talking when I remained silent. "We should have about a two-hour drive back up to the farm, provided we don't hit too much traffic. I'm not sure how much you were told before you came here, but you'll be living there with myself, my wife, and my two children. We live in a very small, rural area, but the people there are nice and I think you'll find you enjoy it soon enough, even if it's not what you're used to."

I let out a short, dry laugh at that, but he reacted strangely, smiling at me as though my laugh had been a genuine, friendly one. "I know you don't believe me," he said, "but it's got a very homey feel to it, our town. There's only one high school, so you'll become very acquainted with everyone in town much quicker than you would back in California. It may be a little bit of a culture shock at first, but after the initial adjustment, it's a nice place to live. Both of my children love it there."

We reached his car a moment later, and he loaded my bags inside. I held back a sarcastic comment about the lack of a pickup truck, trying to stick to my plan. I'd tell him as little as I could about who I was or what my thoughts were on any of the events in my life. He could guess for five months for all I cared.

We got into his car and he kept talking. "As I said before, I have two children. My eldest is Scott; he's twenty years old but thankfully, he's decided to stay home and help us out on the farm while he attends the local college. And I think you'll get along with Cameron, considering you two are the same age and in the same grade."

He pulled out of the parking deck and I stared out of the passenger's side window, hiding my disappointment. The next five months would've been a little easier to get through if I'd had some eye candy around the ol' Marshall family farm, even if I'd have hated the girl as a person. Now it looked like I'd be dealing with two sons, which was far worse.

"You'll be sharing a room with Cam," David continued, and as I looked over at him, alarmed, I finally couldn't keep silent.

"Isn't that inappropriate?"

David looked both surprised that I'd spoken and confused by what I'd said. "Well… I can't imagine why it would be, unless you're referring to the influence you may have while you two are in such close proximity for so long, but I trust both of my children and I'm confident that they'll be the ones to have a positive influence on you. We've already rearranged the beds to put a spare in Cameron's room, so don't worry about not having your own space."

"Oh, so we're not sharing a bed?" I asked rhetorically, my voice dripping with sarcasm. "Okay, cool. *Now* it's okay for me to share a room with a teenage boy."

David laughed loudly and abruptly, his voice booming through the air and making me jump. "Oh! I'm so sorry," he apologized. "I always forget; I like to use her full name a lot when I'm not addressing her directly, but you should know that most of her friends and family call her Cam or Cammie. My daughter."

I took that in for a moment. "…You named your daughter Cameron."

"I consider it a unisex name," he replied calmly, not taking his eyes off of the road. "You've never met a female Cameron?"

"No."

"Well… looks like you'll have yet another first here in Georgia," he told me happily, and I resisted the urge to grind my teeth together. My eyes went back to the window and I thought about taking out my mp3 player. Maybe he'd take the hint and stop talking.

As it was, he kept going. "So, given that it doesn't seem like you're in any mood to tell me what you know about me, how about I go first and tell you what I've heard about you?"

I remained silent. I had a feeling that I was going to end up hearing more from him regardless of what my answer was.

"I talked to your father briefly, but most of my information comes from my good friend Judge Jacobs and your high school principal, so please excuse me if anything's not entirely accurate, and feel free to jump in and correct me at any time." He paused. "It's my understanding that you haven't been attending class at your high school since the start of your senior year, which is why you've been sent here. So my primary concern while you're here is going to simply be that you go to school. Easy enough, right?"

I didn't answer.

"Beyond that, I'd like to touch on some of the behavioral problems I've heard about, mostly from your principal. He mentioned a suspension and a fine you received junior year after alcohol was found in your locker, and although your father himself didn't say much on the subject, both Judge Jacobs and your principal seemed to feel that he was unfit to be your guardian due to a problem with alcohol abuse." I clenched my fists. He was getting very close to hitting a nerve. "But you argued very emphatically in his favor, from what I've heard. You didn't want a different guardian."

"And yet here I am," I said through gritted teeth, but he didn't acknowledge my comment.

"Judge Jacobs also mentioned your father being a single parent."

I wanted so badly for him to stop talking. "My mom's dead," I bit out, hoping it'd shut him up.

It worked, but only for a moment. There was a long silence, and then he said, "I'm very sorry to hear that."

"Whatever."

He was silent for so long after that that I almost thought I'd be able to enjoy some peace and quiet for the duration of the ride, but it didn't last. As we edged our way through Atlanta traffic and finally began to head out toward the suburbs, he proposed, "Why don't I tell you a little about myself, to even things out? I have a Master's in Psychology from the University of Illinois…"

"I read your website," I cut him off, hoping he'd shut up again.

"Oh, did you? Well, then you know the basics: that I live on a farm and that you'll be attending a Baptist church every Sunday." If he noticed my eye-roll, he didn't acknowledge it.

"Your responsibilities will start out small around the house, but they'll increase as you continue to live with us. When we have boys stay with us, Scott serves as their guide and helps them get acclimated, and Cameron does the same for the girls, so you two should get to know each other well. My wife Wendy spends her days at home, so she's quite an expert on everything you'll need to know, as well.

"But anyway: about myself. I'll be working as a counselor at the high school you'll be attending. So if you ever need anything during school hours, I'm just a few hallways away. Most days, I'll be giving you and Cameron a ride to school, but if I'm ever unavailable for some reason, Scott will pick up the slack."

"When do I get phone calls?" I asked abruptly, thinking of Caitlyn, and even my dad. I needed someone at least partially sane to talk to throughout all of this.

"Whenever you want, provided someone else is around," David informed me. "Which should be the case; I don't expect you to ever be home alone. But we'll have to have someone there to listen to your end of the conversation."

"So I can't even speak honestly," I realized.

"No, you're welcome to say what you want. Believe me, whatever you say, we've probably heard worse. I've been doing this for ten years. We only have someone listen to make sure you aren't getting into anything you aren't supposed to be involved with."

"Ten years," I echoed, and then finally asked the question that'd been in my mind from the moment I'd caught sight of him at the airport. "So does this always work, then? Does everyone come out zombiefied?"

"They come out with a greater understanding of themselves, and, generally, more well-behaved, yes. Zombification might be a bit of an extreme word for what I do, but I suppose it might seem like that to you right now." He glanced at me. "I'm not out to change who you are at your core, Lauren. I'm only here to help."

"If you were here to help, you'd send me home," I countered.

"You may not agree with me, but your home wasn't a healthy environment," David said. "You had minimal to no parental supervision there, your school attendance was not enforced, and you've been engaging in substance abuse."

"I've had sex before marriage too," I told him gravely, feigning disappointment. "Tons, actually."

He shrugged his shoulders nonchalantly. "I know you may think I'd take offense to that, but sexual activity is somewhat normal for someone your age. Just don't tell my children I said that. Or my wife."

I quirked an eyebrow at him, alarmed, and he glanced at me

quickly, shooting me a small smile.

"Like I said: I've been doing this for a while, Lauren. It'll take more than that to shock me."

"I have more than that," I countered defensively, resisting the urge to drop the lesbian bomb an hour into my stay.

He smiled at me again. "Then we'll have an interesting seven months together, it seems."

"Five," I corrected mentally, and at last, he let me have my silence.

* * *

We entered the small town of Collinsville, Georgia after another hour of driving. It was like nothing I'd ever seen before. The roads were mostly deserted, both in vehicle and pedestrian count, and there were hardly any streetlights: only stop signs. David claimed we were driving through the center of town, but some of the roads that branched off from ours were made of gravel, and the only noteworthy buildings I spotted were a small convenience store and a bank. I wanted to hurl solely from lack of civilization, and that want only got worse when we finished driving through the main part of town and got back out into the country. It smelled like cow shit.

David was informing me of the lovely fact that the nearest movie theater was a twenty-five minute drive away when we pulled into the gravel road that functioned as the Marshall's driveway.

Their farm was a small one, but their house was actually nice from the outside. It was two stories, with a long porch that ran across the entire front side of the house and along another side of it as well. There was a wooden porch swing at the end of it, and I pictured an imaginary version of twenty-year-old Scott Marshall swinging back and forth with a straw hat and overalls on, spitting sunflower seeds. Then I felt like hurling again.

Behind the house was a pasture. I could see a stable from where I sat in David's car, which confirmed that they had horses, and I saw cows grazing out in the fields near a barn. I tried to remember which animals had been listed on the paper. Horses, cows, and… something else. Hopefully not pigs.

David got my suitcases out of the car for me and carried them to the porch. Grudgingly, I followed, my purse in my hand, and looked down at the ground, trying to watch my step. I was in heels and it was getting darker by the second. Eight o'clock had come and gone just minutes ago.

I was almost to the porch when the front door flew open, and out came a plump blonde woman with her arms outstretched. "Oh, dear, look at you!" she gushed, pulling me into a hug, and I knew then that I'd seen hell.

When she was finished crushing me, she grasped my biceps and pulled away to get a good look at me. I scowled. "David, she's so pretty! Oh, she'll have such a good time here! Come on in, sweetie."

David gave me a small smile, like we were in on some secret regarding how much dislike I already held for his wife, and I glared back at him, letting him know that I blamed him for this.

He was, admittedly, not a Southern stereotype, but his wife was pretty damn close to one. She was just missing a thicker accent.

I became more self-conscious once I was inside. I'd felt enough like an outsider from the moment we'd entered the county limits, but standing in the Marshall's country home's living room, sporting heels, a short skirt, and hoop earrings, I felt more out of place than ever.

"Where are Cam and Scott?" David asked, placing my bags in the living room.

Wendy scoffed. "Being rude, as usual." She looked to me hastily. "Forgive my manners as well, honey. I'm Wendy."

"Lauren," I forced myself to say, but she seemed preoccupied with walking to the bottom of the stairs rather than listening to me. I jerked with surprise when she let out a shout.

"SCOTT! CAMMIE! OUR GUEST IS HERE! GET DOWN HERE!"

There was a thump and a muffled curse from somewhere upstairs, and Wendy practically flushed with embarrassment, glancing at me again. Both of my eyebrows were at the top of my forehead, and I struggled to hide my amusement. Okay, so the parents were intolerable, but maybe their kids wouldn't be so bad.

Scott came downstairs first, running a hand through his hair self-consciously as he reached the bottom. He had the dark hair of his father rather than the blonde of his mother, and he was dressed in a T-shirt and jeans, the latter of which had a small dirt stain on the right thigh. I grimaced even as he raised his own eyebrows, taking me in.

"Hey there." He smiled, holding his hand out. "Wow. Uh, I

mean, nice to meet you and all." His accent was strange: a mix between his father's Midwestern and his mother's mild Southern. Trying to hide my distaste for his hygiene, I shook his hand and made a mental note to wash mine as soon as possible.

Wendy, meanwhile, scowled at him. "You better not let Jill hear you talking like that."

"C'mon, Mom," he sighed out. "I'm not allowed to think another girl's pretty?"

"Not if you wanna marry Jill, you aren't."

I pursed my lips awkwardly as Scott rolled his eyes, and David tried his best to change the subject. "Scott, where's Cameron?"

Scott shrugged. "Probably up there doing her physics homework. You know how she gets."

"Sorry!" a female voice called, and down came Cam, her blonde hair bouncing in a ponytail even as she caught sight of me and grinned.

I felt an immediate sense of anxiety. She wasn't cute. She was *hot*.

Cameron Marshall was not a round-faced, doe-eyed Southern girl that looked like the type to go to church every Sunday and probably wanted to wait until marriage to have sex. If what David had told me was any indication, she probably had the *personality* of that round-faced doe-eyed Southern girl, but she looked like the opposite of all of those things, and while it was relieving to have a hot girl around, my brain and libido were a little conflicted by her presence.

My libido was saying "hot girl," but my brain was saying

"bigoted Southern girl" and they were *both* saying "innocent girl," and it took me a moment to realize she'd offered her hand for me to shake.

"I'm Cammie. Lauren, right?"

"Yeah," I replied shortly, and shook her hand for less time than I'd shaken Scott's. There was no template in my head for how to react to her, no set of dialogue that I knew would guarantee she'd like me. I was completely out of my comfort zone.

"Cool. Well, I don't know if Dad's told you yet, but if you have any questions, I'm the one to ask. You'll be staying in my room."

I nodded. "He told me." The Marshall family was a strange one. They each had different accents, and to varying degrees. Cammie had her father's, with just a barely audible Southern twang. But I'd avoided my worst nightmare: five months full of "y'all"s and "ain't"s.

"Cammie, help Lauren take her bags upstairs, and then we'll have dinner. Scott, help me set the table," Wendy ordered. Both of her kids immediately obeyed. Scott headed into the kitchen, and Cammie brushed by me to grab my larger suitcase. I followed her up the stairs with my smaller one, silently wondering if I'd eventually wind up following instructions robotically the way that they did.

Once Cammie and I were alone in her room, I put my suitcase down and surveyed the area. The room was surprisingly large, featuring a walk-in closet and two single beds with a nightstand resting between them. There was a Bible on that nightstand, and Cam had a couple of posters on her walls. Both were of Ryan Hansen movies. He was this cheesy romance novel writer, and I couldn't stand his stuff.

I also noticed a large, open briefcase on a desk by the far wall, filled with rows of organized colored pencils and pastels. Beside it on her desk was a large piece of paper, although I couldn't see what was on the paper from my position on the other side of the room.

"Here we are," Cammie declared. I could tell she wasn't quite sure how to handle my arrival, and it pleased me to know that I wasn't the only uncomfortable one here. I tried to look at the situation from her perspective. I was a kid that had misbehaved enough to warrant a flight across the country, and I was wearing four-inch heels and an outfit that wasn't exactly modest. I'd probably be intimidated by me too.

I pointed at the open briefcase. "What's that?"

She followed my gesture and her eyes widened. I watched her hurry over, close the briefcase, and then tuck the paper underneath it, thinking her actions strange even as she forced a smile my way. "Nothing. Sorry. I should've cleaned up before you got here, but I lost track of time." She cleared her throat and clapped her hands together. "Anyway, we should get down to dinner. Mom made steak tonight."

She left the room and gestured for me follow. I took one last glance around, murmured, "Fucking Ryan Hansen?" and then moved to trail behind her.

* * *

They joined hands and prayed before their meal. I sat between David and Cammie, and he simply sent me a knowing smile and reached past me to take Cammie's hand under the table, unbeknownst to Wendy and Scott. I could tell Cammie was confused by the gesture, but she didn't protest it, and I feigned joining in until Wendy's eyes had closed and she was no longer paying attention to me. As she spoke, I made a half-hearted effort to listen.

It wasn't that I was an Atheist... well, I guess I was, but it wasn't in an effort to be anti-religion or anything. My parents weren't religious, and the few times I'd gone to church with friends, it just hadn't been my thing. So, in the same way that far more children grow up Christian, I grew up nonreligious. And by the time I hit thirteen or so and realized I wasn't a part of the majority religiously, it was too late to convince me God existed.

It wasn't like I hated Christians or anything, though. I mean, give me a Christian version and an Atheist version of the same person and ask me which one I'd rather hang with and honestly I'd probably pick the Atheist version, but only because that version is a little more likely to avoid telling me I'm a sinner who's gonna burn in hell, and I like that in a friend.

I was dreading fighting with the Marshalls about church in two days. Mostly because I had a feeling its attendees were of the extremist variety, the Marshalls included. But David trying to ease my discomfort by not forcing me to take part in the family prayer was a good sign, at least.

When they finished praying, they immediately dug into their steaks, which were served with mashed potatoes and green beans.

I reached for my knife and fork and was about to cut into my steak when I froze on the spot, a wave of nausea abruptly hitting me. I thought of the cows out in the pasture.

David was the first one to notice I wasn't eating. "Are you okay, Lauren?" he asked.

I shook my head, my lips pressed together tightly. I was sure I was going to vomit. My eyes were trained on the small amount of red juice that had pooled on the plate beneath my steak.

David set his utensils down. I could feel four pairs of eyes on me. "What's wrong? Do you feel sick?" he asked.

I nodded, swallowing hard, and then spoke quickly, eager to shut my mouth again. "Steak is cow, right?"

The entire family was silent for a moment. And then Scott caught on first, clearing his throat just after he swallowed a bite of the meat. "Oh. Yeah, I forgot to let you know, Dad... ol' Bessie put up a fight at first, but by the end of the struggle, I think she knew it was her time to go. Isn't fresh meat the best kind?"

"For God's sake, Scott," Wendy reprimanded even as Cammie chuckled beside me. Wendy turned to me. "We don't eat our own animals, dear, unless you count the eggs from the chickens." She shot Scott another glare even as I felt some of my queasiness dissipate, and he grinned over at me.

"She reminds me of Cammie," he said, nudging his sister. "Remember? You were eight and Dad told you where hamburgers came from? You didn't eat meat for three years."

"Shut up," Cam mumbled.

With a little trepidation, I went ahead and began to cut into my steak. "So nothing that was ever alive out there will ever end up here?" I clarified before I took a bite, pointing first in the direction of the pasture and then to my plate. David nodded beside me.

"That's right," he said.

"Good," I replied. If the Marshalls did eventually manage to force me into making contact with dozens of nasty farm animals, I honestly wouldn't be able to look any of those cows or chickens in the face knowing I'd be eating them later.

They were still gross, though.

* * *

I wanted to go upstairs and take a shower in Cammie's and Scott's shared bathroom after dinner, but David made me stay at the table while everyone else cleared it off and took their plates to the sink. David took mine, much to my relief. I wanted to be a pain in the ass, but I was majorly jet-lagged and didn't really have the energy to argue with anyone today. If they'd made me do my own dishes, I probably would've agreed just to avoid any hassle. Tomorrow, on the other hand, was a different story.

I found out why David hadn't freed me from the table after the dishes were cleaned. The rest of his family left us alone, and he sat down across from me and cleared his throat, lacing his fingers together and resting them on the table. "So what do you think so far?"

"I'd like to go home," I said, and he nodded expectantly.

"I know. But it'll get better."

"You really think I deserve all of this?" I asked him. "Just for not going to class for three months? Since when is being sent to a new home across the country a viable punishment for that?"

David was silent for a moment. When he did eventually speak, he admitted, "I haven't been completely honest with you. I was hoping to get you to open up on your own... but perhaps it'd be better if we just laid everything out on the table, so to speak."

"I'd prefer that," I agreed, narrowing my eyes at him.

"I've heard all about your mother," he told me, much to my surprise.

"But no one knows about that," I countered. "How could you—?"

"Judge Jacobs was provided with your school file, of course. There's a lot of information in there. Everything you've been in trouble for... your grades... and the names of both of your parents. You're here because you're a special case, Lauren, and because you've been through a lot. Whether you realize it or not, growing up without a consistent guardian to watch over you *is* out of the ordinary, and it *has* affected your behavior."

"You act like I'm some sort of heathen," I shot back. "Why would the judge play dumb with me?"

"Did he? Or did you assume he didn't know about your mother because he wasn't as sympathetic to your situation as you thought he should be?" I ground my teeth silently, and that was enough of an answer for him. He leaned toward me. "Listen, Lauren. We are all here to help. The rest of my family doesn't know who your mother is, and we can keep that between us, if that's what you want. But this is a team effort, and you have to be willing to work with us."

"Then we have a problem," I told him, my voice sharp, "because I'm not."

He looked disappointed. "Well… at any rate, at least we can improve your school attendance. But that's honestly the least of my concerns."

As much as I wanted to end our conversation, that piqued my curiosity. This entire trip had been made out to be some kind of attendance reform program. Now the rules had changed? "Then what *are* your concerns?" I asked him.

He rattled off answers like he'd done it dozens of times over in his head. "Substance abuse, lack of guidance, intimacy issues, depression, loss of a loved one…"

"Okay, I do not have intimacy issues," I countered, offended. "*Or* depression."

"From what I understand, you've spent three months lying in bed since the death of your mother," he pointed out. "That seems indicative of depression."

"God, my mother just died!" I hissed out, remembering to be quiet for the sake of the rest of the Marshalls. "Of course I was sad. Or… *am* sad. It's okay to be sad."

"But it's not okay to miss school for three months." He stood without any warning, and I took that to mean I could stand as well. "That's enough for tonight. Tomorrow you'll be helping out on the farm."

I snorted. "Yeah, right. Over my dead body."

He pursed his lips together as I left him there. "Goodnight,

Lauren."

I was up the stairs before he'd even finished speaking. Seconds later, I ducked into Cammie's room briefly to get everything I'd need for my shower, and saw that she was sitting on her bed now, her Bible open on her lap. She looked up too late to see my eye-roll, and smiled brightly at me. "How'd it go?"

She saw my next eye-roll, then, and a moment later, I was out of her room and in the shower, thankful to finally have some peace and quiet. I ran through the Marshalls in my head, trying to work out what exactly I thought of them. I knew I didn't want to be here, and I knew that that wasn't going to change, but what I hated most so far was the way that David seemed determined to pry into my personal life. I didn't like Wendy, either, but at least she was a good cook.

Scott had potential, though. He was a boy, sure, and one that'd looked at my breasts before my face when we'd first met, but he seemed to be the most relaxed of the Marshalls, and I was eager to hang out with anyone who wasn't uptight for as long as I had to stay here.

Cammie, on the other hand, seemed to be a lot more likely to adhere to every little rule her parents made. She was nice, but she was a good church girl who wore parent-approved outfits that didn't show too much skin, and she read the Bible every night from the looks of things. I didn't expect to be having any sort of fun with her anytime soon, sexual or otherwise. She was hot, but I knew her type: a total stick in the mud.

I finished my shower and got ready for bed, even though I

knew I wouldn't be sleeping anytime soon. It was just after ten thirty, which meant it was seven thirty back in Los Angeles. Nowhere near my body clock's bedtime.

Cammie was still buried in the Bible when I returned to her room, but she set the book aside even as I grabbed my mp3 player out of my purse and went to sit on my bed. "You brought that from L.A.?" she asked. I knew she was just making polite conversation, and nodded. "What kind of music do you like?"

"All kinds." A thought struck me and I smirked to myself. "Except for country."

"Not even Taylor Swift?" she asked, sounding genuinely surprised. I practically snorted.

"Uh, no. Definitely not Taylor Swift."

"What about Luke Bryan?"

"I don't know who that is," I replied simply, then put both earbuds in and cranked up my music. But Cammie replied before I could completely drown her out, and I missed about half of her sentence. Sighing, I paused the song. "What?"

"I said, how can you not have heard of Luke Bryan?"

"Because I'm not from the middle of nowhere?" I replied uncertainly. She shot me a knowing smile, briefly reminding me of her father.

"He's on the radio. So what *do* you listen to, really?"

I sighed again and unplugged my earbuds from the mp3 player, then tossed it to her. She caught it easily and proceeded to scroll through my music. Occasionally, she made a comment, like, "The Beatles, cool," or "I can't believe you don't like Taylor Swift but you have Avril Lavigne on here."

46

Regarding the latter, I couldn't stay silent. "I've had that library since age eleven, okay?"

"Suuure," she drawled. "I bet when you get mad at your parents you slam your bedroom door shut and blast 'What the Hell.'"

I scowled at her. "Real hilarious. Can I have it back, now?"

She tossed it back to me. "You're missing my favorite band."

"I'm shocked," I deadpanned. "Look, I'm not gonna get a lot of sleep tonight otherwise, so I'm just gonna listen to music now and hope it helps. My body thinks it's not even eight o'clock yet."

"Okay," she agreed simply. "That's a good idea, I guess. We have to wake up at nine in the morning tomorrow."

"What? Why?" I was most certainly *not* waking up that early, especially when my body would be telling me it was six in the morning.

"To get to work on the farm. We do it every Saturday."

"Then Sunday is church, and then you have five days of school," I realized. "Which days don't suck?"

"Well, I don't think any of them do." She looked amused now. "But Saturday's not as bad as it sounds. If we work quickly, we can have most of the day free."

"Or if I don't work at all, I can have all of it free," I countered, then put in my earbuds and looked away from her before she could reply.

Chapter Three

Sure enough, I woke up to an alarm at nine o'clock on Saturday morning.

It blared for a solid fifteen seconds before I heard Cammie fumble for the button to shut it off. She got out of bed, but I stayed put, wrapped up in my comforter with my face half-buried in my pillow. I pulled the comforter over my head and squeezed my eyes shut, annoyed that I was going to have to start my whole rebellion plan this early in the morning. I wanted to go back to sleep, not spend half an hour arguing with Cammie and the rest of the Marshalls about whether or not I'd be shoveling horse shit today.

After a few seconds of footsteps padding around the room, I finally felt Cammie's hand on me through the comforter. "Hey Lauren, it's time to get up," she said. I didn't move. There was silence for a moment, and then she called my name again. I heard her sigh when I still didn't move. "I know you're awake." After another few seconds, she gave up and left the room. I relaxed a little and tried to go back to sleep, hoping maybe I'd won, but it wasn't long before she returned. This time Scott was with her, and he laughed when he saw the way I'd burrowed beneath the covers.

"C'mon, Lauren. Ready to try some hard labor?" he asked, and I'd finally had enough.

I moved the covers off of myself and glared at them from where I laid. "No. I'm going back to sleep."

"Sorry. I don't think Dad's gonna let you do that," Scott said.

"He can't make me work when I don't want to," I argued.

"Yeah, that's true, but arguing all the time is only going to make your seven months here harder," Scott countered. Behind him, Cammie looked annoyed with me.

"You're already awake. Just get out of bed," she said.

"Have you *seen* me?" I asked them. "I don't do manual labor. In fact, I don't do any kind of labor. But what I *do* do is sleep in. Every day. Including today. Goodbye." I threw the covers back over myself and rolled over to put my back to them, huffing loudly.

"Jeez. Spoiled, isn't she?" I heard Scott murmur. Cammie made a small sound of agreement. I felt redness in my cheeks almost instantaneously even as they both left the room, and my heart sank in my chest, then started beating faster. For a moment, I was back in Los Angeles, walking into class late with a brand new manicure and a coffee as Cassidy Parkinson leaned over to whisper the same insult to the friend who sat next to her.

I swallowed hard and whispered aloud, "I'm not spoiled."

Realizing I couldn't get back to sleep now, I sat up in bed and rubbed at my eyes. I felt like absolute shit, but I wasn't sure if that was because I'd woken up so early or because of what Scott – and indirectly, Cammie – had said about me. I hated that they'd hit a nerve so quickly. "Spoiled" was one of my very few kryptonites. They didn't even know about how rich my family was and yet, they were already using the insult against me. That was what hurt the most. I'd thought before that I'd only ever been called spoiled because people knew I had money.

I went to my suitcase, started rummaging through it for clothes to wear, and found the shirt and shorts I cared about the least. When it was time for shoes, I stared down at my collection with trepidation. I had a case full of heels and one pair of sneakers, but they were white and unworn.

That was when Cammie found me. She walked back into her room, alone this time, and raised both eyebrows when she saw me kneeling by my suitcase. "You're up?" she asked, not bothering to hide her surprise.

"I can't decide which shoes to wear," I told her, only giving her a quick glance. I knew deep down that the sneakers were probably about to be ruined today, but I was hoping there was a chance that she'd offer an alternative.

Cammie was still hung up on the fact that I was out of bed. "Really? For going outside?"

I crossed my arms and stood, looking to her. "This doesn't mean I want to do it, or that I'll have fun," I told her. "But I'm not spoiled."

I could tell she was trying to hide a smile. "My brother hit a nerve," she guessed.

"Just help me pick out shoes." I gestured toward the suitcase and she joined me in looking over what I'd brought.

"All you have is heels," she said, appalled. "Doesn't it hurt to wear them constantly?"

"I've been wearing heels since age five," I explained. "But obviously I can't wear them today."

"Well, you have those sneakers." She pointed them out.

"I don't wanna ruin them."

"What size are you?" she asked.

"A four," I said.

"*What?* Wow, you have tiny feet! I'm a six, sorry. I think you may have to just wear the sneakers." She shrugged her shoulders. "But we won't give you much to do today. You can mostly just observe."

"Good," I said.

She smiled at me. "I'm glad you decided to join us."

"Well, I figured your dad would come force me anyway," I half-lied. I'd been prepared to combat David as well, if need be.

Cammie shook her head. "I don't think so, actually. That's not really how he does things." She paused, and then corrected herself. "Well, he'll force you with school, but only because that's a legal thing. Anyway, do you want breakfast? Mom's making French toast."

"She cooks every meal?" I asked, baffled. I couldn't remember the last time my parents had cooked a meal before Dad's pancakes the other day.

"Of course," Cammie replied, but I was lost in my own thoughts. It felt like so much longer than a day since I'd gotten here. Five months would feel like a lifetime at this rate.

Cammie and I spent a few minutes getting ready in the bathroom, and then she put on some real clothes and we went downstairs together. I followed behind her and couldn't help but stare. She'd chosen a pair of shorts and a tanktop, and I could see now that her arms weren't muscular, but they were toned from what I supposed had to be constant manual labor. She was definitely in shape.

I forced myself to look away and swallowed the lump in my throat. *The roommate is off-limits,* I told myself silently. *You can look, but don't even think about touching.*

I ate breakfast with Cam and the rest of the Marshalls, who all seemed pleasantly surprised to see me up, and David explained the chores for the day. Cammie and I were to take care of the horse today, which sounded like the best job of them all to me. For one, there was no plural "horses," which meant just one animal to deal with, and secondly, I figured Cammie would be willing to do all of the work today. So really, I'd only complied by waking up early, and I'd gotten a good breakfast in exchange for that. I wasn't doing any work, and that made me feel better about giving in to Scott and Cammie earlier.

We went outside after breakfast, Cammie and I bringing up the rear, and I felt the cow shit smell flood my nostrils. I paused, second-guessing myself, and Cammie stopped beside me, putting a hand on my arm. I glanced down at the action and she removed it sheepishly, but told me nonetheless, "You can do this. You're not spoiled, right? You can work just as hard as the rest of us."

"Emotional manipulation—I'm impressed," I sighed out. "Did your dad teach you that?"

She rolled her eyes at me and dropped the act. "C'mon. It'll be over soon."

We trudged out to the stable together, and Cammie listed out everything that needed to be done. I pretended to listen; it wasn't like I'd be willing to do any of it anyway.

There was one horse alone in its stall, and I stood by the entrance to the stable as Cammie went to go pat him on his head. "Good boy, Aerosmith," she cooed, and I raised an eyebrow at the name.

"It's named Aerosmith? Why?"

"*He* is, yes," she corrected. "And I named him."

"Your favorite band," I realized. "Seriously? Why?"

"Why did I name him that or why is it my favorite band?"

"Why is that your favorite band? I assumed it was, like… The Wiggles, or something equally wholesome."

Cammie laughed at that. I liked her laugh; it was a pretty, almost giggly laugh that made the corners of my lips tug upward. "Not exactly. My dad has all their albums; he used to play them a lot in the car when I was a kid. Even if I start to like another band just as much, they'll never beat the nostalgia factor."

"My dad likes to blast Queen," was all I could really think of to say to that.

"What, like, Bohemian Rhapsody?"

"Yeah." I paused. "I know everyone's heard that song, but it still kind of surprises me that you have."

"I don't live in a tiny little country bubble," she said. "We're still in the 21st century."

"Well, it feels like I've crossed over into the 1800s," I admitted. She looked away from me, petting the horse for another moment before she cleared her throat and stepped away.

"Okay, anyway, the first thing we should probably do is clean out his stable. Something tells me you won't have any part of that, so I guess just stand back and don't get into any trouble." She smiled at me to let me know she was joking, and reached over to unlock the stall. I backpedaled instantly, putting some distance between the stable and myself.

"Wait, you're letting it out?"

"Just for a minute. I can't clean this up otherwise. Just... go take a lap around the house or something and I'll be done when you get back." She snapped her fingers, like she'd just had an epiphany. "Actually, you can go grab something from the house. It's gonna get warmer out as we get closer to noon, so you might wanna grab a hair tie and a couple of baseball caps out of my closet."

"Okay," I agreed, eager to get away from the stable. I headed back to the house and was surprised when I didn't come into contact with any of the Marshalls on the way there. I knew from David's list this morning that he and Wendy were with the cows and Scott was with the chickens, but I couldn't remember what they were supposed to be doing with them other than that the cows needed to be milked. That was one job I was sure I'd never do.

I took off my now-muddy shoes before I went upstairs to Cammie's room. I found the things she'd asked for without much difficulty, but paused on my way out when I caught sight of the closed briefcase still sitting on her desk. Sticking out from beneath it was a corner of the white paper, just barely visible.

I took two seconds to pretend like I needed to debate Cammie's right to privacy, and then crossed to the desk and opened the briefcase again. It was exactly as I'd seen it last night. Rows and rows of colored pencils and pastels of every shade lined the briefcase, and most of them were nearly down to little nubs. There were also a couple of paintbrushes I hadn't noticed the night before, along with around seven different small tubes of paint. So Cammie was an artist.

I closed the briefcase and set it aside, taking in the image on the paper beneath it. She hadn't gotten very far along, but I could tell what she was drawing was some sort of cityscape. Skyscrapers stretched up toward the top of the paper, and a couple of street lamps lined what were the beginnings of a road. There was a lot of blue shading, which told me she'd meant it to be a night scene. A car was visible on the not-quite-a-street, but only the tire and a yellow outline had been drawn. It was a taxi.

"New York," I guessed aloud, surprised. What surprised me even more was that it was *good*. Cammie could draw.

I put the briefcase back over top of the paper and moved quickly, not wanting Cammie to wonder why I'd taken so long.

On my way outside, I passed the house phone, which was tempting. But I'd only been here for one day, so it wasn't like I'd have much to report to Caitlyn, and besides, there was still the matter of getting back to Cammie quickly so as not to arouse suspicion.

She was done cleaning the stable by the time I reached her, and instead was brushing the horse. I kept my distance, and she came to me to take the hat. Her hair was already up, so she just pulled her ponytail through the back of the cap, and then asked me, "Do you want any help?"

"Oh," I replied, feeling dumb as I looked at my remaining hair tie and cap. "Uh, I don't wear hats."

She tilted her head to the side quizzically, reminding me of a confused puppy. Then she smiled. "You know, I think you and my best friend would have a lot in common."

"I don't know whether I should be offended by that or not," I replied, horrified at my own imaginary creation of Cammie's best friend. I pictured one tooth and a straw hat.

Cammie rolled her eyes, looking mildly annoyed with me. I suspected she'd read my mind, because she told me, "You have got to stop the stereotyping. She's actually really cool. Her name's Tiffany."

"God," I murmured and put my hair up into a ponytail, then slapped the cap on in hopes it'd get her to stop talking.

It didn't work. "What? You don't even like her *name*, now?" Cammie asked. "You haven't even let me tell you about her. I really do think you'll like her, you know... She doesn't get along with most of the kids that stay with us but you guys kind of seem similar. She hates when I try to convince her to help out around here too."

"Not a farm girl. Okay." I wrinkled my nose. "But her name's Tiffany. Does she wear all pink and carry around a Chihuahua?"

Cammie rolled her eyes at me again. "No. She's our school's head cheerleader, though."

I mimed a gag. "Okay, no. Sorry."

She looked offended. "*I'm* on the cheerleading squad too, you know."

"Voluntarily?" I asked, just to annoy her. I could tell by her expression that it'd worked.

"Yes, of course. And all my friends are." She turned away from me and went back to brushing her horse, and I could tell I'd frustrated her. It struck me then how little I knew about her, even though we'd made relatively easy conversation today.

I was silent for a moment, still keeping a few good feet in between the horse and myself. Cammie stopped brushing him and moved to do something with his hooves that involved scraping with some sort of pick; I couldn't see her actions clearly from my position, and there was no way I was getting any closer to the horse.

Finally, I asked her, "So why do you like cheerleading?"

She took a moment to answer, but when she did, it was simply with a shrug of her shoulders and an, "Oh, I don't know. I guess it's kind of fun sometimes. My mom was a cheerleader when she was younger too."

"So is that what you do in your free time? Just go to

cheerleading practice? Do you have any other pastimes?" I was curious now if she'd admit to her drawing hobby. She'd certainly wanted to cover it up last night. I wondered if even her own family knew, or if she'd gotten the briefcase somewhere else.

She straightened up, done with the hooves, and arched an eyebrow at me. "Why the third degree? Suddenly I'm fascinating to you?"

I suppressed a frown. "I'm just trying to get to know my roommate."

She stared at me, chewing at her bottom lip. She looked like she was thinking hard about something. "You really wanna know what I do for fun?" she finally asked.

"Well, I'm not gonna die if I don't get my question answered, but it beats talking to your dad about whether or not I cry myself to sleep every night," I countered, folding my arms across my chest. She looked satisfied with that answer.

"Okay. I'll be right back. Stay here."

She hurried away into the stable before I could reply, leaving me here with the tied-up horse, who snorted loudly and pawed at the ground when she'd gone.

It was less than a minute later that she returned with several large contraption things in her hand. The only one I recognized was a saddle, but that was enough for me to get the idea. "No way in hell," I protested, taking a step back.

She smiled at me knowingly. "It's only scary until you get up there."

"Bullshit." I shook my head. "I'm not doing it. This is totally not what I had in mind when I asked what you did for fun."

"I own a horse. What did you expect?"

I scowled at her even as she moved to suit up Aerosmith.

"Good point. But yeah, no. Not gonna happen."

"Don't knock it 'til you try it," she recited. "Besides, the horseback riding isn't even the point. I want to show you something."

"You want to show me something," I echoed, disbelieving. "Why do we need the horse for that?"

"To get there," she replied simply.

"Why do you want to show me something? What makes you think I'm worthy of this something?" I argued. "I've known you less than a day."

"Because," she told me easily, "I like you." She finished with Aerosmith and shot me a small smile. "I think you're probably gonna be my favorite person we've ever had, actually."

I raised an eyebrow at her, and then shook my head, dismissing her compliment. "Okay, as flattering as that is, you don't even know me. What makes you think you're gonna like me best?"

Her small smile morphed into a grin then, and she replied, "Because you got out of bed on the first day."

* * *

"I'm a failure," I thought wryly as I reached for Cammie's hand and gripped it tightly. *"A certifiable, bona-fide failure. I might as well just convert to Christianity and start dating boys now. I am weak sauce. No backbone. No spine. Worthless, pushover, doormat—"*

"Swing your leg over!" Cammie instructed, and then pulled harder on my hand. I obeyed, and suddenly I was sitting in the saddle behind her while she gripped the reins and kept Aerosmith steady. "You did it!"

"Yay me," I replied weakly, trying hard not to look on the ground or to think about the fact that a few-inches-thick saddle separated me from touching a horse.

"Wrap your arms around my waist," Cammie told me, and I blinked at her back.

"Huh?"

"You'll fall otherwise," she replied. "Lock your hands together too."

"Oh. Okay." I scooted forward and followed her instructions, overly aware of how close we were sitting in the saddle. I felt more uncomfortable than I'd felt in years, and I was sweating bullets now. It'd gotten hot out quicker than I'd thought it would.

"We'll start off slow. Let me know if you get scared."

"I'm already scared. God, I don't even know you," I mumbled. She found that really funny for some reason.

"Just don't panic, okay? I've been doing this for years. You're safe with me."

"How do I get down?" I realized with alarm, and Cammie sighed in front of me.

"Don't worry about that yet."

"Yet?! Cammie, I'm from Los Angeles, in case you haven't noticed. I feel like I'm riding an alien."

She started laughing again. "Aw! You're gonna hurt his feelings!"

60

"Sorry if I'm a little unconcerned about that at the moment." I was momentarily distracted when the horse started moving, and immediately gripped Cammie tighter. I wasn't worried about the closeness anymore; I was terrified.

"You're okay," she told me quietly, and released one of the reins briefly to pat my hand. "I'll keep you safe."

"Where are we going?" I asked, trying to distract myself.

"Out to the woods," she explained. "See them, ahead?"

I looked up and spotted the cluster of trees in front of us. "Why there?"

"Because what I'm showing you is in there."

"Are you a serial killer?" I asked her, which made her chuckle.

"That's what happened to the last girl," she confirmed. "She was never seen again."

"At least her family was relieved," I played along, but Cammie sounded serious when she replied.

"What makes you say that?"

I considered her question. "Well, people send their kids here because they're problems, you know? They don't want to deal, so they give them up."

"I don't think that's it. Besides, Dad says you're here because his judge friend from college sentenced you to a stay here over attendance issues, knowing Dad would be able to help you. Your parents didn't have any say."

"Yeah, but I could tell," I told her. "I guess maybe he- they, I mean, felt a little bad, but they were still ready for me to go."

"I'm sure they love you." She paused. "And that they'd be sad if your new family had you axe-murdered in the woods near their home."

I forced a laugh and went silent after that, thinking about why I'd just covered up that my mom was gone. I'd known I didn't want anyone to know who my mom was, but now I realized I didn't want them knowing she'd passed away, either. That knowledge I was content to have stay between David and myself. I didn't want pity, and that was the only thing I'd get from Cammie, Wendy, Scott, or anyone else. And I didn't want them blaming her for my problems.

There was a worn path that already wound through the trees, and we followed it for long enough that I lost track of time, although I suspected it only took so long because I refused to let Cammie tell Aerosmith to go any faster than a walk. Eventually, the path ended, and opened up into a grassy clearing, big enough for a few mack trucks to fit inside and in the shape of an oval. "Here we are," Cammie announced, and Aerosmith slowed to a stop beneath us.

I didn't say anything at first, more concerned with watching her dismount. She tied Aerosmith to a tree and then returned to help me. "Okay, Lauren, you just need to swing your right leg over and—"

"What if I just, like, slide off front-first?" I suggested, looking over the side of the horse with trepidation. "It's too high to jump."

"Don't slide off that way; you just have to bend your knees and you'll be fine," Cam insisted quickly, but I was already working to get my legs hanging off of one side of the horse. Beneath me,

Cammie sighed, and I heard Aerosmith whinny nervously beneath me. "You're not listening to me."

I managed to get my right leg over the horse, and sat sideways in the saddle, eyeing the ground beneath me. "Can I just slide off like this?"

"Well, you might as well, now," she admitted, and stepped forward, beckoning to me. "Just make sure you slide rather than jumping. I'll catch you." She reached over and patted Aerosmith to try and calm him, then beckoned to me again. "Don't worry; you're not high up at all. It just looks that way from up there. On three, okay?"

I winced at the ground and nodded.

She counted me off. "One... two... three."

I slid forward and Cammie gripped my arms, helping me stick the landing and then propping me up when I accidentally stumbled forward into her. My hat bumped hers, indirectly yanking at my hair. "Ow!"

"Shh—don't scare him," she retorted, rubbing at a spot on her head and fixing both of our hats. When I'd finally gotten myself together, she gestured to the clearing. "Anyway, here we are. Not much, I know, but I haven't brought many people here so you should feel special."

"Did everyone you've shown it to get to see it on the first day?" I asked, raising an eyebrow smugly.

She rolled her eyes. "It's the second day, technically, and no. But it's different; you're living with me. If you ever need a place to think or be alone, I know it can get kind of crazy back there, so this is where I come. Sometimes alone at night to watch the stars."

"That sounds dangerous," I said.

"There's no one here; we live in the middle of nowhere," she pointed out. "And Aerosmith would notice if something was up, anyway. C'mon." She grabbed my hand and tugged me to center of the clearing, where she sat down and tilted her head up toward the sky. I took a seat beside her.

"Why are you showing me this?"

She was quiet for a moment, and pulled up a few blades of grass with one hand. At last, she shrugged, avoiding my eyes. "I guess… things just get a little rough around here sometimes. I like coming here to get away and I thought you might like it too." She shrugged again. "As for why I brought you here so soon… I know we seem like a stereotype. Our family. But when I was twelve, I slept in a bed a few feet away from a fourteen-year-old cocaine addict, you know? What we do isn't easy."

She looked at me, finally, and I stared back. I hadn't considered that at all since learning I'd be coming here. David mentioned he'd been doing this for ten years. Cammie would've been seven years old, and Scott, ten.

"I still remember the first time we had a girl. I was nine, and she was thirteen. Dad didn't give me any responsibility to watch out for her or anything, but that didn't change how I felt when she told me she was just going to the bathroom and then relapsed and cut herself. The people that come here have issues, and I know that. And I know that you're not just here for attendance. But God, those kids *hated* us. It took weeks for them to even have real conversations. You're different. You're out here with me on the first day."

"I'm sorry I'm spineless," I murmured, humbled by her story. "I meant to be more of a pain in the ass."

"I don't think it's spineless. I think you just have more going on than we can see. Because we knew that that girl had a cocaine addiction, and we knew that the other one self-harmed. Or at least my dad knew, but I could tell the other kids had stuff going on, you know? But you seem perfectly normal to me. Maybe just a little disgruntled, but frankly, you're kind of entitled to it."

"Finally someone admits it." I sighed with relief.

She forced a smile before continuing, "I know about the attendance thing, but I also know that can't be the only reason you're here. I don't know what your other issues are, and I guess I don't know if that's a good thing or not, or if it's scarier. But what I do know is that you're out here, helping – even if I have to use that term very loosely for the time being – and that can't be a bad thing. So I hope that while you are here, we can be friends. And this clearing is my olive branch to you."

She offered me another smile; this one was sincere. "I hope you decide to make an effort while you're here, Lauren."

Chapter Four

I spent most of that Saturday with Cammie after our trip to the field. She talked for most of it, telling me about life in Collinsville and about her family. She told me that her mother was born on a farm but moved up to Illinois when she was a teenager, which was where she eventually met David. Wendy'd always wanted to go back to farm life, and it'd been her idea to move to Collinsville and start a new life and family there after David got his degree in Psychology. So they compromised; they'd live on a farm, and David would run his practice at home as a side job while counseling students at the local high school. And that's what they'd done ever since.

She told me more about Scott too. He'd been dating Jill since their senior year of high school, and they'd gotten engaged recently. After they got married, they planned to move into a place nearby, and Jill would raise their kids while Scott helped out on the farm and worked on cars for a living. That was what he was in school for: to become a mechanic.

I noticed that what she didn't talk about, however, was herself. We were similar in that way. Closed-off, secretive. And although we were getting along, especially after what Cammie shared with me back in the clearing, it seemed that she'd reached her divulgence limit. Now there was definitely a sense of guardedness from both of us, like neither of us wanted to give too much away. For me, it was because I knew I planned to make changing myself difficult for the Marshalls in hopes that I'd get out of Georgia relatively unscathed. But I didn't know what her reason was.

After another admittedly fantastic dinner from Wendy, David wanted to talk to me again. So we spent another half-hour at the dinner table, him analyzing me while I droned on and on about how my day was okay, the horse was okay, Cammie was okay, everything was *okay*. It was my way of giving nothing away. I didn't want him to know that my day wasn't as bad as I thought it'd be, that the horse was terrifying, that Cammie was sweet and a little confusing, and that everything else totally and completely sucked.

Eventually, church came up. I drew the line in the sand there. "Listen. I want to be honest with you. I didn't plan on even leaving my bed today, but I did. But tomorrow's different. I'm not religious."

David was annoyingly accepting of that. "I understand. You made a great effort today, actually. More than we're used to. I think it's fair that if you don't want to go to church tomorrow, you shouldn't have to."

"I'm never going to want to go," I said, not backing down. "Really. Never."

He just nodded again. "If you change your mind, let me know."

"I won't," I said.

"Okay," he replied, and then changed the subject. "I'm just glad to see you're getting along well with Cammie. Honestly, it's been a while since I've seen one of our visitors click so quickly with Cammie *or* Scott. She seems to really like you."

"She's okay," I told him simply. "Can I go now?"

"Sure." And he let me.

I took a long shower after that. I hadn't gotten particularly dirty during the day – although my shoes were completely ruined – but I definitely felt dirty.

By the time I was changed into pajamas and back in Cammie's room, she was in the same place I'd found her last night: in bed with her Bible. I realized we'd apparently have a nightly routine in here together, so I got my mp3 player out. I was halfway under the covers when she finally acknowledged me, looking up from her Bible with her head tilted vaguely to one side.

"Lauren?"

I pulled a bud out of my ear and lifted an eyebrow, looking over at her. "Yeah?"

"Are you really not religious?"

Great. So we were going to have *this* conversation. "I'm not," I confirmed. "Did your dad tell you?"

"He just came up while you were in the shower. He told me you didn't want to come to church tomorrow. If you stay here, I have to stay back with you."

"Why? I don't need a babysitter," I protested, but I knew what her response would be before she even spoke. Admittedly, it had crossed my mind to use the phone tomorrow if they all left without me. I just needed to hear a familiar voice.

"We don't leave people here alone," she told me. "So you don't believe in God at all? In anything?"

"No," I said shortly. I tried to go back to listening to my music, but she didn't let me.

"How?"

I stared at her. "What do you mean, 'how?' I just don't. Can you explain why you believe there is a God?"

"Well..." she trailed off for a moment, "I guess it's just a feeling I get sometimes. Like someone's watching over me and out for me. Keeping me safe. You don't feel that?"

I shook my head, not looking at her as I scrolled through my music library using my thumb. "No, never. I guess it must be nice to believe someone cares about you, though."

She was silent for a while after that. When I finally looked over at her, she was back to reading her Bible, but her mouth was set in a small frown, and her eyebrows were furrowed. I got an explanation for that when she eventually spoke up again. "Do you really think that no one cares about you?"

"Of course they do," I responded instinctively, thinking mostly of Caitlyn, and, more notably, not at all of my dad. "I guess it'd just be easier to feel it on the inside, is all."

There was another long silence. Cammie turned a page of her Bible, and then cleared her throat. "I've never met an Atheist before," she admitted.

I glanced at her briefly, hiding a smile. "I've never met a girl named Cameron before."

* * *

I stuck to my guns about church. Wendy, I could tell, was disappointed, but David stayed true to his word and simply had Cammie stay behind while he drove Wendy and Scott to church with him.

It didn't take me long to realize there wasn't much to do at the Marshall's farm, given that I wasn't allowed internet access other than for homework and that cable television meant only fifty or so channels, some of which were geared only toward Southerners. I slept in after the whole ordeal of turning down church, and once I'd woken up again, I entertained myself by watching a few really uncomfortable local commercials before Cammie plopped down next to me on the living room couch and asked, "Is there anything in particular you wanted to do today?"

I was surprised by her hospitality. Cammie wasn't the type who was happy to get out of reading the Bible or going to church. It was very obvious that she liked being religious, and she liked going to church. I imagined she was pretty disappointed in having to miss out, so her asking me about my own preferences was out of left field for me.

She'd been nice to me so far, so I tried being nice to her. "Um, I don't know… is there anything you like to do?"

She considered my question. "Well, we have to drive about a half an hour if we want to get anywhere close to the sort of area you can kill a day exploring, but there are some cool places around town. Local restaurants and stuff. And we don't have a movie theater, but there is a place for drive-ins nearby. That can only be done at night, though, of course. Other than that… maybe the park?"

"You have a car?" I questioned, arching an eyebrow.

She grinned. "No. But I know where Scott keeps his keys."

"Wait, we can do that?"

"I don't see why not. It's just a trip into town, right?" I raised an eyebrow at her, and she added, hastily, "Maybe we should just try to beat my family back here, is all. Just in case."

And just like that, we were on our way into town, Scott's mud-covered pickup truck rolling over bumpy roads as trees passed by outside my open window.

For a moment, I tilted my head back, closed my eyes, and forgot about where I was, and even who I was with. For those few seconds, I was in Caitlyn's car, and we were on our way to the beach, the sun in our eyes and the wind in our hair. No responsibilities, no one forcing us to do anything we didn't want to do. No five months of farm work in a small town across the country. No David Marshall or his family.

Cammie turned on the radio and I opened my eyes, looking over at the dial even as she turned the volume up on a country song I didn't recognize. I wondered if she'd forgotten I didn't like country music.

I looked to her, next. Strands of her blonde hair whipped back and forth in the wind coming in through her window, and she had both hands on the steering wheel while a pair of sunglasses covered her eyes. The sun was bright and shining directly onto us, and I could see a few freckles on her face that I'd been too preoccupied to notice yesterday.

She glanced at me, and I looked out my window hastily, wondering if I'd been watching her long enough to have crossed over into staring territory. I heard her turn the music down a moment later.

"So did you leave anyone special back home?" she asked, catching me completely off-guard. I shocked myself by thinking of Caitlyn first, before I finally pulled myself together enough to reply.

"Um… define 'special'," I said, trying to avoid answering without having time to think it through first. Cammie had taken my lack of religious beliefs better than expected, but lesbianism was an entirely different issue. I wanted to choose my words carefully.

She laughed at my response and gave me a knowing look. "Oh. Okay."

I waited for her to say more, but it seemed our conversation was over for her. "Wait, what does that mean?"

She smiled through a shrug. "I don't know; I guess… it makes sense that you'd be the type to not settle down with anyone."

"Why? I'm a 'type' now?" I asked, more than a little offended.

"I didn't mean it like that, of course. It's just…" she hesitated, and then glanced to me knowingly. "I mean, c'mon. You're *really* pretty. I'm sure guys are really into you, right?"

I stared back at her, completely baffled at where she was going with this. "So what if they are?" I deflected, and she laughed again. "So you're totally that girl! I bet you hate commitment, don't you? You're like the bad girl who doesn't care what anyone thinks but happens to be popular anyway, yet is way too rebellious to have a serious relationship with any of the guys who fall over themselves trying to get with her. Like… like a female version of Justin from *A Lifetime of Karma*."

"What is it with you and Ryan Hansen?" I asked, scoffing to hide how disappointed I was. She was so, *so* off. "You have posters all over your walls. He just writes dumb, cheesy love stories."

"Every teenage girl enjoys a good love story," she argued. "And anyway, you didn't tell me if I was right or not."

I turned and rolled the window up, tired of trying to talk over the wind. Cammie, seeing what I'd done, mimicked the action and then shot me an expectant look as we pulled up to one of Collinsville's few red lights.

"Well?"

I was silent for a while. The red light turned green, and Scott's truck lurched forward. I looked at Cammie again. "How about you tell me whether or not you think you were right when it's been long enough that we actually feel like we know each other?"

She looked amused by the idea, but nodded nonetheless. "That sounds fair. Are we turning this into a bet?"

"It wouldn't work as a bet," I said. "It's totally subjective on your part. All you'd have to do is say you still think you're right, even if you didn't, and you'd win."

"I wouldn't do that." She pulled into the parking lot of our destination: a local burger joint she'd recommended. The car slowed to a halt and we unbuckled our seatbelts. Cammie turned in her seat to face me. "I guess that means you think I'm wrong, then?"

"A knack for accurate first impressions, you do not have," I confirmed. "Way off."

She eyed me for a moment, analyzing me in a way that was more than enough to convince me she was her father's daughter. "Okay. So no bet. But why don't you tell me what you think of me, then? Let's see if you can do any better."

"Fine," I agreed. It seemed easy enough. I looked her up and down for a moment, and she stared back at me almost defiantly. I smirked. "Okay. You said you're a cheerleader, so you're probably pretty popular. But not *too* popular... just enough so that every now and then a guy asks you out. But you turn them down because you're saving yourself."

She rolled her eyes at that, taking offense to it for some reason. "Oh, c'mon. You don't have to say it like that."

"Like how?"

"Like... in that condescending tone. Plenty of people wait."

"So I'm right, then?" I guessed, and she shook her head at me in disbelief. I ignored her and pressed on. "You don't have a rebellious bone in your body, you do everything your parents say, you're a straight-A student with *maybe* a couple of B's every now and then, and you love it here in Collinsville because like every popular kid, you love high school and you pretty much have your entire life together here… or at least you feel like you do. And you never want to leave. Oh, and you never curse, of course, because that wouldn't be very lady-like." I took a deep breath. "There. Done. Did I cover everything?"

She pursed her lips and stared back at me, but I could see the corners of her lips threatening to turn upward. "Not quite."

"Awesome." I pointed to the building we'd parked in front of. "So you said these burgers are good, then?"

* * *

They were. *Really* good. I ate all of mine and then some of Cammie's, who was so amused by my appetite that she even offered to get a couple more burgers to go. I turned that down for financial reasons, feeling self-conscious. I knew my dad had more than covered the cost of taking care of me when he'd written a check to David, but I had a strong feeling Cammie was using her own money to pay for us, and I felt bad about that. Especially given that she didn't know I had a lot of money waiting for me back in Los Angeles. Maybe I'd reimburse her if I ever got the chance.

We went to one of the local parks after that. It stretched about a half-mile long and housed seven or so fields, some of which were used for baseball, others for soccer. There was a gas station across the street from the park, so we left the truck there, went inside and got ice cream from a bin near the cash register, and then walked to the park. There, we circled the perimeter of the track for a while, occasionally stopping to watch at some of the fields where amateur baseball games had been started.

"Did you ever play sports?" Cammie asked me as we walked. I shook my head. I'd done a little gymnastics at around four years old, but that didn't really count.

"Not really. Did you?"

"Just cheerleading." She cut my next statement off before I could even open my mouth. "It *is* a sport."

She looked so indignant that I couldn't help but grin, so I hid my mouth behind a frozen Snickers bar on a stick. "Of course it is."

"George Bush was a cheerleader," she told me, as though this was supposed to sway my opinion. I chuckled.

"Well, that wasn't exactly the best strategy if you wanted to try and change my mind. If he can do it, anyone can."

She scoffed, but I could tell she wasn't actually upset. "Right. I forgot you're from Los Angeles. Well, *my* parents voted for Bush and for Romney."

"Don't you know you're not supposed to talk about politics when you're first getting to know somebody?" I asked, and regretted it as soon as I'd said it. Cammie didn't really react, but I knew the cliché I'd actually been thinking of was the one about first dates, and I knew it was possible she'd make the connection. I cleared my throat and rushed to continue our conversation. "Okay. I can give you cheerleading if you give me gymnastics at age four."

She laughed at that. If she'd noticed my awkward comment, she'd ignored it. "Deal."

Her phone buzzed, suddenly, and she dug through her purse for a moment before pulling it out and looking at it. "Oh, shit. We really lost track of time. Scott wants to know where we took his truck; he's gonna be pissed." She groaned, and then told me, "We should go."

"Alright," I agreed, trying to keep up even as Cammie quickly pocketed her phone and tossed the remnants of her ice cream into the nearest trashcan.

We were halfway back to Scott's truck before I realized that she'd cursed.

Twice.

Chapter Five

Scott wasn't happy with Cammie when we got back. I took longer to get out of his truck than she did, and so I wound up watching from the driveway as she met him on the front porch and he held his hand out expectantly. She pressed his keys into his palm a little too roughly to appear totally compliant, and he went back inside just as I reached the porch.

"Why'd we take his truck if you knew it'd piss him off?" I asked her curiously. She didn't seem the type to try and purposely antagonize anyone. Or the type to break rules.

She rolled her eyes. "I don't get my family sometimes. They say they want to make you feel welcome, but when I actually try to show you around, I'm in the wrong. It's so stupid."

We went inside, then, to find David and Wendy waiting in the living room. David swept Cammie aside without so much as a real greeting, and Wendy and I stood together awkwardly. I tried to pretend I couldn't hear them arguing in the other room, but their voices carried through the wall just loudly enough that I could make out a few bits and pieces of their conversation.

"...confidential information," David's low rumble of a voice explained as my eyes found my feet uncomfortably.

Cammie's retort followed a moment later, a little louder and easier to hear. "Well, she seems fine to me!"

I cleared my throat and looked at Wendy. "Can I use your phone, please?"

* * *

Caitlyn answered on the sixth ring. "Hello?"

"Oh, thank God," I sighed out, forgetting for a moment that Wendy was listening to my end of the conversation. "Hey."

"Lauren!" she practically shouted when she realized it was me. "Oh my God! Are you okay? What's going on there? Are they listening to you right now?"

"Um... kind of, a lot of stuff, and yes, but not your end," I answered hastily. "I've had the weirdest weekend of my life."

"Are you acting like a little shit?" Caitlyn asked knowingly. I could picture the grin she'd have on her face as she spoke.

"I went outside to a stable yesterday," I admitted, ashamed of myself. "And rode a horse. But no church! I put my foot down on church."

"Girl, what foot? Because from where I'm standing, both of

your feet are missing, along with your *spine*. Why'd you ride a horse? Gross."

I glanced to Wendy, who wasn't looking directly at me and pretended to busy herself with inspecting one of the kitchen countertops. A small frown was visible on her lips. "I got talked into it." I could feel my face reddening slightly; I knew Caitlyn well enough to realize what her next question would be.

"By who? Definitely not the dad. One of the kids?" There was a pause that stretched on for a little too long as I struggled to formulate a response, and then Caitlyn was laughing so hard that I was worried for my eardrums for a moment. "Oh my God! Oh, Lauren. They have a daughter, don't they?"

"Shut up!" I hissed, throwing Wendy another nervous glance. "I didn't say that!"

"You didn't have to!" She quieted down nonetheless, but I could hear the amusement in her tone as she asked, "Okay, so give me a number one to ten, then... wait, no. That's too obvious if they're listening on your end. Let's do one to twenty-five. Is she at least a twenty?"

"What even-?" I scoffed, and then rolled my eyes. "I'm not answering that! Seriously, this is not what I wanted to talk to you about."

"I don't see you sharing any other news that's actually good," she observed. "I'm just trying to focus on the positive."

"There's none of that here," I insisted. "What about you? Are you done being weird?"

"Weird? I'm not weird."

"That's debatable."

"You know what I mean. Not any weirder than usual."

"You were weird at the airport. When I said goodbye."

She sighed, holding off on a response for a moment. I heard the creak of the leather couch in her living room as she shifted. "I'm always weird about that. Doing gay stuff with your gay best friend is weird. I'm cool now, anyway; that's what you were asking, right?"

"I guess," I replied, but nothing felt resolved. I let out a breath. "I guess I just miss hanging out already, is all. I'm sorry I wasn't around more back when... I was around to *be* around."

Caitlyn was quiet for a long time again.

"You there?" I asked her eventually.

"Yeah. I'm just thinking. Maybe Georgia could be good for you in some ways. At the very least, it'll make you realize how much you take L.A. for granted."

"I doubt it. We're still getting out when I get back, right? Like we've always planned?" I asked her.

"Of course. We'll get a dog and an expensive apartment in a new city and be totally gay together, only not gay at all. You just have to get through this, first."

"Okay. I miss you."

"Miss you too. Stand your ground."

"I will."

I heard the smile in her voice as she replied, "Bye, Lauren. Call me again soon."

"Bye," I started to say, and then changed my mind and quickly interjected, "Hey, Caitlyn."

"Yeah?"

"Twenty-five," I breathed out, and then hung up the phone with a grin, cutting her off before she could react.

Wendy still looked vaguely perturbed as she took the phone back from me, and David and Cammie came back into the living room area just a few minutes later, after I'd taken a seat on the couch with the intent of trying out the television again. Cammie looked frustrated, David, disgruntled. She gestured for me to follow her upstairs, and, confused, I rose from the couch and obeyed. Whatever she wanted, it probably beat spending time with her parents.

She shut the door behind us once we were alone, then rounded on me with her arms folded across her chest. "So... Dad says since you've only been here for two days I can't be taking you around town without letting them know where we're going first."

"Okay," I said. I'd been expecting something like that after what I'd overheard. Cammie thought I seemed relatively normal compared to the Marshall's past visitors, and David knew I was nursing several bad habits and still feeling the effects of a close death in the family. I wasn't stupid; I knew that he'd probably told her I needed to be kept close to home and that she'd wondered why exactly that was considering I seemed totally okay.

Cammie was surprised by my nonchalant response. "Wait, you're okay with that?"

"I've gotten nothing but orders since I've been here," I told her. "What's one more?" I moved to sit on my bed, and she stared after me with disbelief.

"Okay... can I ask you a question?"

It wasn't nighttime yet, but I reached for my mp3 player anyway as I replied, "I guess. If I can ask you one." I was still curious about her art supplies, and although it'd only been two days since I'd gotten here, I had a strong suspicion that she planned to never mention them.

"Why are you here?" she asked. "I'll even take just the bare minimum. No details." She sat across from me on her own bed and crossed her arms again. "Drug addiction? Kleptomania? Neglectful parents?" I must have reacted to her last suggestion without realizing it, because she paused there and stared at me. For a moment, she looked like she felt sorry for me, and I felt my jaw tense with aggravation. Pity was the last thing I wanted. "I guess that would make sense," she admitted eventually. "If you didn't do anything wrong..."

"That's not it," I cut her off. Neglectful felt like the wrong word. Neglect implied purposeful lack of care. I didn't feel neglected. I felt... I don't know. Something else. But it wasn't neglect. "I'm here because of myself. And it's none of your business what I did."

I knew I sounded snippy, but I preferred her thinking badly of me to thinking badly of my parents. She didn't understand what life was like for them. How different it was from how she and her parents lived.

Cammie's voice was softer when she next spoke. "I'm just trying to understand. You just seem... really nice. I mean—"

"Really nice people can still have problems. They could even be worse than the mean ones," I told her, rolling my eyes. "At least you know exactly what you're getting with the mean ones." I cranked up my music and lay down, then, tuning her out. My question could be saved for another time; she'd pissed me off and I was done with this conversation.

If she replied to me at all after that, I didn't hear her.

* * *

David drove Cammie and me to school the next day. Collinsville High was a much smaller school than I was used to. It had a parking lot in the front and another in the back, and was made up entirely of only two buildings: a main building with two floors and interconnected hallways that formed three diamonds, and then a second building that mostly just contained the gym.

Cammie went straight to class, as things were still a little tense between us, but David showed me where his office was and then helped me get my schedule. I didn't look at it at first, only following his verbal instructions to get to my first class: Intro to Business.

My teacher was an old woman with a voice that reminded me vaguely of a parrot, and as she found me a place to sit, she reassured me that I'd have no trouble catching up with the rest of the class.

Intro to Business, as it turned out, was not nearly as useful as it sounded. It was a typing class. We sat in our chairs, backs straight, for ninety minutes, literally using a computer program to copy a sample business letter word for word. When we were done and it was printed out, we were allowed to get on the internet for the rest of the period. It was a complete bullshit class.

Once I'd finished my letter for the day, I finally took the time to look at my schedule. After Intro to Business was Music Appreciation. Following that was Home Economics, and then my last class was Health.

I stared down at the schedule for a moment, taking it in, and then abruptly raised my hand. It took a moment for my teacher to notice me. "Yes, Lauren?" she asked.

"Can I be excused? It's an emergency." That was the code David had told me to use if I ever needed to come see him, so I was immediately given a hall pass and sent on my way to his office.

He was scribbling something onto a notepad at his desk when I knocked on the door and then entered without waiting for his response. He barely got out a "What's wrong, Lauren?" before my schedule was tossed onto his desk and I was glaring at him.

"What is this?"

He took the paper into his hands and stared, his eyebrows furrowed. Then he looked back to me, confused. "Your schedule. Is there a problem?"

"Of course there's a problem; do you think I'm an idiot?"

He set the schedule down, concerned, and motioned for me to take a seat. "Of course not."

I remained standing. "Then why have I been given four classes even an untrained monkey could ace? I'm not stupid just because I had bad attendance, and I don't plan on being treated like I'm stupid."

"I don't think you're stupid," he repeated, sighing. "You're entering Collinsville High halfway through the semester, Lauren. There are certain classes you'd have a lot more trouble catching up in."

I bit my lip, trying to find a hole in his logic. I didn't mind having easy classes, honestly. It was the fact that they'd all been chosen for me that was the problem. Like it'd been expected that I'd bomb anything else. "So give me one real one, then. I don't care which of these you replace." I leaned down and prodded the schedule still on his desk. "There has to be something."

He watched me for a moment, gauging my expression, and I kept my own gaze firm. It wasn't about the class, really. It was about proving I wasn't who he'd assumed I was.

"Let me get this straight," he finally began. "You don't want to work on our family's farm. You don't want to go to church. Generally, you seem to want to skate through your seven months here as quickly and easily as possible. And now you're asking for harder classes?"

"I wouldn't have to if you hadn't treated me like a dumbass," I snapped, folding my arms across my chest. "But you did, so yeah. Give me a different class."

"Look, Lauren, I really don't see how that can be done. You'd probably need a tutor that could be available several times a week to help you with assignments, and I don't feel comfortable letting you meet up with someone that often when the majority of your time right now is supposed to be spent at our home."

"So have them meet me at home," I suggested. "My dad can

afford to pay for tutoring. I honestly don't really care what you have to do. I'm not letting you pigeonhole me into an incompetent problem child that needs to be babied for seven months. Sorry."

"That honestly wasn't my intention," he insisted, but he could tell by now that I wasn't budging. He let out a deep sigh, rubbing at his temples. "Alright. You'll need to be tutored by someone you know, who won't have trouble meeting up with you at home..." he trailed off, and then sat up a little straighter, like he'd had an idea.

"What?" I asked him. He moved to access his computer.

"Give me half an hour or so," he replied, "but I think I can get you into Cameron's Physics class. It'd be your third period, replacing your Home Economics course. But it's a very tough class."

I backpedaled quickly when I heard that idea. I didn't want Cammie to tutor me. I'd spent enough time with her this weekend to realize that too much time alone with her would probably just lead to tension and arguing, or else to a different kind of tension I didn't like to dwell on. "Is that the only option, though? On second thought, losing Home Ec would be really tragic; I've actually always wanted to know how to sew my name onto a little handmade pillow."

He shot me an expectant look. "This by far is the simplest and most convenient solution I can come up with, Lauren. Either you want the harder class or you don't. But don't make this decision lightly; I'm going to have to go meet with the teacher today and discuss your situation with her, so it would be best if you didn't go back on this."

I curled my upper lip unpleasantly, but waved my approval nonetheless. "Fine. Cammie can teach me Physics... but you're assuming she wants to."

"Cameron's a responsible student," he assured me. "She'll help you get caught up."

"Okay." I moved to leave, but he gestured for me to come back.

"Wait; stay here for a little while. I'd like to discuss yesterday with you."

"You mean you haven't gotten bored of our talks yet?" I asked, feigning surprise as I grudgingly took a seat. David forced a smile.

"I understand what it's like to be a teenager, Lauren. I know having someone your own age to spend time with is important, and I'm glad you and Cameron are getting along. But it's also important for you to keep in mind what comes naturally with that. Trust. Honesty."

"You want me to tell her about my mom," I deadpanned, realizing where he was going with this. "That's not gonna happen."

"The issue here is not your mother." He paused. "I suppose it's necessary that I stress what I told you before. You truly are a special case. You came here out of a lack of responsibility and guidance. Most of the kids we get have something extra: a bad thing. And I believe you do too, but not on the level Cam and Scott are used to, which is why Cammie is confused the way she is. You're here mostly to add good things – a decent attendance record, a supportive environment – not to remove bad ones, such as addiction. I don't feel it's my right to explain that to her, but it certainly is yours. Does that make sense?"

"I thought I had intimacy issues," I mumbled sarcastically. I was only partially following him, but from what I understood, he was basically trying to say that I was the unfortunate byproduct of a shitty home life, and *that* only made me angrier.

He smiled in a way that told me he'd picked up on my sarcasm. "Perhaps I worded that wrongly. I meant to suggest that you haven't had experience with a healthy relationship."

"So I haven't actually dated anyone. So what? Is that even any of your business?"

"I didn't specify that it had to be a romantic relationship."

It took a moment for me to make sense of that, and when I did, I glowered at him, at a loss for words. "Wow," I finally breathed out, infuriated. "Are you serious? I love both of my parents. I love my best friend. Those are more than enough."

"But do you feel you have a healthy relationship with any of those people?" he pressed gently. I grit my teeth, resisting the urge to bite out an instinctive response.

I considered his question. My mother was always working and then she was gone forever. My dad had had an alcohol problem for as long as I could remember. And Caitlyn... we adored each other, but we were a little bit of a roller coaster friendship, and I wasn't sure the whole "occasionally having sex and then being awkward about it afterward" thing was totally healthy.

"It's not fair for you to judge people you don't even know," I muttered, finally. I felt an ache in my chest start to form as I struggled to shake off what he'd said.

"I only asked a question, Lauren," he told me, his voice still annoyingly gentle. I shot him another glare.

"But you knew what the answer'd be when you asked it."

He offered me a sympathetic smile. The worst kind. "Not entirely. But it seems like you just gave me yours."

* * *

The rest of the day was, frankly, terrible. I missed the first half of my Music Appreciation class, and when I finally arrived, it turned out to basically just entail sitting in a circle with musical instruments in a ceremony vaguely reminiscent of my Kindergarten musical experiences.

After that was lunch, only the lunch periods were beyond confusing, and I wound up sitting alone at a table for two lunch periods instead of one. Then it turned out *neither* of those lunch periods were the one I was supposed to have attended, and so by the time I finally got to Home Economics, they were actually leaving to go to lunch. So I spent another half hour drinking a chocolate milk alone.

Health class at the end of the day wound up being ninety minutes of watered-down Sex Ed. I felt sorry for the lanky, slightly dorky guy teaching the class, until he said something about abstinence that made me snort loudly enough for the whole class to hear, and he shot me a glare that told me he wasn't nearly as much of a pushover as he seemed to be.

All in all, it was about as horrific as I'd expected, and when Cammie and I converged at David's office to hitch a ride back home with him, I didn't pretend that I'd liked it.

David handed me a sheet of paper as he exited his office. "Here's your new schedule, Lauren," he said.

I fixed my gaze to the paper to see that it was the same schedule we'd discussed earlier. My Home Ec class was gone, replaced with AP Physics. I balked.

"Wait. AP Physics?"

"Isn't that what you asked for?" he questioned, confused.

"Nobody specified that it was *AP* Physics!" I exclaimed, trying hard not to panic. I'd never taken an AP class before in my life. "I just thought I was taking regular Physics instead of Home Ec!"

Cammie pulled the schedule out of my hands abruptly, looking down at it with disbelief and mild horror. "You put her in my AP Physics class? Are you crazy?"

"Hey!" I exclaimed, insulted.

Cammie looked just as affronted. "You *just* practically said the same thing yourself."

"Well, yeah, it's okay when I say it; that doesn't mean *you* can act like I'm dumb."

"I don't think you're dumb," she insisted. "This class is hard for me too."

Between us, David started rubbing at his temples again.

"Change it back, Dad," Cammie demanded of him. "How did they even let her in?"

"I pulled a lot of strings," David explained over my scoff. I glared at Cammie.

"Okay, you know what? I think I'll keep it."

"That's really not a good idea," she told me, eyeing the schedule with trepidation. "It's a tough class."

"Well I'm a tough girl. I can pass the class," I snapped, and although she didn't seem convinced, that ended our argument.

On the inside, however, I said a few words for the tattered remains of my already-low GPA. *"Rest in peace, 2.3. You're gonna need a miracle."*

Chapter Six

Cammie, to her credit, started my Physics lessons that night. David had been right; she took schoolwork almost too seriously.

"You know what I don't get?" she asked me as she flipped backwards through the textbook, toward the earlier chapters. I watched her patiently, chewing idly on the end of my pencil. I didn't answer, and she continued, "How do you have the weirdest little pet peeves? Get sent halfway across the country and you're understandably irritated, but call you spoiled or dumb and you fly off the handle."

"I do not 'fly off the handle,'" I argued.

"You were the first kid to ever do farm work on the first weekend, and now you're taking an AP Physics class. This is the handle." She pointed to her book. "This is you." Her hand, pressed to the book, leapt off of it and slowly sank lower toward the ground, Cammie whistling as it went.

"That was more of a 'falling off the handle'," I protested, just to antagonize her. She rolled her eyes and went back to flipping through the book.

"I'm just saying you have strange priorities."

"I just demand respect," I told her. "That's all. I don't like to be judged before people get to know me. I don't think that's fair."

She glanced up at me. "And why is that so important to you?"

I let out a deep sigh and shook my head. "You and your dad, I swear... Are you aiming for a therapy career as well?"

She smothered a grin as her eyes refocused to the textbook. "Not exactly. Are you going to answer my question?"

"It's hard to get in L.A., sometimes."

"Sorry, what?"

"Respect," I clarified. "At school, or when I'm out with friends, or whatever. You have to demand it if you want it. I don't let people just walk all over me, or tell me what to do, who to be, or who I am. Not back there, and not here."

"Have you been in fights?" she asked. I raised both eyebrows.

"Me? No way. Have you seen the shoes I wear? Who fights in heels?"

"But I thought you were such a bad girl back in L.A.," she countered, half-mocking.

I shook my head. "I never said that. *You* did."

"Huh. I guess that's true." She paused. "I don't think you're spoiled or stupid, if that means anything at all to you. You're just kind of confusing."

"You too," I told her shortly, and then nudged her Physics book before she could respond and asked, "So what's the first chapter on?"

"Um... force."

"Like the pushy kind?"

She stared at me. "Yes. The pushy kind."

"Oh, okay. Cool," I said.

She sighed. "Let's just get started."

* * *

My second day of school went better.

I realized very quickly that my switch to Physics had created way more stress than I'd wanted, but my ego wouldn't let me back down on it, so after ninety minutes of typing and another ninety of shaking maracas in a circle of students, I entered my Physics class.

Cammie was already there, sitting by two friends of hers I assumed were from the cheerleading squad. She offered me a smile, but I knew immediately that I wasn't sitting anywhere near her. As much as she'd insisted that I'd get along with her friend Tiffany, I had no desire to try and fit in with the cheerleaders.

I don't know if she expected me to join her, but I do know that she certainly didn't expect me to go take the empty seat that I did. There was a girl sitting off to the side alone, sporting a general look that could be described as nothing other than "alternative." She had jet-black hair and clothes to match it, with a haircut that left the underside of one half of her head completely shaven. I was surprised that was allowed at Collinsville High, given their no doubt strict dress code rules.

At any rate, she looked lonely, and sitting near her beat sitting with the blonde girl next to Cammie I was pretty sure was Tiffany and the brunette on Tiffany's other side who seemed equally intimidating and judgmental.

Cammie shot me a confused look, but Tiffany distracted her soon after that, whispering something in her ear and giving me a furtive glance. I saw Cammie shrug and her friend giggle, and I rolled my eyes silently.

Our assignment for that day – and every day, I would soon find out – was a small problem set that consisted of ten practice problems. Our teacher, a portly, friendly man in his forties, began by introducing a new formula to us and explaining the concept behind it, and then he passed out the papers to us. He paused by me to privately welcome me and to offer his help anytime I needed it, which was nice of him, but I wasn't going to be the kid to walk to the front of the class and basically advertise that I didn't understand anything.

My biggest problem after that was that I really *didn't* understand it. The majority of his explanation went right over my head, and I had no freaking clue how to solve for tangential velocity or acceleration or whatever the hell we were supposed to be doing.

Cammie's two friends spent most of the class period talking in hushed whispers, but Cammie got right to her assignment. I spent a solid fifteen minutes glaring at her back, willing some of her knowledge to osmosis it's way on over to me, but it predictably didn't work.

I cut that out when the girl I'd sat by whispered, "Hey, do you need any help?"

I looked at her, surprised she'd spoken. She'd seemed like the quiet type.

She offered me a smile when I glanced over at her, and continued quietly, "Sorry. I'm Maddie. I've kind of been out of it today; I didn't realize you were new. This class takes some getting used to."

I scratched at my head and looked down at my paper. I wanted to be able to finish some of it myself, but I couldn't even make sense of the first problem, which was supposedly the easiest. I sighed. "Yeah, I'm kind of lost."

"You just have to figure out how to plug in the formula," she explained, gesturing toward the series of symbols written on the board.

"It's like an alien language," I mumbled. That made her grin.

"So you're, like, totally new to our school then?" she guessed. "Where are you from?"

"Los Angeles." I pointed at Cammie's back with my pencil, and, curious to see Maddie's reaction, declared, "I'm with that one. Her dad's next pet project. Do you know them?"

She blinked at me, looking taken aback, and then shook her head abruptly. "Wait. You're the next kid living with the Marshalls?"

"The one and only."

"What are you doing in this class? I mean, no offense, but from what I've heard those kids don't have the greatest track record with grades."

"I'm doing a terrible job of proving a point because my ego is massive," I declared, sighing deeply. "Cammie's tutoring me, but I'm pretty sure she doesn't think I'm too smart, so it's just frustrating for her and annoying and insulting for me right now. And that's just after one study session."

"So why aren't you sitting with her?" Maddie asked. I noticed she looked like she was trying not to smile. As though she already knew the answer.

"I think the girl with the bubblegum lip gloss and the other one doing her makeup in class right now have got it covered. I remember the days when I thought bright pink lip gloss was a good idea..."

She snickered beside me, and I knew then that I liked her. "Nice. Yeah, no offense... you could fit right in with them with some effort."

I rolled my eyes. "I know, I know. I sound like a total hypocrite sitting here judging your school's popular chicks when I don't look much different, but historically I don't exactly share a lot of personality traits with them." I studied her. "I like your haircut; how'd you slip it past the censors?"

"Thanks." She smiled. "My dad's the principal. He went pretty crazy when I came home with it a week ago, but it's a hard cut to fix once it's done, so I get to keep it until it grows back."

"Nice. School principal for a dad. I bet you get out of anything."

"Your reputation doesn't disappoint," she joked, and began to look to my problem set in a way that told me she wanted to get back to helping me out with Physics. I was stuck on her last comment, though.

"I have a reputation?"

"Oh, no. Well... yes. Not *you*... more like the kids that showed up before you. I mean, everyone knows about the Marshalls. Cammie's brother Scott was a big football star back when he was here, and now she's like the cheerleading squad's second in command or whatever, and their dad's worked here for a while now and apparently a lot of the students like him, I guess. Everyone knows who they are; everyone knows what they do. There's usually about one new kid a year, so you're right on schedule to show up."

"So the others were terrible?" I guessed.

"For a little bit. I think a lot of them were in my dad's office on the first day, actually, because he'd come home complaining about the new Marshall kid. But that always stopped eventually as the year went on, so I guess whatever Cammie's dad does seems to work. You actually seem more... together than I'd think. Then again, I never really talked to any of the others."

"Well, I did accidentally stick myself in AP Physics," I murmured. "I bet that's never been done here before."

"You could switch out," she suggested with a shrug, but I shook my head.

"It's this or Home Ec, and I'd like to prove I'm not stupid." I glanced to my paper. "Although I'm kind of starting to wonder if

I actually am."

"I'm sure you're not. Look, the formula works like this…"

We spent the rest of the class period working through the problems together. Maddie did the first one for me as an example, and then walked me through the second one until I could get it right on my own. The third one I *did* get right on my own the second time I tried it, and the same with the fourth, although both took me a while. I was halfway through the fifth problem when the bell rang, signaling the end of class.

After that was lunch. I was excited to finally have someone to share a table with, but Maddie informed me that she unfortunately did not eat lunch, instead spending her time in the library every day doing homework. Despite her style, Maddie did seem to be at least somewhat of a nerd underneath it all. I preferred her teaching me to Cammie, though, so that was okay. It just meant I wound up walking to lunch alone, up until Cammie unexpectedly caught up with me.

"Hey." She fell into step beside me, a strange expression on her face. "Why'd you sit with Maddie Parker in class today?"

"Um, I don't know." I shrugged. "Because there was an empty seat beside her?"

"You could've sat by me," she told me. "And you can come eat lunch with us too, if you want. You don't have to sit alone."

I was quiet for a moment, rubbed the wrong way by her insinuation that she and her friends were the only people I'd be able to get a seat with. I cleared my throat. "Look, Cammie. You're nice and everything. But those girls are your friends, not mine. And I can make my own."

"I think you should give them a chance," she pressed, but I shook my head.

"They would never give me one, and you know it. Just because you and I are getting along doesn't mean your friends will feel the same way about me. I'm gonna find some friends of my own, alright? Like maybe Maddie."

"Maddie's not a good idea," she retorted instantly.

I rolled my eyes, not looking at her. "And why not? She seems kind of cool-grunge-nerd, and her dad's the school principal. Not a bad friend to have considering I'll probably end up in trouble here at least once."

"Maddie's just..." Cammie trailed off with a sigh, and simply shook her head. "Look. If you trust me on one thing, please let it be this. You and I both know high school's rough if you aren't socially savvy—"

"Socially savvy," I echoed, cutting her off with a loud laugh. "Cammie, are you *socially savvy*?"

"Shut up," she mumbled, turning red. "You know what I'm trying to say."

"Be popular or be miserable; I got it." We were approaching the lunchroom now, and I paused outside of it, turning to face her. "So Maddie's not popular, then. Well, I'm already miserable, so I may as well have friends I actually like while I'm here. Do you like your friends?"

She stared at me, eyebrows furrowed, and I entered the cafeteria without waiting for a response.

When I'd gone through one of the lines and gotten my tray of food, I scanned the tables of students, trying to slap on labels in my head. The cheerleaders and jocks were easy to spot; so were the video game geeks. But not every group looked like a stereotype; there were some groups that just seemed to consist of four or five close friends. There was no way I was going to try and worm my way into those.

I found a group of two that I eventually decided to approach, solely because they didn't look unfriendly and there were only two of them. They were a boy and a girl, both were dark-skinned, and they sat across from each other at the end of a table, which was where I paused and worked up the courage to ask, "Hey, is anyone else sitting with you guys? I'm kind of new." I held my breath as they looked at me, hoping they'd take pity on me.

The boy raised his eyebrows. "*You* wanna sit with *us?*" He let out a sarcastic laugh, and the girl rolled her eyes, and then they both proceeded to ignore me.

My cheeks hot and embarrassment coursing through me, I glanced around the cafeteria in search of a table I could just eat at alone. And, abruptly, as though a veil had been lifted from my eyes, I noticed that there were a *lot* of white kids here. Like, a lot. I'd never noticed it before, but literally everyone I could see was white, with the exception of the boy and the girl sitting in front of me, waiting for me to leave them alone. Their reactions suddenly made a lot of sense.

I cleared my throat and tried again. "Look, um... I really am new. I guess maybe I just don't get how things work around here yet but—"

The girl laughed at me there. "Yeah, you got that right."

"Well, I'm all about breaking down barriers. Yay diversity," I tried, raising a fist weakly, and they both eyed me like they thought I was crazy. Then the girl looked to the boy.

"Okay, can we just put this poor girl out of her misery?"

"Go ahead," the boy sighed in response, and the girl chuckled at me again as I hastily moved to take a seat beside her.

"Thank you!"

"I always wondered when some clueless white girl'd be dumb enough to try and talk to us, and now it's finally happened," the girl told me. "What's your name?"

"Lauren. I'm new here. I think I said that, um…"

They exchanged looks, and then the boy told me, "I'm Nate. This is Fiona."

"Are you guys the only…?" I asked, and then trailed off awkwardly. I didn't know what the protocol for this sort of thing typically was. L.A. wasn't by any means some racial equality haven, but it certainly wasn't like this.

"No. But we're the only ones in this lunch period, I'm assuming," Fiona told me. "Which is why we were the only ones sitting here."

"But isn't that creepy? It's like segregation," I pointed out, and felt like I'd put my foot in mouth again when they exchanged another look.

"It's not like it's our choice," Nate replied. "That's just the way things are around here. You wouldn't understand."

We sat in silence, then, and for a moment, I wondered if one of those groups I'd seen earlier had actually been the group for the gay people here. Then I wondered if the gay people even got a group. Maybe they were all closeted, or all ate alone.

"I do," I finally said, nodding my head. "A little bit, at least. I know that might be hard to believe."

Fiona changed the subject abruptly. "What are you doing in Collinsville? Who comes here voluntarily?"

"Not me," I declared. "I'm the new Marshall kid."

Both Fiona and Nate looked at me, wide-eyed. Then Nate started laughing. "Oh, wow. So you thought you'd stir shit up by coming and sitting with the black kids?"

"What? No," I retorted, not sure how I was supposed to take his comment. "Definitely not. You guys just didn't seem intimidating."

"Well, she's got that right," Fiona said, arching an eyebrow at Nate as a smile pulled at the corners of her lips.

"Do you know how to fight?" Nate asked me abruptly. "The last one beat up a kid on the first day."

"Um..." The answer was no. Undoubtedly. I had the fighting capabilities of Paris Hilton. "Maybe?"

"Even if she doesn't, it's gonna spread that she's the Marshall kid," Fiona pointed out to Nate, and then turned to me. "It might be a good idea to keep you around. You'll definitely intimidate people."

"I will?" I cleared my throat and corrected, "I will. Exactly."

"I didn't even think of that," Nate declared, looking to Fiona proudly. "That's a great idea, babe."

I glanced back and forth between them, raising my eyebrows. "Wait, you guys are dating?"

"For two years," Fiona confirmed. "Sorry you'll be third-wheeling every day if you're crazy enough to keep sitting with us."

"It's okay. I can do that," I insisted.

"Cool." Nate grinned at me, and then the three of us spent the rest of our lunch period making small talk. I liked both Nate and Fiona; they seemed guarded initially, but got friendlier as they begun to realize I wasn't sitting with them just as a means to mess with them. Plus, they were cute together.

My second day ended just under two hours later, after another Health class, and for the first time since I'd arrived in Collinsville, I felt like I might actually have a shot at making friends.

* * *

Cammie and I did our homework in her room together that night, although "together" was hardly the right word to describe us sitting separately on our beds whilst silently scribbling equations onto sheets of notebook paper. I got through numbers five, six, and seven in that I was able to get an answer that made relative sense, but after another half-hour of working on number eight, I was back to being convinced I'd made my life one-thousand times more miserable by taking AP Physics.

"I should've just let everyone think I was stupid," I mumbled eventually. "This is impossible."

Beside me, Cammie let out a sigh she seemed to have been holding in for a while. "Right? I've been working on seven for, like, an *hour*."

I paused, the eraser on the end of my pencil halfway to my third sheet of notebook paper, where I'd already erased four other attempts at number eight. I looked at Cammie. "You're stuck on seven? Really?"

"Yeah, the wording on this question sucks. Does he want us to find an answer for the entire wheel or for the hub?"

"You find both and take the difference, I thought." I flipped back through my work to number seven, then reread the question. "Yeah."

"Wait, you've done that one already?" she asked, abruptly standing up and walking to me. She looked over my shoulder at my paper. "How?"

"Maddie walked me through a few of them today. I guess it helped," I said calmly, trying to hide how smug I felt now that I knew I was further along than Cammie. My confidence was majorly boosted. "Maybe you should ask her for help sometime."

I looked at her in time to see her pull a face that told me she had no intention of doing that. She went back to her own bed. "Huh. I guess she always has been pretty smart."

"You've known her for a while, I'm guessing?"

She looked away from me, focusing on her work again. Her response was distracted. "Yeah, sort of. Been in school together and stuff since we were kids."

"Oh." I sighed, looking to my problem set again. "So how much of our grade is this worth?"

Cammie let out a short laugh. "Oh, he doesn't take it for a grade. It's just practice for the test."

I stared at her, hard. I stared until my eyes burned holes into her cheek, and until she finally looked up at me with an innocent, "What?"

At last, I blinked. "Are you kidding me right now?"

Almost immediately, she shot me a knowing look. "Oh. You were doing it because you thought it was due tomorrow, weren't you?"

"Duh. Why else would I do it?"

"To learn it," she said, as though the answer should've been obvious. "How else will you ace the test?"

"I just need to pass," I retorted, pushing every study material on my bed aside and immediately collapsing onto my back with my head on my pillow. "Wow, was that a colossal waste of my afternoon or what? Can we watch a movie or something?"

"You're welcome to it. But you'll have to do it in the living room," Cammie told me. She was back to focusing on her problems again. "You might not like anything from my DVD collection, though."

"I've seen it," I remembered with distaste. And I had. Cammie owned an unnecessarily large amount of romantic movies. Her posters didn't lie; Ryan Hansen did, in fact, seem to be her favorite author, and she had too many of his movie adaptations to count. I mean, I liked a good romance myself every now and then, but she took it way too far.

"So when did the Hansen obsession start, by the way?" I asked, mostly because I got a kick out of distracting her from her work. I was quickly realizing that Cammie was the overly studious type; she didn't appear to have a massively large IQ or anything, but she *did* seem to work really hard.

She sighed at my question. "It is not an obsession. It's like I said before: Every teenage girl enjoys a good love story."

"Even you?" I asked, raising an eyebrow. That, for some reason, got her attention, and she abandoned her work to give me a slightly affronted look.

"'Even me'? What does that mean?"

I shrugged my shoulders, suppressing my amusement at her indignation. "I mean... you just don't seem like the romantic type. You wouldn't have the time to, like, indulge in mushy, pointless stuff."

"I do too have the time," she retorted, turning her entire body to face me from her spot on her bed. I had her full attention now.

"Oh, come on." I rolled my eyes. "You seriously want me to believe that you're the kind of girl who sits around and wastes her time watching movies about bad boys who show up to save the good girl from the monotony of her good girl life while she in turn encourages him to give up his bad boy ways? Give me a break."

"You seem familiar with the formula yourself," she noticed.

I scoffed. "Yeah. Unfortunately my best friend is completely *that* kind of girl."

"What kind of girl?"

I paused, trying to put my thoughts into words. "You know... the kind that acts like she doesn't believe real romance exists or whatever, but deep down she totally wants to be the protagonist of a cheesy romance movie. As if it's actually going to happen. The real world doesn't work that way."

She watched me for a moment, and for a few seconds I thought she actually might laugh. Finally, still trying to suppress a smile, she told me, "You're very cynical."

"Yeah," I agreed, nodding. "I guess I am. And I think you should be *more* cynical. I'd like you more, you know."

At that, for some reason, she finally did laugh.

"You're the strangest girl I've ever met," I murmured, shaking my head at her.

She grinned back at me. "You've only known me for four days."

I occurred to me, then, that it felt like we'd been friends for much, much longer.

* * *

I got a reality check regarding how little I really did know about Cammie just an hour later, when Scott came up to let us know that dinner was ready.

While he was still peering into her room, he suddenly added, "Oh, by the way, Cammie, Jill and I are going to the drive-in this Friday night to see this old black-and-white horror film they're playing. I know you don't like scary movies, but I thought you and Peter might wanna come along anyway." He offered me a smile. "You're welcome too, Lauren, if you don't mind fifth-wheeling."

He ducked back out of her room and I heard his footsteps descend down the stairs as Cammie shifted on her bed. I looked at her. "You have a boyfriend? Why didn't you tell me?"

It was a natural assumption based on Scott's wording, and so I wasn't surprised by Cammie's response. "Yeah, I guess I just forgot to mention him. He's nice. I'd be surprised if you wanted to hang out with him, though."

She got off of her bed to leave the room, and I trailed after her, confused that she seemed eager to end our conversation so soon. "Why wouldn't I?"

"Oh, he plays football," she told me dismissively as we headed downstairs. "Not your kind of person."

Wendy watched us from the dinner table, and perked up when she realized we seemed to be talking about Peter. "Cammie, did you introduce Lauren to Peter yet?"

We joined the Marshalls at the table, and Cammie shook her head shortly. "Not yet."

"Well, if you two are going with Scott and Jill to see a movie Friday night, maybe he could come have dinner with us beforehand," Wendy suggested, and then looked to me. "Peter's a very nice boy. He even helps us out on the weekends every now and then when he's not busy working."

"He came over once, like, a month ago," Cammie corrected hastily, and then cleared her throat and reached for Scott's hand in preparation for prayer. "Can we eat, Mom? I'm starving."

They bowed their heads as Wendy spoke, David and Cammie's hands clasped together over my lap, and I looked around silently, waiting for them to finish. Cammie's eyes were shut a little too tightly, and I watched with furrowed eyebrows as the muscles of her jaw tensed. I wondered if her failing to bring up Peter with me was more than just a coincidence. Maybe they were on the verge of a breakup.

I had to admit that it was weird to me that Cammie had a boyfriend. It was like I'd said in her room earlier: she just didn't seem like the type to be into romance. Although I admittedly hadn't known her long, the Cammie I knew was a workhorse when it came right down to it. She worked hard at home, she worked hard at school, she read the Bible every night and listened to every little command her parents gave her... It was only during our short time in the clearing and when we'd gone out together on Sunday that I'd really seen another side of her, but that side didn't seem the type to have the perfect football-playing boyfriend her mom would approve of, either.

But then again, she was sitting on a great GPA, had a healthy relationship with her parents, was popular at Collinsville High, and looked great. If one thing was certain, Cammie had her life together. So it shouldn't have come as a surprise that with the ideal life came the ideal boyfriend. It was just strange that she hadn't spent any of the past four days gushing about him to me, was all. Caitlyn never shut up every time she so much as spoke to a cute guy she was interested in.

The Marshalls finished their prayer and we all began eating, and as I sat in silence listening to Scott tell his parents about his day, I made a decision: there was no way I was passing up an opportunity to find out just who the two people were that wanted to spend the rest of their lives with the Marshall children.

Chapter Seven

Looking back on my first week that Friday night, I became paranoid I'd been overly complacent. I knew Week One was probably supposed to be the one the Marshalls made the easiest on me, but even so, I'd done all that'd been asked of me as far as farm work went, and I didn't skip any classes on purpose.

To my credit, though, skipping a class would've just meant I'd go sit outside and do nothing but wait for it to be over, and that was never what I was like in Los Angeles. I skipped classes to go have fun, or I didn't go at all because I wanted to stay home. Rebellion for the sake of rebellion just seemed like an asshole move. And yeah, I'd wanted to be an asshole to the Marshalls before I came here, but it took much less effort to just half-listen in class rather than sit around for ninety minutes doing nothing. Plus, I'd missed church, and I was sure that counted for something.

A third reason to attend classes – the second being that David was constantly and openly checking my attendance record – was that I now had a few classmates that seemed vaguely like people I could call friends. Maddie helped me in Physics class every day, which I enjoyed even more when I realized it bothered Cammie, because although I liked Cammie, she was so uptight sometimes that it made her a really fun person to unsettle. I felt like the SpongeBob to her Squidward.

Plus, an added bonus was that the more I talked to Maddie, the more Maddie seemed like a viable hookup partner. She didn't have a boyfriend, she'd already proven she was up for trying new things, and thirdly…there was no other way to describe it other than that she "pinged". There was just something about her that made her a blip on my gaydar, and I was rarely wrong. Maybe she didn't even know it herself, but I was confident Maddie was at the very least a little bicurious.

Then there were Fiona and Nate, who ate lunch with me, which meant I only saw both of them for half an hour a day. But it was a half-hour of getting to know people I could relate to on a very basic level. They weren't teased, or beaten up, or called names, but there was a rapport they clearly had with the rest of the citizens of Collinsville. I got the sense that they spent most of their time only talking to each other, despite the fact that they'd lived in Collinsville for years.

So a week into my stay, I was staying strong when it came to David's prying into my past, Wendy and I were on chilly but polite terms, Scott and I didn't talk much but at least got along, Cammie and I were steadily becoming friendlier and friendlier, and my three other friends consisted of a girl with her head half-shaved and practically the only two students at Collinsville High who weren't white. All in all, I was doing better than expected. And although the first week would no doubt be the easiest, I couldn't help but begin to think I could last five months.

Cammie decided to get all dressed up Friday night, which was exciting for me because I finally got to prove that there was something I was good at: Looking great, and helping others look great. I helped her pick out her outfit, and then, afterwards, I did her hair and makeup. When she got her first look at herself in the bathroom mirror, her eyes went wider than I'd ever seen them.

"Oh my God. How are you so good at this?"

"I do a lot of going out," I told her, ducking into her bedroom with an outfit of my own and beginning to change. "Eventually you perfect this sort of thing."

"You're doing my makeup for Homecoming," she called after me. I finished changing and rejoined her in the bathroom to do my own hair and makeup, and she smiled at me. "You don't have to get dressed up if you don't want to, you know. I'm sure Jill won't for my brother."

"So why'd you for Peter?" I asked, continuing anyway. There was always a chance I'd meet a cute girl, even in a town like Collinsville.

"I care what he thinks," Cammie told me simply, her eyes on me while I worked.

"Jill doesn't care what Scott thinks?"

"I mean, I'm sure she does, but they're engaged anyway."

"So you have to work to keep your man," I said knowingly. "You know, if he dumps you for not wearing makeup, he's probably an asshole anyway."

"Yeah, but my mom really likes him," Cammie replied instantly, and then avoided my eyes when I paused and looked at her in the mirror.

"Oh?" I asked. She looked like she'd said something she wasn't supposed to. "But do you?"

"Of course. He's nice."

"I think that's the only word I've heard you use to describe him since I first heard about him," I said.

"Well… I mean, there are other good things about him too," Cammie told me with a shrug of her shoulders. "He's kind of perfect. Smart, a total gentleman… and he's already got this football scholarship lined up for college."

"He sounds perfect," I told her lightly, finishing up my makeup. She looked at me in the mirror.

"Wow. I mean, you look really good."

"Thanks."

"Mhmm." She stared at me for another long moment, and then cleared her throat abruptly and left. I watched her as she headed back into her room, and then I turned back to the mirror to do my hair, my eyebrows furrowed as I considered what she'd told me. Boy likes girl. Girl's mom likes boy. Girl dates boy.

It didn't seem like quite the cliché a Ryan Hansen fan would hope for.

* * *

Our first stop on the way to the drive-in was Jill's house. She hopped into the passenger's seat of Scott's truck, and I got my first glimpse of her when she turned to look in the back and grinned at me. "Hey! Lauren, right? I've heard a lot about you."

"Nice to meet you," I said politely. Jill was a classic example of a guy ending up with a girl just like his mother, only she seemed genuinely friendlier than Wendy did. Still, she was ultimately a blonde Southern belle who looked like she'd be right at home on a farm. She had the look I'd expected Cammie to have.

But she was nice, and we spent most of the drive making small talk about what I thought of Collinsville and my classes and the Marshalls. I lied about all of it to be polite, and I don't know if Scott picked up on that, but Cammie certainly did, because she spent about half the remaining ride in Scott's truck with her eyes nearly rolling out of her head. That was fine with me, though; in fact, it was nice to know that there was someone here who saw through my bullshit, even if it meant that she also might be able to read me in situations where I wanted to fool her in the future. Besides, I was learning pretty quickly how to read her too.

We met Peter at the drive-in itself; he had his own car. He was about what I'd expected: brunette, tall, and subtly muscled, he stood a couples inches taller than Scott and had a certain confident air about him. Like he knew he was a hot commodity in his small country town. I knew within a few minutes of meeting him that Cammie was the one who was lucky to be with him. Not that I necessarily felt that way myself, but it was clear from the way they interacted that she was the one trying to keep him around. It was kind of awkward to watch, actually, especially after my conversation with Cammie in the bathroom.

We wound up sitting in the bed of Scott's truck as the movie started up, Peter with his arm wrapped around Cammie as they huddled together near the back of the bed, and Scott and Jill sitting together closer to the front. I ended up in a corner by myself, wishing I hadn't shown up in the first place. It felt silly now, but I'd had this strange hope that I'd come here and meet someone to sneak off with. As though there were lesbians in droves in this small town, just waiting for me to offer them a one-night stand. That clearly wasn't going to happen.

What did happen was that Cammie ended up deciding she hated the movie ten minutes in. She detangled herself from Peter just as the first monster appeared onscreen and declared, "I want to go buy popcorn. Anyone else want something?"

"I'll come with you," I offered immediately, anxious to get out of my small corner and away from Peter and the other couple.

I hadn't actually been aware that they sold concessions at drive-ins, but as it turned out, they had an entire booth for them. Cammie and I stood in a small line, and as we waited for our turn to order, I saw her sigh and shoot a glance back in the direction of Scott's truck.

"It's really hot out here," she said eventually. She was right. The moist air was doing horrible things to my hair. "I wish he'd give me some air."

"Ask him," I told her simply, baffled that she'd keep quiet about something as small as being uncomfortably hot. "You have to ask for things if you want them, you know."

She rolled her eyes at me, a smile on her lips. "Yes, I'm aware."

"So he seems like your typical jock," I told her. "Buff, brunette, and beautiful. What's not to like?"

"Yep." She kicked at a wayward stone on the ground in a manner that said otherwise, and then changed the subject. "I can't stand horror movies."

"Too scary?"

"Bad stuff happens, worse stuff happens, everyone dies, and so does the monster if they're lucky. It's all the same. I hate formulaic crap like that."

"Except your romances," I reminded her, only teasing, but she looked like I'd caught her in a lie for just a second.

"Except the romances, yeah."

We fell silent after that. Cammie seemed strangely subdued. I cleared my throat. "Do you want to leave early?"

"Why would I do that?"

I shrugged my shoulders. "I don't know... to talk? You seem kind of down."

"I'm okay. Just not a fan of horror movies."

"Me either," I admitted. I don't think I had as much of a distaste for them as Cammie did, but I certainly hadn't attended the drive-in for the movie.

She asked me about that, next. "Why come with us, then?"

"I didn't have anything better to do on a Friday night."

"Trust me; this isn't exactly my ideal Friday night, either," she said.

"What is?" I asked, curious, but we reached the front of the line at that moment, and Cammie turned away from me to order.

When we got back to the truck, Scott and Jill were gone. Peter replied to our questioning looks with, "I think they snuck off somewhere to be alone. It's kind of a nice night to spend together, don't you think?" He looked at Cammie in a way that told me he wanted me gone as quickly as possible, but if Cammie noticed, she didn't care.

"I don't know; it's kind of hot." She crawled back and collapsed beside him, the bag of popcorn in her hands. I kept my distance from them and resolutely glued my eyes to the movie. With each passing second, I felt more and more uncomfortable.

Cammie broke the silence by scooting away from Peter and over to me, then offering me the popcorn. "Want some?" she asked, and I shook my head.

"No thanks."

"Okay," she said, but I noticed she didn't move back in Peter's direction.

Minutes passed. Eventually, Peter shuffled toward Cammie and asked, "Hey, Cam, wanna go back to my car?"

She was sitting so close to me that our arms were just barely touching, and I felt hers twitch as she turned to look at him. A small smile played on her lips. "What, you don't like the movie?"

"I like you better," he joked, and I suppressed the urge to mime a hurl. Guys like Peter were everywhere in Los Angeles; I knew his type, and although I was sure he wasn't a terrible person, he was certainly a douchebag of a teenage boy. I imagined he was a perfect gentleman in front of Cammie's parents, though.

She wound up leaving with him. I felt some sympathy for her, unsure of whether or not she'd actually wanted to go, until I became more preoccupied with the fact that I was alone in Scott's truck bed. I didn't know whether or not that was a good thing. On the one hand, I didn't have to deal with being the awkward fifth wheel, but on the other hand, sitting alone was awkward too. And I couldn't help but eventually go back to thinking about what exactly Cammie and Peter were doing in Peter's car.

So that was how I spent most of the rest of the movie: sitting alone in Scott's truck bed, marveling at the irresponsibility of the two children who were supposed to be making sure I wasn't getting myself into any trouble. For all they knew, I could be smoking pot or having lesbian sex right now and they'd be none the wiser.

I shook my head to myself and tsked, vaguely annoyed. I didn't *intend* to misbehave, but they were practically asking for it now, leaving me alone like this.

I started to get out of the truck bed, and then paused. I didn't have a plan. It was dark and kind of creepy out here. And, annoyingly, I seemed to have suddenly developed a conscious that sounded like David Marshall. *"You'll probably get into trouble if you do this,"* it said. *"Think about the consequences of your actions."*

I ignored it, realizing what I wanted to do. It wasn't anything I'd get into trouble for, because I wouldn't get caught, and it wasn't anything that'd hurt anyone. It was just something I wanted to do to fill my rebellion quota for the week, especially since I was majorly slacking.

Scott had left his cell phone in one of the cup-holders between the front seats of his truck, and in less than five seconds I'd ducked into the vehicle, grabbed it, and then settled into the back seat, lying down on my back. I dialed Caitlyn's number. I just wanted an uncensored talk with my best friend.

She answered quicker this time than she had before, but I could hardly hear her, it was so noisy wherever she was. And she had to shout into the phone to hear herself. "Hello!?"

"Caitlyn, it's me," I told her, but she didn't reply at first. The noise around her got a little quieter.

"What?!" she repeated, and I heard her exhale heavily against the phone. Finally, the noise stopped, and it was silent. I felt strange, like I'd interrupted her fun.

"Sorry. Um, it's Lauren."

She squealed so loudly into the phone I had to move it away from my ear. "Lauren! Oh, I'm sorry for that." She laughed, loudly and obnoxiously. I realized she was probably drunk, at least to some degree. "I'm at a party, but I went outside so it's okay now. Whatcha doin'?"

"Watching a stupid movie in a truck bed," I told her. "But they left me here so I stole the son's cell phone. I'm not sure when they'll be back."

"So no one's listening?" She laughed. "That's awesome! Now you can tell me about the hot girl you're gonna hook up with."

"I'm not hooking up with her; she has a boyfriend."

"Oh, come on. That's never stopped you before."

"Caitlyn, I called you because I miss you," I told her, frustrated. "Not because I want to talk to you about stupid shit."

"Okay," she replied, but she seemed distracted. "What did you want to talk about, then?"

I sighed, my heart sinking in my chest. I should've known she'd be out on a Friday night. "Just... never mind, I guess. You're busy."

"No way. Look, you might not get the chance to talk to me again without people listening to you. Let's talk." Her words were slurred, but I could tell she meant it. And I supposed talking to a drunken Caitlyn was still better than talking to anyone else.

"I just... I don't know what I'm doing anymore," I admitted. "I thought I wasn't gonna care what these people thought, and I'm kind of thinking I'm starting to."

"Dude, you don't care what anyone thinks," she pointed out with a giggle. "Now you suddenly care about this redneck family?"

"Well, I mean, it's always bothered me when people talked shit in school and all that, but obviously we both know to just brush that stuff off. It's different when it's your roommate for five months."

"So it *is* the daughter," Caitlyn said. I paused.

"Why do you say that?"

"Well, she's the one you're rooming with, right? You didn't say it was different when you're *living* with someone for five months, like the family. You specifically said 'roommate'. You care what she thinks." She laughed, suddenly. "I don't blame you, I guess, if she's hot."

I sighed, rolling my eyes to myself. "She's just the one I've talked to the most. I think maybe we're friends. If we're even that." I sighed again and changed the subject. "I just feel like I'm not doing things the way I thought I would and now I feel really uncomfortable about it."

"Well…" Caitlyn trailed off, and I knew she was trying to think of something to say. I wished she was sober. "Okay. Maybe there's a time to be an asshole and there's a time to not be an asshole? Like if they try to force you to go to church: asshole time. If they try to force you to go to school and graduate: not so much asshole time. If therapist guy asks about your mom: asshole time. If he asks about your day: ixnay on the assholery. And not being a total bitch all the time doesn't make you a pushover, right? Like, maybe you just didn't feel like putting up a fight that day." She exhaled loudly, and I could practically envision the grin on her face as she added, "Damn, I give good advice drunk."

"How about this one?" I proposed, somewhat satisfied with her answer. "We can talk about the hot girl."

"Finally, yes!" she retorted. "Tell me about her."

"She's the only one I've gotten to really know so far. I mean, the brother's alright, the dad's annoying but he could be worse, and the mom's that totally fake 'bless your heart' type. But the girl's cool, I think. Kind of high-strung sometimes, but… anyway, her name's Cammie."

"Do you like her?"

I shrugged, and then realized she couldn't see it. "Not really like that. I mean, we've already established her hotness, so it's not like I'd say no, but she's definitely straight and she's off with her boyfriend right now. Anyway, that's not exactly what I wanted to talk about."

"Okay?" Caitlyn replied, sounding confused.

"The thing is, I'm not sure she likes her boyfriend. I'm kind of not sure she likes anything she says she likes."

"What does that mean?"

"Well, her mom really likes this guy she's dating, but she just keeps telling me that he's 'nice'. And she's a cheerleader. Guess who really likes cheerleading?"

"This is my shocked face," Caitlyn deadpanned, and then after a pause, added, "I'm not making a shocked face, by the way."

"The weird thing is that she seems totally confident about it all most of the time. Like, they're totally that couple that'll win Homecoming King and Queen and all that shit; she has this town locked down."

"Get her to teach you her ways," Caitlyn joked. "You, too, can have a popular boyfriend and be on a team your parents approve of. It beats the team you *do* play for."

"Very funny."

"Seriously, though... What's with the over-analysis? She's just some girl you'll never see again in five months."

"Yeah, I know. Maybe it's just wishful thinking, or something, but I guess I was just hoping I was living with someone sane. It'd be nice if she turned out to be really cool."

"She could still be cool without having some massive hidden whatever you're trying to dig up," Caitlyn said. "Maybe she's a hot country girl with a boyfriend she's 'meh' on but doesn't wanna dump for her parent's sake, and she knows how to work the high school social ladder. Sounds pretty badass to me."

"I guess you're right."

"I'm always right. Now how's your whole hookup plan coming? Since you so *obviously* are gonna be able to get laid in Collinsville?"

"I'm working on it," I told her, rolling my eyes.

"You have a target yet?"

"Gross; I'm not manipulative enough to call her a 'target', Caitlyn. Jesus."

"So there is a girl?"

"She's in my Physics class. She shaved like half her head and—"

"Gay," Caitlyn interrupted.

"Not by itself; Rihanna did it," I reminded her with a grin. "But I'm getting vibes anyway. And I think Cammie might know something, because she's getting super uncomfortable with me hanging out with this girl, and she made some weird comment about how I should be more socially savvy or something."

"Maybe she's jealous."

I let out a dry laugh. "Maybe you're too drunk for this. Listen, I'm gonna try to get us uncensored calls from now on, okay? I'm making friends who might let me borrow their cell phones if I can ever get some time alone with them outside of school hours."

"I want constant updates. Even if you can't give me them uncensored," she told me.

"Deal. Look, they might come back soon, so…"

"It's cool. I've got a party to get back to. And I'll have to

125

update you on what's going on here soon too. You'll never guess what Daniel Hunter and Jaime Lyons did."

"I'm gonna guess it involves sex." I sat up in my seat and looked around, checking to make sure no one was coming back yet.

"Ah, you're too smart for me." I heard Caitlyn giggle.

"Drink some water. I'll call you soon."

"Okay. Love you, girl. Bye!"

The call ended with a click and I spent a minute figuring out how to erase all traces of it from Scott's phone. Another minute later, I was back in the truck bed, alone.

I picked a good time to end my conversation with Caitlyn, because it wasn't long before I heard footsteps heading back toward the truck.

It was Cammie, and she was by herself. Her hair was mussed just slightly; I wouldn't have noticed it had I not known to look for it. It was the same for her crinkled skirt. I realized with muted surprise that she'd had sex with Peter in his car. "Hey," I greeted her, trying to take her rather clear lack of virginity in stride, but it was hard to hide my shock. It honestly had never occurred to me that Cammie wasn't a virgin.

"Hey," she replied quietly, and I wondered if she was aware of how exactly she looked. I wasn't sure if I was just used to spotting those same traits on myself, or if it was actually obvious to anyone with eyes what she'd just done. Either way, it was probably better that she not look the way she did by the time Scott got back here.

"Where's Peter?" I asked her as she collapsed beside me in the truck bed.

She answered with a sigh. "He went home. He said he didn't really like the movie."

"Oh. Okay." I moved my purse onto my lap and dug through it for a moment, then pulled out a tube of lip-gloss and offered it to her. She stared at it. "I thought you might wanna reapply. The lipstick you had on earlier's gone."

She took it from me, and I saw her cheeks redden even in the darkness. "It's that obvious?"

"To someone who's had a lot of sex, yes." I reached up and pressed my thumb to the corner of her mouth, rubbing slightly. "You have a tiny smear, here, too." I took my thumb away a moment later, and saw the smear was still there. "It's gonna need to be wetted; I'm guessing you don't want my spit on your face, so."

She forced a laugh and wiped it away herself, then used the tube of lip-gloss I'd given her. "Anything else?" she asked when she was done.

"Straighten the skirt and the hair," I murmured, reaching up to fix her hair myself, and I don't think she took her eyes off of me the entire time I worked. When I was finished, I leaned away from her and eyed the top half of her body critically. "I think you're good."

"Okay." We sat in silence for a few seconds, and I turned back toward the movie, but I didn't register what was on the screen at all. I was trying to wrap my mind around what I'd learned. But it was no wonder now that Cammie hadn't looked like the typical innocent Southern belle when I'd met her. She *wasn't* that girl.

"So you don't seem that surprised," Cammie finally muttered. "Did you always know?"

I looked over at her to see her gaze glued to her lap. "Know what?"

She let out a dry laugh. "That I'm a total slut."

"You're not a slut for having sex with your boyfriend," I said. "Girls just use that word to try and shame other girls who are hooking up with the guys they want for themselves. And guys use it because they're bitter they aren't the ones being hooked up with, and because it makes them look cool around their douchebag friends."

Cammie didn't reply to that at first, but it didn't seem to help, either. She didn't take her eyes off of her knees.

"You're not gonna tell my family, are you? Even Scott doesn't know."

"They all think you're a virgin?" I asked, dumbfounded. David and Wendy were believable – Wendy in particular – but Scott was a surprise. I didn't have a sibling of my own, though, so maybe it really wasn't something they typically shared.

She nodded. "Yeah. Scott graduated before…" She paused then, like she'd changed her mind about telling me something.

I retreated into my own thoughts. Scott was twenty years old. Three grades above Cammie and me. He graduated at the end of our freshman year.

"I lost my virginity when I was fourteen," I told her abruptly, and she fixed her gaze to me. I stared straight ahead at the ground between Scott's truck and the car in front of us, thinking back. "I made friends with the wrong people my freshman year of high school. They got me a fake ID, got me into this club I wasn't supposed to be in. I met this... this guy there." Girl. "He was gorgeous... handsome, you know? Said all the right things. I wasn't really that naïve or anything, you know. I didn't feel like a victim. And he was seventeen, and hot, and charming. So I went for it."

"In a club?" Cammie interrupted, a look of disgust on her face.

I laughed a little. "No. Um, he drove us back to his house. He was kind of nice about it, actually. It really wasn't a bad first time. I was just... young." I sighed, embarrassed for myself as I continued my story. It all seemed so silly now. "So of course I thought I was, like, totally and completely in love the next morning, being fourteen and just having had great sex with this older guy. He dropped me off at my house, he kissed me goodbye, and I never saw him again." I paused. "Actually, I take that back. I saw him two years later at the same club, but I don't think he remembered me. And then that night I pulled the same stuff he'd pulled on me to get someone into my bed."

Cammie was silent for a while, taking my story in. Finally, she asked, "Do you tell them you love them?"

"No." That was true. I'd never said those words to anyone but my parents and Caitlyn. "I don't lie. And I don't really fall in love, so."

"Anyone can fall in love."

"You watch too many movies," I told her. "Anyway, I just wanted to make you feel better. In case you thought you lost it too young."

She forced a smile. "Well... you do have me beat, at least."

"Sixteen?" I guessed.

"Fifteen," she corrected. I waited for her to tell me about it, but she didn't.

"No story?" I asked.

She shook her head, her eyes shifting to the screen in front of us. The movie would be over any moment now.

"Not yet," she said, and it felt like a promise.

Chapter Eight

"We should play twenty questions."

"No way!" Cammie looked horrified by my idea, and shook her head as she circled me on Aerosmith's back. We were out by the stable, momentarily avoiding responsibility together while the rest of the Marshalls tended to the other farm animals. It was Saturday, which meant farm work for the whole family, and Cammie'd spent the past hour trying to talk me into doing some of it. I'd obviously refused. "Twenty's way too many."

"Ten, then," I suggested, pointing the stick in my hand at Cammie and Aerosmith and slowly turning to keep my eyes on them.

"No. Put the stick down; what are you even doing right now?"

"Defending myself."

"I'm not gonna make you ride him again," Cammie sighed, rolling her eyes at me. "You look like an idiot."

"So, like you do all the time?" I taunted, grinning at her. "What about three questions?"

"Why do you wanna ask me questions? I'm not telling you how I lost my virginity, just so you know."

"I wouldn't ask that anyway," I told her. "Too personal. Stop circling me, dude, it's creepy. I feel like prey."

"He needs to be walked," she argued.

"He's not a dog. Tell me why you hate Maddie. Is it because she's not popular? I didn't take you for that much of a snob."

"I don't hate her."

"Then what's with telling me I need to be more socially savvy? Seriously, that's one of the most pretentious things I think I've ever had said to me in my life. And I've met some pretty pretentious people."

She sighed, and Aerosmith slowed to a stop. I tossed my stick to the ground and folded my arms across my chest as she replied, "You'll find out for yourself; you don't need to hear it from me."

"If I'm gonna find out for myself, I might as well hear it from you. I'm starting to think you just don't approve of anyone who isn't in your little clique."

"That's not true. Tell me who else you hang out with. Did you find anyone to sit with at lunch?"

"Yeah," I said. "Two people. Fiona and Nate."

Her eyebrows furrowed, and Aerosmith started circling again. I reached down and retrieved my stick, and she shot me a look. "Oh, c'mon."

"He's like Hotel California," I declared. "Once you're on him, you can never get off."

"You got off just fine! I helped you get off." She flushed abruptly, and I snickered.

"Nice word choice. Soooo... Fiona and Nate, then."

"I actually don't know who you're talking about. What are their last names?"

"I don't know. I never asked. They probably don't know mine, either; it just wasn't ever said."

"What do they look like? Who do they hang out with?"

"They hang out with each other," I told her. "They're dating. They're black."

She paused, confused. "Wait... you sat with them?"

"If you seriously have a problem with that, we can't be friends," I told her, my tone even. "Really."

"I don't. It's just... unorthodox."

"So?"

"So nothing." She shrugged. "I just don't know anything about them because our groups typically don't mix."

"What, black people and white people?" I asked incredulously. "How do you live like that, Cammie? Is everyone just completely ignorant? I mean, I know you've lived here your whole life, but you *do* realize the race relations in this town are what's *actually* unorthodox, right? Like, they sit alone because everyone thinks like you do."

"I mean, it's not like I'm racist," she told me quietly, and I could sense she was getting defensive.

"I didn't say you were. But this town's what, ninety-nine percent white? How many of those ninety-nine percent do you think ever bother to wonder what it's like for the other one percent? The same goes for any other majority-minority situation. I mean, I'm not much better; I only sat with them because they just looked nice and they were a small group that was easier to approach, but I think Collinsville would be a much nicer place to live in if people gave this stuff some thought every once in a while. Like…" I hesitated, and then pressed on. It was only a matter of time before the subject came up, anyway. "…what do you think it's like for gay people here?"

Cammie was so dumbfounded by what I'd just said that she actually did a double-take. Aerosmith slowed to a stop, and she stared at me, unspeaking.

"I mean, that's gotta suck, right?" I continued hastily. I could feel myself getting nervous. "Living in a small town like this, where everyone's super religious. I bet you can count the kids that're open about it at your school on one hand. The rest probably hide or fake straight. It's not like that in a lot of other places, you know? I mean, do you even know any gay people, Cammie? And if you don't, have you ever even thought about the fact that you don't?"

She cleared her throat at last, and nudged Aerosmith forward again. Something about what I'd said had caused her to completely clam up, because for all my talking, I got only one word in response.

"Maddie."

* * *

I called my dad that night, using the phone in the kitchen while the entire Marshall family watched television in the living room. It rang, and rang, and rang, and then went to voicemail. I tried again and got the same results.

"C'mon, you idiot. Pick up," I hissed into the phone on my third try. David finally came over to me to watch me dial a fourth time.

"Is he busy?" he asked.

"He's never busy," I said quietly, pressing the phone to my ear again and listening to it ring. "He's probably just dr— asleep."

The phone rang a few more times, and just when I was sure it was about to go to voicemail, I heard the click of it being answered. A sense of relief washed over me. "Hey—"

My dad cut me off. His speech was slurred. "Stop. Calling." And then the call died with another click. I swallowed hard, unmoving for a moment, then shook my head and handed David the phone back.

"I thought he answered, but it just went to voicemail again," I told him stiffly. "I think maybe I'll go take a shower."

I was gone before he could reply, taking the stairs two at a time. A minute later, I was stripping down and stepping under the hot spray, choking back a lump in my throat as I slowly cleaned myself off. I wouldn't cry over something as silly as a phone call with my idiot dad. I wished I'd just called Caitlyn again. She might've been at some stupid party, but at least she'd want to talk to me.

When I was finished, I returned to Cammie's room to find her inside. For once, there was no Bible or Physics homework in her lap. Instead, she had my mp3 player.

"You can listen to that, but it doesn't mean I'm reading the Bible," I joked, sitting down on my bed and facing her. She gave me a faint smile, which wasn't unexpected. I regretted bringing up the gay thing; she'd been weird all day since. It wasn't worth having what I'd already suspected about Maddie confirmed, and it was unpleasant knowing that Cammie'd probably wanted me to stay away from her for that reason. I wasn't used to having my good impression of someone ruined by homophobia, but I was afraid that was going to be the case with Cammie soon. I wondered if she sensed that, and if that was why she was acting so strangely.

She handed my mp3 player back, and as I accepted it, I asked her, "So since I'm not going to church tomorrow, do we have plans?"

"My dad's actually staying back with you this time," she told me. "I think he might have something planned, though, yeah."

"Oh."

I stared at her, and she cleared her throat suddenly. "But, um... it wasn't me that made that decision, you know. It was my dad, just now. I'd stay back otherwise."

"Really?" I asked her.

She nodded, smiling at me again. "Really."

"Okay. Good to know." I slid under my covers, Cammie turned the lamp on her nightstand off, and we didn't say anything more.

* * *

David woke me up around noon the next morning, and as I stirred and blinked the sleep out of my eyes, I thought maybe I was imagining things. But I was wrong.

He stood at the edge of my bed, athletic shorts and a T-shirt on, an armband around one wrist, and a tennis racket in his hands. I stared at him. "...No."

"Everything once, Lauren," he chided, beckoning me out of bed. "There are some courts close by, and it'll be good for you to get out of the house."

"I was out of the house all day yesterday. I can't play tennis. I'm not athletic," I insisted, shaking my head wildly. "No. No way."

"I do this regularly every summer with Cameron and Scott," he explained. "You don't have to be good at it; it's not about that. It's about spending time with your family."

"You're not my family," I reminded him sourly.

"You understand my meaning," he said. "Besides," he gave the racket a cheesy swing, "don't you want to see how much skill I've built up this summer? Scott's really been giving me a run for my money over the past couple of years."

"Not really." I let out a deep sigh, rubbing at my temples. "God, you're like the dorky dad from every sitcom ever. What a nightmare."

"Indulge me this one time." He smiled at me. "If it goes terribly, we'll make it a one-time thing."

"It will." I slid out of bed, avoiding his no-doubt triumphant expression, and half-heartedly moved to rummage through my suitcase. I took out my muddy sneakers, paused abruptly, and then glanced back at him. "Is it too late to just go to church?"

"Yes. C'mon, we won't be gone long. What's your favorite food; do you like milkshakes? Maybe we can grab something on the way home afterward."

I rolled my eyes and turned back to my suitcase, finally locating a tank top and shorts I could wear. "I like milkshakes," I mumbled.

I could feel his grin at my back. "Good. We'll do that."

A half hour or so later, I was turning a tennis racket over in my hands, trying to figure out how to hold it correctly while David bounced a ball in front of himself on the other side of the court. "Ready?" he called out. "I'll send you a soft one!"

"No," I said, quietly enough that he wouldn't hear. He tossed the ball into the air and then tapped it my way. It bounced once, over the net in the middle, and then dribbled its way to me at about knee level. I swung at it sideways, my racket slicing through the air and missing completely. The ball bounced past me, and I grimaced at the pain in my arms.

"That's alright!" he insisted, giving me a thumbs-up. "You almost got it; let's try it again!"

I eyed him warily, trying to figure out what exactly the point of this was. I could've slept in today. He was being such a... *dad*.

He tossed the ball into the air and tapped it to me again, and I missed it completely for the second time. That happened again on the third try, and the fourth, and I only got more and more frustrated with each attempt. This was stupid.

David wouldn't give up, though, and tapped the ball to me for a fifth serve. It bounced once, twice, three times...

I gripped the racket with two hands, my teeth gritted tightly and my anger and frustration building quickly as the ball came closer. I reared back and swung the racket hard, like a baseball bat. This time, it connected, and the ball went soaring over David's head and over the fence confining the court. He watched it fly past, and once it was out of view, he turned toward me and stuck both arms in the air, like he was signaling a successful field goal. I raised my racket into the air triumphantly. "I hit it!"

"Great job!" He gave me an encouraging nod. "Now let's try to keep the next one in the court."

We actually only spent another hour or so playing after that, and, in retrospect, it was easy to see that playing tennis hadn't been the point of our adventure out of the house. But I did get good enough to hit the ball about half the time. Unfortunately, even when that happened, it almost never went where I wanted it to. But David didn't complain, surprisingly, even though I could tell he did a lot more running after tennis balls than he was used to.

We picked up milkshakes from a fast food place afterwards, and sat outside at a picnic table, an attached umbrella shielding us from the sun. I was thankful for that; today was a hot day, and I was sweating way more than I was used to after the tennis court.

"So that was your first time with tennis?" David guessed, eyeing me proudly from across the table. "You did very well for having no experience."

"I bet you say that to all the misfits," I dismissed, sipping at my shake without meeting his gaze.

"Not quite. Most of them haven't given me the time of day yet at this point."

"I don't have the energy to argue with you people," I admitted. "I'm too busy bumbling my way through my first week here. I totally blew the rebellious phase, huh? I'm straight into zombification."

"We appreciate it more than you can imagine," he said. "And I'm not just talking about Wendy and me." He hesitated for a moment before he continued. "Cameron and Scott always get a bit wary before we take in a new child. Understandably, of course. I don't mean to put too much pressure on them, but it can't be helped in some respects, obviously. You're… a welcome change from the difficult—as you called them—*misfits* of the past."

"So I've been told," I said lightly, eyes still on my shake. "I just want to get through this. Now, if you can get me to agree to go to church regularly, *then* you've done your job."

"I've wondered… do you think perhaps you feel so adverse to religion because you're caught up in whether or not you have a belief in God, rather than making it more about what's actually being taught?" he asked. "Because I do believe the teachings are the important part, and are what you and a lot of others could benefit from."

"Here's the thing." I cleared my throat. "Say you tell me in church that it's not good to steal things. Like, yeah, that's right, that's a good thing to teach me, and I agree with it. That's cool. But you don't say that it's not good to steal because the action of stealing itself is wrong; you say it's not good to steal because it's one of God's Ten Commandments and he came up with them and stuff. For me, like, no offense, but can you see how it's cheapened? Like I'd be down with church and all the lessons if it wasn't taught using a dude I don't believe exists. I mean, I'll avoid stealing because I believe the action is immoral, not just because God says it's wrong or whatever and I think I'm going to hell if I steal."

"Why do you think you take issue with believing in a God?" he asked me. It aggravated me that he hadn't addressed any of my questions.

"I'm a logical person. I don't see him, I can't hear him, I can't touch him, feel him, smell him. He's just... not there. And if to someone else he *is* there and they get comfort from that, fine, but don't use that belief to—"

I cut myself off abruptly, my heart rate picking up in my chest. I knew my dislike toward religion itself stemmed from the homophobia often attached to it, but I didn't want him to know that. David, I had to admit, was an understanding person. But if Cammie's attitude toward Maddie was any indication, he didn't seem too invested in teaching his own children to accept gay people, so I couldn't assume he accepted us himself.

He was watched me expectantly now. "To what?" he asked gently.

I reached for my straw and stirred my half-melted shake with it, letting out a deep sigh. "Sorry," I mumbled. "I'll talk and everything, but can it be about something else?"

"We won't talk about anything you don't feel comfortable talking about," he agreed. "What would you like to talk about?"

I shrugged my shoulders, still stirring my shake. "I don't know." I paused. "Do Cammie or Scott ever go away anywhere? Summer camp or anything?"

"Not particularly," he told me. "Scott did go on a three-day field trip in the seventh grade, but I think a weekend or so is the longest I've ever gone without seeing either of them."

"Did you miss him?" I asked, not daring to look at him.

"Of course. Terribly. He missed us too. He'll deny it if you ask him, but he burst into tears the second he got off the bus and saw Wendy and me waiting to pick him up and take him home."

I hid a small smile. "I bet his friends teased him afterward."

"I think most of them were the same way. It's hard not seeing your family at age twelve."

I tried to think back to myself in seventh grade. Not much was different than it was now, really. My mom had been alive. But working. Always working. "Yeah," I agreed. I knew my voice sounded empty, lacking commitment. I had no idea what he was talking about. David wasn't stupid, and it was clear he'd noticed.

"Do you think you'd like to try calling your father again today?" he asked. I knew he was trying to be encouraging, but he'd only reminded me of yesterday, and now I felt even worse.

"No, I don't think so. I don't think I'll call him at all."

"I think he'd like to hear from you," David pressed. "His only daughter's three-thousand miles away. I'll bet he misses you."

"You'd be wrong," I told him stiffly. "He's totally out of it. He had one last parenting hurrah right before I left to try and patch things up with us, and even that was just giving me shitty relationship advice I won't ever end up needing. I'm starting to wonder if there'll be anything left for me to come back to when this is all over."

"I know it may feel like that," he told me. "But I've had a lot of kids stay with me over the years. Their parents sent them here because they cared."

"Those kids were messed up by drugs or serious depression or whatever," I said. "You said yourself that I'm a nice change in that I don't have anything bad. I'm just lacking good. So I put up with shit the others didn't, and you guys all like me. Right? That's the good part about me being here under the circumstances that I am."

I paused, and he stared at me silently. "Now here's the bad. I didn't have a bunch of eventually-fatal baggage or life-threatening mental issues. At most, I was just kind of a drunken promiscuous stoner on my worst days. I'm here because I needed different parents. Like a temporary adoption: a court-ordered one. Not one arranged by anyone who actually cared about me. My parents didn't and don't care. In fact, sometimes I wonder if they ever loved me."

He was watching me, still silent, and I knew in the back of my head that I was saying more than I'd ever intended to. I was telling him things that'd make him judge my parents, and that was the last thing I wanted him to do. But I couldn't stop. He was here, and he was listening, and I couldn't remember the last time anyone but Caitlyn had really listened to me.

"I mean, look at what happened to my *mom*. She spends most of my life away, like, trying to earn a living and everything, which I get, but she didn't ever try to get my dad help even though he was always a total wreck. Instead, she let him go over a decade with an alcohol addiction, and then she fucking, like..." I swallowed hard, aware of an ache in my throat that usually meant tears were to follow soon, "...she died because *she* decided to drink and get behind the wheel. Why would she do that after seeing what my dad was like? And even worse, now look at *me*; I drink sometimes too. So how am I any better? Why is everyone here trying to act like I'm some exception, like I'm so nice? I laid in bed for three months straight before I came here; I think you're mixing up friendliness with freaking not giving enough of a shit to put up a real fight with you guys."

I finished, a little out of breath. I could feel my throat closing as David looked back at me. When he spoke, it was with more conviction than I expected. "Lauren, I've learned more about you in the past ten minutes than I learn about some of the kids during the entirety of their stay. That's how I know you're going to thrive here. And that's how I know I can help you. You're not a bad person." He leaned forward, like he wanted to share a secret with me, and lowered his voice. "And you know what's great about you coming here? From now on, you're always going to have someone who'll be there for you if you need them."

I shook my head, wiping at my eyes hastily. "Who? You?" My

voice was dripping with sarcasm. "How can you promise that?"

"Because I've promised it before," he told me. "And I've also made good on that promise."

"Yeah, well… you wouldn't be the first middle-aged man to promise me something and not come through," I told him.

"I can assure you that won't be the case. But in return, you have to stop thinking about cooperation with me as a form of giving in, Lauren. You've spent seventeen years doing things the same way. Give seven months of something new a try. That's all I'm asking. Make an effort for seven months. Do that, and have a little faith, and I know you'll be surprised by the results. You just have to trust that I know what I'm doing."

"But what if I cooperate and then don't like who I am seven months from now?"

"That's where you have to trust me," he said. "And to trust yourself. I've said this before: I'm not here to change who you are at your core. I'm just the guy smoothing the edges over a little bit." He laced his fingers together and leaned back, watching me. "So what'll it be? Will you try things our way?"

I swallowed a lump in my throat. "What's the alternative?"

"Well… I suppose we could keep doing things the way we have been. You can miss out on church, refuse to do farm work, and you can even slack off in your classes, and I have no control over that. But who really wins there? Yes, you'd prove coming here wasn't any help. But then you also wouldn't *get* any help, and where does that leave you?"

"What if I thought my life didn't need any changing?"

"A week ago I'd believe you thought that. Now I'm not so sure you do."

I sat quietly, thinking to myself. I wondered what Caitlyn was doing right now. I wondered what I'd be doing if I were still in Los Angeles. And finally, I looked up at him.

"If I give, I expect to *get* too, you know. I don't want to be treated like a prisoner anymore."

"Understood. To some extent, you can have more freedom. But over time."

I swallowed hard. "I just don't need any more disappointments."

"I won't let you down," he said firmly. His eyebrows were tightly knitted, his mouth a straight line. I clicked my nails on the picnic table, worrying my bottom lip with my teeth. What he said made sense. I trusted that if I started to see a trait developing in myself that I didn't like, I'd be able to easily squash it. And if things got *really* bad, it wasn't like I couldn't just eventually refuse anyway.

Still, Caitlyn was going to tear me to bits for this. I'd be giving up being difficult just for the sake of being difficult, and, even worse, I'd be resigning myself to the fact that there was no way out of Collinsville for the next five months. David Marshall was not going to give up on me, it seemed.

But there was also something oddly comforting about that.

"Shit, okay." I let out a deep breath. "I'll do it. Just... don't tell anyone anything I told you today."

"Of course not," he agreed, breaking out into a warm smile. "First rule of the Marshall household, though, if you're truly going to be a part of our family: no cursing."

"I'm regretting this already," I admitted, but he just laughed and stood to leave.

"Alright. Let's try to get home before Wendy and the kids do."

"Okay." I downed the rest of my milkshake and followed him, wondering what the hell I'd just let myself be talked into.

Chapter Nine

My first Physics test was the following Friday, so as much as I hated studying, I knew it'd be a good idea to get a head start on learning the material if I was really going to give my all in Collinsville for the next few months. There were five tests total that each made up twenty percent of my Physics grade, but I'd missed the first two, so now each of my tests were worth a third of my grade. If I screwed this one up badly enough, my chances of passing Physics would be a solid zero.

Cammie didn't study on Sunday night, but I could tell she was surprised that I did. Instead, she sat in her bed with her Bible, flipping through the pages while I chewed on the end of my pencil and tried to solve some of the practice problems I hadn't bothered to do before. Things were tense between us. I sensed she still wasn't over our earlier conversation about the prejudice in

Collinsville, but maybe that was a good thing. Maybe it meant she'd given some thought to how truly un-cozy her cozy little town was.

I focused on Physics for as long as I could, but eventually, Cammie's page turning became a welcome distraction. I reread the same Physics problem five or six times before I finally asked her, "Why do you read that every night?"

She lifted her head to look at me. "Sorry, what?"

"We have a routine," I said. "Every night, you read your Bible, and I listen to music until I fall asleep. What's in there that's so fascinating?"

"You really wanna know?" she asked, disbelieving. I shrugged my shoulders. I didn't, really, but I *did* want to know why she read it every night.

"I guess. I just mean, like, you went to church today already. Isn't that enough?"

"It's not an obligation to me."

"I know, but… are you honestly learning anything from reading that every night?"

"Of course."

"Like what?"

"Well… here. I'll read you one of my favorite verses." She flipped through the pages for a moment until she finally settled on one. "James 4:3. But when he asks, he must believe and not doubt because he who doubts is like a wave of the sea, blown and tossed by the wind. That man should not think he will receive anything from the Lord; he is a double-minded man, unstable in all he does."

I was unsure how to react. "What does it mean?" I finally asked.

"It's talking about prayer," she explained. "When—"

"Wait, wait," I interrupted abruptly. "Okay, so how can you not doubt something but then also not think you're gonna get anything out of it? That doesn't make any sense."

"That not quite what it's saying," she told me, the corners of her mouth quirking upward in amusement. "You shouldn't doubt that God's listening to you. But you can't expect him to answer your prayer, either."

"And why not? Isn't there another one: 'Ask and you shall receive' or something?"

"Yeah, but that's kind of out of context," she said. "It doesn't mean we always get what we want. It means we get the things that God knows are good for us. If it's in God's will, we'll receive it. He has a plan for us."

I sighed, already feeling overloaded. "Okay."

"Is there anything else you wanna know?"

My first instinct was to tell her there wasn't, but another thought occurred to me. I knew I'd made her uncomfortable today, but I couldn't get a clear read on how homophobic she was, yet. And if I was going to be spending the next five months with her, that was probably something I should try to investigate.

"Yeah. Tell me about the ones people use to discriminate against gay people."

She swallowed visibly at my request, silent for a moment. I arched an eyebrow at her. "Um. Okay. I guess one of the more famous ones would be Leviticus 18:22. 'Thou shalt not lay with mankind as with womankind: it is an abomination.'"

My eyebrow went higher. She hadn't even touched the book in her hands. "Did you just recite that from memory? Wow."

Her cheeks went visibly pink. "Oh... yeah, I guess. It's a pretty easy one to remember."

I tilted my head to one side, appalled, and at last asked, "Cammie, do you hate Maddie because she's gay?"

"Of course not," she replied, her eyes going wide. "No! I don't hate her at all. We have gay kids at our school and they seem okay even if I don't really talk to them."

"Do they get picked on?"

She opened and closed her mouth for a moment, looking uncertain. "I mean... I- well, yeah, sometimes. Some of them."

"If you see it happening, why don't you stop it?"

She went pink again, and I could tell I'd disarmed her. "It's... Would you?"

"I would," I confirmed, nodding. "And I don't even have a book telling me I'll get into a land of eternal paradise for being a good person and helping others and all that."

"That's not fair," she countered immediately, her eyebrows furrowing. "Seriously. You've grown up a lot differently than I have. And you can say that because you're new and you're from across the country, but I've grown up with the people here and I actually care about what they think."

"Maybe a little too much," I mumbled. Cammie stiffened on her bed and didn't reply, instead going back to reading her Bible.

She was clearly willing to pretend she'd missed my comment. But I knew she hadn't, and, given the way the tone of our interactions had begun to shift toward the negative, I couldn't help but think that as quickly as we'd built up our friendship over the course of the past week, it seemed possible we were headed for an even quicker destruction of it.

* * *

I walked into Physics the following day with a plan of action. I was eager to finally have some semblance of my life back in Los Angeles here in Collinsville, and all I needed to do to get it was to find a way to get some quality time alone with Maddie.

After what Cammie'd told me, I knew Maddie had to be pretty open about liking girls, and if she was open in a town like this, I had to imagine she was probably up for hooking up with an attractive girl. And if there were two things I did have, it was a talent for seduction and a big ego. I found it hard to believe she'd turn me down if I played my cards right. The harder part would be the letdown afterward, if she wanted a relationship.

But even that had to be done differently this time. I'd only slept with girls in Los Angeles, where there were lesbians and curious straight girls for miles in all directions. It was easy to avoid ever seeing a girl again, and it was easy to find new girls to hook up with. If things worked out with Maddie, I'd have two new dilemmas I'd never really had before. I had a class with her, and Collinsville wasn't exactly full of out lesbians. So I wasn't an idiot; Maddie was a unique circumstance. But I'd slept with Caitlyn and we were fine, for the most part. Maybe Maddie and I could be too. I sat down next to her silently and waited for her to acknowledge me. I'd dressed up this morning, but not quite enough for Cammie to get suspicious and start wondering about my motivations. I was wearing a skirt that showed a tiny bit more of my legs, my favorite earrings, and a slightly lower-cut shirt.

Maddie was scribbling at something in her Physics notebook, and, finally, I cleared my throat and asked, "Stressing about the test this Friday?"

She gave a short laugh. "Yeah, seriously." Then she looked over at me and paused, arching an eyebrow. "New outfit?"

"You like it?"

She grinned. "Hello, Los Angeles Barbie. Did Cammie pay you to wear that to impress Tiffany?"

My smile died slightly. "Um… no?"

"Oh." She looked embarrassed. "Sorry. That was stupid. I just thought… I mean, you look good. Just even more like them than usual."

"Ouch." I tried to brush her comment off, but my ego had taken a hit, and it hurt. Maddie hated Tiffany's little clique, and if I reminded her of them, it wasn't a good sign. "Well, at least all the guys seem to like it. I've been getting stares all morning."

"Don't you get stares every day?" she looked amused. "The daily short skirts and the heels work for you; your legs look super long. I was just caught off-guard by the cleavage."

I looked away from her, and my smile faded further. Cammie was watching us. I raised both eyebrows at her, as if to ask her what her problem was, and she turned away immediately, embarrassed. I made sure to keep my voice down when I spoke to Maddie again. "We should study together at your place tonight, if you're free."

She looked back at me, and for just a second, I saw her eyes flicker to the dip in the neckline of my shirt. And then they were back on mine, a playful glint in them. She wasn't stupid. She knew. "Are you allowed? You haven't been here long."

"I think I can work something out with Cammie's dad," I said, still keeping my voice down. I did have somewhat of a plan, which mostly involved some begging and demanding and pointing out how compliant I'd been for the past week. And if I was going to get anything out of the agreement I'd made with David yesterday, this would be the prime time to play that card, while our conversation was still fresh in his mind.

"I mean, good luck," she replied with a shrug of her shoulders. "You're welcome to come over if you can somehow get permission. I'll wait for you in the back parking lot near that exit by the gym for ten minutes or so today."

"Okay. I'll be there."

* * *

Cammie was practically horrified by my idea, and I resisted the urge to punch her as David considered my pleas and she shook her head emphatically beside me.

"Seriously, ignore Cammie," I told him. "She has personal issues with this chick."

"I do not!"

"I did farm work. *Twice.* I've been going to all my classes. I'm trying to do well in them, with Maddie's help! Why else would I be going over there?"

"Good point," Cammie cut in, folding her arms across her chest and narrowing her eyes at me suspiciously. "Why else *would* you be going over there, Lauren?"

"I don't know; that's why I asked the question," I retorted simply, and turned away from her to address David again. Cammie glowered at me as I continued, "I agreed to go to *church*, for God's sake—"

"You did?" Cammie interrupted again, but I ignored her.

"So the least you can do is let me spend an afternoon at a friend's house so that I can study for a Physics test I'm going to fail if I *don't* get the chance to study."

David seemed confused. "I thought Cammie was helping you study."

"She is. But Maddie's been better at it than Cammie so far."

"*Hey!*"

"She's already helped me out a ton already. Can't I just go? You can pick me up; I can call you from her place and give you the address if you give me your phone number."

He sighed, and then shook his head. "I'm sorry, Lauren, but it hasn't been long enough and there are certain precautions we need to take. I can't let you go. Not alone, at least." He glanced Cammie's way, and she and I abruptly exchanged looks.

"Uh, no."

"No way."

"That completely defeats the purpose of going!" I exclaimed without thinking. David, understandably, looked confused again.

"I'm not sure how. All three of you could benefit from a good study session."

I pursed my lips, unable to find a good retort to that. Cammie couldn't seem to, either, considering she'd just claimed to have no problems with Maddie.

David smiled at us. "Great. Well, Cammie, just let me know when you two need to be picked up. I'll see you both tonight."

He left us there without another word, and I felt Cammie's stare searing into my skull. I turned to glare back at her. "Don't look at me like that. I didn't ask for you to come."

"I wouldn't have to if you weren't going in the first place. I'm starting to think you're only hanging out with her because you know it bothers me."

"I have to admit it does give her a sort of appeal," I said, baiting her. If possible, her glare hardened.

"You know, you may not be getting into fights or arguing with my dad as much as the others kids who have stayed with us did, but I'm starting to wonder if I shouldn't have given you the benefit of the doubt after all."

"I'm crushed." I placed a hand over my chest, pouting. "I know about your secret clearing and everything now, though. I guess you should've held off on showing me."

The malice in her gaze dissipated slightly, replaced by hurt, and I realized I'd hit a nerve. I was surprised by how guilty I suddenly felt.

"Let's just get today over with," she snapped, brushing past me, and I let out a deep sigh as I turned and hurried after her.

* * *

The car ride with Maddie was one of the most awkward situations I think I've ever been in. And I've been in a lot of awkward situations.

She was surprised to see Cammie with me, obviously, and after a quick explanation from me about how I still apparently needed a babysitter, Maddie grudgingly agreed to let Cammie come along. I wasn't sure how much Maddie'd understood my request to come over beyond realizing I was coming on to her, but it was clear I'd at least gotten the bare minimum across, and there was an air of sexual tension overlaying the already-present awkwardness caused by Cammie's presence, which only made things even more uncomfortable.

I rode in the passenger's seat alongside Maddie, and Cammie sat in the back, staring out a window as we drove past several admittedly nice houses and then turned into what I assumed to be one of Collinsville's richest neighborhoods. The houses were large and the neighborhood was gated, and I was even a little reminded of my own home in Los Angeles. It was a welcome change from the Marshall's farm, and one I probably should've anticipated, given that Maddie's father was the principal of the only high school in Collinsville.

We pulled into the driveway of a three-story brick house with two garages, one of which Maddie parked inside. Once we'd all gotten out of the car, she gave Cammie and me a brief tour before we settled at her dining room table with our Physics notebooks. Neither of her parents were home.

Studying was tedious with Cammie around. Whereas I was only looking to pass our test, Cammie wanted to ace it, and so we had to work on thoroughly covering every little part of the material in order to meet her standards. I guess that worked in my favor, overall, but given that the current situation wasn't one I wanted to be in in the first place, lengthening the time it took to study was an especially unwelcome idea.

After the first two chapters had been covered, we took a snack break, and Cammie went to the bathroom, leaving Maddie and I alone in the kitchen. Immediately, Maddie rolled her eyes at me.

"I can't believe she's in my house."

"Sorry." If she wanted a Cammie bashing session, I couldn't participate. I felt badly about what I'd said earlier, like Cammie'd been snippy and I'd just been downright mean. "I made a mistake. I thought her dad would cut me some slack."

"I get it." She let out a heavy sigh, and I thought of how hard Cammie'd tried to discourage me from getting anywhere near Maddie.

I looked at her. "So am I ever gonna get to know why you and Cammie don't get along?"

Maddie chuckled a little, to my surprise. "Oh, God. That's all on her. I mean… she's not my favorite person, but I don't care if you hang out with her. Her friends suck, though."

"I figured they would," I said. She kept going.

"My freshman year was when I told everyone… you know…" She tilted her head in my direction, a knowing smile on her face, and continued, "All of her little cheerleader friends gave me so much shit for it. Cammie didn't tease me or anything, but she didn't ever say a word to stop them."

"Did you expect her to?" It was hard to believe she would, given what I'd learned about Cammie so far, but then again, they'd been in school together for a long time. Maddie probably knew her better than I did.

"Yeah, actually." She shrugged. "Maybe that was my mistake." Then she looked over at me. "But everyone that mattered was eventually okay with it, which is rare in Collinsville, so I guess I'm lucky anyway." She cleared her throat, a knowing look in her eyes. "So how were your parents? Assuming you aren't just a curious straight girl, of course."

I laughed. "Yeah… no. They were fine."

"That must've been nice. My dad was cool; Mom took a while, though."

"Well, they were lacking in other areas," I admitted vaguely. Our conversation was interrupted by the sound of a toilet flushing down the hallway, and Maddie let out a sigh.

"Great. Back to work. Guess I'll have to get you alone some other time."

She smirked at me as she brushed past me to leave the kitchen, and I grinned at her back, pleased.

"I guess you will."

* * *

David, I could tell, sensed I was upset with him when he came to pick Cammie and me up from Maddie's house. I didn't talk much with him in the car, and Cammie spent most of the drive clammed up as well, and so when we got home, it was unsurprising that she immediately went up to her room and that David pulled me aside for another pseudo-therapy session.

"I hope you understand why I didn't let you go alone today," he told me.

I did. Especially given that I'd been pretty hell-bent on hooking up with Maddie today — something that David definitely wouldn't have approved of.

I was sure he probably wanted me to be celibate or something. Or maybe to be in a stable relationship before I had sex with anyone. Well, he wasn't getting that, and he couldn't keep me cooped up forever. I'd just have to wait him out. Play the game. I wouldn't resist his demands anymore, and then when he gave me enough freedom, I could do what I wanted, to a certain extent. I just had to toe the line more carefully than I did in Los Angeles.

"I get it," I told him simply. "I just thought you felt like you could trust me."

"Give it time," he said.

"Okay," I agreed, and that was that.

Next on my list was Cammie.

I was still a little wary of her, but given that she seemed to be my go-to babysitter and that we were sharing a bedroom, I knew we needed to make peace. Maddie herself had said that Cammie hadn't ever said anything homophobic to her, and Cammie claimed to have no problem with gay people. So even though it was still possible Cammie was lying, it was equally possible that she was actually just kind of a little too into the high school social hierarchy, and was standoffish toward Maddie because of her social status, not her actual homosexuality. That'd also explain the popular asshole of a boyfriend she had.

And while that kind of shallowness wasn't exactly a desirable trait in a person, it was better than homophobia. I could forgive it and look past it. High school was rough; I could see the appeal of keeping an intact reputation.

As I climbed the stairs to Cammie's room, I wondered for a moment if I'd fit all of her puzzle pieces together. If I understood her. The boyfriend, the cheerleading, the friends. None of it fit the girl I'd spent two weeks getting to know. But it did fit a girl who desperately wanted to fit in. I'd been an outcast at my old school, and so I could understand how someone who felt like an outsider would do whatever it took to avoid becoming one.

When I peered into her room, she had my mp3 player again. I raised a questioning eyebrow at her. "You gonna keep stealing that?"

"I like your Avril Lavigne songs," she mumbled, raising a half-hearted middle finger in my direction. I hid a smile; vaguely enjoying this side of her. I liked seeing her do things her parents wouldn't approve of.

"Do you still want to teach a prissy city girl how to ride a horse?" I asked.

She arched an eyebrow, removing the earbuds and pausing the song she'd been listening to. "What?"

I swallowed hard, shrugging my shoulders. "I was kind of a dick earlier. I thought maybe you'd get a kick out of watching me be terrified."

I could see her struggling not to smile. "You…" she trailed off, and then shook her head abruptly. "Are you sure?"

"I need you to keep me sane," I told her simply. "So let's go visit your big metaphorical olive branch clearing in case we're about to royally screw our friendship up before we've even gotten a chance to be friends. Okay?"

I'll never forget the way she looked at me, then. It was in that moment that I got the first inkling that Cammie Marshall wasn't going to just be a five-month friend. That she was going to change my life.

She looked at me like I mattered.

* * *

"Drug use, um… mostly pot, though. I stopped that for the most part by my senior year. No hardcore stuff; no addictions. I tried LSD once. Never again, though, Jesus. The drinking… mostly casual. I still do that, but I'm not as bad as my dad. He's a mess; just drinks his life away. I got caught with alcohol in my locker once, but I was holding it for a friend and there was no way I was ratting her out. I only get blackout drunk sometimes. So I'm *definitely* not as bad as my dad. Although that's not saying much."

I paused for air, eyes on the grass between us, and then

continued, "He got worse after... after my mom died. That was three months ago; she was killed in a car wreck. Your dad thinks I might have depression because I haven't really been out of bed since she died, but I don't know... I think I was maybe just really sad, and I think there's a difference between that and depression. But anyway, that's why I had the attendance stuff.

"Your dad also thinks I have intimacy issues because I haven't really had parents for several years now and I don't really... love anyone, I guess. I mean, I do, but... I guess I'm just not really into being... intimate. With people. Other than in the biblical sense, of course, because I *do* have a lot of sex. Or I did. Well, when I say it like that, I guess it does sound like I have intimacy issues." I let out a short, awkward laugh, and shifted uncomfortably. Finally, I looked up at Cammie.

She chewed on her bottom lip, her gaze turned slightly upward, and then, to my surprise, she sniffed a little and reached up to wipe at her eyes. I raised both eyebrows in genuine confusion.

"Are you okay?"

She let out a watery laugh. "Jesus Christ, am *I* okay? God, your mom *just* died. No one would be okay after that."

"I know." I swallowed the lump in my throat. "I mean, we weren't that close. Not since I was young. It was kind of like... maybe losing an aunt or something. I don't know. I don't have any aunts or uncles. I guess maybe it is different, then, since she raised me." I swallowed another lump and fell silent, suddenly uncomfortable. I felt open and vulnerable, and I didn't know how to respond to the fact that Cammie was doing a worse job of not crying than I was.

"Why weren't you close?" she asked, her eyebrows furrowing. I wasn't sure I was ready to divulge that yet. This felt so raw and genuine, exposing all of this to her. I wasn't ready to potentially ruin it with questions about my mom's movie star career.

"She was really into her job," I summarized. "She worked a lot. She didn't get really busy until I was a little older, but after that I was basically at home alone with my dad all the time."

"Okay." Cammie sniffed again and seemed to decide better of asking more questions about my mom. Instead, she asked, "Can I hug you?"

"Okay," I echoed, and she got up onto her knees across from me and then scooted closer to wrap her arms around me. I leaned into her, not hugging her back, but resting my forehead on her warm shoulder. I didn't want her to let go.

When she did, she moved to sit beside me instead, and pulled her knees up to her chest even as she grabbed my attention with her next sentence. "I know it's not much after what you just told me, but... I've never told anyone the whole truth about my first time having sex." She took a deep breath and began, "I lost my virginity to this guy named Trevor."

I looked at her, but her eyes were closed, like she couldn't bear to look at anything.

"You'll meet him soon, actually. Or see him, I guess. He goes to our church. He's nineteen. When I was a sophomore, he was a senior. Scott had just graduated back then." She let out a breath, then shook her head and opened her eyes. "I thought he was so cool. He played basketball and he was, like, the leading scorer of our team or something like that. I don't even remember. Anyway, he was the guy every girl wanted to date. But he picked me."

She paused there to force a laugh, and shook her head again. "I was fifteen, and this seventeen-year-old guy with a nice car was paying attention to me. All of my friends were telling me I was so lucky. We went out on three dates or so, and after every one, they'd just spend hours grilling me on everything that had happened. Really gushing over it, you know? And after school one day, he wanted me to come with him to his house. So I told my dad I was going home with Tiffany, and I went with him. His parents weren't home, and..." She trailed off, then shrugged her shoulders, as if she was frustrated with herself. "And he told me that I was special, and that he loved me, and that it'd be our little secret."

"Asshole," I murmured, and she shot me a bitter smile.

"Yeah, well, I was fifteen, and so I was actually shocked when *everyone* knew the next day that I'd 'given it up' after just a few dates to a guy who wasn't even officially dating me. He lied about what we did too. Just like that, I was spending about the next year or so as the school slut."

"But you're not," I reminded her. "That guy was a complete and total dick."

"Yeah, I told myself I wasn't for the first few weeks or so," she murmured. "But hear something about yourself often enough and eventually you start to believe it. What are the odds that everyone else is wrong and you're the only one that's right, you know?"

I thought back to my high school back in Los Angeles. No one there but Caitlyn had anything nice to say about me anymore. Especially now that I'd been shipped off to Georgia to have my behavior corrected. "Yeah. I know."

"But no one will say that stuff to my face anymore, at least," Cammie continued. "Not the cheerleader who was on the Homecoming court with her quarterback boyfriend last year."

I stared at her as she yanked at a patch of grass almost angrily, and I felt strangely at peace. I understood her, and I knew instinctively that I did, and that I understood her better than her brother and her parents and her classmates. And there was something really, *really* nice about understanding someone in a way everyone else had yet to.

"Sucks that we can't do them all over again, huh?" I asked her, shooting her a wry smile. Past her, Aerosmith pawed at the ground near the tree he'd been tied to. I looked away from her and around at the clearing, and then up at the sky above us. It was bright blue today. It made me feel like things were going to be okay here. Like *I* was going to be okay. "I like it here, Cammie. We should come here more often, okay?"

She opened her hand and let the grass flutter back to the ground at her side. "Even if you have to ride a horse to get here?" she asked.

I nodded.

"Yeah."

Chapter Ten

"No cell phones or any kind of electronic devices, guys, and keep your eyes on your own paper. You have until the end of the class period. Go ahead and turn 'em over."

I flipped the sheet of paper on my desk onto its front side and immediately felt a sense of relief. Multiple choice. I scanned the first question: "*Determine the tangential speed of a wheel in circular motion given that its radius is .5m and the time it takes to complete a rotation is 2 seconds.*"

I stared. Then I reread the question and stared some more.

I spent a lot of time doing that over the course of the period. Some of the questions had ridiculous answer choices I could eliminate, and others were actually solvable, but I knew right away that I hadn't studied enough to do well.

Maddie finished the test really early, and she was the only student our teacher allowed to leave the class after turning it in. I'm not sure if the special treatment was due to the fact that her dad was the school principal or if it was just because she was really smart and only planned on going the library anyway, but either way, she gathered her things, murmured a sincere "Good luck" to me, and then left the class with almost an hour to go until lunch.

And so, I stared. There were five or six questions I wound up feeling really confident about out of the fifteen on the test and about three more I was split fifty-fifty on, but the rest felt like complete guesses. I didn't feel well about how I'd done after I'd finished, but it helped that after Cammie turned in her test, she looked nervous too. I knew she'd do well, so maybe I'd also done better than I thought.

As I handed my paper over, an idea struck me, and I murmured, "Do you mind if I go ahead and leave now? It's an emergency."

I received a knowing look in response, and then, "Go ahead. Send Mr. Marshall my regards."

"Thanks." I grabbed my stuff, left the room, and then immediately headed for the library. I was curious as to what exactly Maddie did in there every day, and I knew spending time with her had to beat sitting in my Physics class for another twenty minutes.

As I entered, a woman in her late sixties behind the front desk immediately zeroed in on me and croaked, "Sign in here, please."

There was a small, open area nearby, filled with lounge chairs surrounding a table covered in magazines, and Maddie looked over at us from her spot in one of the chairs. "Oh, Ms. Harris, she's with me." She beckoned me over and I sat down beside her, looking around at the rest of the library as Ms. Harris let us be.

Shelves of books lined the room, and there appeared to be several other lounge sections just like ours. The center of the room was filled with computer desks. There were a few students there using the computers, but otherwise, the room was mostly empty.

"So you're friends with the librarian," I observed, smirking over at Maddie. She had a thick book in her hands that looked almost as big as her head.

"It's one more friend you don't have," she teased, shifting in her chair to face me. "What are you doing here?"

"I just wanted to see what all the hype was about. You stay in here every day instead of eating, so I figured it had to be amazing."

She forced a laugh. "So how do you think you did on the test?"

"Not too hot. If I bombed it I might have to go back to Home Ec," I admitted. "I can't make up, like, a forty on a test with only two tests to do it."

"You could. We'd just have to study together a *lot.*"

"Every day," I agreed, nodding. That made her laugh loudly enough to get hushed by Ms. Harris. I raised an eyebrow at her. "Uh oh. I think you may be fighting with your friend."

"Shut up," she hissed, smacking my arm, but she had a grin on her face. "You're gonna get me banned."

"What do you do in here anyway?" I looked around again.

"Don't you run out of ways to pass the time?"

"Well, there's always homework," she said. "I do that first. Then, if there's time left over, I'll read. I only have to kill a half-hour."

"What are you reading?"

She colored slightly, which only made me more curious. Then, grudgingly, she showed me the massive book in her hands. "It's not what it looks like."

"The M encyclopedia," I read aloud, and then looked to her judgmentally. "Ew. And I thought Cammie's reading habits were bad."

"I'm only reading it because we're studying the Mongols in my history class right now, so I looked up their entry for some background info."

"Dig the hole deeper, girl." I waved my hand in a circle, gesturing for her to keep going.

She rolled her eyes at me, still smiling. "Whatever. How is Cammie bad, then?"

"Oh, she likes that guy with the romance novels. Ryan Hansen?"

Maddie raised her hand to her mouth to smother a laugh, and we got another suspicious glare from Ms. Harris. I was a little confused; I didn't find it *that* funny, but Maddie seemed to really think that what I'd said was hilarious. "There's no way. That's the guy that did-?"

"*A Lifetime of Karma* or something like that, yeah."

She shook her head emphatically. "No way."

"Right? So cheesy."

"No, I seriously mean 'no way'," she insisted. "She told you she's into that crap?"

"She has the posters up on her walls."

Maddie raised both eyebrows at me, then exhaled loudly and shook her head, going back to her book. "Wow. Okay."

"Anyway." I shifted, hoping she wasn't truly planning on going back to reading while I was sitting right here. "I was thinking we could hang out tonight. Are your parents gonna be home?"

"Right after school, yeah," she told me. "But not later tonight. They go out to dinner together every Friday." She looked over at me. "We could kill some time together right after school, maybe go take a drive to a restaurant and then come back at a time when my parents won't be home?"

That sounded a lot like a date, but I'd take it over nothing. "Okay."

"Are you gonna be allowed to come alone this time?"

"Hopefully," I sighed. "If I can't come alone, I won't meet you."

"That's probably better," Maddie admitted. "I really don't wanna deal with Cammie being mopey third wheel again."

I frowned a little, instinctively reacting negatively to her description of Cammie. I felt slightly protective of Cammie after what she'd told me earlier this week. I couldn't help but think a lot of her peers had inaccurate impressions of her, Maddie included. "Okay."

The bell rang minutes later, signaling the start of lunch, and so I left Maddie in the library and headed down to the cafeteria, where I met Fiona and Nate at our usual table.

As we sat down to eat, Fiona eyed me curiously, in a way that made me feel distinctively uncomfortable. "Hey, Lauren, can I ask you a question?" she asked, and when she had my attention, she finished, "What's your last name?"

"Hey, that's right," Nate jumped in. "We never even got your full name."

"I never got yours, either," I said, and he grinned.

"Nate Davis. Fiona's last name is Lawson." They both looked at me expectantly, though Fiona seemed much more interested than Nate.

"Lennox," I told them. Fiona's eyebrows shot up, and then she sat back in her seat, going strangely silent.

"Cool," Nate said. "Lauren Lennox. Has a certain flare to it. So anyway, are you going to the Homecoming dance next Friday night?"

"Probably not," I said.

"Maybe you should," he told me. "Your roommate's winning Queen."

"How do you know that for sure?"

Fiona finally spoke again, there. "Cammie and Peter are *that* couple. They'll probably snag the cutest couple superlative this year too, if she hasn't cheated on him before then."

"Cheated?" I echoed dumbly. "That doesn't seem like Cammie."

"Well, she's done it before," Nate said, shrugging.

I sat in silence with them for a moment. That couldn't be right. "Are you sure she would do something like that? Maybe they're just rumors."

"Nah, they got in this big fight about it in the middle of the hallway last year," Nate recalled. "It was a big deal. But it was a long time ago so I guess the dude's over it by now. Not sure how, but I guess it's hard to let go of a hot cheerleader." He caught the look Fiona shot him and backtracked. "If you're into that, I mean."

"Why would she do that?" I asked, dumbfounded.

"Like I'd know. But anyway, now she kind of has a reputation for that kind of stuff," Nate replied simply, but that only left me more confused. "Maybe you should ask her yourself."

"Maybe," I echoed, and then ate my lunch silently.

* * *

David shut down my plans with Maddie that afternoon, and I was forced to grit my teeth and take it well as he told me, "I know you're probably not happy with the decision, but like I said: you just need to give it a little time." He paused, and then decided, "You know what? How about I let you and Cammie go to the football game next Friday alone?"

"It's not alone if I'm with Cammie," I pointed out sourly. She was quiet on David's other side as we walked to his car in school parking lot.

"Cammie will be on the field during the game," David said. "Aren't they announcing Homecoming King and Queen afterward too?"

"Yep," Cammie spoke up, nodding her head. "There's the game, then they'll call the whole Homecoming Court onto the field and announce the King and Queen. And then later on is the dance."

"Tiffany's taking care of giving you a ride, right?" David asked, and Cammie confirmed with another nod. He looked to me, proud of himself. "There you go. You can do that. I won't be at the game or the dance."

"Except I don't wanna go to a football game *or* to Homecoming," I argued. "And Cammie's still playing babysitter."

"I'll be on the field," Cammie echoed. "And I think you won't regret coming." She shot me a knowing look, then, while David's attention was distracted, and I responded with a confused look. I could tell she was trying to tell me something, but I didn't know what it was.

"Okay," I gave in uncertainly. "Maybe I'll go."

"Good," David replied, smiling. "I bet you'll have fun."

* * *

"A lot of us don't actually go the Homecoming Dance," Cammie explained later that night, as I was getting ready for bed. I shot her a confused look, and she continued, "I have to be at the football game, since I'm up for Queen, but afterward, there's supposed to be this party at one of Peter's friend's houses."

"So that's where all the cool kids are going," I realized with a laugh. "Okay. Whatever. I didn't peg you for the partying type, though."

"I'm a good dancer," she told me, grinning. Her grin died with my next statement.

"Your parents don't know very much about you, do they?"

She stared at me for a moment, and then cleared her throat and slid under the covers in her bed. "Why do you say that?" she asked eventually.

"I mean, you're not some terrible kid, from what I can tell, but you're not exactly an angel, either. Nate told me today that you've cheated on Peter before. Is that part of the reason you work so hard to keep him around?"

She went stony-faced, and I saw her swallow hard. "Why were you guys talking about me and Peter?"

"I don't know; it just came up." I shrugged my shoulders. "I mean, what you do in your relationship is your business, but I just didn't think it seemed like you. And after what you told me before, I thought maybe it was just a rumor."

She sighed, deeply, and then shook her head. "Not a rumor. It's a long story. And before you ask, I'm not explaining it. Just… it's not as simple as it sounds."

"Okay. I'm satisfied," I told her honestly. "If you say it wasn't simple, then it wasn't."

She looked over at me gratefully. "Thanks. And, uh… can you not mention that to anyone in my family?"

I shot her a bemused smile. "And you wonder why I think they don't know you."

* * *

I was due to get my first taste of real farm work the next day, per my new agreement with David. Cammie and I headed out to Aerosmith's stall, where, much to my disdain, she gave me my first lesson in horse grooming.

"This is a curry comb." She held up this weird spirally-looking thing that didn't really look like a comb at all. I stared. "I use this one first. Then after that are the hard brush and the soft brush. Usually when I'm done with those, I'll brush his mane and his tail. And at some point, I'll use a horse pick to pick his hooves."

"You do all of that every week?" I asked, alarmed.

She laughed. "You have to do it every day! Or at least a few times a week. My mom does it for me some days, if she doesn't have much else to do, but otherwise it's my daily responsibility. Whenever you see me going out here to ride him, chances are I'm doing all of this beforehand. You also have to clean the hooves again after you ride."

"That's so much work." I shook my head. "Not worth it."

"Oh, yes he is," she cooed, more to the horse than to me. She patted him on the head and he blinked in what I'm sure she assumed was a very loving way. "Anyway," she faced me again, "today I'm gonna teach you how to do all of it."

"Great." I nodded, trying my best to look somewhat determined, but Cammie shot me an amused look as she moved toward Aerosmith with the currycomb.

"I'll be honest," she said, "I'm not so convinced you're actually gonna make an effort. Did you and my dad make some kind of deal?"

176

I crossed my arms and feigned offense. "I resent that."

That got a chuckle out of her and she made her way around the horse with the comb. "I mean, are you seriously going to church tomorrow? You were so against it. I don't think you're a bad person – the opposite, actually – but I'm still not really convinced you actually wanna do any of this." She ran the comb over the horse's back and explained, "I'm doing this to get the dust and dirt on him to the surface, to make it easier to brush out in a minute."

"You think I'm a good person?"

She paused and shot me a strange look. "Of course. Lauren, if I'd lost my mother, I think not going to school would be the least of my problems. I'm sure my dad mostly only has you here because he wants you to get some time in with a functional family."

I didn't respond at first. I didn't like her insinuation that my family wasn't functional, but it seemed pointless to argue it. "I'm not broken," I finally told her. "And I'm not out to hurt anyone. I just don't want to be tied down or forced to do something against my will."

"That seems to be a common theme with you," she noticed. I watched her move on to a different brush. "Not being tied down. Tied to relationships, tied to a family…"

"I just want some freedom," I insisted. "No psychoanalysis necessary. I'm walking on eggshells here just trying to prove I'm not about to go snort cocaine off of a stripper's ass or something." She laughed then, and I told her, "I figured maybe if I made an effort I'd get to have my own life here. I'm trying." My eyebrows furrowed. "Anyway, where do you get off criticizing me? You have so many secrets you put the chicks from *Pretty Little Liars* to shame."

She stood up straight and faced me, arms folded across her chest. She raised an eyebrow. "Like what?"

"Oh, c'mon. The perfect boyfriend you don't like, the lack of virginity and the reputation you got after losing it, the obvious experience with partying, the fact that you can draw but you won't do it unless you're alone. The general discord between the way your friends and family see you from how you actually are, and all that. Like, I'm not stupid; I notice things. We've been roommates for nearly a month now."

She tilted her head to the side and eyed me carefully, a thoughtful smile on her lips. Then she crossed to me and offered me the brush. "Congratulations, you've summed me up."

"Oh, c'mon," I murmured, accepting the brush with distaste. "All I'm saying is that maybe we can both admit we were wrong."

"About what?"

"Our first impressions. I'll admit you're not the perfect little church girl."

"Okay. But I still can't be sure you weren't your school's token bad girl. Undeservedly or otherwise."

"I'm brushing a damn horse and I'm here because of a death in the family," I countered, rolling my eyes and approaching Aerosmith with caution. He blinked at me and I hesitated, pausing a foot from his face and then looking back at Cammie. She watched me with crossed arms and a knowing expression on her face.

"You forgot the part about the substance abuse."

"Forgive me. Anyway, that was all before Mom died. The worst of it, anyway."

"What changed?"

"It took effort to go buy pot," I explained. "I lacked motivation. And the friends to encourage me."

"I'm sorry that that was what it took for you to stop," she said.

"Yeah, me too. But I'm not really that averse to starting again, you know. I just won't do the harder stuff. It's just pot." I stalled, lingering a safe distance from Aerosmith. Cammie finally realized my hesitance, and sighed, approaching me.

"Well, maybe that's what my dad wants to fix. C'mon, he won't hurt you." She passed me and gestured for me to move closer to Aerosmith even as she stood at his side.

"Why doesn't he focus on you and Scott as much as he does me?" I asked, abruptly. I was thinking of when he'd taken Cammie and I home from Maddie's house. He'd pulled me aside to talk, but he'd let Cammie go up to her room alone, even though she'd been just as upset as I'd been.

"Because he knows we've got it covered. You need it more than us. We're fine," she said, and tugged me over to her by my arm. I was too focused on her to be scared of the horse now, and she reached for my hand.

"But what if you're ever *not* fine?"

Her fingers brushed mine and then stilled for a brief moment, her arm tensing, but then she took my hand and guided the brush to Aerosmith. I didn't take my eyes off of her as, together, we ran the brush across his side. Her hand was gentle and soft on mine. "Like this," she said, her voice a whisper. I pulled away abruptly and offered her the brush, ignoring the slight tension in my chest.

"You're way better at this than I am."

"Of course I am; I've had him for years. You're learning."

"Well, I've learned enough for today," I decided. Cammie took the brush back from me, looking a little disappointed. "Will you tell your dad I tried?"

She nodded, her gaze lingering on me for a moment. I shifted uncomfortably, and she went back to Aerosmith, finishing up with the second brush and moving on to a third. I watched her as she worked.

"I didn't know you knew I could draw," she finally said, right around the time she was starting to pick the hooves.

"You had that briefcase on the first night," I recalled. "And a picture you drew."

She paused, then, halfway through her second hoof. "You saw that?" she asked, looking over at me.

"Yeah. It was really good, actually."

She smiled. "Really? Thanks." There was a brief pause as she went back to working, and then she added, "I've never told anyone about that before."

"That seems to be a common theme with you," I echoed, teasing her. She laughed as she moved onto the last hoof.

"Fair enough."

* * *

I called Caitlyn later that night, in Cammie's room with her reading the Bible on her bed beside me. I was exhausted, sleepy, dreading church, and a little homesick, and I surprised myself by tearing up a little when I heard her voice, despite the slight slur in her speech.

"I helped take care of a horse today," I told her, sniffling a little, and I saw Cammie look over at me with concern as Caitlyn replied.

"Aw, Lauren. You're almost a month down, okay? Just four more to go."

"I don't know what I'm doing," I admitted. And I didn't anymore. I felt like I'd never fit in in Collinsville, and I wasn't sure how far I was willing to take my deal with David. I didn't know what else he'd want me to do in the future.

"Me either," Caitlyn replied. "It's so shitty here without you. There's nothing to do. I'm literally sitting alone drinking at home right now."

"But you still have parties to go to," I reminded her.

"There aren't any there?" she asked.

"Just one. Next week."

"Is anyone listening on your end?"

"Yeah."

"Okay. On a scale of one to eight, how well are things going with the girl you're trying to get with? The Physics one."

"I don't know. Six?"

"Does she wanna hook up?"

"Yeah. I think so."

Caitlyn let out a sigh of relief. "Good. Okay, here's what you're gonna do, Lauren. I want you to do whatever you can to get to this party. Take her with you; have some fun there. And then go back to her place. You'll feel like yourself again. That's my advice."

I sniffed again, considering what she'd said. Maybe she was right. When I was with Maddie, I felt more like I was back in Los Angeles than when I was with anyone else. Granted, I wasn't particularly fond of L.A., but it was familiar. It was home. And I was my old, non-horse-brushing self there. "Okay."

"Okay," she echoed. "Call me again soon? When no one's around, if you can. I want you to be able to tell me what's actually going on with you."

"I'll try."

"Bye, Lauren." She hung up and I immediately handed the phone over to Cammie, who still looked concerned for me.

"Are you okay?"

"I'm fine. Just miss my best friend," I mumbled, wiping at my eyes.

"You never told me who you'd been calling this whole time," she said.

"Caitlyn's been my best friend for years," I explained. "She's the only person I can call, and the only one I want to."

"What about your dad?"

"No, I can't call him," I told her stiffly. I think my tone intimidated her, because she backed off and was quiet for a while. I laid down and stared at the ceiling, waiting for sleep, but she spoke again when my eyes were just beginning to struggle to stay open.

"Can I ask you something?"

"Mhmm," I murmured, closing my eyes at last. I trusted that she'd leave the topic of my dad untouched, at least for now. Cammie, unlike her father, seemed to realize he was a subject I didn't like to broach.

"What made you think I don't like Peter?"

I smiled faintly, my eyes still shut. "You mean what gave it away?" She didn't answer, and I told her, "I've never been in a relationship, but I think if I went through the trouble of getting into one, I'd call that person something other than 'nice'." She started to say something, but I added, "And I'd rather be sitting by him in the back of a truck bed than by a girl I hardly know."

I heard her shift on her bed, and she finally replied, "He's okay. I don't hate him or anything. I just don't..."

"Love him?" I finished for her. "That's cool. Who *does* in high school, right?"

There was another moment of silence, and then her response came, quiet and subdued. "Right."

Chapter Eleven

I took my first trip to church with the Marshalls the next day. I didn't really have anything in my suitcase that Wendy deemed appropriate enough to wear, so Cammie had me try on some of her clothes. They fit, and they weren't terrible, but I'd have never picked them out myself, so I was already in a bad mood before we were even out of the house.

As we drove to the church, Wendy and Cammie took turns prepping me in the car. Scott and David wisely stayed silent.

"You'll be joining Cammie and Scott at their weekly youth group, which is in a separate part of the church," Wendy explained from the passenger's seat. I sat in the back, squashed between Cammie and Scott. "Pastor McKinley's a very nice man, so be sure to show him some respect. He's expecting you."

"Just don't say anything and smile at him," was Cammie's

translation, which she whispered into my ear as soon as Wendy was finished speaking. "He's pretty cool."

"Doubtful," I murmured back, and was unsurprised by the soft sigh she let out at my response.

"It's actually fun," she whispered.

"You're crazy," I hissed back to her, and she elbowed me in the side to get me to shut my mouth. I rolled my eyes to myself and felt Scott shake with laughter on my other side while David and Wendy chatted obliviously up front. I made a mental note to spend church with Scott instead of Cammie; it seemed to be an area in which she was distinctly less tolerable than her brother.

Our drive wasn't long, and Scott helped me out of the car when we got to the church, then promptly turned away to greet Jill, who, as it turns out, attended the same church. Of course.

Frowning, I slunk over to Cammie and stood at her side, arms folded across my chest. Wendy and David were already making their way over to the large double-door entrance at the front of the church. I looked around. It was a pretty big place, and there were more people heading inside than I'd expected. There were so many churches in Collinsville it seemed impossible for any of them to have a lot of followers.

"C'mon," Cammie demanded, gesturing for me to get moving. "We'll be late if we don't get inside."

"Wouldn't want that," I agreed with another eye-roll. She sighed at me and tugged me along by my wrist, Jill and Scott just ahead of us.

We took a sharp right upon entering the church, and Jill told me more about it as we descended a flight of stairs, presumably heading for the separate teen service. The youth group, so it was apparently called.

"I think you'll really like it here. Pastor McKinley's very friendly and he's always willing to answer any questions we might have. And every week he talks about something different. Last week it was the importance of giving and charity."

"Right." I tried my best to sound engaged. "Selflessness. That's... good, I guess." Cammie nudged me sharply, and I shot her a confused look. "What? It is."

"Just... try to say as little as possible during the actual service."

"Aw, Cammie," Jill said, shooting me a sympathetic look. "She's doing fine. It's not every day a girl goes to church for the first time, you know."

"I just want things to go smoothly," Cammie sighed out.

"That's because you're a perfectionist," I informed her. "Just go with the flow. I'm not gonna jump up in the middle of your youth group demanding we all kneel before Satan and shi—" I cut myself off at Cammie's sharp look and corrected, "and crap like that. I know how to keep my mouth shut." I looked to Scott to see that he'd turned to raise an eyebrow at me. "What? C'mon, I'll be a perfect angel. Ha! Church humor."

"Just c'mon," Cammie mumbled, promptly grabbing me and yanking me down another hallway.

* * *

Pastor McKinley was a dorky guy in his forties with an ugly

checkered shirt on that quite literally hurt my eyes, but I didn't really care about him. We exchanged a couple generic greetings and he told me he hoped to see me back every week, and then I took a seat with Cammie, Scott, and Jill in this circle of chairs that surrounded the pastor.

The person that *did* catch my attention was an older boy I instinctively knew had to be Trevor. He noticed me too, while I was talking to McKinley, and I saw him watching me as I took a seat. I felt slimy just having his gaze on me after hearing Cammie's story about him.

Cammie noticed me glancing his way and stiffened, then murmured a quiet, "Stop. Please." That was enough to make me force my gaze to Pastor McKinley.

He stood in the center of the circle of chairs as they continued to fill, and when at last it seemed like everyone had arrived, he began his lesson for the day. I half-dozed through most of the opening remarks, and tuned in just in time to hear him ask, "So, a show of hands: How many of you know where exactly your name comes from?" He surveyed the circle as a few hands came up, then pointed to a small boy in a suit. "Joseph, go ahead."

"All of the guys in my family are named Joseph. I think it goes back at least three or four generations."

"Okay, so family tradition. How about you, Tina?"

"My mom was a big Tina Turner fan."

There were some chuckles at that. Pastor McKinley swiveled around to Jill. "Yes, Jill?"

"My mother found it in a baby book."

"Excellent. My point here is that we're all named for some reason. Some more significant than others, but a reason all the same. How many of you are familiar with the story of Jacob?"

He went on for a while after that, telling the story of Jacob from the Bible and how he'd tricked his father at one point and his name basically meant "trickster," and I honestly didn't pay very much attention. I wanted to just get through church, especially on my first day, and more importantly, I wanted Trevor to stop looking at me.

McKinley ended, a while later, with the moral of his story: that names held important meanings, and that we should be careful of what we call each other and other people. I guess it was nice to know there was a positive message in there somewhere.

We went out to lunch with Jill afterward, and I stayed mostly silent. Cammie talked a mile a minute, running over every little detail of McKinley's sermon with her mother, and I realized with a start that it was the first time I really saw any semblance of a bonding moment between Cammie and Wendy. So church was *their* thing.

We got back to the farm in the afternoon and I slept for a while, exhausted both after waking up early for church and actually attending it. All in all, the day was uneventful. I hadn't magically become a Christian, and I hadn't been pushed any further into Atheism. It all just... *was*, and then it was over and I was home. My Georgia home, that is. My home that didn't feel much like a home.

Cammie spent a lot of time with her mother that day, but when she did finally check up on me, she found me curled up in bed after my nap.

"Thanks for today," she told me, sitting down at the edge of my bed. Her voice was gentle, and I could tell she was being sincere. "I know you could've made things a lot more difficult."

"Well, that's what I do," I reminded her quietly. "Avoid making circumstances difficult even when they make me unhappy."

She fell silent after that, and eventually, she left me alone. I burrowed under the covers after that, hiding my face, and I think that right then, by myself in Cammie's room after an unfamiliar day with unfamiliar people in an unfamiliar town, I felt more alone than I'd felt in a long time.

* * *

My next week with the Marshalls went by pretty quickly. I got a 60 on my first Physics test, which was pretty much amazing given my lack of confidence after taking it. With two tests to go, I now had to just make up ten points and I'd actually pass an AP class.

On Thursday, I leaned over to Maddie during class and muttered, "Please tell me you're going to this football Homecoming thing tomorrow night."

She looked up from her sheet of Physics problems – our assignment for the day – to grin at me. "I wasn't planning on it. I hear there's a big party afterward, though."

"I thought only the cool kids had heard about that one," I teased.

"My cousin's throwing it," was her response. "So I get special treatment."

"Come with me to the game, and then we can go together," I suggested.

She laughed and went back to her homework with an idle, "Uh, no."

"Why not?"

"Let's just say I've had some bad experiences with my cousin's parties in the past."

"You?" I raised an eyebrow. "No way, as cool as you are?"

"Shut up," she murmured, barely containing a smile. "I'll go the game and keep you company, okay? But I don't know about the party."

"I'll convince you," I told her, nodding confidently.

She laughed quietly and shook her head. "We'll see."

At lunch, I had a similar conversation with Nate and Fiona, but with opposite results. When I asked them if they were going to the game, they said no, but when I told them about the party they hadn't been invited to, they liked the idea of crashing.

"I'll get my friend to text you guys the address," I promised them, and for the rest of the day, I actually felt a little excited. I'd had Caitlyn back in Los Angeles, which was nice, but now I was making plans with multiple people, multiple *friends*, for the first time in a while, which felt pretty cool, actually.

So Tiffany would pick up Cammie and me and drive us to the game, where I'd meet up with Maddie. I'd convince her to come to the party, where we'd join Fiona and Nate while Cammie went off with her friends and Peter. From there, I'd follow Caitlyn's advice and try to go home with Maddie. And all I had to do after that was make sure I got home without David and Wendy realizing that Cammie and I hadn't gone to the school-sponsored dance.

Simple.

* * *

"How do I look?"

Cammie turned away from her bathroom mirror to look at me, her outfit and makeup on full display. Her hair was straightened and I'd done her eye makeup, showing her how to make their blue color really pop. Then I'd let her finish the rest. She actually looked beautiful, but I wasn't going to tell her that.

"Like a Homecoming queen," I said instead, unplugging my hair straightener from the bathroom wall now that we were both finished getting ready. "Shouldn't you be wearing your cheerleading uniform, though?"

"Yeah, I'm changing into it. But this is what I'm wearing to the party. You're sure it looks fine?"

"Yes," I groaned. "You're hot. Is your friend gonna be here soon? No offense, but I need to get away from your family for a little while before I start reciting Bible verses from memory." She rolled her eyes and turned away from me, biting her lip to hide a smile as she studied herself in the mirror. I watched her, one eyebrow raised. "What?"

"Nothing," she replied. "Be nice to Tiffany, okay? She's doing you a favor."

"No, she's doing *you* a favor. I'm just cargo. Gorgeous, unappreciated cargo."

"I appreciate you," she told me, and then patted me on the head and ducked past me, out of the bathroom. I trailed after her with a sigh.

Downstairs, Wendy, as it turned out, waited with endless compliments and basically screeched about how pretty we were until Tiffany arrived. I never thought I'd be happy to see Collinsville's head cheerleader show up at my current residence, yet I was filled with relief the instant the doorbell rang.

As Tiffany entered and exchanged greetings with the rest of the Marshalls in a high-pitched, bubble-gum sweet voice, David pulled me aside and asked me, "Will you be okay tonight?"

"I'm fantastic," I told him. "Never been better. In fact, I'm actually itching for a sleepover, and Tiffany seems like *such* a nice girl."

"Uh huh. Nice try." He shot me a knowing look. "I want you guys back by midnight, okay? Cammie knows her curfew. I'll be up."

"Yes, sir."

"Alright. Go have fun. And stay out of trouble!" he called after me. I practically flew past Tiffany and out through the front door, she and Cammie hot on my heels. The front door shut behind us, and Tiffany immediately let out a breath.

"God, I hate catching up with your mom, Cammie. She wants to know everything about my life; it's exhausting."

I saw Cammie force a smile as she got into the passenger's seat of Tiffany's car, and I climbed into the back. I frowned openly, feeling strangely defensive. Wendy wasn't my ideal mother, but she was nice enough.

"At least she cares," I said. Tiffany turned around in her seat to look at me.

"So what's your name? How long are you staying here, again?"

"Lauren. Until graduation."

She pulled a face even as we backed out of the Marshall's driveway. "Wow. So you have to share your room for that long, Cammie? That sucks."

My lips parted in surprise and I stared in disbelief at Tiffany even as Cammie cleared her throat up front.

"It's actually not bad. It's like having a friend over every night."

"Yeah, except it's a friend you don't know and didn't ask to have stay over," Tiffany laughed. I clenched my fists at my sides and forced myself to stay silent.

We got to the high school after a painfully awkward few minutes, and Tiffany announced, "I'm gonna go get changed into my uniform. Be out on the field in fifteen, okay?" She directed the last sentence to Cammie, who nodded her response. And then she was gone, and Cammie and I were walking toward the field alone.

"Wow. Your friend's a bitch," I said immediately. "I mean, I knew she was somewhat of a bitch, but she's even worse than I thought. Like, I don't know if I've ever met anyone that bitchy before in my life. And I'm from *Los Angeles*."

"She's just kind of abrasive sometimes," Cammie told me. "You have to get to know her."

"Yeah, right. She just trashed your mom. *I* wouldn't even trash your mom."

"Look, I need to go change," Cammie sighed. "Are you okay to get in and everything on your own?"

"I guess." I shrugged my shoulders neutrally. "Good luck with the Homecoming thing."

"Thanks."

She left me alone, and I, using money from David, paid my way into the stands surrounding the field and took in the students around me with trepidation. I didn't recognize anyone, and I had no way of knowing whether or not Maddie was already here.

There were a couple of concession stands nearby – one selling hot food and one selling candy and chips and drinks – and on the field, there were a few students that seemed to be setting up big tanks of water and Gatorade and draping some neatly-folded spare towels over the benches. I smiled to myself, amused. The people here treated the football players like gods.

After spending a few minutes wandering around and failing to spot Maddie, I finally took a seat in the back row, near the entrance, and just hoped she'd find me there.

And that was where I stayed until the game started. And then throughout the duration of the first quarter. *And* the second quarter.

It was around the halftime show that I embraced the fact that I'd been stood up. Maddie wasn't coming, and I had no way to contact her, or even to contact Fiona or Nate and get a ride to the party, which now didn't seem worth going to anyway. But there was no way Tiffany would want to take me home, so now I was going to end up riding with her and Cammie to a party I no longer wanted to attend.

It was a strange feeling, being stood up. It'd never happened to me before, mostly because I'd never given anyone the chance to go on anything remotely similar to a date with me. For the most part, I just felt disappointed. Not sad, really, because I hadn't known Maddie long and although I liked her, I wasn't interested in dating her. But disappointed. And confused, because she'd seemed genuinely interested in hooking up with me.

The mood of the crowd at halftime was just as sour as mine. Collinsville High was losing the game by a field goal. The cheerleaders came out to do the halftime show, and as I watched them, I couldn't help but focus on Cammie. It was clear now more than ever that she was probably the prettiest girl on the squad, and I wondered if that was only so obvious now because she had makeup on and was apparently about to be crowned Homecoming Queen.

Before I could ponder it any further, someone took a seat next to me and let out a relaxed sigh. I turned, hoping for Maddie, and my stomach twisted when I saw it was Trevor, of all people. He kept his eyes on the field rather than looking at me at first as he asked, "Close game, huh?"

"Don't people typically stop going to high school events after they've graduated?" I retorted. He grinned at me, finally making eye contact, and offered his hand.

"I'm Trevor. I saw you at church last Sunday. But I don't think you ever mentioned your name?"

I ignored his hand. "Gertrude."

He laughed, unfazed, and took his hand back. "C'mon, I'm trying to be nice here. You looked lonely. Were you supposed to meet someone here?"

"None—" I started to say, with the intention of letting him know that my plans were none of his business, but I trailed off, chewing on my lip as I watched the cheerleaders on the field. I glanced to him to see him watching them now too, and held back a shudder. "Seems kind of like you have a thing for younger girls," I told him, struggling to keep my voice from sounding too icy.

He raised an eyebrow at me. "And now why would that be of interest to you?"

I swallowed back a biting retort and turned away, falling silent for a moment. It took everything I had to fake kindness, knowing what he'd done to Cammie, but as a plan formulated in my head, I let out an inaudible sigh and told him, "I was actually kind of supposed to meet someone here tonight."

"Yeah? Like a special someone?"

"Like a special someone," I confirmed, keeping my eyes trained on the field. "But I got stood up."

"Guy must be a massive idiot," he said, chuckling. "Who'd ditch *you*?"

"I don't know; I guess I can be kind of a bitch sometimes," I said.

"Good," he said. "I like bad girls."

Inwardly, I cringed. He was so gross. "That's not what I've heard."

He looked amused. "And what've you heard?"

"Oh, I don't know." I looked at him. "You tell me."

Trevor pondered that for a moment, rubbing at his chin thoughtfully. Then, he declared, "Well, I think rumor has it I'm a pretty decent guy. I'd imagine you've heard about my impeccable dining skills; I can eat several hotdogs in under a minute."

"You must get all the girls," I said. He grinned, and for a moment I could see why Cammie'd liked him at age fifteen. Back then, he'd have seemed charming.

"Not all of them, evidently," he said.

I let out a deep breath. "Well... it's been nice to talking to you, but I'm kind of thirsty, so..."

"Oh, don't worry. I've got it covered," he insisted, as I'd figured he would. He got to his feet, flashing me another smile, "Coke okay?"

"You read my mind," I said, and then he was gone. I scowled at his back as he headed for one of the concession stands, then mentally cursed Maddie for leaving me alone in the first place.

But now that I *was* alone, I was gonna make this night worthwhile, goddammit.

Trevor came back about two minutes later with a bottle of Coke, and I put up with his stupid flirty chatter for another five minutes before I forced a sickeningly sweet smile and asked, "Wanna take a walk?"

He smiled widely and immediately got to his feet and offered me his hand. I took it, and together we walked out to the parking lot.

"Did you drive here?" he asked me as we walked. I looked

around us before I answered the question, and noted that there were quite a few people within sight of us, but none close enough to hear our conversation. That was ideal.

"No, I got a ride from a friend," I said. "A couple friends, actually. Tiffany and Cammie."

"The cheerleaders?" he asked, and then seemed to recall something. "Oh, right! Cammie was with you at church. I remember now." He paused, and during his brief silence, I watched him, appalled that he could barely remember seeing her at church while she clearly hated so much to have to be in his presence. "Has she said anything about me to you?"

I unscrewed my Coke for the first time, and then took a brief sip. Then I shrugged my shoulders. "Oh, not much. Just a few comments here and there."

"Oh? Like what?"

I sipped my drink some more before I replied, thinking of the way Cammie'd acted at church. She was stiff and more uncomfortable than I'd ever seen her when she'd realized that I'd been looking at Trevor. And, to some extent, ashamed. I wanted him to feel that shame.

"Well. Frankly, from what I've heard you seem like a complete slimeball," I said. His smile dropped instantly, and I took more pleasure in it than I thought I would.

"Why are you here, Trevor?" I continued. "Some of these girls are fourteen and fifteen. What are you, almost twenty now? Shouldn't you be done manipulating high school girls at this point?"

His upper lip rose and he snarled, "Who the hell do you think you are? You don't know me."

"I've met a dozen guys like you." I stepped toward him and he stiffened. "So since you publicly humiliated Cammie, I'm gonna publicly humiliate you now."

I turned the Coke bottle upside down and dumped it out all over his head and shirt. He grabbed my arm and tried to push me away, but I was ready for that. I gripped his forearm with my free hand and stepped into him, bringing my knee up into his crotch. He crumpled to the ground with a groan, and I looked around hastily, then hurried away as a few bystanders watched the two of us with surprise. A couple girls nearby who'd seen most of our exchange were laughing and pointing at him.

I got back to the stands and showed my ticket to regain entry, but only made it halfway back to my seat before I felt a hand on my arm. I pulled away instinctively, thinking of Trevor, but it was Maddie who'd grabbed me. She was out of breath and looked a little disheveled as she declared, "Oh my God, there you are! I've been looking for you!"

"I was right here by the gate all game," I told her with disbelief, but she shook her head.

"I am so sorry. I only just got here during the halftime show. My car door didn't shut all the way when I got home earlier today and the battery died; I had to have a friend come over with jumper cables because both of my parents are out for the night. I couldn't let you know because you don't have a phone. I'm really, *really* sorry, Lauren."

"That's okay." I felt a sense of relief wash over me. "I'm just glad you're here now."

"Thanks. I'll totally come to the party with you tonight to make up for it," she promised.

"Good." I grinned at her, then took her wrist and yanked her toward the stands. "I had some fun without you, at least."

"Oh yeah?"

"Yep. C'mon, I'll tell you all about it while we finish watching this dumb game."

We took a seat a short distance from where I'd been before, and I offered some of my drink to Maddie. She accepted it with a grateful smile. "Thanks."

"No problem. I didn't pay for it," I explained. Then I proceeded to tell her what had just happened with Trevor. She was laughing hard by the time I was done.

"I remember him! He was such a douchebag. I'm glad he finally got some payback."

"Yeah, well… what he did to Cammie was really awful," I mumbled, taking my drink back from her. I turned to look at the field, and sensed Maddie's gaze on my cheek.

"You're protective of her," she observed.

I shrugged. "I guess so. Yeah."

* * *

After the game, the announcer called out the names of everyone who'd been nominated, and they went out in pairs to the center of the field, where they awaited the winner announcement. As had been the popular prediction, Cammie and Peter both took home the crowns, and even though I honestly didn't give a shit about Homecoming, I knew it meant a lot to Cammie, so I cheered loudly along with everyone else when her name was called. Beside me, Maddie was even polite enough to cheer too.

It didn't take long after that for the stands to begin to clear. We made it back to Maddie's car amongst the pandemonium, and as we pulled out of the school parking lot, she told me, "So these parties can get kind of crazy. I hope you're prepared."

"You've gotta be kidding me; this was my life back in Los Angeles," I said. "This'll feel like home."

"Do you like it back there?" she asked, glancing over at me as she drove.

"Sometimes. More often than not, no. But it has its benefits. There're more girls."

She laughed. "I don't know; I've been with a lot of girls here."

I grinned. That was a good sign. "Yeah? Well, I've been with a lot in L.A."

"So you think it's better than here?" she guessed.

I shrugged, looking out of the window. Now that we'd left the school, we seemed to officially be back in no man's land. I'd have been convinced we were in the middle of nowhere if I couldn't see a red light and an intersection up ahead. "Well... here is better than expected." I offered her a smile, and she bit her lip. "I like being here with you," I told her honestly. "You're one of the few people I can stand to be with, actually."

She checked her rearview mirror as we slowed to a stop at the red light, and I watched as she shifted the car into park. I shot her an amused look. "What are you doing?"

"*This*, before I lose my nerve," she declared, and before I could even begin to formulate a response, she was leaning over and kissing me.

I closed my eyes without thinking, and immediately kissed her back with an enthusiasm that surprised even me. It felt like it'd been so long since I'd done this with anyone who was genuinely interested in me, and Maddie *was*. She asked me questions about myself, and cared about how my day was going, and yet she had the experience to be what I wanted.

But kissing her now was leaving me a little confused about what it was *she* wanted. We were in a car at a red light; this wasn't about to go anywhere. She wasn't kissing me because she wanted to hook up right now; she was kissing me because she liked me. And I didn't know if that was a good thing or a bad thing, to be liked. I wasn't sure I'd ever been liked before.

She pulled away when a car horn blared from behind us, and I sank back in my seat, my heart hammering unpleasantly in my chest as she maneuvered the car forward again. I swallowed hard as my instincts began to let me know how I felt: this was bad. I'd wanted Maddie to be my home away from home, but this was new and unfamiliar and the exact *opposite* of what I'd thought it'd be. We were on what felt like a date and now she was kissing me like she wanted to be my girlfriend.

We drove in silence, tension building, and she finally cleared her throat and said, "I'm sorry. I didn't mean—"

"No," I cut her off, embarrassed. "It's okay. It was nice."

She glanced over at me. "Really?"

"Yeah. Of course," I said. "Kissing a cute girl's always nice."

There was another long silence after that, and I sensed I'd said something wrong. Eventually, we pulled up to the party and parked near the curb of a nearby street. I let out a sigh, trying to ease some of the tension in my body as the audible bass from the house rumbled in my chest.

"You ready?" I asked Maddie, who offered me an obviously forced smile and a nod.

"When you are," she agreed, and together, we got out of her car and made our way toward her cousin's front yard.

Chapter Twelve

The house was packed with people, and even more arrived after Maddie and I were already inside. I scanned the crowd for Fiona or Nate and, after having no success finding them, pushed my way into the kitchen, where the alcohol was being kept. Maddie stayed with me, but when I offered her a drink, she shook her head.

"I'm driving," she reminded me, and I didn't argue. I just thought, inwardly, that had she been Caitlyn, she would've accepted the drink. And for a moment, I wished she *was* Caitlyn. I couldn't remember the last time I'd been with a girl without both of us drinking first, which I know sounds awful, but it was mostly only due to the fact that I always met girls at clubs or parties.

Still, I accepted Maddie's answer and took her hand to lead her into another crowded room. "Are you looking for Cammie, or for the friends you had me text the address?" she asked. "I know this house if you need help navigating."

"The other friends," I told her. "Fiona Lawson and Nate Davis."

"Oh, you know them?" she looked surprised, but not unpleasantly so.

"I'm surprised you do," I said.

"They've been dating for years, I think," she told me unnecessarily. "Fiona's in one of my classes. They've always seemed really nice."

"I eat lunch with them." I scanned the crowd in the new room and spotted Fiona and Nate in the corner. I guessed Nate was driving, because Fiona had a drink and he didn't. I furrowed my eyebrows, wondering for the first time if Caitlyn and I were the ones with the weird drinking routine. She liked to do it at the beginning of the night because she'd be sober by the end of the night. I thought that was a thing people did.

I led Maddie to Fiona and Nate, who lit up when they saw us. "Hey!" Fiona greeted a little too loudly, and I grinned at her. "Can you *please* convince Nate to dance with me?"

"I'm not a good dancer," Nate deflected, and then changed the subject. "So I didn't know you two were friends." He smiled at Maddie in a way that relieved me. Maddie was openly gay, but they didn't seem to care. I'd chosen the right lunch table to sit at.

"We're in the same Physics class," Maddie told him.

"He actually *can* dance," Fiona cut in. "He's just too embarrassed to be seen with me because he thinks I won't be any good at it." She took a sip of her drink and shot him a knowing look. "You know, I should challenge you to a dance-off one day, Nate Davis."

"Okay, I so need to get on your level," I declared, and tipped my drink back to down it all in one fell swoop. I saw Nate and Maddie exchange disbelieving looks.

"You look like you've done that before," Nate said.

"More than a few times," I agreed, grinning. Maddie tapped me on the shoulder.

"Hey, I've gotta use the bathroom. Do you need to? We should probably go in pairs."

"I do," Fiona told her, and handed her drink to Nate. "Mind if I come?" she asked me.

"Oh, no problem. You guys can go; I'm fine."

They left me alone with Nate, and I shot him a grin. "She's fun when she's buzzed."

"Maybe for you, but I'm taking care of her tonight," he said.

"Then she's in good hands. You should dance with her."

"Nah. I'm fine with watching other people make fools of themselves."

His eyes moved to the crowd in the center of the room, and I followed his gaze. Most of the people dancing seemed to have paired off, and there was some dubstep song with a heavy bass playing, leaving a constant buzzing feeling within my chest. I remembered, abruptly, that Cammie had claimed to be a good dancer, and searched the crowd for her.

She was there, pressed against Peter with her back against his front, his hands on her waist as she tilted her head to the side so that her neck was exposed. I watched him kiss down it as she raised her hands to tangle them in his hair and pull his head lower, and I couldn't look away.

Nate seemed to know who I was watching, because a moment later, he leaned over and said, "Yeah, and you wonder where she gets the reputation from, right?"

"Reputation," I echoed, eyebrows furrowing. The alcohol was beginning to hit me, and I couldn't quite remember what he was referring to.

"The slutty one," he clarified, and I swallowed hard. "They say her parents think she's an angel too. But you'd know more about whether that's true or not than me. Do you two even actually get along?"

I was saved from answering by the return of Fiona and Maddie. Fiona had a new drink in her hand, now, so I took her old one from Nate and sipped from it as we hung out in the corner for a little while. I felt antsy; I wanted to dance with someone.

"Okay," I finally declared, tilting my head toward the crowd. "We're all going, c'mon. Nate, you too."

Fiona laughed and nodded her agreement, moving behind him and then pushing him toward the crowd as Maddie and I led the way. We forced our way in and then let ourselves be jostled by the crowd until we found some space to move around. Fiona and Nate naturally drifted together after a minute, and I found myself moving closer to Maddie. She offered me a smile, but I could sense something was off with her.

I leaned into her and asked, "Are you okay?"

She nodded simply, and I let out a sigh. She wasn't okay.

"Let's go talk," I declared, and pulled her away from the crowd before she could argue.

We detoured through the kitchen, where I grabbed another drink, and then wound our way through the house until I found the backdoor, which led to a deck that was completely deserted. I tugged Maddie outside and then closed the door behind us. I sipped from my cup as I faced her, then set it aside.

"What's wrong? You aren't having fun."

"I'm fine," she sighed. "I just… tried one of these parties my freshman year, and it wasn't really my thing."

"What happened?" I asked her. "Whatever it was, I can make sure it doesn't happen again."

She crossed her arms and looked away from me. "I can't tell you."

"Why not?"

"Because I just can't." She shot me an accusatory look. "I thought you wanted to have fun with your friends. You should just go back and dance, or whatever. Grind on a random."

"Okay, I'm a little confused," I said, finding it hard to think clearly. "Why are you mad?"

"I'm not mad."

"Seriously? God, this is why I hate getting to know girls," I said. "Just stop being passive aggressive and say what's on your mind."

Her eyes narrowed dangerously. "Gee, thanks, Lauren." She took a step closer to me. "You know what? Fine. I'm not upset because we're at a party, even though I didn't want to come here. I'm *upset* because of what happened in the car. I'm not here to play games, okay? Do you like me or not?"

"Of course I like you," I told her. "You're pretty, smart, funny, easy to talk to... what's not to like? It's seriously that simple for me."

She let out a deep breath, and I could see the anger disappearing from her gaze. This time, I knew I'd said the right thing. "Don't overthink it," I insisted. "We like each other, right? So what's the problem?"

"Okay," she said quietly, and glanced to the backdoor. No one inside seemed to have even noticed us yet. "Okay," she repeated, and then caught me off-guard by stepping into me to kiss me again.

It progressed quickly this time, now that we were out of a cramped car and had more time alone. I was tipsy and turned on and kissing a girl against the side of a house at a party, and I grinned against Maddie's lips, feeling more like myself than I had in months. *This* was what I'd been waiting for.

She linked her hands behind my neck as we kissed, and I pressed my hips into hers, my hands on her waist as our kisses grew deeper and deeper.

She pulled away first, long after I'd lost track of time, and moved her hand to cup my cheek as her thumb caressed the skin there. I dropped my head and kissed her neck, and her head rolled to the side. I heard her breath catch, and I murmured, "We should just go back to your house."

Instantly, she froze, and I felt her body tense against mine. I pulled away, confused. Had I screwed up again?

Her eyes searched mine intently, her eyebrows furrowed, and then, abruptly, she moved away from me. I sighed, exhausted. We'd done another 180.

"Why?" she asked, her tone clipped.

I colored. "Um." And I couldn't really think of anything else to say. The reason seemed kind of obvious, honestly.

"Really? You want to go home with me. Right now?" She laughed suddenly, more at herself than at me, I think, and then shook her head in disbelief. "Wow," she deadpanned. "I am *such* an idiot."

"No you're not," I said instinctively, my speech vaguely slurred. "You're smart."

"Shut up, Lauren," she dismissed with a roll of her eyes. Then she pursed her lips and shook her head again. "You know… when I said I'd been with a lot of girls here, you know how many I meant?" I didn't answer, and waited for her to continue, a feeling of trepidation quickly building in my chest. "Four," she told me. "*Four.* How many did *you* mean, Lauren? *Forty?*"

I colored abruptly. "No… less than that."

"Twelve, twenty, forty… I guess it doesn't make a difference. I've slept with four girls. I was dating all of them at the time. That's a lot for a seventeen-year-old girl, so yeah, I'm experienced. But I'm not like you."

I furrowed my eyebrows, a little offended. Or a lot offended. I couldn't tell; my brain was a little sluggish at the moment. "Like me?" I echoed.

"Yeah, like you. Was this just a hookup to you the whole time?" she asked me, appalled.

"Only if that was what you wanted..." My cheeks were on fire now. I was totally and utterly humiliated, and still too tipsy to fully comprehend what was happening.

"So I could sleep with you if I wanted to, great. What about a relationship?"

I swallowed hard again and didn't reply.

"Have you *ever* been in a relationship? With *anyone?*" she asked. When I stayed silent, she nodded. "Should've known. How on earth can you talk shit about guys like Trevor, being the way you are? How is what you're doing here any better than what he's done? You let me think you wanted to get to know me; that you actually liked me. Here I was, actually catching feelings for a girl I was spending time with, and meanwhile you just wanted to sleep with me."

"But I do like you," I mumbled, my voice barely audible at this point. I wanted to crawl into a hole and never come out. I realized with a pang that I'd just punished Trevor today for essentially following through with the same sort of plan she was accusing me of having now. But I couldn't comprehend the idea that I was no different. I'd actually gotten to know her, I genuinely liked her as a person, and I'd never slept with anyone who didn't want it, so how was I in the wrong?

She folded her arms across her chest, her gaze steely. "You know exactly what I'm talking about. You were getting to know me, coming to my house, wearing clothes to impress me, letting

me know you were willing to go hang out with me around town...
How else was I supposed to interpret that? You just assumed that
I wanted what you wanted, and if there were signs that I wanted
more, you ignored them. So if you don't mind, I'm gonna go
home, and I don't want to talk to you ever again, okay?" She
moved to open the back door, and threw over her shoulder, "You
can get Nate to take you home." The door slammed shut behind
her.

My vision a little fuzzy, I fumbled my way to a chair and sat
still for a moment, trying to process what had just happened. I felt
like I was going to vomit, and I didn't know whether it was from
the upset stomach the alcohol had given me or if it was because of
what Maddie had just said. The idea that I was comparable to
someone like Trevor was sickening. I didn't *trick* people. I didn't
lie. If Maddie had told me she was looking for a girlfriend from
the beginning, I'd have said I wasn't interested. Or at least I
believe I would have.

I sighed, placing my head in my hands. The deck was starting
to spin if I kept my eyes open.

I heard the back door open, and then a hand was on my
shoulder and Fiona's voice was in my ear. "Hey girl, is everything
okay? Maddie just stopped by to tell us she was leaving. Nate and
I can give you a ride home when we leave?"

"Yeah, okay," I agreed quietly. "I just have to talk to Cammie;
we need to get home at the same time."

"I haven't seen her," Fiona said. Her speech was still a little
slurred. "But Nate might have. He's putting my jacket in his car,
so I told him I'd go and find you." She fumbled her way into the

chair beside me, and, once she was seated, asked, "What happened? You know I'll always be here for you, Lauren, right? You seem super nice. Like, I'm really glad you came here."

"Thanks," I forced a smile at her, trying to put my fight with Maddie aside for a moment. "I'm glad I picked your lunch table. I was really worried everyone here would be really closed-minded and awful but you guys are so sweet. And you were really nice to Maddie. You didn't even care that she was gay."

"Of course not," Fiona waved the air away with a shake of her head. "That doesn't matter. People have their stuff and you've just gotta accept them for who they are. Like you. I bet you have plenty of stuff going on in your life, since you came all the way from Los Angeles to stay with the Marshalls. I mean, the thing with your mom, like…"

She shook her head disbelievingly, and I raised my head to stare at her, my gaze suddenly sharp. Then she realized what she'd said, and gasped, raising a hand to cover her mouth. When she removed it, she apologized, "I'm *so* sorry, Lauren. I really didn't plan on ever mentioning it unless you did first. I haven't even said anything to Nate."

"You know about my mom?" I asked, dumbfounded. "How?"

"My mom loved her show. The one she was on as a kid. She was actually a really big fan; she was really upset when… well, I mean, not like you were, but…" She bit her lip, and continued, "I guess I told her at one point that I'd made a friend from Los Angeles named Lauren who'd been flown all the way here to stay with the Marshalls, and she told me that if your last name was

Lennox, you might be Nicole Erikson's daughter. So after you told me your last name… I just figured you were. It made sense. You kind of dress like you have money, and you're here for a reason, you know?"

I looked away from her and put my face in my hands again. This was too much for one night.

"I'm sorry, Lauren." She sounded so sincere that for a moment I thought she might start crying. "Please, are you okay? What can I do?"

I let out a shaky breath. Fiona wasn't going to start crying, I realized. *I* was. And as hard as I tried, I couldn't stop thinking about what Maddie had said. "I think I'm a bad person," I admitted.

"No, you're not," she told me. "Nate and I really like you." She hesitated, and then added, "No matter how close you and Maddie are. Or were." I raised my head to look at her, wiping away the tears blurring my vision. She smiled at me, and asked, "Do you want to go inside? We can find Cammie, then find Nate and leave. It's almost eleven-thirty anyway, and I don't know about you, but Nate and I have to be back by midnight."

"Me too," I murmured, and she nodded and took my hand, helping me get to my feet. Together, we made our way to the door, and Fiona giggled a little when we both had some trouble making it.

"We need Nate," she joked.

"Yeah," I said.

We spent ten minutes searching for Cammie without any success, and I decided eventually that she'd probably be heading

214

home soon anyway, so instead we found Nate and then walked out to his car together.

"So these parties aren't really worth all the hype," Nate decided as we drove away. "You guys drank, we danced, and we left."

"That's kind of the gist of it," I admitted. "Only if you're lucky, you meet someone during the party and go home with them afterward."

Nate laughed at that. "You must be the first girl I've ever heard talk like that. Do people even *do* one-night-stands in high school? Isn't it usually assumed that if someone's talking to you they're interested in more than a hookup? Or am I just being optimistic?"

I slunk back in my seat, feeling lower than dirt again. "I don't know."

We got back to the Marshalls' farm with five minutes to spare. Nate and Fiona dropped me off in a hurry, already late to get back to their own homes, and I gathered myself quickly and tried to practice walking straight. I'd sobered up a lot since my talk with Fiona, but I couldn't tell if it was enough to get me past David. Still, I had to try.

I was halfway to the steps of the front porch when I noticed Cammie waiting for me on the porch swing. I started to wave and call out to her, but she raised a finger to her lips, motioning for me to be quiet, and then beckoned me forward. I took in her appearance. "Disheveled" was putting it lightly. Her hair and the makeup I'd worked so meticulously on were now a mess, and her clothes had so many wrinkles I wasn't sure even an iron would fix them.

"Jesus," I murmured as I reached her. "Who the hell did you hook up with tonight?"

"Just Peter," she sighed. "Look, I can't let my parents see me like this. Can you fix it?"

"I can try." I shook my head, marveling at her. "What did you do before me?"

"Tiffany, when I looked like this," she admitted. "But I only just got back a few minutes ago; she didn't have time."

"Okay." I rummaged through my purse for a moment, then went to work on her makeup first.

With just inches between our faces, she looked back at me with sudden concern. "Hey," she said, quietly, "your mascara ran a little. Have you been crying?"

I shrugged. "Yeah, a little. Dramatic night."

"What happened?"

"Got in a fight with Maddie; Fiona knows about my mom now. The usual."

"What? How?"

"How did I get into a fight with Maddie or how does Fiona know about my mom?"

"Both."

"Well, I don't want to talk about Maddie, and Fiona's mom was a fan of my mom."

She pulled a face. "A fan? What does that mean?"

I froze, realizing I'd slipped up. Then I shook my head and went back to her makeup, murmuring, "Goddammit."

"Hey." She caught my eye and then reached up to rub some of my mascara away. Her hand was gentle on my cheek as she told me, "We don't have to talk about it if you don't want me to know."

"Thanks." I smiled at her, genuinely grateful.

"You've done the same when it comes to my secrets," she said. I knew she was talking about her cheating on Peter, and I was surprised to learn that she considered the rest of that story a secret. I'd thought it was simple: She didn't like Peter and she'd liked someone else for a little while. But maybe there was more to it than that.

"You shouldn't let him do this to you," I told her eventually, "if you don't enjoy it." I frowned at her. "You look like a chewed up rag doll."

She let out a bitter laugh. "Thanks."

"But still somehow beautiful," I added somewhat nervously, and tucked a strand of her hair behind her ear. She stared at me for a moment, and I saw her swallow visibly. Then, so quickly I'd later convince myself I'd imagined it, her gaze flickered down to my lips.

The front door opened, and she and I moved away from each other quickly as David stared out at us. I knew without looking in a mirror that both Cammie and I almost certainly looked like we hadn't just been to a tame high school dance. His eyes narrowed. "Come on in, girls."

David was alone, thankfully; Wendy'd apparently elected to go to bed in preparation for all of the farm work we'd be doing tomorrow. My heart sank at the thought of waking up early.

We were directed to sit on the couch, and David leaned in

close to Cammie's face, arms crossed, and demanded, "Exhale."

She breathed out into his face and he sniffed at her. "Mints. Very nice." She bit her lip guiltily and sat back as he focused his attention to me. "Your turn."

I pressed my lips together and shook my head, wary. I'd never gone through anything like this before. So *this* was having parents. Huh.

"Lauren," he demanded, his voice stern. "I won't ask again."

With a roll of my eyes, I leaned forward and exhaled. He sighed, no doubt at the alcohol on my breath, and then, to my surprise, shifted his attention to Cammie.

"Cammie, I expected this from Lauren, but not from you. Who gave the two of you alcohol?"

"Just some guy at the dance," Cammie mumbled. I hid an impressed look; she was playing the part of a regretful daughter with ease even as she continued to lie to her dad.

"Who? Was it your idea to accept it from him?" He let out a sigh. "Cammie, I've told you and Scott about how dangerous underaged drinking is. You don't know where those drinks have come from or where they've been. Especially given that I trusted you and asked you to make sure Lauren stayed out of trouble after the game, I can't believe this is what you went and did tonight."

"It wasn't her idea," I cut in swiftly, sick of watching him berate her. Even if she wasn't as perfect as David thought she was, I knew she deserved a punishment less than I did. Everyone deserved to let loose once in a while, and besides, David would go easier on me than he would on her.

Cammie, who'd bowed her head as her dad was laying into her, now stared at me with surprise as David's gaze shifted to me instead. "I saw some guys with flasks and asked if I could have some. Cammie said it was a bad idea, but I talked her into it." I arched a defiant eyebrow. "Try everything once, right?"

David seemed conflicted, and spent a long moment looking between the two of us. Then, at last, he shook his head and stood up straight. "Alright. Up the stairs, both of you. You'll need a lot of sleep tonight because you're doing double the work tomorrow."

I heard Cammie let out a sigh ahead of me as we both got off of the couch and made our way upstairs. David watched us from the bottom until we were in Cammie's room and the door was shut behind us.

She turned around to face me as soon as we were alone. "You didn't have to do that, you know. I'd have gotten a few weeks of grounding. He'll never trust you again, now, and you won't be able to go anywhere without me."

I shrugged my shoulders and moved to my suitcase to find pajamas for the night. I knew she was right, but it wasn't like I could change my story now, even if I'd wanted to. "I'm used to spending a lot of time with you by now, anyway," I said.

She was quiet for a moment. I straightened up with clothes in my hands to see that she'd moved to her bed. The light of the lamp on her nightstand caught her neck, and I stared at the red circle on her skin as she told me, sincerely, "Thank you."

"Did Peter do that?" I asked, and she followed my gaze, then raised a hand to her neck and flushed. "Don't worry," I reassured her. "I think your dad was too caught up on the alcohol thing to notice it. Seriously, though... is that *enjoyable*? He seems pretty aggressive. It's gonna take a lot of makeup to cover it up."

She shrugged her shoulders. "Oh, I don't really know. It's okay, I guess."

"Okay, but... is that a 'yes'? A 'no'?" I asked her. "I mean, do you look forward to hooking up with him? I know for a fact that you can still enjoy sex without being in love, so do you?"

She just shrugged her shoulders again and didn't answer. I decided to cut her some slack, and went into her closet to change my clothes. She changed after me, and then, together, we settled into our respective beds. Cammie turned off her lamp, sending us into complete darkness.

I shifted around for a moment in my bed, and then rolled onto my side, thinking of my fight with Maddie again.

"Cammie?" I asked, when I heard rustling from her bed and was sure she was still awake.

"Hmm?"

"The guys you've slept with... did you think, going in, that any of them meant anything? Like, that they were going to be the love of your life and they were just this perfect guy that you'd dreamed about dating and couldn't wait to... you know, *be* with? After Trevor, I mean?"

She was quiet for a long while; for so long that I was sure she'd fallen asleep. But then her answer came. "That's a loaded question. Why?"

"I'm just... trying to figure something out," I mumbled.

"Well... I think that I started off with high expectations back when I was first starting to date. But if you sleep with enough people that don't think you matter, maybe it starts to hurt a little less when they turn out to just be another jerk. Eventually, you can see it coming, I guess. Eventually you realize that as much as you hope a frog could be a prince, it's probably actually just a frog."

"How do you avoid getting hurt if you *are* the frog?" I asked.

There was a long pause. And, eventually, she murmured, "The frogs don't get hurt, Lauren. You can't break a heart that doesn't exist."

That, I think, stung more than anything Maddie could've said to me in a million lifetimes.

Chapter Thirteen

I didn't sleep well that night.

Instead, I tossed and turned until sunrise, caught in a strange and horrifying dream where I was watching a fictional retelling of Cammie's first time with Trevor. He spent the entire lead-up whispering sweet nothings into her ear, and then, at some point, his hair grew out and the tone of his voice climbed higher until it was me in bed with Cammie, spouting bullshit to get her to sleep with me. Then I blinked and Cammie had turned into Maddie.

The nine o'clock alarm saved me from the rest of the dream, and I stared up at the ceiling as Cammie got out of bed, wondering what on earth was in store for me today.

Cammie couldn't look at her mother throughout breakfast. A tension had filled the house overnight that left everyone on edge, with the exception of Scott, who seemed to find this whole thing hilarious. I was almost relieved to find out I'd be spending most of the time on cow duty with him rather than my usual horse job with Cammie. She, meanwhile, was ordered to help her dad out while Wendy took care of Aerosmith.

Scott led me out to the barn after breakfast, and almost immediately shot me a knowing grin as he pulled its front doors open. "So why'd you take the heat for Cammie?"

I took a moment to respond. There was a cow waiting for us in the barn, standing upright on the straw floor, and I knew instantly that I wasn't going to like whatever Scott was about to make me do. Finally, I looked to him, still slightly distracted. "Um... who says I took any heat I didn't deserve?"

"Dad told me your alcohol story," Scott said. "I used to play football for Collinsville, remember? I went to Alex Parker's parties every year too, you know."

"Right." I followed Scott to the cow, keeping a safe distance, and he brought out a pail and set it under the cow's stomach. My own stomach dropped. *Oh no.* "Do I have to?" I asked him, and he grinned.

"If I want my parents to trust me, yeah. You've just gotta learn and get a decent bit of it done, and then I'll take over." He set a stool down next to the cow and then patted the top of it. "C'mon."

"Can I at least get some gloves?" I asked. He laughed and nodded, moving to rummage through a nearby set of cabinets for a pair. "Anyway," I continued as he searched, "I covered for Cammie because your parents are kind of harsh on you guys and I knew your dad would cut me some slack. He expects *me* to screw up, not her."

"Huh. You're more observant than I thought," he admitted, and, at last, found me a pair of gloves to wear. "Yeah, Dad gets pretty into his job."

"He puts a lot of pressure on you two."

Scott shrugged his shoulders. "We're used to it. I mean, it's definitely frustrating at times, but Cammie and I have grown up with it. We know there are expectations we have to meet."

"Yeah. I've noticed."

He motioned for me to take a seat, and I grudgingly complied even as he kept talking. "I mean, take me and Jill. Of course, my mom really likes her, which I'm happy about because I like her too. But I'm not in a hurry to get married and have kids, you know? I'm only twenty. But I'm also mature enough to know that what I want isn't necessarily what's best. And I trust their judgment."

"You don't want kids?" I asked, and he laughed.

"Uh… I didn't exactly say that, but not really, I guess. I mean, I'll have them because I know it'd kill my mom and Jill if I didn't, but if it was up to just me I probably wouldn't. Anyway, stop trying to put off milking the cow."

"It's gross." I wrinkled my nose even as Scott kneeled down beside me and reached for an udder. "Ew."

I spent the next fifteen minutes verbally going over technique with Scott, and the next ten working up the courage to actually touch one of the udders. When I did, I gagged, and Scott grinned at me.

"C'mon, it's not that bad. Just squeeze."

"Gross gross gross," I murmured, reaching out and gripping the udder again. I followed Scott's instructions, half-ready to vomit all the while, and milk shot out of the udder and into the bucket.

"Nice! You're a natural," Scott told me, but I shook my head and stood abruptly, already moving to pull my gloves off.

"No way. Uh uh. I am *not* doing that again. That is so gross."

"We haven't gotten nearly enough, you know," he said, but I just shook my head again.

"I said I'd milk the cow, and I did. Mission accomplished."

He smiled over at me again, then wordlessly took a seat on the stool and began to milk it himself. I let out a sigh of relief and thanked him.

"Yeah, just don't let my dad find out I did this for you," he replied. "And the kid thing stays between us."

"Deal."

We worked into the afternoon, all five of us. I got off easy with milking the cows, which took a while because there were more than just one, and spent most of my time in the barn, chatting with Scott and watching the field for signs of any of the other Marshalls. In the time I'd been here, I hadn't really gotten to know Scott, so it was nice to finally get a chance to talk to him alone.

At two o'clock, we finally stopped and came inside for lunch. Things were still tense, but considering Cammie looked like she was going to pass out at any moment after what were evidently several hours of hard labor, her parents were a little nicer to her this time. I couldn't really look at her; every time I did, I felt guilty that I hadn't really gotten a punishment.

After lunch, she was set free at last, and so was Scott, who immediately grabbed his keys and left to go pay Jill a visit. Wendy cleared the table by herself, and David asked me to come join him outside again. I grew nervous as I followed him, realizing that he probably had some sort of special punishment prepared for me given that I'd taken the blame for last night. I tried to brace myself for cleaning up animal poop or lifting heavy bales of hay.

But that didn't come. Instead, he motioned for me to sit down on the grass with him just outside of the house, and told me, "I thought now might be a good time to talk."

"About what?" I asked dumbly. Of course he wanted to talk about last night.

"I know my kids very well," he said. "I know their hobbies, their friends, their favorite colors... and despite that, I'm a little baffled by what you and Cammie did last night. She's a good kid."

"Well, you straightened her out," I said, a hint of sarcasm in my tone. "She learned her lesson. A whole extra two hours of work in the sun."

His jaw tensed, but he didn't otherwise react to my comment. Instead, he said, "I'd really hoped you were improving. I put my trust in you and let you go off by yourself. Now I'm not even sure I can trust you alone with Cammie. I didn't realize you'd have the kind of influence you're having on her."

"Maybe you don't know your kids as well as you think you do. That stuff you said you knew was all shallow. Like, do you know they want to do with their lives?" I tilted my head to the side, eyeing him curiously. "Do you know that? Because I do, I think, and I've known them for three weeks. And if you *don't*, I don't really get why you're out here talking to me instead of them. I already have a father, and he may not know my answers, but that doesn't mean you should be trying to figure them out in his place if you don't even know them for your own kids."

"I watch out for them, Lauren," he replied, his tone calm. He offered me a small smile. "You may take more focus to get a read on, but I certainly know my own kids."

"Okay, so what *do* they want to do with their lives?" I challenged.

"Scott would like to start a family with Jill, once he gets out of school. And Cammie wants the same, a family of her own here in Collinsville... although only after getting into a good college, and, I'll admit, probably not with Peter, as much as Wendy likes him."

It surprised me that he'd picked up on Cammie's feelings toward Peter. But for the most part, he was wrong. Completely wrong about Scott, certainly, and, if my hunch was correct, at least partially wrong about Cammie.

But I didn't tell him that. Instead, I just got to my feet and asked, "Can we be done now?"

"I suppose," he said, but he was pretty clearly disappointed as he watched me turn and head back inside. He wasn't the only disappointed one. David Marshall, counselor extraordinaire with the ability to turn any "bad" kid good, seemed have only achieved that title by putting his own kids on the backburner.

And as a girl who'd grown up without much of a father, I had no desire to be the one responsible for Cammie and Scott losing theirs.

* * *

When I got upstairs, Cammie'd just gotten out of the shower and was already changed into her pajamas.

"Exhausted already?" I asked her, reaching down into my suitcase for a change of clothes. I was eager to take a shower of my own.

"Yeah, I might need a nap," she sighed, and rubbed uncomfortably at her shoulder. "Sleep off the ache."

"Did you pull a muscle or something?" I asked. She kept rubbing at the same shoulder, and winced even as she nodded.

"I think I strained, like, my shoulder or my neck or something. Too much heavy lifting."

I tossed my clothes onto my bed and moved to her, motioning for her to stand up. "Here."

"What?" she asked, watching me with mild amusement even as she got to her feet. "Do you know how to fix it?"

"Maybe. I got sore muscles a lot from gymnastics. My mom used to make it go away."

"You got sore muscles at age four?"

I grinned. "I was a very intense toddler, okay? I fell down a lot."

"Possibly on the head area?" she asked, grinning.

"Very funny. Just let me—" I reached out for her shoulder and she winced when I pressed down. "Sorry."

"Just be gentle."

"I'm trying," I insisted with a laugh, and rubbed at a spot between her neck and shoulder with the pads of my fingers. Cammie tilted her head to the side and closed her eyes. I realized this had been a bad idea right around the time she let out a small moan. "There. Feel better?" I asked, abruptly pulling away. Her eyes opened and she nodded.

"Yeah, a little."

"Cool." I turned away from her to retrieve my clothes. "I'm gonna go take a shower."

"Wait, um…" I paused, and turned to look back at her. She hesitated, and then continued, "You mentioned your mother helping you when you'd get hurt. So she *was* around when you were younger?"

I nodded. "Yeah. A little bit. I just don't remember much about her from back then. I was too young." I waited for her to say more, but she didn't. "Anyway… shower."

She nodded and I left, wondering what her questions had been about. I knew a lot about Cammie, most of it deduced after heavy observation, and she knew a lot about my problems, but I guess beyond why I was here, I hadn't shared much about my personal life with her after all. Was this her way of trying to get to know me?

I got back to her bedroom twenty minutes later. She was in bed, and her eyes were closed, but they fluttered open as I sat down on my own bed. "Trying to nap?" I guessed.

She shrugged her shoulders, her voice quiet. "I don't know.

Not really." She paused, and then asked me, "Do you ever just get kind of lonely out of nowhere?"

"I spend my life lonely," I laughed. "Especially recently. I'm alone *here*."

"You have me," she said. I smiled at her, a little surprised.

"Good to know. And you have me."

She swallowed hard at that. "That's not what I mean. Or... I guess..." She trailed off and fell silent, deep in thought, and I smiled at her again.

"You should tell me about the stuff you draw," I suggested.

She arched an eyebrow. "No way."

"Why not?"

"Because. I'll tell you that when you tell me whatever you're hiding about your mom."

I knew she was only saying that because she figured I'd never go for it, but honestly, I considered it. Cammie wasn't going to tell anyone; I trusted her not to now. That was what mattered to me. I was Nicole Erickson's daughter in Los Angeles and it wasn't fun there. The good thing about Georgia was that at least I was just Lauren here. But maybe it was time to give that up – at least partially.

"Okay," I said at last, and without giving her time to retract her offer, I told her, "My mom was a famous actress."

She stared at me blankly for a moment, and I waited for it to click with her. When it did, her eyes widened and she asked, "Nicole Erickson? Oh my God."

"Yep." The only famous actress who'd passed away recently enough to make sense. "The one and only."

"Wow." She shook her head, her eyebrows furrowing. And then she asked, "Why didn't you tell me?"

"Because I like being Lauren, and because it didn't seem necessary. You knew my mom died recently; why flaunt that she was famous?"

Cammie was quiet for another few seconds. I watched her take a deep breath, and then nod her head. "Yeah. That makes sense."

"It does?" A sense of relief washed over me.

"Yeah. Being the daughter of a famous person... that must be all you are to a lot of people. Or at least to the ones who knew who she was."

"Which would be everyone at my school," I told her. "Which, contrary to what you may think, did *not* make me popular. Everyone thought I was a spoiled little shit."

She cracked a smile. "You kind of are."

"Only on my bad days," I countered. "And I'm trying to be better. Anyway, now you have to show me your drawings."

"Wait. You still haven't told me what she was like."

"Oh. Right." I didn't consider my answer for long. I'd been asked this question a lot. *Everyone* wanted to know what my mom was like. "Well... I mean, you've seen her stuff, right? I know she used to think her comedy could be better, but she was pretty funny, I thought. She was just a really good actress in general. And she loved her job but didn't like the pressure, I don't think. She loved her fans too; would always worry about disappointing them—"

"Lauren," she cut me off, shaking her head. "Not what Nicole

Erickson the celebrity was like, okay? What your *mom* was like."

I blinked at her. *That* was a new one. "What do you mean?"

"Like, as a person," Cammie pressed. "As the mom you got to know, even if it was just for a little while. Did she read you bedtime stories? Did you guys do things together? You know, the mom from your childhood."

"Oh." I tilted my head to the side, thinking back. And then I smiled. "Yeah, she did read me bedtime stories, didn't she?"

"What kind?" Cammie asked. She was grinning at me now, for some reason.

"I don't know. I don't remember," I admitted. "She did the voices, though. And she liked to take me out for ice cream a lot, after my gymnastics classes. Back then, she didn't get recognized so much. We'd go to the park and eat ice cream and there was this big playground set with three slides... I liked to hide in them and she'd guess which one I was in." I laughed, abruptly. "Oh, wow. I'd totally forgotten about that." With Cammie still staring at me, I fell silent, resting my chin on my hand. "Huh."

"What changed?" she asked me.

"I got older and she got a big movie role. She had her faults, though, you know. Even when I was a kid, my dad was an alcoholic. I think she thought that if she ignored it for long enough, he'd fix himself. And eventually, she was too busy to dwell on it. So I became old news and daddy dearest became my only real guardian."

"He could still get help," she pointed out.

"He won't without someone to motivate him, and there's no one to do that."

"Well, there's you," she said.

I chewed on my lip for a moment, and then glanced toward her desk, eager to get away from the subject of my dad. "Anyway, your drawings?"

"I wasn't being serious about talking about those," she replied, her cheeks pinking slightly, but I rolled my eyes at her and shook my head.

"We had a deal. Are all of them of New York City, or what?"

She pinked further, and crossed her arms in front of her chest, almost defensively. "I didn't know you could tell exactly what city I was drawing."

"The skyscrapers and yellow cabs gave it away." I tilted my head to the side, studying her while she pursed her lips together. "So... what, you want to live there one day? Small town life isn't all it's cracked up to be after all?" I guessed.

She was quiet for a moment. Her eyes moved to the bedspread in front of her and, at last, she shrugged her shoulders. "I don't know." She looked up at me. "I don't mind the farm stuff. I like animals, and the work isn't too hard. But I guess..." She trailed off, and then let out a deep sigh. "Okay, yeah. I guess I've thought about it a little. There's this art school in New York City I've done some research on. It's just this small private college, but..."

"You should go," I told her immediately. She seemed surprised by my sudden response.

"I can't just leave my family after graduation to go to school halfway across the country, Lauren."

"Why not? You should do what you love. If it's what makes

you happy, then go for it."

"It's not that simple," she said. "I have... commitments here."

I watched her as her gaze sank back to her lap, and my eyebrows furrowed in realization. "Your mom and your boyfriend and your imaginary future family?" I guessed. Her lack of response was an answer in itself. "But you don't want that," I said.

"I never said that," she retorted.

"You didn't need to, Cammie. I paid attention."

Her eyes jumped back up to look into mine. I could no longer get a good read on her; she seemed a little... affronted?

"Why would you do that?" she asked. "You know, it's really... *annoying* how you can see right through me. You came here with your own issues. It's not like you actually have the time to sort *mine* out."

I offered her a small smile. "So you're admitting you have them, then? Everything isn't perfect after all in Cammie Marshall's world?"

"Nobody's perfect."

"I know that, Hannah Montana, but you walk around like you have this town in the palm of your hand. I mean, I watched you win Homecoming Queen. And there may be people who don't like you here, but they'll never say it because you're almost, like, too high up on the hierarchy to be torn down. Like you're socially untouchable. And I know you worked hard to get that way. But I also know that everything isn't as okay as you like to pretend it is."

She sat quietly as I spoke, and didn't make any moves to interrupt me. So I kept going.

"I think you let other people dictate who you are. I think

you're the innocent good girl around your dad, the sweetheart church girl who reads cheesy romance novels around your mom, a total whore around your douchebag boyfriend because you know that's what he wants, and a shallow boy-crazy ditz around your cheerleader friends. At first I wasn't even sure if *you* knew who you really were." I paused, watching her clench and unclench her jaw as she stared at me.

"But I'd like to think that maybe you feel like you can be honest with me? Or at least more honest than you can be with anyone else. I mean, *I'm* so fucked up that I'm in no place to judge your whole multiple-personality game anyway."

There was a long silence, and I watched Cammie as she sat back and chewed on her lip. Her hands fidgeted with a clump of her comforter for a moment, and then she released it and looked to me.

"I thought *I* was supposed to be the future therapist." She cracked a small smile, and, relieved, I returned the gesture.

"You don't have to be all of that, Cammie. There are people who will like you for being who you are instead of who they want you to be. You should live your life the way you want. Go to art school."

She shook her head, shooting me a knowing look. "I can't."

"Not true. You can do anything you want to."

"You don't really believe that."

"Sure I do. You're smart. Pretty. Clearly you're eerily socially aware. You get good grades. If you just get over this thing about being who everyone wants you to be and actually start being yourself for a change, you can do whatever you want. Just stop caring so much about what everyone thinks of you."

She shook her head again. "I can't do that. What everyone thinks of me matters way too much here. And people would hate me if I were totally myself."

"That's not true," I immediately cut in.

"Oh, yeah?" She arched an eyebrow. "How do you know?"

"Because I'm the closest thing you've got to someone who knows the real you, and I don't hate you. I'll take the Cammie who likes drawing, hates her friends and wants to live in New York over popular cheerleader romance-novel-loving Cammie any day."

She laughed. "You would."

I smiled over at her as her laughter died down, and the mood abruptly became somber. We sat in silence together for a minute or so, and I laid down on my bed, folding my arms behind my head and staring up at her ceiling.

"Sucks, doesn't it?" I said at last. "To not feel at home where you grew up? I used to have these elaborate fantasies about escaping Los Angeles one day. This wasn't exactly where I imagined I'd end up, though."

Cammie didn't respond at first, but when she did, I had to hide a grin.

"Yeah. But I'm glad you're here."

Chapter Fourteen

"Look."

Cammie's arm stretched up overhead between us, and she pointed to a cluster of stars off to our left. I followed her finger.

"What?"

She chuckled. "Looks like a dick."

"Nice."

I rolled over onto my side to watch her as she grinned up at the stars. We were in the clearing ten minutes from her house, and Aerosmith was tied up to a tree just a few feet away. We'd brought a blanket to lay beneath us. It was one in the morning on a Friday night, and the rest of the Marshalls were asleep. I guess that meant that technically we'd snuck out. We'd been doing that often lately. Things had changed a lot over the course of the past few weeks.

With Maddie refusing to talk to me and my time with Fiona and Nate limited to school hours after Cammie and I'd been busted for drinking, Cammie was kind of the only friend I actually got to spend time with now. But part of me was okay with that. The more time we spent together, the more I liked her. *Really* liked her.

I swallowed hard as I watched her, then forced myself to close my eyes. The Sunday after I'd dumped soda on Trevor came to mind. He hadn't been at church that day, and no questions had been asked about it.

But then he hadn't been there the next week. Or the next. Or the one after that. And soon enough, Cammie had started to wonder why. So I told her. When I was finished with my story, she'd hugged me so tightly I'd ached on the inside. Right around the chest area, actually. Things hadn't really been the same since.

I opened my eyes to find that she'd turned her head and was looking back at me. "Tired?" she asked, smirking.

"Yeah," I mumbled, not quite looking her in the eyes. "Farm work tomorrow. Gross."

"You should be used to it by now," she pointed out.

"I'll never get used to shoveling horse shit."

She laughed. "*One* time! You big baby, you just stand around and watch me do it. Don't complain."

"I'm not," I whispered, letting my eyes flutter shut again.

"I have a date with Peter tomorrow night," she told me abruptly. "Will you help me get ready?"

"Sure," I agreed. There was a long silence.

"So… remember how you asked me about cheating on him?"

Cammie asked.

I opened my eyes again, wondering why she'd bring that up now. It was long forgotten. I wanted to know more about her, but I wasn't going to pry anymore.

"Yeah. What about it?"

She took a deep breath. "Ironically, I think he might be the one cheating on me now. With Tiffany."

I propped myself up on an elbow, curious. "What makes you say that?"

"I don't know. I guess they've been acting weird around each other lately. Maybe after all this time he still wants to get even."

"He's supposed to love you, you know."

She shot me look. "Yeah, right."

"I mean, do you care if they did hook up?"

"I haven't decided."

"It might put a wrench in the whole 'marry him to make your parents happy' thing."

"Yeah."

I watched her for a moment, studying her. She seemed let down, but not very affected. "Cammie, have you ever really had feelings for someone?" I asked, curious. "And not like Trevor. In the way that it wasn't about social status or who your friends thought was cute or who they told you you should text back or whatever, but someone you genuinely wanted to be with?"

She arched an eyebrow at me. "Don't sound so accusatory. You know, I could practically ask you the same thing. Ever had feelings for anyone you didn't just want to sleep with?"

"I asked first."

She frowned, and then admitted, "Twice."

"Who were they?" I asked. She shrugged her shoulders, and I nudged her. "C'mon, Cammie. At least tell me about one."

She sighed deeply, and then grudgingly replied, "Alright. But I'm keeping it short. It was when I cheated on Peter." She rolled her eyes. "I was losing interest in him, and I met this guy. We were getting along well and I guess I thought maybe I liked him. We hooked up; it wasn't what I'd thought it'd be. He moved away a few months later."

"That hardly counts," I said. "You changed your mind."

"Okay. Then... once, I guess."

"Who?" I tried, but she blushed and shook her head.

"You said one, so I talked about one. That's all you're getting. Your turn."

I considered her question. Did Caitlyn count as someone I had feelings for? I cared about her, sure. I missed her terribly even now; the last time I'd talked to her, I'd stolen Cammie's cell phone and chewed her out for her bad advice after the whole fallout with Maddie. I felt terrible about it now, which only made me miss her more. But I knew I didn't want to date her. Maybe she'd just been temporarily filling a void I hadn't realized I had.

"Never," I said at last. "Like I've said: I've never really been the relationship type."

"Why not?"

"It's easier to not let anyone get close. I never get burned that way, romantically or otherwise."

She shook her head at me and let out a light laugh. "You're

such a cliché. Am I going to hurt you, then, now that I know so much about you?"

I rolled my eyes at her and feigned a laugh. "Yeah, definitely."

She grinned, and her hand brushed against mine as it rose to hit me on the shoulder. "Shut up," she laughed. My hand burned.

* * *

"Can we talk?"

"No."

The call ended with a click and I sighed deeply, trying to be as quiet as possible as I hung up the Marshalls' house phone. David was in the shower, Wendy was in bed, Scott was at Jill's for the night, and Cammie was out on her date with Peter. That meant I had a brief window of opportunity to sneak another call to Caitlyn. She'd been ignoring me for a while now, but tonight, it seemed, was the breakthrough night, because when I called again, she answered with a growl of, "Are you just gonna keep doing this until I talk to you?"

"Yes. I'm still trapped in Hillbilly Hell and you're gonna ignore me? I know I was a bitch—"

"Understatement."

"--I *know*, okay? I'm sorry. I'm sorry I'm sorry I'm sorry. What else can I say?"

"Maybe: Caitlyn, I am an idiot for trusting your drunken advice and it's my own fault I lost a chance with a girl by being my usual douchebag self."

"Fair enough. All true," I admitted. "I shouldn't have blamed you. I was just upset."

"Yeah, well… historically there's a direct correlation between your bitchiness and the length of time since you've had sex," she mumbled. "Should've expected it."

"How are things going there?" I asked her. I mostly meant with my dad, and she seemed to catch my meaning.

"Well enough. Same as usual. And with you?"

"It's okay, I guess."

"Yeah. Things are pretty okay."

We fell silent for a moment, and I listened to her breathing on the other end of the line. "Cait?" I asked at last, keeping my voice down to a whisper.

"Hmm?" She sounded tired.

"Can I ask you something?"

"Yeah. Shoot."

"Okay. Do you ever think about what being in love would feel like?" I wished I could ask her what it did feel like, but I knew she'd never been in love before. Neither of us had even come close back in California.

"Yeah, of course. But I'm kind of disturbed that you're the one asking me this question. What is Marshall doing to you there?"

"It's not David. I mean… we don't talk about love. Not much, anyway." I paused. "If I tell you something can you not be weird?"

"No guarantees," she yawned.

I sighed. "Well, after that whole thing with us right before I left—"

"Lauren," she cut me off, sounding much more awake now. "I

get that you haven't seen me in a while, but if you're about to tell me you're in love with me, I'm hanging up right now."

"You're so full of yourself," I sighed. "It's not that bad."

"*That* bad?"

"Just listen. After we hooked up, I had this feeling. I guess for like half a day I thought maybe it was about you, but maybe... *probably...* I got a glimpse of what it could be like to be with the same person every day, and I guess I didn't mind it. Maybe I just wasn't open to the idea before now. Maybe I just had to meet the right person." I shook my head. "I don't know; or maybe this trip has me wigging out or something."

Caitlyn was silent for a moment, and I waited with baited breath. I wasn't prepared for what came next.

"You wanna daaaate me, you really loooove me," she sing-songed, and I scoffed at the phone and rolled my eyes.

"Shut up!"

"Lauren has feeeelings..."

"Idiot," I snapped, glancing over my shoulder toward Wendy and Scott's room. "Can we have a real conversation for like two seconds here? Jeez, it's easier to talk to Cammie than it is to talk to you at this point."

"Ouch," she replied, stopping at last. "So you've officially replaced me."

"You know that's not true. She's just..." I cleared my throat. "She's a cool girl. That's all."

Caitlyn was silent on the other end again. I bit my lip and let out a sigh. Some part of me was already expecting her response, because I wasn't surprised when it came. "You really like her, huh?"

I swallowed hard, and then shrugged my shoulders. "I don't know."

I closed my eyes as Caitlyn replied. Her tone was somber now. "I'm sorry, Lauren. I wish I could be there."

"It's like there's this constant ache in my chest and I don't even know when it started," I told her. I knew I was about to start rambling, but I couldn't stop. "From the first week she was like a puzzle I could pass the time trying to figure out, so I started paying attention. And pretty soon I was paying attention because I cared, and we were getting along, and having these conversations about... *everything*. Like me and you, but... it's different." I let out a deep breath, but Caitlyn urged me on.

"Keep going, girl. Let it all out. This is the only place you're gonna get to do it, you know."

"I know," I sighed, and chewed on my lip for a moment. "There was this guy who did this really terrible thing to her a few years back. She told me and I was the first person she ever told. I kicked his ass next time I got the chance. I didn't even think twice about it. And she's got this boyfriend who – just, *God*, I can't stand him—"

"Whoa, whoa. Stop there," Caitlyn cut in. "She still has the boyfriend? Like, as far as you know, she's *still* straight?"

"Yeah." I exhaled sharply. "But she's only dating him to make her mom happy. Another thing she only told me."

"She's probably still straight."

"Yeah," I repeated lamely. Then I shook my head, as though

bringing myself out of a stupor. "Yeah, you're right. I need to stop this. I'm not getting my heart broken. Jeez, first girl other than you I actually have a heart-to-heart with and I'm talking like this. Forget it; I don't wanna be in love with anyone."

"Good luck with that. What are you gonna do? Just tell yourself you don't care every time you start to feel all fuzzy inside?"

"Exactly."

"That's not going to work. My advice would be—"

"Uh uh," I interrupted. "After last time I'm not taking advice from you. Just let me get myself through this." I glanced over my shoulder and realized the shower was no longer running. "Look, I have to go. I'll be in touch."

"Good luck," she repeated, amused, and I hung up the phone.

I spent the next couple of hours lying in bed with my music. As I grew drowsier, I tried to pinpoint when I'd changed. I'd wanted so badly to give the Marshalls a hard time here. I'd wanted to be the same person at the end of this trip that I was when I came here. But I knew that was no longer going to be the reality. David – slowly but surely, and much to my own chagrin – had become the father figure I'd never really had, and Cammie, almost from day one, had attached herself directly to the throbbing organ behind my ribcage. I was sick with dread now, aware that I'd be hearing about every second of her date with Peter when she returned.

The movies really didn't do this feeling justice. Falling for a straight girl was *hell*.

245

She got back after I'd fallen asleep, I'd later find out. Told David she'd had a good time, removed her makeup and let down her now-messy hair. Took a shower because she didn't feel very clean anymore, and then changed into sleepwear and fell asleep with a heart aching worse than mine.

* * *

Cammie fell ill a week or so later and missed a couple of days of school, which left David and I to ourselves on our early morning drives. On the second day we were alone, he turned the radio down and asked me, "So Collinsville isn't as bad as you thought it would be, hmm? You're about halfway done and honestly, you're doing great."

"Negative, Dave-a-rino," I retorted, only half paying attention to him as we made our way across town toward Collinsville High. "Just because my nose is used to the smell of crap doesn't mean I don't still know it stinks."

He laughed heartily at that, and I raised an eyebrow at him. "Well, regardless, just know that I'm proud of you. You've been pleasant to be around, you've stayed out of trouble for the most part, and you're going to school and doing well."

"I'm going to fail AP Physics," I reminded him. After the 60 on my first test, I'd studied obsessively with Cammie and pulled a 68 on the second. The last test was in two weeks and I needed an 82 to pass the class. That wasn't going to happen. I'd studied harder than I ever had before for that second test and still failed.

"Cammie will help you if your other friend is busy again," he insisted. I hid a frown. I'd hoped he'd forgotten about Maddie. *Cammie* certainly hadn't, but thankfully she'd refrained from asking questions. "You'll be okay, Lauren."

"I'll take regular Physics next semester," I told him. "It's no big deal. I'll still graduate on time."

"Still, don't write off your class. An 82 might seem impossible, but I think you underestimate how intelligent you are."

"Ahm more smarter than y'all country folk," I drawled, and he laughed again.

We pulled into the school parking lot, he dropped me off, and I proceeded through my day as I normally would until around the end of Physics. I now sat on the opposite side of the room from Maddie, and relied on Cammie to explain what had happened in class that day once we'd gotten home. With her being sick, I was totally lost on yesterday's lesson and so far was equally confused about today's.

If there was ever a time to fix things with Maddie, now would've been it, but I couldn't so much as get near her these days without her glaring two holes through my face. I somewhat deserved it, but it was still frustrating. I'd yet to even get the chance to apologize.

When class ended, the hallways flooded with students. Most of them were headed toward the cafeteria for lunch, but Maddie, as usual, went in the opposite direction, toward the library. I glanced over my shoulder, intending on just getting a quick glimpse of her, but instead I turned just in time to see the notebook she'd been carrying get slapped right out of her arms. The guy who'd done it smirked at her. "Dyke."

I moved without thinking, and intercepted him even as Maddie stooped to retrieve her notebook. "Hey," I snapped. "Don't fucking do that again."

He grinned and let out a laugh. "I'll do whatever the hell I want."

Maddie cut in there, surprising me. "Leave me alone." She wasn't looking at the guy, but at me. "I don't need your help."

"Ooh, catfight. Have fun, ladies," the boy said, and then left, high-fiving one of his friends as he went. I rounded on Maddie, frustrated.

"Really? You're gonna be pissed at me for standing up for you?"

"I've been handling this myself for years before you showed up. I don't need you now." She turned and tried to move away, but I reached out and grabbed her arm. She yanked it out of my grip and snapped, "Don't touch me."

"Look, Maddie. Can you hear me out for two seconds?" I lowered my voice and checked around us for eavesdroppers. The hallways, luckily, were beginning to thin out, and in a few moments we'd be alone. "I'm sorry that I screwed up. I've been doing that a lot lately. With everyone." She watched me, eyes narrowed, as I continued, "I was wrong. I suck at relationships, I suck at communication, and… a part of me did know I wasn't being totally honest with you. I've never really met someone who wanted to be with me for more than one night. You caught me off-guard, and I threw away a really good friendship. I've wanted to say that for a while."

She studied me for a moment, and, at last, echoed, "Friendship."

"Yeah," I agreed. "I don't think I'd be very good at an actual relationship, and if I'd known for sure that that was what you wanted, I would've never gotten involved with you in the first place. So... we could've been really good friends."

She shook her head, unsatisfied. "You know, I really don't get what the deal with you is. You've got this weird hang-up, like you're so damaged you can't catch feelings for anyone, and it's bullshit, Lauren. Can't you just grow a pair and admit I wasn't the right person? Stop hiding behind your stupid player shtick. Anyone can fall for someone. You've just chosen to close yourself off to it, maybe because you're afraid of getting hurt."

"I don't believe that."

"We're in a class together with Cammie, Lauren. Just because you're scared to make eye contact with me doesn't mean I haven't been looking at you. And *you*, as it turns out, spend a lot of time looking at *her*."

I felt my face heat up at record speed. "That's—"

"But you definitely just want to sleep with her. That's all it is." She nodded, feigning sincerity, and I flushed deeper. "If she's the reason it didn't work out with me, then I get it. But if you're not going to admit it, unfortunately I'm still going to operate under the assumption that you're just a manipulative ass. So, you want things between us to be okay again? Be honest. Right now." She crossed her arms and waited, and I stood silently with her, glancing around us. We were completely alone. Inwardly, I groaned.

"Okay. I, uh… I don't know how I feel about Cammie," I said at last. "It's kind of new to me." I didn't make eye contact with her; instead, I examined my fingernails nervously. "I just like being around her. Hate when she's with Peter. That kind of stuff. We've gotten pretty close." I shook my head. "But I'm not dwelling on it because she's straight, so. Yeah." I looked up at her and sighed. "Honest enough?"

To my surprise, she was trying to hide a smile. "That was pretty painful, wasn't it?"

"Incredibly."

"Well." She took a deep breath and then sighed. "Alright. Look, you're still an ass and I'm still pretty pissed at you, but give a little more time to cool off and then we'll talk. You're lucky I'm a nice person."

"I know."

"And yes," she added, shooting me a frustrated look, "I'll help you study for the Physics test, you douchebag."

She left, and I headed for the cafeteria, put only somewhat at ease by our conversation. I'd fixed things with Caitlyn, and now Maddie was at least willing to talk to me. But she'd given me something to think about.

I felt close to Cammie in a way I hadn't felt with Maddie. But acknowledging that I could feel something, *anything* deeper than a solid friendship and aesthetic attraction to her was utterly terrifying. Her religious family would crucify me, and there was a mild chance that she'd help them do it. Let alone actually return my feelings.

And if by some miracle she felt the same way – which she didn't – I'd be in new territory. Vulnerable in a way I'd only been back when I'd been young and naïve and so adoring of my own parents. That, obviously, had crashed and burned and left a permanent bruise on my chest. Loving Cammie certainly would leave the same result. And handling a new father-daughter relationship with David was precarious enough; love absolutely did *not* need to be thrown into the mix.

I shook myself out of my thoughts and focused my gaze to the end of the hallway. There was a janitor's closet at the end of it, just past the cafeteria, and I'd looked up just in time to see Peter slip out of it, grinning at someone still inside. I didn't have to see her to know it was Tiffany.

I carried a weight in my chest for the rest of the day. Cammie didn't love Peter, and she'd said she didn't care what he got up to with Tiffany. But I no longer loved my dad in the way I'd used to, and it still hurt when he disappointed me.

* * *

David and I drove home together, and he took note of my silence right away. Familiar with his tactics by now, I should've realized he'd be more likely to start interrogating me, but I was lost in thoughts of Cammie, Tiffany, and Peter. I knew she should know that I'd confirmed her suspicions, but I hated the idea of being the one to tell her.

"You're awfully quiet," David said, when he could take my

silence no more. "Everything okay?"

It occurred to me that maybe David could be the one to tell her. I cleared my throat and glanced to him. "I caught Cammie's boyfriend with her best friend today."

David adjusted his grip on the steering wheel, and his eyebrows furrowed. "...Peter and Tiffany?" he asked at last.

I nodded. "Yeah. She said she kind of suspected it, but now it's for sure."

"What are you going to do?" he asked me.

I shot him a disbelieving look. "Me? Don't you want to tell her?"

"Well, I think she'd probably prefer to hear it from you, to be honest."

"So you think I should tell her?"

He seemed to struggle for an answer. "Well... I'm not sure I can answer that objectively. As a father, yes, she should know. As a therapist, what you share is your decision. But would you want to know?"

I shrugged my shoulders. "I don't know. I've never been in a relationship."

"You know Cammie very well," David told me. "I think you know what she'd want." I could hear the silent implication in his words. He may as well have said, "Dear God, please tell my daughter so I don't have to be the one to watch her heart get broken." But I did know Cammie very well. Possibly better than David did. And I honestly didn't expect tears from her.

We got home a few minutes later and I cringed at the droplets that splattered against my head and shoulders as I abandoned

David's car. It was beginning to sprinkle out. I hated the rain back home, despite its rarity, and I hated it even more here. Here at the Marshall's, a rainy day today meant a muddy one tomorrow.

I went to Cammie's room to drop off my backpack and was surprised to see her out of bed and drawing at her desk. "Hey," I greeted her, and she jumped and moved to block the paper. I scoffed. "Oh, c'mon. I know all your secrets; let me see."

"Never," she retorted, quickly putting her things away. She swiveled around to face me. "How was Physics?"

"Gross. *That's* the first thing you're gonna ask me?" I dropped my backpack onto the floor and collapsed onto my bed. "You seem better, though."

She nodded. "Mom fed me soup and medication all day. Sniffles are gone, fever is nonexistent. I'm good as new."

"That's good." We fell silent, and I looked around the room, suddenly uncomfortable.

"What's up?" she asked me. When I finally made eye contact with her again, she seemed concerned. "Did something happen?"

I hesitated, and then nodded. "Yeah." I bit my lip. It was best to just get it out now, before I talked myself out of it. "Um, I saw Peter coming out of a janitor's closet with someone earlier today. Right before lunch. When I got into the cafeteria, I didn't see Tiffany at her table."

She sucked in a breath, raising both of her eyebrows. Her hands rested on her knees. "...Oh."

"I know he wasn't your favorite person in the world, but... if you need... I don't know..." I shifted, only growing more uncomfortable. "If you need someone to vent to or something. I'm, you know, here."

She sat still for a moment, and then, to my relief, shrugged her shoulders and relaxed a little. "Thanks." A small splat on the window beside her caught her attention, and she twisted her body around. "Is it raining out?"

"It was sprinkling a couple of minutes ago." I was confused by the abrupt change in subject. "Are you sure you don't want to talk about Peter?"

She got to her feet and shot me a knowing look. "I'm not holding anything back, okay? You don't have to try so hard to figure me out sometimes. My mom's gonna be much more disappointed than I am. I'll just find another guy, I guess."

"Find another guy?" I echoed. "Why? It's okay to be single. Your mom will understand, Cammie."

She didn't answer me. Instead, she moved to stand directly in front of me, her hand outstretched. "I like the rain. Come outside with me."

"My hair," I retorted instinctively, only to be yanked to my feet by her instead.

"Don't be such a brat," she said, amused, but I resisted.

"Wait. Can't we just talk for two seconds? Besides, you've been sick all day!"

"And now I'm better, which means my immune system is at the height of its power. *You're* more likely to get sick than I am."

"All the more reason not to go outside in the rain..."

"It's sprinkling." She released my hand and crossed her arms, giving me a judgmental look. "You asked what you can do to make me feel better. This is it. We're going to stick our tongues out and drink rainwater while spinning around in circles. Like adults."

"If this is some metaphorical Baptism, I'm out," I retorted, but changed into my one pair of tennis shoes and followed her downstairs nonetheless.

"No Baptism necessary. Peter didn't define me, and losing him doesn't mean I'm starting anew. I'm the same person I was half an hour ago. I just want to get out of the house and away from my mom before she finds out and goes crazy. Trust me, Peter cheating on me is not going to go away for a while, as much as I'd like to just forget about it and move on."

"So you're really going to break up with him?" I asked her as I followed her through the living room. Wendy and David were in their bedroom, which I suspected was David's way of trying to keep Wendy away from Cammie while I broke the news. "He didn't break up with you when you cheated on him. It probably *should* be a relationship death sentence… but it doesn't have to be if you want him around for whatever reason."

She spun around, her hand on the knob of the back door, and I stopped abruptly, surprised and half-expecting her to chastise me. But she was smiling at me instead, albeit sadly. "Peter's family is just as bad as mine, Lauren. He's under a lot of pressure too. We both made mistakes. If he doesn't break up with me, I don't know what I'll do. I don't know a lot of things right now. I'm glad that you get that keeping him around was important to me even if he wasn't exactly my type, but… can we just go outside and forget about this stuff for a little while?"

She ducked outside without waiting for a response, and I grudgingly followed after her. Luckily, it was still just drizzling, and I only got mildly damp following Cammie out to the stables. When we were safely under cover, she headed for Aerosmith's stall. "What are you doing?" I asked.

"I would think you'd know by now," she retorted, smirking, and led him out into the rain.

* * *

So I found myself huddling alone under a tree a few minutes later, shivering slightly as Aerosmith pawed at the ground a few feet away. In the center of what had become Our Clearing, Cammie had removed her shoes and was standing still, her face tilted up toward the sky and her tongue outstretched to catch the falling droplets of water. It'd started raining harder since we'd gotten here. Her parents, it occurred to me, were probably wondering where on earth we'd gone.

"Cammie, we should get back soon!" I called out, but she just spun around and spread her arms out to her sides, dousing herself with splashes from puddles of water with every shift of her feet. I couldn't fathom how she wasn't freezing yet. "The things I do for this girl," I mumbled to no one, shuddering harder. I was literally huddled under a tree in the middle of nowhere during an increasingly heavy downpour, soaking wet, in order to watch a recently-pseudo-dumped blonde girl dance around and drink rain. Caitlyn would die of laughter if she could see me now.

Cammie, meanwhile, had elected to splash her way on over to me. Her mascara, carefully applied this morning, was running, and her hair was plastered to her head, but she was grinning widely and there was a spring in her step I'd never seen before. She nearly collided with me and I had to place my hands on her arms to steady her. "I've never seen you this happy before," I admitted, somewhat surprised.

She laughed at me. "It's weird. I thought if I ever lost Peter the world would end. I put so much effort into keeping him around because I knew I wouldn't be as popular anymore and because my mom would be disappointed... I couldn't be the one to get broken up with. But this isn't my fault. *He's* the ass. Even if I was the ass first, he's the ass now. Mom won't blame me if I end it."

I nodded, smiling back at her. "You kind of seem like your mind's made up, then."

"Yeah." She nodded back. "Yeah, I think so. It just hit me that I could really be free. And best of all..." She spun away from me and exclaimed to the empty woods, "I don't have to have bad sex anymore!"

"Oh my God," I mumbled, clapping a hand to my forehead even as my chest panged at the reminder. "You're so crazy."

"I don't care." She pulled away from me and backed up into the clearing again, and, arms outstretched to her sides, shrugged her shoulders overdramatically. "I really do not care about anything right now. It feels like a weight the size of an elephant has been lifted from my shoulders."

"Getting to put your own happiness over other people's is

fun," I agreed. "You should try it more often. I've been trying to tell you this."

She was quiet for a moment, her smile fading as she examined me critically. Finally, she demanded, "Come out here, Lauren. C'mon."

"It's cold," I protested.

"The rain's kind of warm. Please?"

I took a deep breath, held back an eye-roll, and finally stepped out into the rain. Cammie smiled and pulled me forward, out into the middle of the clearing. My hair, which had been somewhat sheltered by the tree line, immediately grew damp again, along with the rest of my body. But I did feel warmer.

"Why did you and Maddie stop hanging out?" Cammie asked me, still gripping me by the hand, and my blood abruptly turned to ice. I looked back at her, wide-eyed and completely caught off guard.

"What? Why?"

"People have been saying for a while that she came onto you and you rejected her," Cammie admitted. "I mean, even I can tell she's been angry at you for a while now. It makes sense. I've been waiting for you to talk to me about it. Why haven't you?"

"That's an awful rumor," I replied, dodging the question. "People just assumed that?"

"So that's not what happened," she guessed.

I glanced away from her, letting out a heavy sigh. "Look, Cammie, it's pouring out. This isn't exactly the ideal place to have a meaningful discussion."

"The way she's treating you is the way she used to treat me. It was like I didn't exist." She raised her eyes to look into mine. "You're all about being yourself. Not being someone who makes themselves into whatever anyone else wants them to be." I didn't understand where she was going with this. Not at first. But then she swallowed hard, and, avoiding my eyes, added, "If you like her, Lauren, it's okay."

My lips parted with surprise and I choked on my own words as I struggled to deny it. But I could feel my cheeks heating up. "It wasn't like that. We're not even friends anymore."

"So she wanted to date you and you weren't interested," Cammie guessed. She eyed my flushed cheeks for a moment, and then added, "But you like girls. In all the time you've been here, you've never talked about boys. Not boys you've met here, not boys you were with back in Los Angeles. Not by name, anyway. And you never go into detail. I'm right, aren't I? If I wasn't, you'd have told me what happened with Maddie by now."

I pulled away from her and immediately headed back toward the tree line. "I'm leaving." I could feel my cheeks burning brighter and brighter, and although a part of me knew not only that I was lucky to have kept it from Cammie for this long, but also that she was okay with it, the rest of me was fleeing on instinct.

"Lauren, wait," Cammie sighed from somewhere behind me, and before I could break out into a run, she caught my arm and forced me to stand still by the edge of the trees, still several yards from her horse. "Just talk to me. You can be honest with me, okay?"

"Oh, like you could with me?" I blurted. "I had to figure out most things on my own. You figure this out and think you can pass judgment? I'm in a small town in the South, Cammie; do you really think I'm going to be open about my sexuality here?"

"I just thought you knew you could trust me," she replied, her voice quiet.

"I can, but considering you've literally freaking memorized the Bible verse that demeans gay people, *and* you don't like Maddie, there wasn't and isn't much you can do to prove we're seeing eye to eye here."

She chewed on her lip, looking near tears, much to my surprise. At first I convinced myself it was the rain, but then she sniffed and wiped at her eyes. Trying to break the tension, I quipped, "It's raining. That's not going to help."

"Shut up," she murmured, pushing me slightly. My back hit the tree behind me and I winced. "I'm sorry," she added, her voice still quiet.

We stood in silence for what felt like minutes, Cammie looking everywhere but at me, and at last I spoke first. "Cammie, I haven't been able to talk to anyone the way I talk to you in a while. You're so important to me. You're getting me through this trip. But I couldn't tell you everything."

"I know," she agreed. "It's not-... I mean, I get it. I'm just..." she paused, and then finished, "confused."

"About what?"

"Why Maddie?" she surprised me by asking. "Was it because I told you she liked girls?"

I nodded simply. "Yeah."

"So that's it? That's the criteria? *Any* girl who'd be up for it?"

I ran a hand through my damp hair. "I don't know, Cammie. I don't know how I feel about it anymore. Being a slut's kind of tiring." I forced a laugh, and she gave me a small smile. We didn't break eye contact as I added, "I guess sometimes I think it'd be nice to love someone. To be able to tell them anything and everything and... I don't know, learn all of their pet peeves and favorite books and movies and where their ticklish spots are. But as nice as it'd be, I figure it's equally scary. If you leave your heart in someone else's hands it's so much easier to get it broken. And sometimes I think it could be worth it, but then I tell myself I'm being crazy and to just cut myself off emotionally because it's easier." I shrugged my shoulders and let out a sigh.

"This would be one of the reasons I'm in therapy, I guess. Anyway, regardless, I know Maddie wasn't the right person for any of that, if that's what you're asking. Maybe someone else could be, I don't know. I'm probably too screwed up to love someone the right way anyway, so there's that. Sorry, I'm totally rambling."

"A little." She smiled again, eyes still not leaving mine. "But it's okay." I wondered fleetingly when she'd moved closer. I could see every freckle on the bridge of her nose and splashed across her upper cheeks. "I think you'd make a great girlfriend. You just have to try," she told me. She was so close. I could feel her breath on my face. My brain was working overtime to try and decipher what exactly she was doing, but, pathetically, all it could process was her name.

"Cammie?" I managed to mumble. Her hand slid to my cheek and her eyes closed. Mine fluttered shut when I felt her lips brush against the corner of my mouth. She kissed me there, half on my lips, half on the skin of my cheek, and my heart hammered in my chest.

She stepped closer, her stomach and chest flush against me, and her nose brushed across my cheek as her mouth hovered millimeters from mine. My brain function was gone; I didn't know what she wanted. A sign that this was okay? A confirmation that this was what I wanted too?

Too? was the last thought I had before she kissed me again. I forgot my back was pressed into the hard bark of a tree; I forgot that it was raining heavily around and on us; I forgot that there was an impatient and equally-soaked horse just yards away. Cammie filled my senses and I wrapped my arms around her waist, too hesitant to actually grip her or force her closer. Her hands were soft on my cheeks, and I was so lost in the feel of her lips and body against mine. It was different than kissing other girls had ever been. It was *so* different.

She kept me close as we kissed over and over, and soon her hand was fumbling its way under my shirt and clutching at my waist. I kissed her harder, tightening my hold on her, and then abruptly panicked as hundreds of thoughts came spilling into my brain at once. I pulled away, accidentally banging my head against the tree in the process. "Shit," I mumbled instinctively, reaching up to feel my head. I saw stars, and as I blinked them away, Cammie reached up with me, wide-eyed.

"Oh my God, are you okay?"

"Fine. It's fine. I'm fine," I stuttered, looking anywhere but at her. "Sorry. I mean—"

"Okay. Okay, you're sure?"

"Yeah."

She swallowed hard and we fell silent. I opened and closed my mouth several times, trying to find the right words, and then eventually let out a slow breath.

Cammie'd just kissed me. I pinched myself to make sure this wasn't some elaborate dream, and then sank back against the tree. "Wow," I murmured, mostly to myself, but I could tell from the shift in Cammie's behavior that she'd heard me. She was hiding a smile as she turned away to squint through the trees at Aerosmith. When I realized she wasn't going to say anything else, I pushed through the awkwardness and just went for it. "You just kissed me."

She bit her lip and avoided my eyes. "I'm aware."

"Soooo..." a thought occurred to me and my heart sank. "Was this, like, a 'woo-hoo I'm free from Peter' rebellion type of thing, or...?"

She shook her head and cleared her throat, still refusing to look at me. "No."

"Spur of the moment 'why the hell not' kind of thing?"

"No, Lauren."

"'Why not try a girl out since it didn't work out with-'?"

"Oh my God, stop," she laughed, flushing bright red. "Just stop."

I chewed on the inside of my cheek. "Okay. I'll stop." I looked around us abruptly, shuddering. "It's still raining. If we're gonna have this talk, can we please do it somewhere else?"

* * *

With Aerosmith safely in his stall, Cammie and I sat down together on the floor of the stable. We'd barely made it back here in one piece. Mostly because wrapping my arms around her waist felt strange now. Looking her in the eyes felt strange now too.

She spoke after some time, her voice so quiet I could barely hear her over the rain. "When I was eight, I had this friend. We were inseparable. Closer than most girls were. One day I told my parents I wanted to marry her. My mom wasn't too happy about that, and I got this massive lecture about how girls belong with boys and God doesn't like girls to be with other girls. All the stuff you'd expect from someone like her, you know? My parents think I've forgotten about that, but I always remembered." She shrugged her shoulders. "For the most part... I always knew."

I stared at her, dumbfounded. A large part of me had still been convinced on the ride back here that she'd just kissed me on impulse. The rest entertained the idea that I was some sort of exception. But this? She'd seemed nothing but straight, and I'd spent daily time with her for *months*.

"But all of the guys," I blurted, shaking my head. I couldn't fathom it. Lesbians didn't sleep with men. Lesbians didn't enjoy sex with men. I looked up at her, realizing with horror what she was about to say. "Oh, God, Cammie."

"I want to make my parents happy. My mom happy," she

murmured. "I still do. That means living the life she imagined for me. You have no clue how much pressure there is in this town to be what everyone expects of you. To be normal." She shifted, pulling her knees up to her chest and resting her chin on them. "I thought I could fix it, so I tried with Trevor. I did what my friends said I was supposed to. When that didn't work, I kept trying. I thought maybe it'd get better. It didn't. When Peter didn't work, either, I cheated on him with someone I thought might. Someone I really liked as a person. But I still wasn't attracted to him." She paused, bit her lip, and then admitted, "I kissed Maddie at one of her cousin's parties a while back. I was drunk and she was the only lesbian I knew; she'd been out for a while and I'd watched her go through hell because of it. It was impulsive and stupid and... nice." She trailed off again. I could fill in the gaps there.

"But when it came down to it, you couldn't be what she was. She had no one in her corner and you couldn't even stand up for her." I couldn't identify my own feelings. I was angry at her, but I understood.

She shook her head and squeezed her eyes shut tightly. She was beginning to cry again. "I'm so fucking awful, Lauren. She knew and she's known for so long and she's never said a word to anyone, and I've been terrible to her just to keep up appearances. And the worst part is that I'm okay with myself, you know? I wanted it to go away for a while: prayed for it and everything, and it didn't. I think I'm meant to be like this, and I can accept it. I *want* to be happy. But if no one else will accept it, I don't think I can disappoint them. I can't look my mom in her eyes and see hatred in them."

"You come first," I told her, setting my jaw. "Cammie, look at me. *You* come first."

She stared back at me, her eyes red and swollen. "I'm not strong enough to think that way. I'm not like you and Maddie."

I bowed my head and ran my hands through my hair, letting out a heavy sigh. I closed my eyes, paused, and then looked up at her. "So you kissed me and that's it? It *was* just something to try out?"

"Of course not," she retorted, shaking her head. "I've wanted to kiss you for a while now."

I watched her for a moment, not quite daring to believe her. But then I remembered. "You almost kissed me the night you were crowned Homecoming Queen. On the porch after the party. I thought I was imagining things."

She tucked her head behind her knees and sniffled. "God, I'm a wreck."

"That's okay," I told her. "Me too."

She was quiet for a while. I leaned back against the door to one of the stalls and let out a deep sigh, trying to make sense of everything. The girl I had feelings for was gay. She was gay and she'd kissed me and now my heart ached in a way it never had before.

Cammie got to her feet first, after some time, and crossed to me, offering me her hand. I took it and rose beside her, taking care to keep a foot of space between us. I wasn't sure where her head was at. "What now?" I asked her.

She shook her head. "I don't know."

"We can't just act like it didn't happen," I pointed out. "We spend hours a day together. Some of it alone."

"Yeah. Alone." She paused, and then turned red. "Sorry. That was supposed to stay in my head."

My lips parted as a new thought occurred to me, and I turned to her accusingly. "I've changed in front of you before."

She forced a weak laugh and left my side, walking to the edge of the stable and then beckoning me toward her. "C'mon, one last run and we're safe inside."

"Jesus Christ," I mused, and with a shake of my head, took off after her.

Chapter Fifteen

I kissed your daughter.

David was talking to me. We'd taken our usual places on opposite sides of the dining room table. This was nothing compared to the awkwardness of dinner, but I was still struggling to fight off the flush creeping into my cheeks.

I literally just made out with her about two hours ago.

"What do you think?"

I blinked at him rapidly. "Huh?"

He sighed. "Lauren, you're not even listening to me. I was asking what you think about coming white-water-rafting with our church this weekend."

"I have a choice?" I asked, surprised. "I thought I had to go now."

"That's to the actual service. I'd like for you to go, of course, but I understand if you'd rather spend your Sunday relaxing. Especially after that stunt you and Cammie pulled today, no matter how well-intentioned." He shot me a critical look. "Cammie's health is up in the air, but if I were you, I'd expect a cold at the least by the end of the week."

"Okay. I'll think about it," I mumbled.

* * *

"Maybe you should skip it."

I looked across the room to Cammie's bed, an eyebrow arched. A day had passed since our trip out into the rain, and it had certainly been an eventful one. Tiffany and Peter had remained silent about their hookup, and so Cammie'd confronted them in the hallway and caused a big scene. Then she'd been sent home early by the principal.

Wendy was probably downstairs mourning the death of Cammie's relationship right about now, but Cammie, meanwhile, seemed unfazed for the most part. She'd gotten a few cheers in the hallway today, mostly because Tiffany didn't appear to be very well-liked, and I think that helped her feel better. Her social life was mostly intact, her mother didn't blame her for the breakup, and she didn't feel she needed a guy around to cover up her sexuality... for the time being.

"What?" I asked her, confused.

"The trip this weekend," she elaborated.

"You want me to stay home," I said flatly. "How flattering."

"I want you to stay home because I might choose to stay home," she explained, examining her fingernails idly.

"You have that option?"

She nodded. "I just broke up with my boyfriend and I've been sick this week, remember? I might need to stay home. Just to be safe." She feigned a cough into her hand and grinned. My eyebrows went higher, and I glanced toward her bedroom door. It was wide open, and I shifted my gaze quickly toward the mp3 player in my lap.

"Oh. Okay."

"Think about it," she advised.

"Oh, I'm thinking about it," I mumbled, just loudly enough for her to hear. She grinned and let out a laugh just as footsteps thundered up the stairs. Cammie's grin hadn't quite faded as Wendy peered into the room.

"Cammie—" she paused, and then looked appalled. "How can you be smiling at a time like this? This boy broke your heart!"

"I know, Mom," Cammie sighed. "Lauren's telling me jokes to make me feel better. Am I not allowed to smile?"

"I just don't want you to keep all of your feelings inside, honey. If you need to cry you can let it out."

"I *will*, Mom. I'll come talk to you later, okay? I'm just not ready right now."

"Okay. Well... dinner will be ready in a few minutes. Keep your door open, remember, the exterminator stopped by today and he said to keep the house aired out."

"Okay, Mom."

Wendy disappeared back down the steps and Cammie shifted

on her bed with a quiet groan. "God, I love her and all, but she's such a cartoon character."

"At least she cares?" I offered.

"I guess." She glanced around her room for a moment, and her eyes settled on one of the posters pinned to her wall. "I hate romance novels, by the way," she said out of nowhere.

I forced a laugh. "Should've known. Everything's a lie with you."

"Not everything." I turned to look at her, and she offered me a small smile. But the mood had gone somber, and I stared back at her with furrowed eyebrows.

I was looking at a girl who'd spent years carefully crafting herself into the ideal small-town girl. She'd endured countless boyfriends and friends she didn't like, forced herself into doing things she wasn't interested in, and hid her real interests and feelings. All because she'd been told at age eight that being herself wasn't an option. As much as she was trying to be light-hearted now, that wasn't just something that went away.

"Cammie?" I asked her, dropping my gaze to my lap. "What do you want with me?"

She raised her eyebrows. "What?"

"I mean... what is this turning into?" I asked her. "You lost your boyfriend. I've been here for a while; I've seen the things you did to keep him around. If you're gonna want another boyfriend soon..."

I glanced to her and she avoided my eyes. "I don't know what I'm doing," she said at last. "I like you."

"Okay. I like you too." I paused, and then, embarrassed, I mumbled, "I like you a lot. In a way I haven't ever liked anyone else."

She smiled at that. "Me too."

"But this," I pointed back and forth between the two of us. "It's so complicated. I don't *date* girls, and you don't date *girls*. So we're both equally lost, not to mention the fact that you're not sure you won't get insecure and seek out another guy to pretend to like and *I'm* not sure I'm ready or able to have a relationship. I'm gonna screw it up, and if I don't, you probably will. This is so high-risk."

"We don't have to label anything. We like each other. Can we start with that?"

"And go where?" I arched an eyebrow at her, watching her chew at the inside of her cheek.

"...I don't know." She sucked in a breath. "Lauren, part of the reason I was so ready to dump Peter today was because of what happened with us. I don't have any answers. I just know that I like being around you." She flushed abruptly and shook her head. "God, I'm really not used to talking like this."

"Me either," I admitted. My thoughts went back to Peter, Trevor, and all of the nameless guys Cammie hadn't mentioned, and my heart lurched. I closed my eyes. "I don't think I could watch you hook up with guys after what you told me. Can we at least agree on that being something that needs to stop? Don't put yourself through that, Cammie. Not while I'm around. You don't deserve it."

"Okay," she said. Her voice was quiet, and her arms were

folded across her chest. "I can do that."

* * *

I kept Fiona and Nate out of the loop about what had happened with me and Cammie, although I figured Fiona would inevitably catch on, given that she knew I liked girls.

Maddie, however, got to hear the whole story. Cammie and I didn't get much alone time over the course of the rest of the week; in fact, things just got more tense between us anytime we were together. At school on Friday, I convinced Maddie to come pick me up on Saturday so that we could spend the day studying at her house. She wasn't too happy about that, and neither was Cammie, but Maddie agreed when I told her I had big news to share.

So the second we were inside her house and placing our things at the dining room table, she demanded, "Alright. What's the big secret? Tell me so we can move past it and get this thing over with."

"I'll tell you," I said. "You just have to promise not to be mad."

"When have you seen me get mad? Unless you're about to tell me you love me and then try to get me to sleep with you, I think we're good."

She crossed her arms, waiting impatiently, and I chewed at my lip. "Okay. Um. Cammie and I kissed."

She raised her eyebrows, but didn't seem as shocked as I'd thought she'd be. "Huh. That happened sooner than I expected it to."

"What? Are you serious?"

"Well, once I turned you down, it was kind of a matter of time. She's a repressed lesbian and you're a hot slut who spends a lot of time with her, so."

"That is such a flattering assessment of the situation," I deadpanned. "C'mon, be serious. I know you knew she was gay all along. I get why you didn't say anything, but now you have this smug look on your face like you know I've got bad karma coming."

"Well…" she trailed off and sat down, and I joined her at the table. "Here's the thing about Cammie. She grew up with parents who have super high expectations. I mean, these screwed up kids show up once a year with problems that make *you* look like a model citizen, and her job is to sit back, not stir up any trouble, and be the perfect kid so the screw-up can copy her. So she's not supposed to have problems. Naturally, because she isn't supposed to have problems and because she's gay in a small town, she's probably *more* fucked up than you'll ever be. And you want to have *sex* with her now?"

"It's not like that," I mumbled.

"Of course it's not," Maddie agreed. "You have feelings for her. So now you're even more screwed. I may have had a crush on a so-called player," she pointed to me with a smirk, "but *you're* falling in love with the most damaged girl in Collinsville. I mean, she sleeps with guys to keep them around because she's terrified that if she's single for more than a minute her super religious mother and the rest of her family will think she's a disappointment and everyone will hate her. Her giving up Peter for you is so huge. But still, can you imagine what it'd be like to have a mother like that, and how far you'd go to make her happy if you really cared about her?"

"No. I hardly had a mother," I replied, stony-faced.

Maddie deflated slightly. "I'm sorry. I guess I'm not trying to be as harsh as I sound, I'm just—"

"Still bitter?" I arched an eyebrow.

She gave me the finger, rolling her eyes. "Look. I *am* over you, and knowing what you have coming to you is making it harder to stay angry with you... but you wanted to know more about Cammie. There it is. She'll say and do anything to make her parents happy. So if it comes down to you or them, you should know that she'll choose them. Which makes her a very dangerous person to fall for."

"So... what, I should end it right now?"

"Is it worth it not to?" she asked me.

I shrugged. "I don't know. I think it might be."

"That's your decision." She sighed. "Just... coming from someone who got to know you, and got a glimpse of how emotionally insecure you are—"

"I'm not emotionally insecure," I cut in, but she dismissed my protest with a shake of her head.

"Coming from someone who got a glimpse of how emotionally insecure you are, you should probably find someone more stable. That's all. And before you throw in another jab, I don't mean me. I don't mean anyone in Collinsville. I'm only telling you how to avoid getting your heart broken. That's what your top priority is and always has been, right? So if you want to avoid that, genius, don't take the leap of faith with Cammie."

I swallowed hard and moved to reach for my notebook. "Maybe we should study now," I said, and kept "*Maybe my priorities should change*," bouncing around in my head, unspoken.

* * *

I spent some time with Scott out around the farm later that day. I'd taken to hanging out with him in the barn some days on the weekends while he milked the cows, under the guise of helping him out. Cammie, I'm sure, knew exactly what was going on, but her parents were none-the-wiser.

"Jill and I are getting married next month," he told me. "Our moms have been collaborating on details."

"January seems like a weird month to get married," I said. "I thought most people did it in the summer."

"Not sure." He shrugged his shoulders. "I've been kinda getting the vibe that Mom and Dad want me to move out soon, though, so I guess January it is." He let out a small laugh. "Cammie's thankful for it, I'm sure. It'll take the attention away from her love life for about ten seconds."

"So your parents have always been like this," I observed.

"Just with Cammie, and it's mostly Mom. I've heard Dad telling her she should be with whoever makes her happy, but of course he's also got high standards for the guys she dates. Between you and me, I don't think he really liked Peter."

"Your Mom did."

"Mom just saw a cute boy who goes to church and freaked out. She'll get over it. Especially when Cammie moves on to the next one."

I frowned once he'd turned away from me. He reached for a fresh bucket to place under the cow in front of him as I asked, "So she does that often?"

"Eh, it's not that bad. Give her a few months or so. Peter was pretty long-term, so by the time she moves on you'll nearly be out of here."

"But before Peter," I pressed.

"There weren't a lot of actual boyfriends, really. There were a lot of guys, but I think most of them were one-time dates. Cammie does a lot of test runs. *She's* gotta like him, *Mom's* gotta like him, then Dad... it's a lot of checkpoints to get through." He turned back to me and raised an eyebrow. "Why so curious? Trying to figure out who you can get away with fooling around with while you're here? Because if that's the case, I can tell you right now that Dad won't want you dating anyone. He says it's a distraction and that it's not what you're here for."

"No. The people here aren't exactly my type," I explained, grimacing, and to my relief he laughed and dropped the subject.

"Right. So Dad mentioned you've got a make-or-break test next week? Is that why you and Cammie are skipping rafting tomorrow?"

"Yeah. Lots of studying to do." I cleared my throat awkwardly, glad he couldn't see my face at the moment. "I, uh... need an 82."

* * *

"What's your *real* favorite book?"

Cammie arched an eyebrow at me, stretched out on her bed just feet away. We were both lying down on our sides, facing each other, and she was wearing a low-cut tank top I'd scoffed at last night when she'd put it on. For now, I was content to stay in my own bed.

"I would've bet my *life* that with my family finally out of the house your first question would've been 'Can we make out now?'"

I shook my head silently, only barely smiling. "Talk to me."

She shifted slightly, pressing her elbow into her pillow and resting her head on her hand. "Really?" She smiled, amused.

"Yeah."

"You've slept with more girls than you can count back in Los Angeles. But you won't even kiss me again."

"Does that bother you?"

"No, it confuses me."

"Does it really? Obviously I don't want things to be the same with you as they were with the other girls. That's kind of the point. Tell me what your favorite book is. And *don't* say the Bible, because I know you play up the religious stuff for your mom."

She grinned at me. "That verse I shared with you was the real me, you know. It helped me come to terms with being gay."

"You could just not be religious," I joked, and she gave me a stern, knowing look. "Kidding! Seriously, answer my question, though."

"It's lame."

"Don't insult my question, douche."

"I meant my answer's lame!" she laughed, and it was my turn to grin.

"What is it?" She shook her head. "Tell me!"

"Ugh. Harry Potter."

"Oh my God, Harry Potter is not lame. That's blasphemy."

"It's just such a generic answer; I feel so un-unique. And it's lame that I would sneak them at night and read them. My mom didn't want us to."

I envisioned a preteen Cammie huddled under her comforter with a flashlight and a book the size of her head, and laughed aloud. "That's so sad. But very adorable."

"So what's yours, then?"

"I don't read."

"Yeah, you do."

I rolled my eyes. *The Catcher in the Rye.*

She laughed harder than I had, this giggly, happy laugh that was almost contagious, and rolled over onto her back. Then she turned her head to look at me. "Shut up. No it's not."

"It could be."

"Lauren!"

I bit my lip to hide a smile. "It's this lesbian novel called *Fingersmith*. I read it when I was fourteen, actually, when I wasn't busy getting into trouble anyway."

"You knew you liked girls that far back too?" she asked.

"Yeah. But I didn't grow up learning there was something

wrong with being gay. It was a pretty easy transition. I hooked up with no one, then I hooked up with girls."

"You've never even kissed a guy?"

"No." I shrugged my shoulders. "I get the girls that have, though. For some people they don't realize… they think they're just weird, or that mediocre is just as good as it's gonna get for them. Or they feel pressure, like you."

She was silent for a moment, thinking, and then she turned her head to look to the ceiling and sighed. "I'm so… or I *was* so set on what my life was going to be. There are jokes everywhere about how marriages are sexless and terrible. I know I could get through it. But I don't think I fully realized what I was missing out on until you came along. I don't know what to do now."

"You don't have to figure it all out in one week," I suggested, mostly because she'd already heard my opinion a few days ago in the stable. There was nothing more I could add there.

"The semester's almost over, Cammie. We have a massive test in a couple days, then Winter Break, the holidays, and Scott's wedding. There's plenty of other stuff to focus on for a while. And I've been here just over two and a half months, so I'm not leaving for another, what, five months?" *Three*, I corrected mentally, but pushed that aside for now. "So slow down. Not that I know much about it, but I hear it's okay to take things slow every now and then."

She rolled her eyes, albeit smiling, and took the pillow out from under her head to throw it at me. I deflected it and blew her a kiss mockingly, and she hopped out of her bed and raced to mine, pecking me quickly on the lips before I could react. By the time

I'd blinked, she'd already left the room.

"Hey! Cammie!" I stood up and trailed after her, calling, "I need to know your favorite color before we do that again!" Then I followed the raucous laughter, grinning all the way.

Chapter Sixteen

"I love you."

Maddie looked like the last thing she wanted to do was be near me, but I ignored her scowl and wrapped my arms around her, mildly crushing her against her locker. "Thank you thank you thank you! You're a miracle worker. You literally, just, like, taught a monkey calculus. That is the kind of miracle you've pulled off."

"You're not stupid, Lauren," she deadpanned. "You know that."

"I am at this!" I released her to jab at the test paper in my hand, grinning. "An 83, though?! This is a total and complete act of God. Coming from an Atheist, here, by the way. Thank you."

"You're welcome," she said at last. "Please go away."

"Let me make it up to you," I insisted. "We can go to the drive-in, or... I don't know, anywhere you want. Cammie showed me that awesome burger place you guys have; we could go there."

"Lauren," she sighed. "We're not friends, okay? Things aren't going to go back to how they were. I can tolerate you, and I'll help you out if you need it. Occasionally, you might be able to get a smile out of me. But I'm not going anywhere with you. Especially not to all of those weirdly date-y places you just listed."

"Those aren't date-y," I mumbled. "I went to them with Cammie."

"Okay, now you're purposely being an idiot," she hissed, then glimpsed over my shoulder and added, "Speak of the devil; it's the Homecoming Queen herself here to talk to her subjects."

Cammie glanced awkwardly to Maddie as she arrived beside us, and then focused her attention onto me. Her voice a whisper, she asked, "Hey, um, do you think we could talk for a second on the way to lunch?"

"Sure." I instinctively raised a hand to wave goodbye to Maddie, but thought better of it and turned away to walk with Cammie instead. "What's going on?"

"Things have just been getting worse every day with Tiffany and me," she explained. "I can't take another lunch period with her."

"You can sit with us, if that's what you're asking. If your rep can handle it, that is."

She shrugged her shoulders. "I've been caring less and less about that lately. Particularly on rainy days."

I hid a smile at the reference and settled for bumping her shoulder with mine. "It'll be okay," I murmured. "Fiona and Nate are nice." Then I showed her my test paper and grinned. "Guess who's not a failure?"

* * *

Watching Cammie interact with Nate and Fiona was like watching a baby bird take a nosedive out of its nest. Cammie being the baby bird, of course, and her usual social group, the nest. She was so out of her comfort zone that just looking at her made it hard to keep myself from choking on my own laughter.

"You're so paranoid, oh my God," I told her openly. "Nobody cares that you switched tables. You're so lame." I arched an eyebrow at Fiona and Nate, who looked just as amused as I did. "I see what you meant on that first day; popular people suck."

"It's not that I don't like you guys," Cammie insisted. "I'm just not used to this. Being practically kicked out of my social circle. Ever since Peter and I broke up and I chewed Tiffany out, they've all been passive-aggressively letting me know I wasn't welcome there."

"The dark side of the cheerleaders," Nate confirmed gravely. "Now that you've seen it, you can never go back."

"We won't kick you out unless you're a raging racist," Fiona added casually. "Or a homophobe, for Lauren's sake." She paused, then, frozen and wide-eyed, and clapped a hand to her mouth. "Oh my God, Lauren, I'm so sorry."

"Cammie knows," I explained, holding back laughter. "It's okay."

"But I didn't," Nate cut in, though he didn't look surprised at all. In fact, he was grinning. "I assumed, though. You and Maddie went through all of the stages of a relationship in the span of, like, two weeks."

I felt Cammie shift uncomfortably next to me, and rushed to change the subject. "Anyway, now that we're all caught up, and we've all established that nobody is racist or homophobic, can we eat in peace?"

Nate gave me a thumbs-up, then proceeded to shovel a glob of macaroni into his mouth via spoon while Fiona looked on with disgust.

* * *

Winter Break came a few days later. Fiona's family took Nate on vacation to some ski resort, so with Maddie still upset, I had no one to hang out with other than the Marshalls.

Scott and Wendy busied themselves with Scott and Jill's upcoming wedding, and David busied himself with keeping Wendy in check and giving me the occasional check-up as well. Those had been getting less and less frequent the more of a non-entity I became, and now David only sat me down once or twice a week to talk about my problems. With Scott's wedding impending, it slowed to a solid once a week.

Cammie, meanwhile, busied herself with me.

"Girls are so soft."

"Mhmm." I hid a smile and kept my eyes closed as her fingers trailed across my cheek.

"You're seriously so soft."

"My lips are softer, you know."

She gave a sarcastic laugh and whispered, "Uh, and my parents could come upstairs at any moment."

"Except it's past their bedtime, and you're already in my bed. I think we'd be caught regardless right now." I puckered my lips. "How many times have we kissed? Like, less than five."

"We're taking it slow, remember? *Your* idea."

"I was thinking, like, turtle slow, and this is snail slow."

"Fine, let's just strip down right now."

"Right now?" I echoed.

"Right this second."

I grinned. "You first." She tapped my cheek with her hand, huffing, and I winced. "Careful. I'm sensitive."

"Yeah, right." She smirked down at me, hovering over my head, and I stared back defiantly, struggling to keep the corners of my lips from turning upward. She bit at her own lip just for a second, and her gaze flickered down to mine. I reached up to tuck a strand of her hair behind her ear, and just like that, the mood had changed.

"I haven't told my friend from back home about us," I admitted quietly, letting my hand fall to my side. Hers stayed at my cheek, her thumb rubbing back and forth across the skin there.

"Why not?" she asked. Her tone was simple, casual. She wasn't being judgmental, only curious.

"I'm afraid she'll tell me I can't do this. She's my Maddie."

Her eyebrows furrowed with concern. "What does that mean?"

"My friend Caitlyn knows me better than anyone else back

home does. Just like Maddie knows *you* in a way no one else does here. I talked to Maddie about us the Saturday I went to her house to study, and she said she doesn't think you can do this. She practically laughed at me for wanting to try it out."

"You shouldn't have talked to her about us," Cammie replied, removing her hand from my cheek. "It's none of her business."

"I needed someone to talk to."

"Talk to *me*," she pressed. I could hear the frustration growing in her voice. "Has it ever occurred to you that maybe I know more about my own feelings than some girl I've hardly ever talked to who just *happens* to know that I'm gay does?"

I sighed deeply and reached up to cover my face with my hands. "I know. I know, Cammie, you're right."

"And maybe if your friend says you're incapable of falling in love with someone then she's not really your friend. Maybe she doesn't know you as well as she thinks she does, because I know you pretty damn well and I'm not worried about you."

"You've known me three months, Cammie," I mumbled, taking my hands off of my face. "She's known me for years."

"I don't care. I trust you." She leaned closer and brushed her lips across my cheek, up to my ear. "I trust you, okay? And you can trust me."

"Can I?" I whispered.

She tensed briefly. I heard her sigh into my ear, and then she moved to kiss my temple, murmuring against my skin, "*Yes.*"

I pulled away, turning to look at her, and she reached out for my cheek again, a small smile on her lips.

"Promise?" I pressed.

She nodded. "Promise. You promise I'm not a booty call?"

I let out a short laugh, nodding back. "Yes, I promise."

"Then we're good."

"We're good," I echoed. She glanced from my eyes to my lips, and I knew before she moved that she was going to kiss me.

I pressed close to her, cupping her cheek in my hand and rolling her backward onto her back, my body positioned half on top of hers as she sighed into my mouth and wound her arms around my neck. She pulled me closer and I was suddenly overly aware that she wasn't wearing a bra. Neither was I.

As our kisses grew heavier and heavier, so did the pounding in my chest. I was sure Cammie could feel my heart hammering against hers, and the thought embarrassed me. Kissing someone had never gotten my heart pounding so hard so quickly.

Moments later, I pulled away to take a breath, and she bit her lip and arched her body up into mine. A soft little noise I almost missed escaped her, and she repositioned her hands behind my neck and gently pulled me closer again. Her normally bright blue eyes had shifted toward a darker hue, and I swallowed hard as I moved to close the distance between us again. My skin tingled everywhere she touched: my neck, my cheeks, the strip of bare skin just above my waist where my tank top had ridden up.

We kissed for what felt like hours, and at last I broke away from her only to see that her eyes had remained closed. With her breathing audible, a slow smile spread across her lips, and at last her eyes fluttered open to look into mine.

"Every night," she whispered, still breathless. "We're doing this every night."

I leaned back down, chuckling, and buried my face into her neck. "Okay, Cammie." My hand slid to her collarbone and I managed to get a small part of my palm over her heart.

It was racing faster than mine had been.

* * *

I'd like to say that Christmas with the Marshalls was fun. I'd like to say that we all baked cookies together and shopped for a Christmas tree and decorated it as a big happy family and I felt like I *belonged* and like everything was going to be okay in my life forever because I wasn't spending Christmas with Caitlyn and a bottle of vodka.

But that wasn't even close to the truth.

Christmas with David, Wendy, Scott, and Cammie was somewhere between "mediocre" and "mildly unpleasant." For one thing, I'd always learned that Christmas was about giving and receiving presents. Basically it was a lesson in generosity. And an awesome holiday – when I actually ended up getting to give and receive presents, that is.

With the Marshalls, it was about Jesus. Jesus this, Jesus that, Jesus was born, Jesus in a manger, songs about Jesus, baby Jesus, which church baby is gonna *play* baby Jesus, and much more. Then I had to actually sit through the play, which was only manageable because I got to sit by Cammie and mess with her while the lights were dimmed. She was unamused.

The presents were the highlight. I was given money to shop for each of the Marshalls, and they each bought me something as well. I mostly got clothing, which I was thankful for. I'd needed stuff for a while that could actually survive farm work.

The tree ordeal was a pain in the ass. Wendy and David argued about which tree was prettier while Scott and I chased each other up and down the aisles of trees like a pair of twelve-year-olds. Between the two of us goofing off, David's arguing, and Cammie getting distracted by constant texts from a still-pissed-off Tiffany, Wendy threw a fit, gave up, and headed back to the car, demanding David choose whatever tree he wanted.

Then David, being David, picked a tree that was too tall, so we wound up with a Christmas tree that bent over at the top. Scott managed to get an angel to stay up there anyway. For about a day. It fell and broke apart at the neck the next morning. I took one look at the decapitated angel lying on the living room floor and laughed so hard I cried. Wendy wasn't pleased with that.

Too soon after the tree incident, Cammie and I baked cookies while we were home alone and left them in for too long. When the rest of the Marshalls came home to a smoky kitchen, we had to find a way to explain it without mentioning the part where we made out for ten minutes while we were supposed to be extracting the cookies from the oven.

All in all, it was a train wreck. But it beat home by just a little bit.

Only a little bit, though.

I called Caitlyn on Christmas morning, eager to hear about what she'd gotten. Zeke always gave her the best presents. He worked as a golf caddy and last year it'd been a golf cart.

Cammie sat alone in the living room with me as I dialed, and nudged me pointedly just as the phone began to ring. "You should do it," she mouthed, and I dismissed her half-heartedly. She was right about the timing, though. Her family was outside feeding the animals.

"Maybe," I mumbled.

Caitlyn picked up a few seconds later with an ecstatic, "Hey! How was your Christmas? You'll never guess what Zeke got me."

"A puppy?" I tried.

"Better. He made me a promise."

"A promise?" I scoffed. "Your Christmas present was verbal?"

"Lauren, he said he wants to live in New York, and that he'd go with us if we were up for it."

My jaw dropped. "What? Why New York?"

"He's tired of Los Angeles. I told him our plan to get the hell out of dodge after you come back, and he wants in. One of the guys he caddies regularly for is super rich and owns a house there, so he has connections. And this way you don't even have to go back to Los Angeles. If my brother's coming with us, then after we come get you we can just go straight to New York and start fresh. I can bring you everything you want with you; clothes, electronics, whatever. It just has to be able to fit into your car."

"Oh my God," I murmured, reaching up to put my free hand on my head. "You guys are insane. We have to find somewhere to live! An apartment or loft or something."

"We have three months. Let us figure it out. You just might

have to pull the financial weight at first with the down payment and rent while we get jobs, but we're totally cool with working for our own money, and we'll pay you back, I swear."

"Cait, don't worry about that," I insisted. "Just... wow, okay, I'm up for it if you are. Let's do it."

"Yes!" She let out an excited squeal and I laughed at her. Cammie, beside me, looked a little alarmed by what I assumed were the noises Caitlyn was making. I remembered what she'd wanted me to do.

"Hey, Cait," I began, once she'd finally calmed down. "I should probably tell you something."

"What's up? You sure you're okay with this?"

"Yeah, it's not about that."

"Okay...?" She trailed off, and I glanced to Cammie, who reached over and gave my free hand a quick squeeze.

"I'm just gonna say it. I've kind of been... hooking up with the girl I told you about." Cammie smacked my arm and rolled her eyes. "We're dating, I mean. Like relationship dating. Maybe. I don't know." I got another smack from Cammie for that, and shot her an alarmed look. "What? It's not like we've talked about it."

"Wait... *what?*" Caitlyn cut in. "You're dating someone? Physics girl isn't pissed at you anymore? *And* you're dating her? Romantically?"

"Yes, romantically," I sighed. "And I don't mean Physics girl."

"Oh my God. The straight one?"

"Not so straight. Yeah." I leaned forward so I could see toward the back of the house. Through the window, David was visibly walking back toward the door. "Um, so I kind of can't talk about this anymore right now. I'm really sorry!"

"Oh hell no, you are *not* gonna leave me hanging like this. You have a *girlfriend?*"

"Her family's coming inside; I can't talk about it. I have to go; they don't know I'm calling."

"Bitch if you hang up this phone I swear to—"

Cringing, I pushed the button to end the call and thrust the phone into Cammie's arms. She fumbled with it for a moment and then reached over to plant it back where it belonged seconds before the back door opened.

"Anything interesting going on, girls?" David asked as he entered, gesturing toward the television in front of us. I glanced to it, saw it was on ESPN, and then shook my head, my expression carefully neutral.

"Nope. Not really."

Chapter Seventeen

Our break soon came to an end, which meant a new semester at Collinsville, and four new classes. I didn't pay much attention to the schedule David drew up for me. These were the classes I didn't plan on finishing. I was still getting out of Collinsville the instant I turned eighteen.

At the end of our first day back, Wendy and David took Scott to pick out flowers for his wedding, much to his chagrin, which left Cammie and I alone for a while in her room.

Cammie drew at her desk as I relaxed on my bed with my music and a magazine, and I watched the side of her face as she worked. She was totally enraptured with whatever she was doing, and I loved the look on her. I had this brief image of her in art school, coming home to Cait, Zeke, and me in our apartment, and my heart fluttered at the idea.

"I like you drawing in front of me," I spoke up at last, and she blushed immediately and shot me an accusing look.

"You promised you wouldn't say anything!"

"I promised I wouldn't ask to see," I corrected. "Look at you; you love it."

She twirled the colored pencil in her hand between two fingers and bit back a smile. "Stop looking at me like that."

"Like what?" I asked, grinning.

"Like *that*. I'm working here."

"Sorry," I said, not meaning it at all. She huffed and went back to drawing, and I watched her again for a moment, unable to keep the smile off of my face. Before I could think about it, I'd blurted out, "Come to New York with me."

She froze and then faced me, raising an eyebrow. And then her expression was warm and her tone was dubious. "Lauren..."

I winced. "Sorry. It slipped out."

She stared at me for a long moment, and then her gaze dropped to her pencil and her eyebrows furrowed together. "I applied to that art school, you know. Just to see if I could get in. I don't plan on actually going or anything, but I figured... maybe if I don't get in, I won't feel as bad about staying here. It'd be nice there, though, I bet."

I nodded earnestly. Now that I'd said it aloud, I was quickly realizing how easily it could work out. I was headed to New York straight from Collinsville in March. If Cammie were to come along...

"Cammie, you'll get in. I know it. And then you could go to

school where you want. You wouldn't have to live in Collinsville and deal with people who can't accept you. New York's really gay friendly. I bet people wouldn't even stare at us if we held hands. It'd just be so... easy."

Cammie, understandably, had her reservations. "You'd want that life with me, really? We haven't even used the word 'girlfriend' yet." She forced a laugh. "It still feels weird to say aloud."

I bit my lip and stared at her. "You could be my girlfriend," I said at last.

She snorted. "Such a romantic."

I let out a deep sigh. "I know. I'm bad at this. I'm... I'm a fucking frog, goddammit. I don't know how to do this."

"A frog?" she laughed. "What exactly are we talking about again?"

"The night of that party," I clarified, "you said all of the awful guys were frogs and you had to go through a few frogs to find a prince."

"Oh my God, you're not a frog," she sighed. "You can't take half the things I say about guys seriously when I don't even *like* them."

"But you were right about that," I pressed. "You were with a lot of awful guys. Just because your prince is actually a princess doesn't make me not a frog. I'm the froggiest frog to ever freaking frog; I was a frog for, like, more girls than I even know."

"Not for me. You're my princess," she replied, getting to her feet and joining me on my bed. She gave me a sickeningly sweet smile and kissed me on the cheek.

I hit her with my magazine. "Stop that. I'm terrible. I don't know how to do relationships. I can't even ask you to date me the right way."

"And I don't know how to do lesbianism," she joked, crawling forward until she was hovering over me, our faces inches apart. "So I'll teach you how to do monogamy," she proposed, leaning forward until her lips brushed against mine. My eyes fluttered shut and she murmured, "And you teach me how to be with you."

"It's not hard," I insisted quietly. "You just have to feed and water me three times a day."

She pulled away to shoot me an exasperated look. "Alright, I'll go back to drawing, then."

"No, no," I insisted, catching her by the wrist and pulling her back into me. "I'm sorry." I moved my hands to her waist and leaned in to kiss her, and she sighed into me and cupped my cheeks in her hands. She left me breathless, my heart thudding in my chest and my cheeks warm.

I pulled away and watched her eyes slowly open to look at me. We shared a smile, and she leaned forward to brush her nose back and forth against mine. "You're a softy deep down," she declared quietly. "You just got a little bit lost somewhere along the way here."

Her words left a deep ache in my chest. For an instant, I envisioned myself with a normal childhood and a normal life. What I had with Cammie was special, I knew, but I could've spent my high school years having actual relationships. I wasn't sure it'd compare to how I felt here and now, with Cammie, but this feeling was so addicting that even anything that came close wasn't worth missing out on.

"Fuck my dad," I murmured at last, my voice cracking on the last word. Cammie leaned away to get a better look at me, concerned. I shook my head. "I had the most screwed up childhood, holy shit. They abandoned me." *That* was the word I'd been searching for all those weeks ago, in lieu of "neglected." Abandoned. There'd been a total disconnect between my parents and me, unlike that of parents who didn't pay as much attention to their children as they should. As the years had progressed, mine just hadn't paid any attention at all. And I'd come here defending them.

"They love you, Lauren," Cammie murmured, leaning in to press another kiss to my cheek. "They had to have loved you." I shook my head wordlessly, and she pressed another kiss, this time to my forehead. "*I* do," she murmured into my skin.

I couldn't bring myself to say anything back.

* * *

"I think I'm fucked up."

Across the dining room table, David thankfully realized now was not the time to interrupt me just to correct my language.

"I don't think I'm normal. I don't think I do well with emotions. I don't know how to show that I care about people."

"Why do you say that?" he asked, studying me.

"Because." I squeezed my eyes shut. "It's like... I want to be normal and have these normal reactions and emotional abilities and to be well-adjusted and all that, and I'm just not like that. I've always had this mentality, like... people aren't supposed to get too close because they'll just disappoint you or hurt you, and I never really learned how to let anyone in, and now... now when I want to let people in, I have all these alarms going off in my head and I get nervous and... I feel vulnerable and it feels wrong and awkward and like I'm doing the wrong thing." I let out a deep sigh, aware that I was rambling. "I don't know how to be normal."

He pursed his lips together and nodded. "Well, Lauren, I think you're right."

I looked to him sharply, eyebrows raised. "You do?"

"Yeah. Yeah, I do." He offered me a smile. "It's pretty remarkable that you came to that conclusion on your own."

I shook my head and shrugged my shoulders. "I just keep thinking about the way I was with girls back in Los Angeles. I'd be with a new one every week and I didn't care what they felt or why they were with me. I didn't care about *them*. I'm sick of that. My mom's gone, my dad and I have given up on each other, and I just want to move on and have a normal life and not feel like I have a bunch of baggage to carry around because of who my parents are and how I was raised. I just want to learn how to be *normal*. I want to be in a relationship and not feel like I don't deserve it or can't do it justice."

He studied me for a long moment, almost like he was trying to find the right words to respond with. At last, he replied, gently, "You never told me you were attracted to other girls."

I froze, not daring to believe I'd slipped up. "No. Guys. I said guys, right?"

"You said girls," he confirmed. "It's alright, Lauren."

"Fuck," I murmured, sitting back in my chair and covering my face with my hands. "Goddammit."

"Language," he reprimanded shortly.

My hands slid off of my face and I stared at him, feeling nauseous. "I didn't mean for you to find out about that."

"Why not?" He seemed genuinely confused, which baffled me.

"Uh, check out your homophobic town and your Baptist church," I replied. "This isn't a welcoming environment."

"Regardless of my personal beliefs, I'm still here to counsel you," he told me. "That means I leave my judgments at the door, and I keep what you tell me confidential."

"So that's your way of saying you don't approve but your profession forces you to not judge me," I deadpanned.

"Let's keep the focus on you," he said. "All you need to know about me is that my opinion on you hasn't changed. I'm still here to help you, and I'm still here to listen. I don't believe you're gay out of some childhood trauma or that it's a disease that needs to be cured. You can talk to me about it."

"I don't have issues with being gay. Just change the pronouns on everything I've ever told you about my love life and we're updated," I said shortly.

"Done." He smiled. "So where were we? You were saying you feel vulnerable in emotional situations?"

"When my emotions are out in the open, I guess." I shifted uncomfortably, trying to adjust to being newly out to him. I hadn't expected him to just take it in stride like that. "Yeah."

"Well, the first step to combatting that is to change your pattern of thinking," he suggested. "You're closed off because you're worried about getting hurt. So if you open up and *don't* get hurt, you've taken the first step to not associating emotional vulnerability with negative consequences. Does that make sense?"

"Yeah." I frowned. "Easier said than done, though."

* * *

I tried my best to take David's words to heart. There was an invisible hurdle I couldn't get over, and I knew deep down that it was entirely mental, but that didn't stop it from being hard to get past. I knew it was my problem and my problem alone; I felt that in the way Cammie, despite her issues, had thrown herself wholeheartedly into our relationship, kissing me first and telling me how she felt and then never looking back. She had so much to lose, and yet she'd transitioned so flawlessly into the person she'd deep down always wanted to be. And that person was beautiful inside and out, and all I could ask for in a girlfriend. That person deserved all of me. And instead I was second-guessing her, entertaining what Maddie had said about her going back to dating guys to please her parents.

David, meanwhile, had started watching Cammie and I with a certain look in his eyes I hadn't seen before. If Cammie was right, he remembered the comment she'd made about marrying her friend at age eight, and now she'd broken up with her boyfriend and she and I were inseparable. I could see that David had made the mental jump and was wary, to say the least. I wasn't sure if that was because he didn't want a gay daughter, or because he didn't want *me* dating his daughter.

But I took his advice.

A few nights later, when I was sure everyone else was asleep, I grabbed a spare blanket from the linen closet and nudged Cammie awake. She mumbled something intelligible and batted at me, and I hissed, "Cammie! Wake up!"

She blinked the sleep out of her eyes and squinted at me in the dark. "What are you doing? It's, like, one in the morning. We have church tomorrow."

"We can sleep through it." I got a glare for that. "Please?"

She sighed, and her gaze dropped down to the blanket in my arms. "Okay, seriously, what are you doing?"

"Come with me and find out," I offered, extending my hand to her. "C'mon."

She sat up and rubbed at her eyes, then groaned and moved to get to her feet. "You're so strange."

* * *

She was wide-awake by the time she was tying Aerosmith to a tree in our clearing. I stretched the blanket out across the grass and then went to Cammie, clutching both of her hands in mine and leading her back toward the blanket. She was smiling now.

"You're ridiculous."

"I like stargazing with you," I insisted.

"Oh, is that what we're calling it now? Half the time we've

come out here lately it's just been to make out for an hour."

"I didn't bring you out here for a make out session." That was only partially true.

"Well, now I'm even more confused."

I laughed and pulled her down onto the blanket with me, and she grabbed one of my hands with both of hers and studied my fingers. I grinned at her as she played with my hand and turned to look up at the stars.

"Imagine if we were the only two people in the world," Cammie mused. "Every day would be like this."

"You'd get lonely," I assured her. "I wouldn't be enough."

"But at least I wouldn't have to worry about what anyone thought about me."

I rolled over onto my side, and she released my hand as I looked at her. "You can do that now."

"Can't," was all she said.

I propped myself up on an elbow. "I've been talking to your dad about the way I grew up. I told him I feel vulnerable when I get close to people. I meant that I feel vulnerable around you, of course... but anyway, I think you grew up learning to keep up appearances the same way I learned that getting close to people gets me hurt. I'm trying to undo my parents' damage. Maybe you should try to undo yours."

"I know." She reached out and caressed my cheek with her hand. "I want to." Her palm drifted across my lips and I kissed it. We were silent for a while, just watching each other while crickets chirped and the wind rustled the trees around us. At last, Cammie shifted closer to me until our noses were touching, and moved her hand to my thigh. "I'll start here," she murmured.

"Me too." And, mind buzzing, I closed the gap between us

There was something different about this time, and I knew immediately that Cammie realized what this was. I often forgot when I was with her that she was experienced; that she may have not been with a girl before, but she was still familiar with sex. I was determined to make this different; like a new first time.

I was kneeling above her within a minute or two, and she wound her arms around my back and urged me closer, her mouth on my neck and my hands pressed into the blanket on either side of her head. When she pulled away and rested her head on the blanket again, I stared down at her, breathing heavily. She reached up to run her thumb over my bottom lip, eyes hooded. I swallowed hard, and then broke eye contact with her to watch my own hands reach down and tug at the hem of my tank top. Once it was up and over my head, I shivered and covered my exposed chest. "God, it's cold."

"I can tell," Cammie whispered, grinning.

"Don't make fun of my boobs," I hissed. She just giggled and pulled me down for another kiss.

The jokes stopped there. Cammie reached down mid-kiss and fumbled for the waistband of my pajama bottoms. I broke our kiss abruptly, but she reached up with her free hand and pulled me back down for another kiss, her hand on my neck. I broke the kiss again to insist, "Cammie, you first."

"Why?" she whispered, other hand still dancing along my waistline. I stiffened, and she moved her hand away, then cupped both of my cheeks instead. Eyes on mine, she whispered, "Let me. You don't always have to be in control."

I stared back at her, heart pounding hard in my chest. I knew exactly what she was asking. I'd let other girls do what they wanted to me before; I had no qualms with that. But it was different with Cammie.

"Okay," I stuttered at last, and she rolled us over so that she was over top of me, kissing me deeply. When we parted, she hovered over me on her hands and knees, eyes raking down my body. Very quickly, I felt overexposed.

"You're gorgeous," she told me. "And I love you, even if you never say it back. I love you."

She kissed my cheek, my jawline, and then down my neck, lower and lower, and I closed my eyes and reached down to take her hand in mine.

Maddie'd called it the leap of faith. David had called it opening up.

I took the plunge.

"I love you too, Cammie."

She paused, mouth on my collarbone, and then pulled away to look at me. I opened my eyes. Hers were alight despite her darkened irises, and as I watched, a slow smile spread across her lips. She leaned down to kiss me again, all traces of her smile gone by the time our lips touched, and I pulled her close and kissed her fervently, acutely aware of her hand as it brushed back down my stomach toward my waist.

This time I didn't stop her.

Chapter Eighteen

"Scott came up to me today."

I looked up from the magazine I'd been reading. It was an old one of Cammie's I'd found in her closet. She was on her bed, Bible in hand. We'd been reading to pass the time until her family went to sleep.

I raised a questioning eyebrow, and she elaborated, "He knows we've been sneaking out, like, every night this week."

"Oh." I hid a smile at the reminder, and she buried her face in her Bible, most likely to cover a blush. I hadn't been able to get the image of her in the moonlight out of my head since that first night together. "Wait... does this mean we're staying here tonight?"

"Yeah. I told him we've been going stargazing."

"And he believed that?"

"I think so." She avoided my eyes. "I'm not sure my dad would, though."

"He wouldn't. He knows about me. You see the way he's been looking at us lately, right?"

She didn't respond at first. But when she did, her voice was quiet. "Yeah." I waited for her to say more. "My mom's got like this massive list of her friends' sons and boys from our church waiting for me."

"Is it tempting?" I asked her, but I wasn't sure I wanted to hear her answer.

She looked offended, to my surprise. "Of course not. It's just... easier."

"Is it really, though?"

"Yes. Maybe. I don't know." She sighed and dropped her head into her hands. "Coming out to my dad, though? My brother? They'd be hard enough, let alone my mom."

"Not as hard as getting married on someone else's terms." I paused, hesitated, and then added, "Just ask your brother."

She looked up at me with surprise. "My brother?"

I nodded. "Yeah."

* * *

"We are gathered here today to join Scott Marshall and Jill Stephens in holy matrimony."

I watched Scott carefully as the proceedings wore on, half-wishing Cammie wasn't busy being a bridesmaid so I didn't have to sit alone with David and Wendy. Several members of the Marshall family had flown in, as well; just on my other side were two sets of grandparents that practically refused to acknowledge my presence. I was sure I was only sitting with the family of the groom in the first place so that David could easily keep an eye on me.

Scott didn't look away from Jill throughout the rest of Pastor Mckinley's speech, and it was easy to see that he loved her. But his body was tense and I wondered if I was the only one – bar Cammie, of course – who could see how uncomfortable he looked. He was only twenty years old. He was *so* young. And I knew he didn't feel ready to be married or have kids.

Cammie and I made eye contact across the room and I watched her swallow hard. She glanced from me to Scott, and then back again, and I could see the worry on her face; could see exactly what she was thinking: "This could be me."

When the wedding itself was over, everyone headed out to the Marshalls' farm in droves for the after-party. Cammie and I had helped Wendy set everything up earlier in the day. Soon, the normally-quiet house was packed with several dozen people, and even though Scott and Jill's wedding had been relatively small, it was still hard to get any privacy.

I caught Cammie in the Marshalls' walk-in pantry eventually. She was getting silverware for Wendy and looked drained. "Are you okay?" I asked her.

"I'm fine," she replied shortly, and hurried past me, accidentally bumping my shoulder a little roughly on her way. I sighed as I watched her go. I understood that she was stressed, but I still wished she'd talk to me. I wanted to know exactly what she was thinking. Watching Scott get married seemed to have jarred her a little.

When I got back to the living room, I saw Jill was occupying a group of at least eight women with the story of how she'd met Scott, but I couldn't find Scott himself anywhere. Then I noticed the backdoor had been left cracked open.

I wandered out to the barn in heels, avoiding mud along the way, and peered inside once I'd reached it. Scott was sitting on one of the bales of hay, a glass of champagne in his hand. He was alone.

"Hey. Looks like you kind of ditched your own party," I said by way of greeting.

He forced a laugh. "Yeah. I'm hiding. Can you bring me more alcohol?"

"You're under-aged," I joked, but that seemed to upset him. He frowned and set his glass down.

"God. I am. I can't even legally drink alcohol and I'm married."

"At least you two love each other," I said. "Look. Jill cares about you a lot. If you tell her you want to slow down, I bet she would."

"It's not about her," he replied. "It's Mom. *She* won't understand."

"Maybe she's not as bad as you guys think she is," I proposed. "A little controlling and uptight, yeah, but she cooks you dinner and asks you how your day was and hugs you and tells you she loves you. That's something. You and Cammie don't realize how good you have it."

"Cammie?" he echoed, confused. "Cammie loves Mom. They get along great."

"So do *you* and your mom," I pointed out. "You get along great because you're never honest with her. She signed up to have kids, you know. I think when people do that, they should be willing to support and love them no matter what."

"I'm not putting the brakes on this," he declared, shaking his head. "I just have to do it. I don't have a choice."

"You always have a choice."

"Then this is the one I'm making." He picked up his glass again and downed the rest of the drink in one gulp. I watched him sadly as he set it down and looked back at me. Suddenly, he was curious. "Cammie never went stargazing before you showed up, you know. Not like she does now, anyway. She likes that clearing because she's always liked having time to herself. Now I never see her go out there without you, and you've only been going in the middle of the night lately."

I felt a flush crawl up my cheeks. "I guess I got her into it. I'm big on Astrology."

"Astronomy," he corrected, and I could see that he'd stiffened.

"Yeah. That's what I meant."

He studied me. There was a long pause. "...You're lying, aren't you?"

I could feel my face turning redder. "I—"

"You two are inseparable. You've been going out alone every

night to that clearing and you're lying about why."

I was panicking now. "Anyway, I should go—"

He rose to his feet, eyeing me with furrowed eyebrows, and moved closer. I could see his eyes lower from mine to look at my flushed cheeks, and my heart rate doubled.

When he spoke, his voice was rugged, gravelly. His jaw was so tensed I could see the veins of his neck, but he was so, so quiet. "Are you *screwing* my sister?"

I opened and closed my mouth. My mind was blank, buzzing with something akin to terror, and my brain was telling my legs to run. I gripped the barn door so hard my knuckles turned white, and stayed put. I finally got a word out. "N-no."

I knew as soon as I said it that it wasn't nearly convincing enough. Scott's whole face went beet red and he started shaking with anger.

"Hey, what are you doing all the way out-?"

That was Cammie, who paused beside me at the entrance to the barn, then glanced inside and cut herself off when she saw Scott. She looked back and forth between my reddened face and his, and then down to his clenched fists, and immediately went to him.

"Scott, you have to understand—"

"What about this am I supposed to understand?" he cried, sounding near tears. The anger drained from his face and he gestured to me hopelessly, looking seconds from a nervous breakdown. "This is my wedding day, I'm fucking terrified and Mom's already talking kids and now that I finally get along with one of Dad's experiments she's turned you gay and you're having sex with her?! What part of that is okay?! What am I supposed to understand here?!"

"I'm not a child, Scott. I can make my own decisions. I'm eighteen. I know it's a lot to take in—"

"It's a sin," he spat out, shaking his head. "You're going to hell."

"You don't believe that." Cammie dropped her hand from his arm and shook her head. "I know you don't believe that. I'm a good person. So is Lauren. I'm the same sister you've had for eighteen years, Scott. And you like Lauren."

"Not now. Not anymore. She needs to go. She's messed you up." He moved to push past her, but Cammie grabbed at him. I caught a glimpse of her face and saw her expression had hardened.

"You're not saying a word to Mom and Dad. Don't even think about it, or I'll tell Mom how you really feel about your wedding day."

"That's nothing compared to you sleeping with a girl Dad's supposed to be fixing," he snapped.

"Probably not. But do you want to test them?"

They stood facing each other, gazes locked, and, at last, Scott broke eye contact to glare at me. "She's out of here in four months. And then you'll get over this stupid phase and go back to being normal again."

He brushed past her and left the barn without another word, and Cammie watched him go with reddened eyes. I could tell she was seconds from bursting into tears.

"I'm sorry," I started to say, but she left before I could even get a full apology out.

* * *

I didn't get a chance to talk to her again until long after Scott and Jill had left for a weeklong Honeymoon in the Bahamas. Her grandparents on both sides were staying at a local motel a few miles away, but all four of them stayed late into the night, along with a couple of aunts and uncles who also had flights to catch early the next morning.

I kept to myself. That night, more than ever, I was aware of not only how much of an outsider I was, but also of just how much of who I was was unacceptable. I didn't fit into Wendy's worldview or the worldview of her parents; I wasn't one of them. I wasn't supposed to exist, and I was only around until I wasn't anymore. I was a burden to them. I felt invisible.

As everyone began to crowd around for goodbyes, I finally felt myself relax. The hours of listening to old Marshall family stories, watching Cammie's grandparents ask her about boyfriends, and taking in Wendy's overeager grin at those questions had left me exhausted.

David sidled up to me as the last of the guests were leaving and wrapped an arm around me, squeezing me to him. I furrowed my eyebrows and looked up at him thoughtfully.

"I think I get why you wanted me go to church."

He seemed surprised that I'd have this epiphany now of all times. "Oh?"

"It's a family thing. It's a weekly family tradition. You wanted to force me into family activities. Like regular parents do." I swallowed hard. "But I don't feel like a part of your family. I'm not the kind of person any of them like having around."

"I like having you around," he told me, patting my shoulder. "And so does Cammie. You make her happy. I'm a fan of anything that can do that."

"Really?"

He smiled, a knowing twinkle in his eyes. "Yes."

It occurred to me, then, that maybe things weren't as hopeless as they seemed.

I climbed the stairs to Cammie's room when it was finally time for bed, and entered to see her buried beneath her covers, her entire body hidden from view.

I went to her bed and sat beside her, placing a hand on her arm. I felt her flinch. "Will you talk to me?" I asked her.

"I'm really not in the mood." Her voice was muffled, but firm, and it was my turn to flinch. Sadly, I got back to my feet.

"Okay." I hesitated. "I love you."

She shifted beneath the covers as I watched, and then sat up in bed and let them fall to her lap. She pulled her knees up to her chest and I saw her eyes were red-rimmed. "What did you tell him?"

"He figured it out," I said. "I'm sorry."

"He hates me now."

"He doesn't hate you. He just needs time to adjust."

"You don't know that." She sniffed and wiped at a tear on her cheek. "You don't know what this feels like. I feel like I'm drowning. First it's Scott, and then who? My parents? My classmates?"

"You shouldn't care about the kids you go to school with."

"But I do!" she bit out. "I care a lot. For as long as I'm living here, I'll care."

"You don't have to live here," I reminded her. "You can live anywhere you want. I have the money. I'll give you anything you want, Cammie. I'll buy you your own art studio; I don't *care*. I just hate that this hurts you so much." I was red-faced and earnest, I knew, but I couldn't stop myself from continuing. "Your Dad knows about me, and I know it's different when it's your own kid, but he just wants you to be happy. I know he'd be okay with this; I can feel it, and he can talk to your mom. It doesn't have to be this hard forever. You can be honest with him, and things will get better."

"How do you know? You didn't even have to come out to your Dad, right? He just didn't care about you regardless."

I stiffened, and she deflated, squeezing her eyes shut. "I'm sorry, Lauren. I didn't mean that."

"Yeah, you did." I stared at her, my gaze hardened. "You're right. My dad and I didn't spend weekends going out to dinner together or playing video games or watching sports or going shopping. He didn't wake me up in a dorky tennis outfit and buy me milkshakes. But your dad does. And you're *so* lucky to have that. I know you're used to sharing him, and I know that's not easy. But even if he's missing some details about your life here and there, he cares a lot about you. You should give him a chance and be honest with him. *I did.*"

She didn't respond. I moved to change into my pajamas and then sank underneath the covers of my bed, letting out a deep, slow breath. Scott's angry gaze came to mind every time I shut my eyes, and it took me hours to finally fall asleep.

Chapter Nineteen

Pastor McKinley wasn't at church the following Sunday.

Instead, Cammie and I were greeted by Pastor Jenkins, a younger, even dorkier-looking guy I was instantly annoyed by. If McKinley was vaguely aggravating, this guy was intolerable. He was far too excited and upbeat, and he made it hard to sleep through his little lecture. At least when McKinley droned on about crap I didn't care about, it was easy to tune him out.

After a long three or so hours, we met back up with David and Wendy and drove to our usual lunch spot. On our way there, I asked Cammie, "So what was up with the new guy? I don't like him."

"You didn't like McKinley, either," she pointed out, but frowned nonetheless. "I don't know, though. Maybe he took a week off?"

"Seems like something the other guy should've explained," I said.

Wendy was stiff in the passenger's seat in front of us, and David changed the subject.

"So I hear there's a new family lunch package we could try out. Four orders for just $35, plus a free desert. Not a bad deal, huh?"

"You sound like such an old person," I told him, grinning, but Cammie was still stuck on McKinley.

"That was really weird, though, wasn't it?" she asked, looking thoughtful. "Usually if he takes a week off we have someone introduced as a guest and the guest explains why they're here instead of Pastor McKinley. I think this guy's just replaced him, and they didn't mention him at all…"

"Honey, this isn't polite conversation," Wendy cut in, her tone clipped. I glanced from her to David as the two of them exchanged looks up front. Then I shot Cammie a strange look. Her eyebrows were furrowed, and I knew she'd seen her parents' reactions too.

"Did something happen to him, Dad?" she asked.

David hesitated. "I think perhaps the church wanted a fresh face. Pastor McKinley was getting a bit old to be interacting with and trying to relate to young children."

"He was only in his thirties," Cammie argued. "And he has kids. He was nice; I liked him. What really happened?"

"He was caught with someone he shouldn't have been with," Wendy cut in abruptly. "The church felt it was necessary to cut ties with him."

"Oh," I mumbled, but Cammie shook her head.

"Didn't he and his wife separate over a year ago?" She looked appalled. "Wait, was he with a *kid?*"

"Well, he may as well have been," Wendy bit out. "He was with another man. It's no wonder he was fired; he's meant to spend hours alone with kids every Sunday."

David looked like he wanted to be anywhere but here right now. I felt my face heat up. "Are you serious? Gay people aren't automatically pedophiles."

Wendy turned away to look out her window, sighing deeply. "I suppose you'd say that, with the liberal education you received back in that terrible state. I encountered the same sort of agenda back in college."

Wide-eyed, I glanced to Cammie, expecting her to look just as shocked by the things her mother was saying. Instead, she swallowed hard, her eyes fixed pointedly to her lap.

"You're crazy," I told Wendy promptly. "Wow. Your fucked up family makes *so* much sense now."

"We're here," David announced abruptly as Wendy's face reddened to match mine.

"Excuse me?" she asked me, her voice high and sickeningly sweet. David parked the car and immediately got out and came to my door, yanking it open.

"Lauren, out," he demanded, and I followed his orders with malice. He shut the door behind me and guided me away from the car by my arm.

"You put up with that," I deadpanned. "You're just as bad as she is if you let her say stuff like that around her kids."

David paused and released my arm once we'd put enough distance between ourselves and the car. "Wendy is misguided, but she's a good mother. Don't think you can judge her based on one belief she holds."

"She loves her children conditionally. That's not being a good parent." I folded my arms across my chest. "Believe me, I know a bad parent when I see one, and you're just as bad for letting her get away with that shit."

"You've been here a few months, Lauren. You may be a part of our family while you're here, but don't think you know everything about how I do my job as a father."

"A-plus fathering, then," I bit out. "Your son's off getting a girl pregnant when he isn't ready after a wedding he didn't wanna have, and it's a miracle your daughter doesn't hate herself. I'm *so* jealous I wasn't born into this family. Hell, my drunk dad back in Los Angeles is ten times better than this. You don't communicate with your fucking *kids*, and neither did he, but at least I can be honest with him."

He turned away from me and let out a deep breath. Yards away, Wendy and Cammie left the car, and Wendy pulled Cammie into the restaurant by the hand. I watched David as he took a seat on the curb.

"Scott doesn't love Jill," he said at last, as though his world was crashing down around him. "I didn't know that."

"No, he loves her," I corrected. "But as it turns out, getting married and having kids at age twenty wasn't his dream. Shocker."

"He never complained," David murmured, almost

thoughtfully.

"Well I know *that's* how I determine what my kids want to do with their lives," I mused sarcastically. "If they don't complain, they must love the idea."

"I was busy with Cammie," he admitted. "I was *too* busy with Cammie and I didn't pay close attention with Scott."

"No, you were too busy with me," I corrected. "And the other kids before me." I took a seat next to him. "You know a lot about me now. And... I do feel included by you." I paused. "But did you know Cammie's an amazing artist?"

He raised his head to look back at me, eyebrows furrowed. "I didn't."

"She draws New York obsessively. She wants to live there so badly. She doesn't want to stay here; she wants to go to art school there and she applied without telling you, but she doesn't plan on going because she doesn't want to disappoint her mother. And I don't know if she wants kids, but she certainly doesn't talk about how much she *does* want them. She doesn't really like cheerleading, and she never liked Peter, although at least you picked up on that last one." I paused. "And I shouldn't be telling you all of this. You should hear it from her."

He didn't respond, and I chewed at my lip for a moment, almost certain that if I hadn't indirectly outed Cammie before by being so close with her, I most certainly had now. I closed my eyes, sighed, and pressed on.

"Why would you let Wendy make comments like that? I know you don't agree with her."

"I don't," he said immediately.

"Don't let her or don't agree?"

"Both. I try to keep the subject out of conversation altogether because I don't think we'll ever agree."

"Maybe if you talked to her—"

"Oh, believe me, I've tried," he cut in. "As early as college, when we were dating. I remember we'd have discussions about potentially getting married and then having a gay child. She believed as long as we raised our children right and taught them that homosexuality was wrong, we'd have nothing to worry about. Obviously I disagreed. I guess I just let the subject die, eventually."

"Why?"

He shrugged. "I guess... subconsciously, I just hedged my bets that it would never truly be an issue." He hesitated, and then added, "Around the time Cammie was eight, I realized I might've been wrong. But then she grew up, started showing an interest in boys... and that worry went away, even despite the fact that she didn't seem to like Peter very much. But now that's over, and there's you." He let out a deep sigh. "And here we are."

I wasn't sure what to say to that. Even though he seemed to have more than an inkling that Cammie was gay already, I didn't want to confirm it for him. That was her right, not mine.

"You should talk to her, not me," I told him. "I'll be okay. I don't have long left here. I can ignore Wendy and then get on with my life; I don't have to get along with her. Cammie's her daughter, though, and she cares *a lot* about what she thinks."

"Enough to date someone she wasn't interested in," he

realized.

I glanced over my shoulder, toward the restaurant's entrance. I felt guilty about everything I'd shared with him, and the last thing I wanted to do was give him any more information he should've been hearing from Cammie instead. "Talk to her," I told him, and then stood up and turned to head inside.

* * *

The lunch was mostly silent. I sat beside Cammie and tried to reach for her hand at one point, but she moved it away the second I made contact. I realized pretty quickly what was happening. Cammie and David had something in common: the longer Wendy went without reminding them of her bigotry, the more they relaxed and tried to forget about it. With Cammie's default setting for the past few years already being at "sleeping with boys", there was no way she was getting anywhere near me in front of her mother now. I understood, but it still made me feel like crap.

When we got home, I wandered out to the stables alone. I had nothing to say to David anymore, and I wasn't in the mood to be anywhere near Cammie or Wendy.

I went to Aerosmith's stall and leaned over, resting my arms on the door and watching him for a little while. He snorted at my face and then stared back.

"I'm sorry I called you an alien," I told him, reaching out to scratch at his face. He closed his eyes and let out a long breath. "I'm also sorry that you've seen some shit out in that clearing. We didn't have anywhere else to go. Just try to block it out; you can do it."

He let out another slow breath, eyes still closed, and I nodded at him.

"There you go."

I stood with him for a long time, an odd, almost nauseas feeling in my stomach. I hoped Cammie wouldn't hate me for what I'd told her father.

She joined me a half-hour later, coming out in a heavy coat with the hood up. She eyed me in my church outfit and asked, "Aren't you freezing?"

"I forgot it was cold," I admitted. "Been distracted."

She sighed and stepped closer. "I don't hate you. I had a long time to be honest with him before you showed up."

"It should've happened on your terms," I insisted. "But everything just sort of came out. He looked so defeated."

There was a long silence, and she stepped closer and reached for my hand. "I told him about us."

I looked to her sharply. She smiled at me as I asked, "What?"

"He already knew, but... I got to say it. And he was okay with it. Well, in front of me, anyway. He's probably in there freaking out now, but that could be because you're his patient. I told him about Scott's reaction, too, and he thinks he'll get over it." She looked down to her feet and bit at her lip. "He also said I could go to New York if I wanted. But I think that pretty much everything he's okay with would make my mom hate me if I followed through. I don't know if I can deal with that. Losing a mother."

I watched her as she turned toward Aerosmith and reached out to pat him on the head. There wasn't much I could say to that. I knew firsthand how hard it was to lose a mother, and mine hadn't been around even before she'd died. Wendy and Cammie were very close, even if their relationship had been built on the foundation of a feigned personality on Cammie's part. Wendy was still her mother, and I couldn't ask Cammie to choose me over her.

So I didn't know what to tell her. She was faced with a choice I'd never had to make.

She kept her eyes on Aerosmith as she told me, "I've never seen my dad cry before today. He kept apologizing and talking about how he might not take in another kid after you so he can focus on being a better parent to me." She withdrew her hand and turned to me. "You did that. I never thought I'd hear him say that. He loves his job so much, and the rest of us tried to hide how uncomfortable it made us because we could see that it made him happy and that it was making a difference. Is it wrong that I'd be glad to see him stop?"

"I don't think so." I shook my head. "It's his choice, but you shouldn't feel bad about wanting more attention from him." She looked satisfied with my answer, and I bit my lip and added, "I guess that means no New York, though?"

"Well... I'm not going to be with guys anymore, so my mom will eventually find out about me and then she'll be hard to be around," Cammie admitted. "Maybe it's better if I go, after all. If I get into art school, that is. You're leaving with your friend after graduation?"

I hesitated. A lot had come to light today, but I'd avoided telling Cammie about my plan to leave early. I didn't want to upset her. And although graduating didn't sound as awful as it had back in Los Angeles, I wasn't going to spend one more minute in Collinsville than I had to. Maybe I'd even transfer to a new high school in New York for my last two months, if I could.

"What if," I replied, and then paused briefly, trying to find the best way to break the idea to her, "we could just leave here and go to New York. Start the next chapter in our lives. We could transfer schools and finish out up there, and then—"

"Whoa," she cut me off, laughing a little. "I've already applied for college. I need to graduate on time, and I need to graduate from the high school I'm at now."

"Not necessarily," I corrected. "They're not gonna revoke your acceptance just because you finished up somewhere else, Cammie. Just as long as you still graduate in May, you're fine. Caitlyn and Zeke are already going to have a place ready for us to move into. Caitlyn's transferring schools, and she's not worried about colleges."

"And how are you getting up there, then?" she asked, folding her arms across her chest.

"They're picking me up."

She shook her head. "You can't arrange that. Not with Mom and Dad monitoring all of your phone calls. You can only do it around me, and you haven't."

I took a deep breath, and then let it out. "Don't hate me."
"What?"

"I arranged it before I got here. I turn eighteen in March.

They're coming on my birthday. At night."

She stepped away from me, eyebrows furrowing. "And you didn't tell me this until *now*?"

"Well, I didn't know if I could trust you not to tell your parents," I admitted. "And I didn't want you to be mad at me."

"Of course I'm mad!" she replied, nostrils flaring. "Were you just going to leave in the middle of night without telling me?"

"No!" I groaned. "Cammie, that was before. Now... I want you to know, because I'd really like if you came with me."

"How can you ask me to make that decision? I can't run away from my home and switch high schools with two months left; are you insane?"

"You could," I mumbled as my cheeks began to heat up. It did sound ridiculous, now that she'd said it aloud. "I know it sounds crazy, but I have the money to back it up."

"But I don't. I have a life here. You don't have that. You're the one who has nothing to lose."

"But I don't have anything to gain, Cammie," I pointed out. "I'm going to New York because it's where my friend and her brother want to go. I'd go anywhere that wasn't here or Los Angeles. But *you* have so much to gain by going! You can go to your dream school and live your dream life, and you'd get some distance between yourself and your mom while she cools off. Maybe the time apart would make her realize it's not worth it to shut you out because of who you love. *And* your dad would have both kids out of the house and can still do his job if he wants to. It all fits."

"Except for the part where I ditch my family and hometown in the middle of the night without any warning," Cammie deadpanned.

I sighed and reached up scratch at my head. "Maybe if you thought about it—"

"I can't go," she interrupted. "I'm sorry. I can't."

I swallowed hard. "But... I'm already set to go. I'm leaving on my birthday. If you don't come with me..."

"Don't put that pressure on me," she retorted. "You made your decision before you even met me. It's on you to change your mind, not me. This is my home. Maybe after graduation I can think about New York, but until then, I'm staying here."

She turned and hurried away, wrapping her arms around herself to shield her body from the wind chill as she left the safety of the stable.

I watched her go, cold and shivering, and let out at a soft curse as I kicked out at the stall door closest to me. Aerosmith shifted backwards with surprise, and I muttered, "Sorry," then left him there, my heart somewhere in my stomach.

Chapter Twenty

David spent an unnatural amount of time sitting at Cammie's desk in her bedroom that night. He kept glancing back and forth between our beds.

I sat on mine, silent, and listened to music while Cammie took a shower. Every now and then, I'd glance up at David to see him resting his chin in his hands, looking deep in thought. Eventually, I had to speak up.

"Figured it out yet?"

He shook his head simply, and then let out a heavy sigh. "I have to say… as a parent, I have absolutely no idea how to handle this."

I pressed my lips together and nodded, feigning sympathy. "Quite the conundrum."

He glanced to Cammie's bed, where it rested just feet from mine, and then back to me again. "Can't put you on the couch or Wendy'll notice," he muttered, thinking aloud. "Can't move you at all, really, because we'd risk her noticing. Can't move you out of the room but can't have you in the same room..."

"I'm a child of God now, remember? I go to church," I reminded him. "I would *never—*"

"Don't finish that sentence," he warned me. I smirked and broke eye contact, glancing back down to my mp3 player as David rose from his seat. Newly inspired, he declared, "I've got it. Cammie will stay in Scott's room until he returns. If her mother asks, she'll claim she misses him."

I snorted. "That's so weak."

"When he gets back, we'll address this again," he declared, ignoring me.

I arched an eyebrow up at him. "So how does this plan account for the fact that we're teenagers, so we don't respect authority and we're pretty much constantly hor-" He shot me a horrified look and I finished, incredibly amused, "-*monal?*"

"Cammie will respect my rules," he said, though he didn't sound entirely convinced.

"Cammie's a liar," I sing-songed, scrolling absentmindedly through a playlist I'd made recently. When he didn't immediately reply, I felt bad and added, "But a better person than me. And there's no way I'm getting anywhere near Scott's dirty-sock-smell-infused room, so to be perfectly honest, this is probably the best idea you're gonna have."

"I think so too."

The bedroom door opened and Cammie paused in the doorway, pajamas on and wet hair up in a towel. "Dad? What are you doing in here? Didn't you and Mom go to bed?"

"Working out your new sleeping arrangements," David explained. I sighed at Cammie as he continued, "The rule used to be that you couldn't share a room with boys. Now it's only fair that it's changed to not being able to share a room with girls." He paused awkwardly. "Or… at least it seems to me that it's only fair. I'm still new to this."

Cammie stood in the doorway for another long moment, her eyes unwavering on him as he shot her an uncertain look. Then, without warning, she moved and threw her arms around him. I blinked at them, wide-eyed. David seemed even more surprised than I was, but he hugged her back all the same, even as an intrigued smile spread across his lips.

"I love you, Dad," Cammie mumbled, voice muffled by his shoulder.

"I love you too, Cam," he murmured, squeezing her tighter. "And if I get hugs from banning you from your girlfriend, all the more reason to keep doing it."

She sniffled lightly as she pulled away and wiped at one eye with her hand. "I'm just happy we can talk about it like… like it's okay and it's all the same. It was boys and now it's girls. Simple."

"Seems simple to me," he agreed. They shared a smile and then he moved away from her, toward the door. "I'm gonna go change the sheets on Scott's bed…and find some air freshener. Cammie, if your mother finds out you're in there for the week she might ask questions."

"I'll come up with something," Cammie assured him. "I know how."

David seemed perturbed by her answer, but nodded anyway. "Okay. I'll come get you when the bed's ready."

He left, and Cammie immediately let out a soft sigh and turned to face me. I stared back at her, silent. Things had been tense since our talk earlier in the day, but she seemed, for a moment, to have put it from her mind.

"I can't believe he's this okay with it," she marveled.

I nodded, and said, simply, "People surprise you."

"Not him. Not my family. Not usually, anyway. I mean, you saw how my brother reacted."

"And you saw how your dad reacted. Maybe he can help ease your mom into the idea." I wasn't delusional enough to think that Wendy was going to react the way David had. She'd probably be even worse than Scott, and both Cammie and I knew that.

She laughed at what I'd said. "There's no easing her into this. If she finds out, she'll lose it. And I'll lose her."

"I think it's more of a 'when' than an 'if,' Cammie."

"I know." She moved to sit down on her bed, troubled. "I wish this could all just go away, you know? If I knew she'd have no problem with it, I'd tell her, let her know that I might be moving to New York with you after my graduation, and that'd be the end of it."

"I think that even a normal mom who's super attached to her daughter would freak out over all of that," I said, chuckling. "I'm supposed to be messed up and in need of some serious therapy, and you're dating me."

"Who says you aren't?" she quipped, smiling over at me.

"That's fair. I still probably need therapy. But I wasn't supposed to be sleeping with their daughter or talking her into moving across the country."

"You didn't talk me into it. I wanted to before you ever showed up." She paused, and then shrugged. "You were just the first person who ever made me feel like it was a real possibility."

My heart warmed as she stood to give me a quick kiss, and then I asked her, "Do you know when you'll find out if you got into art school?"

"Any day now."

"Are you nervous?"

She laughed. "Uh, yes."

"Don't be," I said, confident. "You'll get in."

David reappeared in the doorway a moment later. "Cameron, the room's all set up," he told her. "If you don't mind saying goodnight to Lauren now, I'd like to talk to her alone for a few minutes."

I shifted uncomfortably at that, wondering if this was the inevitable father to daughter's significant other talk that seemed to happen in every teen romcom. I'd never been put through one before, but if it had to happen, I was glad it was with David about Cammie.

Cammie nodded at her father and then glanced to me awkwardly. "Um. Goodnight, Lauren."

"Night," I offered, swallowing hard. Cammie looked like she

wanted to kiss me, but thought better of it in front of her father and simply reached out to briefly touch my arm before turning and leaving the bedroom. David closed the door behind her and then moved to sit at her desk again, across from my bed. I watched him, wary.

"This isn't new territory for me," he began. "At least, not as far as Cammie dating someone. With her past boyfriends, I'd sit down with them, make sure they had good intentions, and then send them on their way. I don't tell them not to hurt her, and I don't threaten them. I don't think that's an appropriate way to address someone my daughter could potentially spend the rest of her life with. I don't like getting off on the wrong foot."

He paused, and I sensed I wasn't going to like what he said next. "Lauren, you and I already got off on the wrong foot, and I think we've managed to get back on track, so I have no problem telling you right now that I am not messing around here, and if this is some sort of game to you – although I don't believe it is – you and I are going to have a serious problem."

I was uncertain how I should respond to that. "I like Cammie," I mumbled at last, and knew it sounded weak. David seemed to realize how much he'd intimidated me and sat back in his seat, backing off a little.

"I know you do. I know you better than I've known any of her past boyfriends, and I consider that a good thing. But you didn't come here for this. You came here to get help."

There was my opening. I took it earnestly. "Cammie's helping me. She's the whole reason I'm doing okay. You're alright, and I like you more than I thought I would, and I know we get along, but… I couldn't tell you before, obviously, but it was all Cammie, all along. She gave me something to like here. She's good for me."

"I'm not so sure you're good for her," he replied. That stung. "You have a lot going on right now. You have a life that… Well, it's not as simple or easy as I'm sure you'd like it to be, and you can't help that. But Cammie—"

"Hasn't had it easy, either," I reminded him. "She's told me things I know you'd never want to hear. You love her, and her mom loves her, but she's spent years wondering if that love was conditional. That screws up a person. I know what it's like to doubt your own parents like that too. So this isn't…"

I paused, struggling for the right words, "This isn't me taking a girl from her simple, easy country life and throwing her into the middle of all my family crap and then whisking her away to a city too big for her, okay? This is me seeing that she isn't happy here and offering an alternative option she's wanted for a long time but felt like she could never pursue because of her parents. You have so much power over her and you don't even realize it. She's spent so much time being told that what she wants isn't okay, that what she'd do and who she'd love were set in stone, and if you told her that wasn't the case, I know that'd mean the world to her. I know it would."

"This isn't about her dating a girl, or about her going to New York," David insisted. "It's about you. There are things in your life that have forced you grow up before you were ready, and I'm afraid to have Cammie involved in that. I don't want her to have to grow up before she's ready, too."

"She already has," I shot back. "That's what you don't get. Normal teenagers don't put their own wants aside for their parents as soon as they're old enough to realize what those wants are, but Cammie did. And that's *your* fault. Maybe she knows what she's getting into. Maybe it's worth it to her. And maybe the last thing I wanna do is hurt her." I hesitated as he watched me, and then added, "With all due respect, I'm not the bad guy here. You and your wife are."

His eyes narrowed. "That's crossing a line."

I shrugged. "Maybe. I know you care about her. I know her mom does too. But before I showed up, Cammie would've done *anything* for you two, particularly Wendy. She would've thrown her life away to make her mom happy. She'd have been whoever you two wanted her to be, and she'd already perfected becoming that person when I got here. I think what she liked about me was that I saw through it."

I sucked in a breath abruptly, shaking my head. This was getting too personal. "You know what? She's eighteen. I'll be eighteen in a few months. We're adults, and I don't need to justify this to you any more than I already have. It's personal. We're good for each other. You're going to have to trust me, and if you can't, then you can trust your daughter. *Please* trust your daughter."

There was a long silence as he stared back at me. "You may be adults," he spoke up at last, "but you're under my roof. I like you, Lauren, and I absolutely meant what I said about wanting my daughter to be happy. If it's what Cammie wants, then I would love for things to work out between the two of you. But the fact remains that you've got a lot going on. Both back home, and within your own head. Your time here can't just be about Cammie. I'm not naïve enough to think I can stop the two of you, or that I can force you to do anything, really. But if you want me to feel confident that my daughter's in good hands, then you can start by showing me."

I fixed my eyes on his, my gaze sharp. And then, folding my arms across my chest, I asked, "What would you like me to do?"

Chapter Twenty-One

I went straight to Cammie's bedroom after school the next day. The eight hours had gone by in a blur, as had every moment since my talk with David, really. At breakfast, Wendy had hardly acknowledged my presence, which was a nice preview of what was to come when she finally found out about Cammie and me.

I sat down at Cammie's desk and withdrew a notebook from my backpack, then snagged a pen out of a cup that rested on the desk. After a moment, I thought better of it and grabbed a pencil instead. I'd need the eraser.

I tore a page out of the notebook, placed it on the desk, and then dated the first line. Once I'd finished that, I moved down a line, pressed my pencil to the paper again, and waited. Minutes passed, and still I couldn't bring myself to write more.

Soon, the door swung open behind me. "Hey!" Cammie

sounded a little out of breath. "Wanna go for a ride out to the clearing? I just got Aerosmith all warmed up."

"Um..." I glanced from her to the paper in front of me. "I can't. Homework."

"Oh, what class?" she asked, and crossed the room to me before I could make up an answer. She leaned over to look down at the paper, saw there was nothing written but the date, and shot me an amused look.

"Essay," I elaborated before she could ask.

"You can use my computer for that," she reminded me.

"Has to be handwritten," I said shortly.

"Oh. That's weird. Hmm."

"Yeah, um, it's for that home economics class I just started." I turned away from her in my chair, flushing. I really needed to work on my lying.

"Huh." She didn't sound convinced, and there was a long pause as I stared down at the paper and willed her to leave. When she spoke next, her tone was gentler. "Okay. I'm sure you'll figure it out. Don't think too hard." She leaned down and kissed me on the cheek, and then left the room. I pressed my pencil to the paper again as the door shut behind her.

Dad,

I paused again and moved down a line, then reached up to rub at my face with my free hand. My chest ached. I didn't want to do this.

I hesitated, and then made a decision. I didn't want to bullshit some sort of reconciliation letter to my father. When David had given me this assignment, all he'd said was to write a letter to try and establish some sort of understanding with my father. He'd said to reach out to him. I didn't have to be nice.

The words flowed easily after that.

I'm only writing this because I was made to. I didn't actually want to contact you, especially after what happened when I tried to call. I know you were drunk and probably didn't even know it was me, but... well, here I am making excuses for you. I'll stop that now. I haven't felt close to you in years and although I want to say you tried your best with me, I know that you didn't. You've been half-assing parenting for as long as I can remember, and I put up with it for so long. I think I might be done.

When I was younger, I looked up to you so, so much. You have no idea. When you weren't as invested in being around me as I was in being with you, I thought there was something wrong with me. I think deep down, a part of me still wonders if I screwed up somehow. Like maybe if I'd been more worth sticking around for, you'd have been able to make yourself be the father I needed. I can tell myself a hundred times that you were the problem, not me, but I'm not sure I'll ever lose that insecurity. I want you to know that you did that.

I turn eighteen in March, in case you've forgotten, and I get my trust fund money then. As he always planned to, David Marshall will be helping me get that sorted out without me having to go back to Los Angeles. After that, I'm moving to New York. You will never have to see me again, and I will never have to see you again. I'm not going to sit around and wait for you to pay attention to me anymore. If you send me a letter or give me a call, it should be to tell me you're going to rehab. Otherwise, there's nothing more I need from you. – Lauren

My hand ached when I put the pencil down, but I felt better.

Putting my feelings into words had been strangely cathartic, and I felt at peace with what I'd written. When I'd pictured my future with Caitlyn, Zeke, and Cammie in New York, my father hadn't been involved at all. If he wasn't going to change, I really had no reason to keep in touch. Now he'd know that, if he ever bothered to read the letter.

I stood, stretched, and then moved to put my shoes back on, wondering if that offer from Cammie to go to the clearing still stood. *Then*, feeling somewhat dense, I wondered what she'd meant when she'd asked me to go. "Going to the clearing" had been code for something else more often than not lately.

"Idiot," I muttered hastily, and moved faster, nearly tripping over my own feet in my haste to get my shoes on.

* * *

Cammie's nails left small little half-moon marks on my biceps, and I laughed heartily as I examined them. "Ow. Jeez."

She swatted at me from beneath me, red-faced and still breathing hard. "Shut up!"

"The *abuse*." I pursed my lips and shook my head at her in disapproval. "What would your parents think?"

"Ew. No. We are so not talking about my parents right now." She shoved me off of her and I collapsed beside her, grinning. She straightened her clothing and then rolled over to face me, surprising me by leaning in and kissing me deeply. I was halfway on top of her again before she stopped me, her tone gentle. "Mm, wait."

I blew my hair out of my face, frowning. "What?"

She brushed it away for me, tucking it behind my ear. Then she cupped my cheek in her hand. "You don't wanna talk about your essay?"

I deflated. "That was an awful lie. You didn't have to pretend to believe me." I flattened myself against her, resting my chin on her stomach and looking up at her.

"I figured it'd be good for you, whatever it was. It took me a few minutes afterward to figure out you were probably writing to your dad."

"I'm sending it tomorrow," I told her.

"That's good. If you feel good about it, I mean."

"I think I do." I paused, and then amended, "Yeah. I do. I told him I don't need him around unless he goes to rehab."

She sat up, forcing me off of her. I moved to sit next to her as she watched me. "You seem pretty nonchalant."

I shrugged. "Well, it's out of my hands. I wish things could be different, but it's been a long time and nothing's changed. Nothing's worked with him. If he cares, he'll make an effort. If he doesn't... well, I feel like I've done all I can. You can't force change on someone who doesn't want it."

She watched me for a moment, her legs pulled to her chest and her chin resting on her knees. She smiled. "I love you."

"*I* love *you.*"

She grinned, her eyes bright, and then chewed on her lip for a few seconds. "So what'll it be like if I go to New York with you?" she asked.

"Truthfully?" I began, and she nodded her head.

"Paint me a picture. Warts and all."

I smiled back at her. "Okay. Totally realistically... Well, if you come along, we wait until after graduation to go. So I get my trust fund, move some money over to Caitlyn's bank account so she and Zeke can afford the first few months of expenses. They get us an awesome place: three bedrooms at the very least, and a great view of the city."

"We'd share a bedroom?" Cammie cut in.

"Hell yeah. We do now, anyway. And I know you'd want something with big windows, so I'd tell Caitlyn to look for that. We'd make sure to be close to the art school you'll be getting into shortly. Zeke will have a steady job already set up, and Caitlyn and I will get jobs, too. Waitress or bartending jobs at first, but they'll get better. Maybe I'll try acting or something since it's in my blood; I don't know."

"Would you enjoy that?" she asked me.

"I don't know. I'm kind of still figuring out what I wanna do with my life," I admitted. "I have the money to do anything, so the only thing to really figure out at this point is *what* to do. Maybe it's okay that I don't know right now. Maybe in a couple years I'll try college out." I shrugged. "Anything could happen."

"Your friend doesn't want to go to college?" Cammie asked. "Caitlyn?"

"You know, I'm actually not sure. I'm thinking maybe not, given that she was so willing to go all the way to New York, but maybe she actually had the time to apply somewhere there. The only thing that's a guarantee with Caitlyn is that there *will* be a lot of partying, but you'd fit right in with that, as I recall. However, I'll never get blackout drunk again. I won't end up like my dad. I guess, all in all, I just expect it to be like a new beginning. There's no solid plan, and honestly, I'm financially secure enough not to need one."

"You're lucky," she murmured.

I scoffed. "Oh, like I'm not gonna help you out too?"

"You don't need to help me," she told me. "I'm not with you for that."

"I know. But it's a perk. I'm helping Caitlyn and Zeke too, until they can get jobs. You could get one too. Waitress nights or something and go to class in the daytime. If it gets to be too much, I'll be your fallback plan."

"I'd like that," she admitted and leaned over to rest her head on my shoulder.

"Shall we paint a picture of your post-high-school life in Collinsville?" I asked, sweeping my arm dramatically across the clearing.

"Please, god, no," she replied, wincing. "I applied to two local schools and I'm dreading getting the acceptance letters, because the instant I do, the pressure will be on from Mom. And I'll feel even worse if I don't get into art school."

"That's not happening," I assured her.

"Be realistic," she insisted. "It could."

"Well, if it does, we go to New York anyway and you keep trying, because it's what you love," I said simply. "How about that?"

"That sounds nice," she mumbled, tilting her head to kiss my neck. "And scary. But nice."

I wrapped an arm around her and squeezed her tight, then pressed a kiss to the top of her head. "Just give me the word and it's a plan. Caitlyn doesn't come for another month and a half."

She nodded against me, and I felt her exhale against my shoulder. "I'll let you know."

* * *

I went outside after school the following day to put my letter to my father in the Marshall's mailbox. I'd offered to let David read it, but he shook his head and told me he was satisfied that I'd written anything at all. Then he'd asked me if I wanted to send it, which had surprised me. What mattered to him was that I'd written it.

I decided to send it anyway. I meant every word I'd written, and I felt at ease with this being the final chapter in my relationship with my father, if the alternative was to keep painfully chugging along like we had been.

When I opened the mailbox to put my letter in, there were several pieces of mail inside that hadn't been collected by the Marshalls yet. I took them out and sifted through them, curious, and then paused at the next to last letter. The return address was in New York. This was Cammie's letter from her art school.

I folded that one up and put it in my coat pocket, and then looked to the one behind it. It, too, was addressed to Cammie.

This was one of the two other colleges she'd applied to.

I carried the mail inside, where Wendy stood in the kitchen making dinner while David finished tidying up the living room and Cammie set the dinner table. "Mail," I announced.

Wendy heaved a sigh and moved to me. "Oh, thank God. They were late today." She snatched the stack from me without looking at me, but I kept a tight grip on Cammie's letter.

When Wendy looked to me expectantly, I elaborated, "This one's for Cammie. It's from a college." I offered it to Cammie, whose eyebrows rose in surprise as Wendy let out an excited gasp beside me.

"Oh, Cammie, open it!"

"We're about to have dinner," she pointed out, looking uncomfortable. I felt bad about bringing the letter in then, and wished I hadn't said anything.

David appeared between Cammie and me and rested an encouraging hand on her shoulder. "We can wait. Go ahead."

"...Alright." Her expression carefully controlled, Cammie opened the rather thick envelope and withdrew the letter inside. She unfolded it, scanned it, and then, almost disconcertingly, sprouted a smile and announced, "We are pleased to inform you that you have been accepted—"

Wendy let out an excited shriek, and I winced as she wrapped her arms around Cammie, who hugged her back with just as much enthusiasm. "Oh, honey, this was the one we wanted most, too! Now we have nothing to worry about!"

David, beside them, had an uncertain smile on his face, like Cammie's excitement had rattled him just as much as it had rattled me. That was unsurprising, given that he knew about Cammie's application to art school and that she'd be in New York in an instant if Wendy gave her the go-ahead.

When Cammie and Wendy parted, Wendy returned to the kitchen with a spring in her step. As did Cammie, to a degree, when she resumed setting the table.

"Years of that," I marveled quietly, and didn't realize David had heard me until he glanced my way, his eyebrows furrowed. I tried to leave quickly to go hide the other letter upstairs, but Wendy called out that dinner was ready, and I had to leave it in my pocket instead.

Dinner was tense. Wendy talked a mile a minute about what Cammie's college would be like and how close by she'd be and how much she'd love it, and eventually, David couldn't take it anymore. I watched him throughout dinner and spotted the exact moment where he ran out of patience.

"But if Cammie gets accepted to another school she prefers more than this one, she'd be welcome to go there, I'd think."

I saw what he was doing: testing the waters with Wendy, who immediately looked confused. "What do you mean? Cammie only applied to two schools, and this is the one we agreed would be better for her."

"Better how?" he asked. "Because it's closer?"

"Well, yes, that's one reason," Wendy replied. "It's also harder to get into than the other one, and it's got a wider variety of majors for her to choose from."

"For you to choose from *for* her, you mean," David corrected.

347

My mouth dropped open in surprise before I managed to quickly shut it, and beside me, Cammie straightened up and stiffened. Wendy seemed stunned into silence for a moment as she and David stared at each other.

When she finally found her voice again, she seemed genuinely surprised. "No, of course not. I want what Cammie wants, and she and I happen to want the same things."

"How convenient." David cut a piece of meat off of the steak on his plate and casually took a bite even as Wendy continued to stare at him, appalled.

"What's that supposed to mean?"

David chewed and swallowed, then cleared his throat before he replied. "What would happen if Cammie made a life decision you didn't agree with? Hypothetically."

Wendy let out a short laugh. "Honey, that hasn't happened. I'm not sure why we're having this discussion."

"What if it did?" David pressed.

"Dad," Cammie cut in sharply, and then subtly shook her head. "Mom's right. I agree with her about where I should go, so I'm not sure what the big deal is."

David stared hard at her. "Cammie—"

"*Dad*," she cut him off.

Meanwhile, I was just eager to leave before things grew any tenser, or before Wendy caught on and then somehow found a way to blame me. "I'm done eating, thanks for dinner," I announced, standing quickly. Then I froze and looked down as the folded letter left my coat pocket and, as though in slow motion, fluttered down to the ground beside Wendy's chair. It landed with a soft tap, and she looked down as my face grew red. I moved quickly to grab it, but not before she caught sight of it.

"What's that?" she asked.

When I straightened up, the letter was visible in my hands. I shot Cammie a panicked look, and she returned it with one of her own. David looked back and forth between the two of us and immediately caught on.

"Just a letter from my friend," I squeaked out, and then abruptly reconsidered pursuing acting as a profession.

Wendy wasn't buying it anyway, but David shot me down immediately, getting to his feet. "No, it's not. Give it to me."

"Dad, stop," Cammie insisted, rising too. With everyone but an uncertain Wendy on their feet, she too stood and faced me. "You think you're helping but you're not."

"And you think you're doing the right thing, I get it," he countered. "But this isn't right for you, and now that I know that, I'm not going to let it go on. I wouldn't be a good father if I did." He turned to me, his arm outstretched. "Lauren, give me the letter."

"What on earth is going on?" Wendy cut in. "David, what's gotten into you?"

Beside David, Cammie's face had gone red. For a moment, I considered trying to get the letter to her, but deep down, I had a feeling she'd do something with it she'd regret. An image of Cammie glancing back and forth between her parents and then ripping the letter into tiny pieces came to mind, and I immediately handed the letter over to David.

"Thank you," he said shortly, and opened it himself. He scanned it quickly, and then offered it to Cammie. "You were accepted."

"Accepted? Where, to her other school?" asked Wendy, who, beside me, was still understandably lost. I hid a grin at the stunned look on Cammie's face. When it truly sank in that she'd gotten into her dream school, even she could no longer completely hide behind her usual mask.

"To the art school she applied to in New York," David elaborated for her. "She'll be going there in the fall."

Cammie jumped in quickly there. "No, wait. Only if it's okay with you, Mom, I swear. I should've told you I applied. I won't go if you don't want me to."

"Yes, you will," said David, his voice firm.

Wendy looked back and forth between them, lips parted in surprise. At last, she let out a short laugh and shook her head, her gaze falling to Cammie. "Sweetie, this is ridiculous. What are you two talking about? New York? Art school? You're not an artist."

Cammie swallowed hard and the nodded her head shortly, as though that was the end of the discussion. "Okay."

"Cameron, that's enough." David held out a hand to silence her. "You're not doing this anymore. It ends here. I want you to tell your mother the truth."

Cammie looked back and forth between her parents, clear panic in her eyes. "Dad—" she tried again, but he shook his head, speaking next to Wendy.

"I love you, honey, but you have to let our kids do what they want with their own lives. We can't control them."

"I'm not controlling anyone!" Wendy insisted. "Scott's off having the time of his life on his honeymoon, and Cammie's never said a word about art school. How is this my fault?"

"It's not your fault. We're both at fault." David hesitated, and then told her, "We can talk about this in private. Cammie, I'm very proud of you." He led Wendy away to their bedroom, and Cammie and I stood in the dining room in stunned silence. I watched her look down at the letter in her hands.

"I can't believe I got in," she murmured. Then she added, "I can't believe I just told my mom I wouldn't go."

"Your dad will talk some sense into her," I promised. "She'll be okay."

"What if she's not?"

"Then you go anyway." Cammie started to shake her head, and I repeated, more firmly, "Then you *go anyway*, Cammie. You think your dad would let you give this up?"

"It's my decision."

I heaved a sigh, frustrated. "*Stop.* You have no idea how hard this is to watch. We're *all* in your corner, okay? So just... get there yourself, and we can help. The whole world isn't against you. In fact, most of us are on your side."

I jumped and Cammie winced as shouting abruptly started up from the bedroom. Cammie looked to me, wide-eyed, and I asked, "Do you think he told her about us?"

Cammie shook her head. "If he had, it'd be *much* worse than that."

* * *

Wendy cried a lot that day. I felt bad for her. I didn't think she was a bad person — way misguided, perhaps, and a little controlling, but never downright evil — and, in a way, she was mourning the loss of her daughter.

David, in true therapeutic fashion, sat them down together while I watched from the sidelines and had Cammie, against her will, spill all but two things: the promiscuity, and everything and anything involving me.

What she *did* spill was her aversion to cheerleading and all of her friends. The truth about the movie posters. The boys she'd dated only because her mom had approved of them. The colleges she'd never wanted to go to. The drawings and briefcase she'd kept hidden.

She talked for hours about how hard she'd worked to be everything Wendy'd wanted her to be, and I knew it didn't make any sense to Wendy, who didn't really have the full story. Without explaining the way it'd all started back at age eight, Cammie left a massive gap in her story that couldn't be filled until she put the last puzzle piece in: her sexuality. And even David wasn't about to make her do that yet.

And Wendy asked the question that made the most sense, knowing what she knew: "What did I do to make you feel like you needed to do this? Did I pressure you? I thought it was all what you wanted?"

Cammie opened and closed her mouth for a moment. "I just... I felt like you wouldn't like me otherwise. I wanted you to like me.

I wanted to make you proud."

"I can be proud watching you do what you love. I can do that. You can be who you want. I thought you knew that." Wendy was sobbing out her words, and I shifted uncomfortably, wondering if this was all really going to happen today. Cammie looked so badly like she wanted to say more.

"But you can't say that and then..." she trailed off, inhaling sharply and then letting out a shaky breath. "I just don't want you to hate me."

"Honey, I don't hate you. I would be lying if I said that this wasn't shocking, or that I wouldn't prefer you'd stay here... and I really wish you *would* consider staying here... but ultimately I'm going to support you doing what you love. You didn't have to go to all this trouble just for me."

"I can consider staying here," Cammie admitted. "I will consider it. Nothing's set in stone."

"Good." Wendy looked relieved. "Can I see some of your drawings?"

Cammie paused, stunned, and then a grin spread across her lips. "You want to? Really?"

"Of course. Where are they?"

"Upstairs; I'll get them. One second!" Cammie rushed off to do just that, and I saw David and Wendy exchange a warm look. Wendy still had tears in her eyes, and I had no doubt she'd be doing more crying by herself later, but I was so, so happy for Cammie. Today was a big deal, and I knew it'd given her hope, because it'd given me hope, too.

But I was also under no delusions regarding Wendy's unchanged views on homosexuality. Any decent parent would feel terrible upon learning their daughter had sacrificed her own happiness to make her parents happy. But make that parent religious and make the issue of choice sexuality and it was a whole different story. Wendy accepted that enjoyed activities and pastimes couldn't be changed and that Cammie liked what she liked, but I had a feeling that sexuality was an exception to the rule.

When — or *if* — Cammie dropped *that* bomb, Wendy'd go nuclear. And even David knew it.

* * *

Scott and Jill returned a few days later, and David pulled Scott aside on his first day back to talk to him, most likely about the situation with Cammie and Wendy. They went out together afterward to go look at the house Scott had been working on buying since a week or so before his wedding. I found out when they returned that Scott would be moving out in another week.

He was cold to me while he lived with us. I didn't expect anything else from him; I was just thankful he kept Cammie's secret from Wendy. And even better: David noticed his coolness within a couple of days and had a talk with him, at which point his attitude seemed to approve considerably. By the time his week was up, he'd occasionally exchange a few sentences with me, even if he still seemed emotionally distant. With Cammie, he seemed to feel sorry for her more than anything, but she was too busy enjoying her time with her mom and her nights back in her own bedroom with me to care.

I helped Scott pack up his room on his last day while David, Wendy, and Cammie were at the other house moving him in.

"Do you want these all in boxes?" I asked him, gesturing to the books on a small bookcase by where his bed used to be.

"Huh?" he glanced over to me. "Oh, yeah. Thanks."

"No problem."

We worked in silence for a half hour or so, packing things up and then moving them downstairs one by one, until Scott finally spoke up again as I was finishing up another box.

"Hey." I glanced over to him, acknowledging him, and he arched an eyebrow. "You ever been with a guy?"

I snorted and shook my head, looking back to the box in front of me again. "No."

"Why not?"

I rolled my eyes. "Same reason you haven't. Never felt the need to try it out."

"Girls are made for guys," he grunted out as he lifted his box. "Like puzzle pieces."

I wrinkled my nose and followed him out as we carried our boxes to the stack by the front door. "Gross."

"Cammie'll find one she likes," he called over his shoulder. "Dad doesn't think so, but I know it. There's someone out there for everyone."

"I'm gonna be really sad when that happens," I said. "Do you think she'll give me a warning?"

"She's not like you." He set his box down and shook his head at me. "You might be too far gone, but she knows what's right."

I folded my arms across my chest. "You're an asshole."

He laughed lightly and adjusted the cap on his head. "I'm just looking out for my little sister."

"I know this is like arguing with a brick wall, but I'll bite. What have I done to make you think I'm not good for her?"

"You're here. No one good ends up here." He walked past me to head back up the stairs, and I trailed behind him.

"You liked me before you knew."

"Yeah, well, turns out finding a girl's a dyke who's screwing his little sister changes a guy's opinion on her."

"It's not like that," I called after him, growing genuinely annoyed now. "I actually care about her."

He was waiting for me in his bedroom, a fresh box already packed. "Not like a guy can," he countered, and moved around me to leave again. I stood alone in his room, jaw clenched as I heard him heading back downstairs.

We didn't speak again.

Chapter Twenty-Two

Another week passed and I found myself walking with Cammie to our shared lunch period, hands brushing and shoulders bumping as I resisted the urge to tangle our fingers together.

When we sat down with Fiona and Nate, Fiona smiled at Cammie and told her, "I like your shirt today. That shade of green's my favorite color."

"Aw, thanks. I like your earrings."

"Thanks!"

Nate and I exchanged amused looks from across the table. Cammie'd been sitting with us for a while now, and she fit right in at this point. I wasn't sure what her and Tiffany's status was anymore, but Cammie no longer talked about her, and I never saw them talking to each other, so I assumed that the whole Peter fiasco had been the downfall of their friendship. Cheerleading season was over, so they were no longer hanging out then, either.

"So are you guys going to Prom?" Fiona asked us. "It's on March 18th. Just a month to go."

"Whoa, hey, that's my birthday!" I told her. Then I frowned. "What a lame way to spend it. Ugh."

"Of course you'd hate Prom," Fiona laughed out. "Dismantle the establishment! Boycott Prom!"

"Oh, shut up," I mumbled to laughter from Cammie and Nate. "It's just expensive."

Fiona and Cammie both shot me knowing looks, and I heaved a sigh.

"*What?* There are just better ways to spend my night."

"I think you should ask Maddie to go with you," Fiona teased with a wink.

Beside her, Nate added, "Bow chicka wow wow…"

"You guys are *way* too late," I told him, and reached down to pat Cammie's thigh under the table. "Do I seriously need to remind you that Maddie's hated me for a while now?"

"Well, she's like the only other lesbian at this school," Fiona pointed out. "Go forth, and… settle for your only option!"

"I'm seriously not going," I said, and held back a wince when Cammie pinched my side in a very clear, *"Oh yes you are."*

"Well, we are," Nate told me. "What about you, Cammie? Any guy you're interested in going with?"

Cammie coughed abruptly, mid-bite, and grabbed for her napkin, startling Fiona and Nate. "Oh, um," she finally mumbled when she recovered. "I don't know."

"You have to go," Fiona insisted. "You were Homecoming Queen. Just because you don't have Peter doesn't mean you can't find a date just as hot."

"And less douchey," added Nate.

"I'm not winning Prom Queen," Cammie said. "I've been ostracized from that clique for daring to have a cheating asshole for a boyfriend, in case you haven't noticed."

Fiona and Nate exchanged an awkward look, and then Fiona evidently made the decision to speak up. "Didn't you cheat on him first?"

There was tension for only a moment before Cammie smirked. "Shh."

Nate chuckled as Fiona grinned at her. "I'll help you find a date. There are plenty of cute boys who'd jump at the chance to go with you. Maybe not star athlete cute, but there are plenty of other fish in the sea."

"Don't try too hard," Cammie insisted. "Maybe we can all just have fun as a group."

"Yeah. That sounds fun," I added hastily, and ignored Fiona's arched brow. "Let's do it."

* * *

Fiona and I stayed after school together that day. I had a project in Home Ec that involved creating my own recipe, and she was a decent cook, so she offered to help.

We sat down on a bench together just outside of the door to

the gym, and I asked her, "Before we start, can I borrow your cell phone?"

"Definitely." She handed it over immediately, and I nodded thankfully. I'd told her about Caitlyn a while back.

I dialed her number and waited as it rang, then grinned when I heard her pick up. "Cait!"

"Lauren. Oh my God. Hey, how are you!?"

"I'm actually doing pretty well," I told her. "I have an update for you, though. It's kind of important. I need you to hold off on that ride. I, um… I decided I want to stay and graduate."

"Seriously?" she sounded surprised, but not upset. "Wow. What do you want me to do, then? Are you sure you're okay staying the full seven months?"

"I can make it," I said. "Once I get the money in March, I'll transfer some to you to help pay for where we live. I'll call you again soon to work out details with that. We can do the whole New York thing, I just won't come up until after I graduate. And also, we might have a fourth."

"Who?" she sounded genuinely curious, and I hated that she'd asked the question, because now I'd have to answer it beside Fiona.

"Um… the same one?"

Fiona looked curious, but I figured I'd been vague enough.

"Wait, you're still with her?" Caitlyn laughed. "Wow."

I furrowed my eyebrows, a little taken aback. "Yeah. Of course. It's different. I told you that."

"I know, it's just… It's kind of a 'you have to see it to believe it' thing, you know?" There was a long silence, and when I didn't respond, she sighed. "I'm sorry, Lauren. You've changed a lot. But you're still my best friend, and I'm really glad you've found someone. Please don't be upset. You two can come up in May and we'll take her clubbing; introduce her to our world, right?"

I smiled and nodded. "Yeah. Sorry. I'm just a little stressed right now."

"I bet. Her family still doesn't know?"

"Just Mom," I said, still thinking of Fiona.

"How did the others take it?"

"Dad was good. Brother not so much, but he'll live." I paused. "How are things there. Anything from my dad?"

"Oh. Um." She was silent for a moment, and I began to get nervous.

"Cait..."

"No, it's okay. He's just the same, is all. I know you sent him a letter; I've kind of been bringing the mail inside every few days for him. I don't know if he's opened it."

I sat back in my seat with the sigh. "Okay."

"I'm sorry. I wasn't sure if I should say anything..."

"No, I'm glad you did. I'll try to call more, I'm sorry. It's just been..." I shifted uncomfortably, eager to change the subject. "A lot's been going on here."

"I get it. Momma drama. So if I don't hear from you before your birthday, I'll wait until May to come get you. If I don't hear from you by May, I'm gonna be at your front door on May 1st with a battering ram."

"Got it." I forced a laugh. "Sounds perfect. You'll hear from me soon."

"Okay. Muah." She kissed the air. "Two more months apart! What am I gonna do?"

"You have your hand," I joked, and she snorted.

"Inappropriate! You have a girlfriend now!"

"Bye, Cait," I said, chuckling.

"Love you!" she replied, and ended the call. When I handed the phone back to Fiona, she looked amused.

"So you were planning on busting out of here early," she said. "That's good to know."

"Can you blame me?" I asked her.

She laughed. "I can't. But I'm glad you're staying a little longer. What changed your mind?"

"Your beautiful face," I sighed out, watching her dreamily.

"Knew it. Now give me your assignment so I can do it for you."

"You're the best," I told her, leaning down to dig through my backpack.

"Don't forget it."

* * *

David and Cammie went out to eat alone that evening for some father-daughter bonding time, which, unfortunately, left me alone with Wendy.

The drawings Cammie had done over the years had been removed from their hiding place in her closet and now rested in a folder on the living room coffee table, which was where Wendy sat flipping through them for the dozenth time when she called out, "Lauren?"

I was in the kitchen, making a bagel for dinner, and peered over the counter at her. "Yes?"

She made eye contact briefly and patted the seat beside her. I swallowed hard and nodded, abandoning my bagel and moving into the living room with trepidation

"Come sit," said Wendy. "Have you seen these?"

"Yeah," I told her. I sat down, trying my best to keep some space between us. "It took her a while to show them to me, but yeah, I saw them."

"So you knew about this." She closed the portfolio and turned to face me, and I swallowed hard again. Scott was bigger, stronger, and taller than Wendy, but she was easily more intimidating.

"Yes," I said uncertainly.

"Did you know about the rest of it?" She paused, and then wondered aloud, "Did she sit up there with you for *months* talking about what a horrible mother I was?"

"She doesn't think you're a horrible mother," I rushed to correct. "Neither do I." I paused, struggling for the right words. At last, I said, "When I came here, it was made very clear to me that I was meant to be a certain way. I knew that if I wanted to get the stamp of approval to leave here, I couldn't be the way that I was beforehand. And yeah, there were some aspects about me that really *did* need to change, so that whole philosophy worked with me. But Cammie? Cammie's a good kid."

"Of course she is, and it's because we raised her that way."

"You raised her alongside people with more issues than *me* and expected her to be the perfect model for them. You put that pressure on her and taught her that she had to be a certain way too. She felt like she had these impossible standards she had to meet because she had to *prove* constantly that she was the perfect child. Or else risk messing up the setup you've got here. On top of that, she knows how much she means to you and once she was in too deep with making you happy, she didn't think she could bring herself ruin the illusion."

Wendy looked away from me to the drawings, cycling through them silently for a moment. At last, she declared, "You've become my daughter's best friend. And I'm not sure how I feel about that."

"I just waited and listened," I explained. "That's all. That's what it took to get her to open up."

Wendy let out a quiet sigh, then turned and offered me a small smile. "I guess I should've told her sooner that I preferred her with my friend Dottie's son over Peter, anyway."

I couldn't tell if she was joking or not until I replied, "You should probably let her make that call," and she laughed.

"Yes, I suppose I should." She stood, turned, and bent down to wrap her arms around me. I blinked twice, surprised, and then hugged her back until she withdrew. "Now: were you making bagels in there? For dinner? I don't think so; let me get the oven preheated." She bustled off to the kitchen, and I watched her go, realizing with mild surprise that I was beginning to like Wendy.

* * *

"Holy shit."

I stared at myself in the mirror, eyes wide, and then leaned in closer, not daring to believe that I was actually looking at myself. Cammie giggled beside me as I turned and asked her, "Seriously, when did this happen? I'm, like, *hot*."

"Uh, yeah." Cammie nodded very emphatically, looking me up and down. I turned back to the mirror and reached for them of my shirt.

"I mean, I was skinny before, but I have *abs* now." I lifted my shirt and gawked. "Are you seeing this? *When did this happen?!*"

"Well, when you go from your only exercise being dancing at clubs and having sex to working on a farm daily for a few months, your body changes." Cammie shot me a pleased smile and joked, "Now you're as hot as me!"

"Impossible." I arched an eyebrow at her. "Also, I haven't completely cut out my *whole* old exercise routine."

"I'm surprised you haven't commented on your arms yet," she replied, gesturing toward the mirror. I raised an arm and flexed, and my eyes widened.

"Oh man. I'm not, like, ripped... I'm like that perfect middle ground you've got going on, too. I wish I could sleep with myself."

"Muscle building kinda works this way," Cammie explained. "At first it's not there, and then, one day, it springs itself on you and you notice you've changed. If it were summer, you'd be a lot tanner, too."

"I bet I could, like, lift you onto things," I mused aloud.

Cammie snickered next to me. "Okay?"

"It'd be hot. I'd be all, 'Cammie, let's do it,' and lift you onto the counter and—"

"Hey Dad!" Cammie cut in brightly, looking past me with flushed cheeks. I whirled around to see a thoroughly disturbed David at the top of the stairs, watching us.

"Lauren, I'd like to talk to you."

"Okay," I mumbled, unable to look him in the eyes as I followed him into Cammie's room. The bathroom door shut behind me, and a moment later I heard Cammie running her shower. "Sorry I—"

David shook his head at me, and I dropped it, thankful. "I'm glad you took the time to write your letter to your dad."

I perked up, eager to have this conversation. I'd been waiting for it for a while now. "Yeah, I did exactly what you said. And I go to church every weekend, *and* do farm work so often that I have an awesome body now because, like, exercise." I paused. "Oh, and I haven't been sneaking drugs or alcohol into your house, so there's that. I've kind of been awesome."

"And if I give my okay for Cammie to go up to New York with you, you don't think that'll change?"

I hesitated. "With all due respect... college is college. Cammie won't be shielded from that stuff no matter where she goes. I'm not gonna hand her a joint and a handle of vodka, if that's what you're asking, but she'll be around people who can get ahold of those things. That's kind of just what it's like to be a college kid. Her being in New York will just mean that if she screws up I'll be the one bailing her out instead of you. And I'll do that." I sighed, then forced a laugh. "I don't know what I have to do to convince you I'd do anything for her."

"Dad?"

David and I both looked to the doorway, where Cammie stood, looking uncertain.

"I forgot a change of clothes," she elaborated. "You can trust Lauren. You know that, right? *I* trust her."

David pressed his lips together tightly, and, after a moment, nodded his head. "I think she could leave here right now and be okay, actually." He turned to me with a sigh, and I raised both eyebrows in surprise. That meant a lot, coming from him. "I just... only have one daughter."

"Well..." I said, drawing the word out. "You *could* have two. Maybe. Eventually. Or now, if you wanted. Like an honorary daughter."

He laughed and stood to leave, patting me on the back. "Alright. Just give me some time to adjust to that idea."

"We'll work on it!" I called after him, and heard him laugh as he descended the stairs.

Cammie and I went to bed shortly after that, and with over five and a half months of my time in Collinsville gone and the memory of David and me at the tennis courts together playing back every time I closed my eyes, I knew I'd meant it. Even if things somehow changed between Cammie and me down the road, David would always feel like a second father.

And maybe, one day, like a first father.

Epilogue

I won't go into detail about the rest of my time in Collinsville up until graduation, because honestly, not much happened, and not much changed. There was no fallout from Wendy, no nuclear blowup from her, and no screaming or crying. That'd come later, eventually, but it didn't before graduation, because Cammie didn't come out to her, and I didn't ask her to.

Cammie never did get a date to Prom. Not officially, anyway. Neither did I. That was okay with Fiona and Nate. Nate didn't care much anyway, and Fiona, as the weeks went by, seemed to finally begin to get suspicious of the way Cammie and I sat just a little too close to each other at lunchtime.

I didn't talk to Maddie much anymore, which was okay with me, even though I knew she'd have made a cool friend. Not everything had an easy fix. I'd screwed up, I'd apologized, and now we weren't really anything, despite Nate continuing to tease me about there still being "sexual tension." I think what he saw was honestly just regular tension; I don't know if anyone ever really moves past being used for sex, even if things never actually went that far.

Wendy and Cammie took me dress shopping with them two weeks before Prom. Wendy, obviously, believed Cammie didn't have a date, but that was okay, because *Wendy* was okay, and that was a nice first step. If she could accept that her daughter was going dateless to Prom, and could accept that her daughter was considering moving to New York for art college, then maybe soon she'd be able to accept if Cammie actually chose New York, and that she'd be moving in with her girlfriend.

Well, maybe not soon. But eventually. I wasn't going to push. Maybe Cammie'd tell her right after graduation and I'd have to hide behind David in the days that'd follow, or maybe it'd take a couple of years. Either was okay, because there was a good chance I'd never hear from my dad again, so I wanted Cammie to not have to say the same about her mother. *Or* her brother, who I could only hope would warm back up to me eventually. As for the rest of the kids in Collinsville, like Peter and Tiffany, they'd never know, and that was perfectly fine with me.

All in all, my assessment of my time in Collinsville was this: I'd shown up in Collinsville, according to David, for the following reasons: substance abuse, lack of guidance, intimacy issues, depression due to the loss of a loved one, and a lack of school attendance. So: substance abuse? Nonexistent. I wasn't naïve enough to think I wasn't going to have some fun in New York, but I had confidence I'd do a better job of respecting my own limits. No more blackouts. No more waking up in bed with anyone other than Cammie.

Lack of guidance? Well, now there was David for that. And Cammie, to an extent, given that she was still more responsible than I'd ever be.

Intimacy issues? Definitely not, thanks to Cammie. My chest consistently warmed over at the sight of her, and if that wasn't the most embarrassingly mushy feeling I'd ever had, then I wasn't sure what other feeling could've even come close.

Depression? I'd always be sad about my mom, but I don't think I'd ever been depressed in the first place. When I'd come to live with the Marshalls, only three months had passed since her death. They say time can heal anything. I wasn't sure who 'they' were, but they seemed to know what they were talking about, because when I did think about her now, it never hurt quite as much as it used to.

And lack of school attendance? The diploma I'd earn in May said otherwise.

So, my final assessment: I was unabashedly, irrevocably, and *undoubtedly*.... zombified.

But that was okay. Because when Fiona snuck me and Cammie out of Prom on my birthday and into a deserted section of the parking lot for a private dance to a slow song blasted from her smart phone, and Cammie, having not yet made her final decision about New York, leaned in close, kissed me, and then made that decision clear with a whispered, "I'd go anywhere with you, you know," zombification felt totally and completely worth it.

About the Author

Siera Maley was born and raised in the Southern Bible Belt. After coming out as a lesbian as a teen, she relocated to a more suburban area and is now living with her girlfriend and very adorable dogs. Her two previous novels, *Time It Right* and *Dating Sarah Cooper* are available on Amazon. You can visit her online at www.sieramaley.weebly.com or follow her at twitter.com/SieraMaley.

CPSIA information can be obtained
at www.ICGtesting.com
Printed in the USA
LVHW04s0130260518
578529LV00002B/198/P